THE MAN WHO NEVER RETURNED

THE MAN WHO NEVER RETURNED

PETER QUINN

OVERLOOK DUCKWORTH
NEW YORK • LONDON

This edition first published in paperback in the United States
and the United Kingdom in 2011 by Overlook Duckworth

NEW YORK:
The Overlook Press
Peter Mayer Publishers, Inc.
141 Wooster Street
New York, NY 10012
www.overlookpress.com
For bulk and special sales, please contact sales@overlookny.com

LONDON:
Duckworth
90-93 Cowcross Street
London EC1M 6BF
www.ducknet.co.uk
info@duckworth-publishers.co.uk

Cataloging-in-Publication Data is available from the Library of Congress
A catalogue record for this book is available from the British Library

Book design and typeformatting by Bernard Schleifer
Manufactured in the United States of America
2 4 6 8 10 9 7 5 3 1
ISBN 978-1-59020-641-6 (US)
ISBN 978-0-7156-4159-0 (UK)

For Danny Cassidy,
my missing pal—
until we meet again.

Part I

Mystery of the Missing Person: An excerpt from Louis Pohl, *Going, Going, Gone: Famous Disappearances in American History* **(Jersey City: The Wildcat Press, 1970).**

Missing persons have been a source of fascination since our ancestors first climbed down from the trees and began their bipedal wanderings across the planet. In some cases, it was obvious that the vanished had been devoured by a predator, swept away by a deluge, or captured by a rival band of primates. In others, the disappearance was less explicable and, without any obvious or easy explanation, those left behind had to struggle to supply one.

Such incidents gave birth to tales of elves and fairies who kidnapped the unwary and whisked them away to the netherworld. Common to most human cultures, similar yarns have continued to fascinate right down to the present day. They are at the heart of Lewis Carroll's fanciful masterpiece, *Alice in Wonderland*, as well as the legendary Bermuda Triangle and numerous accounts of people shanghaied aboard UFOs to the far reaches of the galaxy.

For the first European settlers who forced themselves on the New World, penetrating its virgin wildernesses, the possibility of being swallowed whole by the vast unknown was especially real. In 1587, Sir Walter Raleigh recruited a party of a hundred or so to establish the first permanent English settlement, the 'Cittie of Raleigh,' on Roanoke Island, in the new colony of Virginia. John White, the governor, came with his wife and pregnant daughter, Eleanor Dare, who on August 18th, 1587, delivered Virginia Dare, the first Anglo-Saxon child born in North America.

Soon after, John White returned to England on what he planned as a quickly executed attempt to gather more settlers and supplies. But larger forces intervened. White was trapped by Spain's Great Armada, and two years passed before he was able to return. When he did, he found the tiny settlement ruined and devoid of any living soul. A single word—"Croatoan"—was carved into a tree. No other trace of Virginia Dare or the other settlers was ever found.

This warning was fitting prelude to what followed, as myriad opportunities for vanishing were built into the new undertaking. The dense, immense forests stretching into the hinterland were the natural habitat for tribes of "savages" who fell upon settlers with horrifying suddenness, and who were sometimes actively recruited for the work of marauding and kidnapping by the French and Spanish. Settlements swelled with transient strangers who arrived one day and left the next. People disappeared constantly.

While some fell victim to the resistance of indigenous peoples, others were done in by the greed of fellow settlers, or stumbled off cliffs, or fell into rivers, or perished from exhaustion or thirst, with no trace left behind. Many of those who went missing, however, did so of their own volition. Indentured servants, enslaved Africans, vagabond Irish, debtors, bankrupts, philanderers, convicts, deserters, criminals, heretics, adventurers—those who fled forced labor, stifling conventions and ancient distinctions, or were drawn by the ways of the Indians, or were driven by a hunger for the next horizon—they all shook the dust of civilization from their feet and drank deeply from the pure, swift-flowing waters of the land beyond the pale.

From the earliest times, then, from Virginia Dare in the 1580's through the unsolved case of New York jurist Joseph Force Crater in the 1930's, Americans have been intrigued by those who vanished: Were they victims of malevolence, murdered, scalped, thrown in some gulley or ravine? Did they perish on a lonely mountaintop or sink into the muck of the riverbed? Or did they go off in a self-propelled search of a fresh start, a new destiny, throwing off the ties of family, class, religion, and finding freedom from ordinary drudgery? Whether celebrated or obscure, the mystery of America's unsolved missing persons will be forever haunted by these questions.

New York City
1955

"Sharpen thy sight now, Reader, to regard
The truth, for so transparent grows the veil,
To press within will surely not be hard."

—DANTE, *Purgatorio*, Canto VIII

THE FIRST TELEVISION FINTAN DUNNE VIEWED (THAT'S THE WORD the newspapers kept using, with their regular updates of how many million more sets were sold and how many more television *viewers* there were) was in Wanamaker's on Astor Place, just before Christmas, the winter the Red Chinese entered the Korean War. The usual holiday attractions were in place: monorail around the ceiling, ornament-laden tree, cartwheeling midgets from circus winter quarters in Sarasota, Florida, dressed as Santa's elves cavorting in front of the grand staircase. But it was the television console, resting on a raised crimson-carpeted platform, that commanded attention.

The placard on the easel beside it gave the details: *The Brentwood by Stromberg-Carlson brings television to life as never before. Features include mahogany veneer console, super-powered steady-locked picture, full-floating speaker for superb sound, and unique single-knobbed feature for easy picture adjustment. Visit the new TV WORLD section of our Appliances*

Department on the first floor for our full line of offerings.
WHAT BETTER WAY TO CELEBRATE CHRISTMAS THAN
WITH A TV!

On the round, porthole-like screen, a small gray figure in a dark suit puffed on a cigarette, extolling in clear, solemn tones "its smooth taste and fine tobacco blend." A crescent of morning shoppers stood in reverent silence, as if war had just been declared or the president had died. Oblivious to the antic blandishments of the elves, a crowd of children was sprawled in front, chins propped on hands.

More and more, Dunne had found himself leaving his office and wandering into stores like Wanamaker's with no real purpose except to get out of the office. When he'd returned to civilian life after the war, Dunne had gone back to the private-investigation business. Though he hadn't planned to build a large operation, it happened anyway. Some clients were still attracted by his pre-war reputation; others came as a result of the extensive contacts he'd made while serving in the Office of Strategic Services. He'd been recruited not long after Pearl Harbor by his former commanding officer, Col. William Donovan, and after nearly two years in Washington, D.C., he had spent the rest of the war overseas.

Within a few years of re-establishing his business, he'd hired almost a dozen full-time and half-time assistant investigators to help handle the volume of business. His role quickly evolved into that of desk-bound executive. He affiliated his office with outfits in Chicago, Detroit, Kansas City and L.A. as the All-American Detective Agency, an arrangement that led to Louis Pohl showing up in his office in the late fall of 1954 with an unsolicited sugar-plum offer from International Service Corporation—ISC—to acquire their loose association and integrate it into a tightly run national operation.

It wasn't until the early summer of 1955 that a highly lucrative deal was worked out on cocktail napkins over a prime-rib-and-scotch lunch at Cavanaugh's on 23rd Street and Third Avenue. The sums being discussed were unreal to Dunne. The zeroes spelled out more money than he'd ever dreamed of having (or desired, for that matter).

The terms they finally agreed on were simple enough. He would retire from management of the agency, which would be integrated into ISC over a three-year period. Pohl offered the full price of sale upfront, as well as a "consultant's fee" paid out for the first three years. This included an agreement not to sign on with any other agency during that time. There was a small banquet in a private dining room at the Hotel Astor for Dunne and the executives at ISC. The cocktail hour went on for two and was followed by champagne and lobster tails. At the end, Pohl handed him an envelope. Inside were all those zeroes once again. This time, instead of a cocktail napkin, they were on a cashier's check.

Roberta asked him several times if he was sure he was ready to retire, but she didn't try to argue him out of it. When he said he thought they should get away from the city, with its sweltering summers and miserable winters, she went and scouted a new home for them in Florida. Without even seeing it, he told her to go ahead and buy it, which she did.

On their last night in New York, after they'd packed up the apartment in Washington Heights and sent everything ahead, they stayed at the Hotel Pennsylvania. Next morning was hot and close. They threaded their way across Seventh Avenue through a hopeless choke of traffic. The gray-brown brew of car exhaust, humidity and overheated air was the same dull color as the gargantuan Roman-style railroad station. A single honk set off a storm of blaring horns that cascaded up and down the avenue. Roberta put her hands over her ears. Barely able to hear what she was saying, he read her lips: *Fin, let's get the hell outta here.*

The train to Florida gave them a chance to relax. Roberta mostly read. He mostly slept. As soon as they arrived, she got to work fixing up their new house. Dunne thought everything looked fine, but she kept pointing out where she intended to have a wall torn down or a new patio installed. He napped, read, took a long swim in the pool each afternoon, until, gradually, at no particular moment he could recall, it dawned on him that this wasn't a vacation but a life.

Sometime in the autumn, he began to have trouble sleeping. Reading didn't help. He sat by the pool and blew smoke rings at the stars. Roberta urged him to try golf. He quit after three lessons because his right shoulder hurt. She signed them up for weekly dance lessons, an hour of constant motion. Mambo. Conga. Rumba. "Listen to the dance instructor," she said. Handsome, agile Felipe Calderon. "See, Fin, he never looks at his feet." *Cha cha cha.* Left knee bent, left foot forward, right knee bent, left leg straightens to receive the weight. As long as he took time to flex his knees beforehand, he not only enjoyed the class, but it became the high point of the week.

Early one morning, as the sky grew light and bird chatter became hysterical, he sat by the pool, which was drained for cleaning, resealing and repainting. A horizontal scum line, like a bathtub ring, marked where the water had been. He decided to take a trip. At the behest of the executives at ISC, he told Roberta. They wanted a report on the Chicago regional office, make sure the new guys weren't screwing up. A white lie—or, more accurately, off-white, like the color she had the bathroom painted above the blue tiles. ISC hadn't asked, but they hadn't put the kibosh on his trip either (though admittedly, since he never sought permission, it never had the chance).

He went by train. Just outside Chicago, he rescued a movie-fan magazine abandoned by a portly woman in a peach-colored coat and matching hat who'd been next to him in the lounge car.

He opened to a gushy article about Humphrey Bogart and Lauren Bacall: "True Love Trumps Gap in Age." Hard not to like Bogart as an actor, despite the way he had ruined the detective trade with that Sam Spade and Philip Marlowe hokum that acted like a magnet for out-of-work, no-talent dreamers who imagined they'd found the easiest way to turn the world's fastest buck. Never was, especially not now, with independents being eaten up by corporate subsidiaries run by former G-Men and the like, to the point there was no getting through the door without a diploma and government experience, a sure-fire formula for turning out bureaucrats instead of bloodhounds.

He dropped in unannounced on the Chicago office only to discover the premises had moved from the basement of a building near the Loop to the upper floor of a glass-and-steel crate with dramatic views of Lake Michigan. The receptionist stared blankly when he gave his name. The agency manager was standard military issue from his salt-and-pepper crew cut to his highly polished wingtips, polite in stand-offish G-Man fashion, doing his best to hide his irritation at the surprise visit. After enough time had passed that it wouldn't seem rude, he fussed with some papers on his desk, mumbled about the need to get back to "implementing the many opportunities for expanding our business," and stood. Dunne resisted the urge to salute.

Next morning, before checking out of the Drake, he took a stroll. The day was unseasonably mild until the wind from the lake switched direction and blew in an armada of lead-colored, sleet-laden clouds. By noon, it was wet, blustery, and rapidly getting nastier. He decided to continue his trip, and sent a wire to Roberta to let her know Chicago had gone so well, ISC asked him to drop in on the L.A. office. Then he wired Jeff Wine, a pal from the OSS and head of the ISC's L.A. office, to inform him he'd be in town on some personal business and would love to get together.

He booked a compartment on the *Super Chief*. Except for an occasional foray to the dining car, he mostly slept, soundly and dreamlessly, lullabyed by the monotonous, comforting clickety-clack of train and track.

Wine met him at L.A.'s Santa Fe station. Tanned and relaxed, with mailbag-sized pouches beneath his eyes and mahogany-dyed, Duco-finished hair, and clad in a green sports jacket with no lapels, Wine was plump and ripe, the epitome of Fred Allen's quip, "At fifty everybody in California looks like an avocado." But Wine seemed a most ripe and happy avocado: divorced with grown kids, grateful ISC had left him in his job as local agency head, and infatuated with life in southern California after cold, dark New York. "A yesterday city," he put it, "if there's ever been one."

Dunne checked in at the Beverly Wilshire and left his winter duds in his valise. Wine took him to buy a new wardrobe of slacks and short-sleeved shirts at Sulka's. They cruised in Wine's chrome-rich Studebaker Speedster beneath the stately palms of Beverly Hills. Poking at the car's push-button radio, he strayed from station to station, never listening for more than a minute, except for Nat King Cole's rendition of "Darling, Je Vous Aime Beaucoup," which he listened to in its entirety.

Wine did most of the talking. He had a radio announcer's voice, as buttery and smooth as Cole's crooning. Airplane and defense industries, concerned over spying and the stealing of trade secrets by rival companies, were fast becoming the agency's biggest sources of revenue. But the studios remained big clients. Still reeling from allegations of Communist infiltration and trying to fend off television's mortal threat with gimmicks like CinemaScope, Cinerama and 3-D, they paid whatever it took to keep tabs on dwindling stables of stars and would-be stars, and to head off scandal.

Wine kept a special file cabinet under lock and key in a windowless room in the basement beneath the office. Like a Great White Hunter with his wall of stuffed lion and tiger heads, he insisted on displaying his trophies to Dunne, opening file after file of surveillance reports and plucking out photos of various well-known Hollywood personalities, past and present, caught in situations and positions "indelicate, indecent, immoral or illegal—pick your category," Wine said.

He removed several glossies from a file and held them to his chest. "These are from the all-of-the-above category." They were taken some time ago, he said, while the agency kept tabs for a studio on Merry Lane, a promising starlet (improbable as it sounded, Merry Lane was her real name) whose fiery temperament and passion for liquor and South American pool boys incinerated her promise. He laid them out in front of Dunne. Though shot from a distance, they were clearly of a couple enjoying carnal relations on a chaise lounge.

Wine jabbed a finger at the couple. "Look close."

Dunne craned his neck and squinted. What at first appeared a twosome turned out to be a ménage à trois. And the trois had a tail. "Don't tell me that's a dog."

"Could be a mutt, or maybe a studio executive. It's not always easy to tell the difference." Wine put the photos back and locked the cabinet. "Merry was a stunner. Had Hollywood in the palm of her hand but went her own merry way too many times. AWOL from the studio for extended periods. Public spats with lovers. Too much booze. Last I heard she was reading palms in the Silver Moon Tea House, a clip joint on the Strip not far from where the Garden of Allah used to be in the old Hollywood days. Salesmen and tourists go there to get their fortunes told, which sometimes includes a rendezvous with one of the neighborhood B-girls, and musicians from the local clubs stop in to stock up on marijuana cigarettes."

Three consecutive nights, they ended up in the same after-hours club, sharing stories from their days in the OSS. Wine reminisced about the troop ship they traveled on to England in 1943 amid a furious winter storm that hit halfway across the Atlantic and sent towering, green-blue waves crashing onto the ship, making it shudder as though hit by a torpedo. "I kept praying a U-Boat would send us to the bottom. That way I wouldn't be remembered as the guy who died puking his guts out on a Navy tub." Finger for stirrer, he twirled the remainder of his drink around in the glass, a miniature maelstrom, and shook his head. "Good God, Fin, it's like it all happened a lifetime ago, not a decade."

"Sometimes," Dunne said, "a decade is a lifetime."

They listened to the trio of Negro musicians play elaborate, looping improvisations over *Body and Soul*, expert and sad even if it wasn't Coleman Hawkins or Charlie Parker. If it didn't relieve the dim smokiness of the room, at least it made it feel appropriate.

Wine launched into a story about the late actor John Garfield. They'd both been fans of his. A kid from the streets of New York, he'd possessed the same tough presence as Jimmy Cagney, the genuine article, the kind that can't be faked. Garfield's fame as a film star, earned in movies like *Body and Soul*, had been overwhelmed by his death *in flagrante delicto*. Dunne expected a funny anecdote. Instead, Wine related how on the night Garfield's little girl died, his friends had called in a panic, unsure of where he was and afraid he was going to kill himself or somebody else. When Wine finished talking, they sat and drank in silence.

For the third morning in a row Dunne woke with the same painful, distracting half-buzz, half-ache above his left eye that reminded him why he hated hangovers. *Pace yourself.* A golden rule, on the job and off. He took a long swim in the pool. Same rule there: *pace yourself.* He left a message for Wine: *Thanks for everything. Have to get back to Florida.* Instead of packing the clothes he'd bought, he hung them in the closet with a note letting the maid know they were there for the taking.

With several hours to kill before his train was scheduled to depart, he sent his bag ahead to the station and took a cab to a Greek lunch shop on the Strip that Wine had recommended. He ordered a large glass of freshly squeezed orange juice and a lamb and butter sandwich served on thick white bread with the crust cut off. After, he strolled along with no thought of a particular destination. Two blocks later he came upon a moldering Spanish-style stucco storefront in general agreement with the seen-better-days musical instrument store and dingy jazz club it was sandwiched between. Above the door was a modest, sun-blistered sign with several letters bleached and weather-beaten into oblivion: PALM REA ER AND ORTUNE TELLER TO TH STARS.

The door was locked and no hours were posted. Unsure he'd go in even if it was open, he admitted to himself he wasn't incurious about what had happened to Merry Lane, the fallen starlet. ("Rhymes with harlot, don't forget," Wine joked.) He'd seen her years ago as the sensational centerpiece of "Earl Carroll's Vanities," the raciest review on Broadway; she was a performer with that rare and priceless combination of gorgeous looks and genuine talent. At the time Merry signed with a Hollywood studio for an outrageous sum, half the countrys population was wondering where their next meal was coming from. Her picture had been splashed all over the newspapers.

He put his face close to the chipped, rusted iron bars on the window. The glare and grime-streaked glass made it hard to see anything. He groped between the bars, swiped clear a swath of dirt and dust with one hand, and shaded his eyes with the other. Tables and potted palms were arranged around what looked like a dance floor. A counter near the door held a large silver samovar and several bottles of yellow and green liqueurs.

The dented metal door opened enough for a skull-like head, with gray stubble on chin and on top, to stick out. "Hey, peepin' Tom, who you lookin' for?"

"Merry Lane work here?" Dunne stepped back from the window.

"Sometimes."

He brushed his hands together to rid them of dust and flakes of rust. "When?"

"Later."

"How much later?"

"What's your hurry?"

"Train to catch."

"Need your fortune told before it goes?" The door swung open. The skull was wired by a scrawny, thin neck to a tall, spindly frame. At the top of his patched, frayed plaid shirt, a tuft of silver hair sprouted through. His oversized khaki army pants looked as though they'd been through both world wars. "What's the matter? 'Fraid the train might jump the tracks?" He came out and leaned against the door.

"Never know, do you?"

"You do when you spot a cop creepin' up to the window." His mouth was full of brown teeth and empty spaces. Swollen, red-veined eyes logged the end of well-soaked nights followed by increasingly fuzzy-headed, dry-mouthed mornings, the wasted look of someone paying the price for decades of hard living, ex-boxer, ex-bouncer, now janitor, on his way to being an anonymous ex-everything breathing his last beneath the chicken-wire ceiling of some Skid Row flophouse.

Dunne approached him. The sour, damp odor from inside was more barroom than tea room. "Better trade in the old crystal ball. I'm a tourist."

"And I'm Mandrake the Magician. Don't need no crystal ball tell me we're paid up full. You think you're goin' to do a little freelance shakedown of your own? Go on, take a walk, or I'll let your compadres on the local patrol know you're tryin' to horn in."

Dunne moved near enough to grab his collar, ball it in his fist, twist tight. An old reflex, almost irresistible. What he'd done, minus a second thought, to plenty of back-talking punks. But not a grumpy wreck like this, a geezer filled with harmless sass, the real menace gone out of him. Dunne reached into the breast pocket of his jacket, took out the travel agency envelop that held his ticket and waved it in his face, tauntingly. "Got a train to catch, pal, otherwise I'd stay and finish this conversation."

"Ain't no pal of yours." Hostility yielding to curiosity, the man leaned close, as if scrutinizing a notice of dispossess or a search warrant. He squinted to make out the name on the envelope. "So go catch your choo-choo, Mr. Dunne, Fintan."

"Congratulations, you can read. Now learn to talk nice. Might bring in some customers. Who knows? Maybe you'll be able to afford a fresh coat of paint."

"Paint my ass." He turned to go back inside. "Got all the customers we need." The door to the Silver Moon slammed shut behind him.

Re-pocketing the ticket, Dunne's fingers touched his chest, registered the hard, accelerated heartbeat. He breathed deeply, exhaled slowly, and glanced at his watch. If he lingered much longer, he might miss the train. He headed to the corner and hailed a cab. It idled, waiting for the light to change. In the window of the Silver Moon, in the space where he'd cleared the grime from the glass, was a small, feminine, oval-shaped face, deathly pale, wide-eyed, with an estimating gaze, the kind worn by the very young and the very old, a cross between fright and surprise. After a second or two, it was gone.

He spent the first hour of the train trip regretting the stop at the Silver Moon. Innocent enough, motivated by curiosity, that's all. But in the case of a career fallen as far as Merry Lane's, maybe curiosity was just another word for cruelty. A lesson worth remembering: There are those who want nothing more than to be forgotten and enjoy whatever peace obscurity provides. In Merry's case, better to let sleeping dogs lie, he decided, if that's who her companion had been, and not a studio executive. He went to the lounge car and ordered a Scotch.

One afternoon soon after he returned to Florida, as Roberta was driving him back from a haircut, he noticed a black Plymouth following behind. He had the distinct feeling it was tailing them. He told Roberta to go to the next light and make a U-turn without signaling.

"What's this all about?" She sounded more annoyed than skeptical.

"Indulge me, that's all."

Stopped at the light, she murmured in a voice so low he didn't know if she was talking to herself or to him, "Lately, that's all I do." The light turned green. She swung the car around sharp enough that the tires squealed. The Plymouth kept going straight. "Grow up, Fin." This time it was clear who she was talking to.

The next two weeks dragged by. On Saturday morning, when he came into the kitchen, Roberta was already dressed and was putting corn muffins in the oven that she'd made from a box of mix. As she sat down at the kitchen table to read the newspaper, she mentioned her plan to go to Miami the next day to visit Elba and her children. Did he want to come? Glancing down at the newspaper cover story on the upcoming inauguration of Cuban President Batista and his country's newfound prosperity, he replied casually, as if he'd been planning it for some time and it hadn't just popped into his head, that he decided he'd take a trip to Havana.

He poured himself a cup of coffee and sat across from her. He'd told her before he didn't care for corn muffins. He preferred a single pastry as a breakfast treat, like the ones at the little Italian bakery next to their apartment building in New York. But there wasn't a decent cannoli or sfogliatelle within several hundred miles.

She opened the newspaper to the horoscope. Familiar routine that he knew by heart. She read aloud in a business-like voice, beginning with his sign: Virgo. Attributes: melancholy, analytical, practical, earthy, on and on. She repeated the predictions as if they contained a corn-muffin crumb's worth of truth and weren't the concocted mumbo jumbo of some booze hound who could no longer handle the rewrite desk.

"'Virgos should stay close to home and avoid new departures.' Listening, Fin?"

"To that superstitious crap?"

"Like dreams, superstitions can reflect experience. They've lessons to teach." Roberta got up and went over to the stove.

He knew instantly that not only *what* he'd said but *how* he'd said it—the irritated tone—hurt her feelings. He came over and slipped his arms around her waist. "Trip out west left me more tuckered than I realized. Few days with nothing to do is all I need." He pulled her close. No wedded bliss without marital piss. Recipe every married couple eventually learns, or doesn't: half cup of spats, disagreements, silences and scars; full cup of things forgiven, forgotten and endured; mix, stir, pour, bake. Let cool before serving.

She pressed her hands against his shoulders, arched backwards, looked into his eyes. "It's as easy to do nothing here as in Havana."

"Havana is more relaxed."

"Maybe what you need is less relaxation and more stimulation." She kissed him on the neck, then rested her head on his shoulder.

It struck Dunne that though neither the original Spanish explorers nor the hordes that followed had found the Fountain of Youth in Florida, Roberta did better than most. She'd closed up her successful interior-decorating practice in New York and segued into their new life with a grace and ease not unlike what she displayed on the dance floor, never missing a step, always in sync with the music. He doubted she'd ever slide into retirement's flab-happy cycle of too much food and too little movement.

When he first met her in 1938, he thought she was detached in the cold-blooded way of those who grew up as she did, father dead and gone while she was still a small child, raised by her mother, a widowed garment worker, stint in the reformatory, early and unsuccessful marriage, illegitimate child she had to give away, time spent working as a hooker. The street was a finishing school of sorts, its graduates as soft and sympathetic as reinforced concrete, skilled in the etiquette of commercial sex, tit(s)-for-tat, you only get what you pay for, nothing more, never on the house.

Lizzie Scaccio was people's exhibit number one. When he was still on the homicide squad, they got called to the cat house Lizzie ran on Grand Street. Two hoods in a stiletto fight over one of the girls had sliced each other with fatal precision. A double homicide. Black-haired, eagle-beaked Lizzie sat honing her talon-like nails with an emery board. "Call the morgue," she said, "and get these shitheads outta here." It was a busy night, she was told. Be a while before the morgue boys arrived. She made a fist with thumb protruding from the middle and flicked it away from her front teeth. Sicilian gesture that didn't mean thank you. "Get the garbage men. They'll know what to do."

Roberta always had more class than the Lizzie Scaccio type, for sure. She carried herself with a high-toned style that belied her background. Beautiful, self-assured, long and svelte, she had a

24

cool poise that he'd taken at first for a stony indifference to anything but her own self-interest. She hired him to work on a case. That was that. He wasn't about to get romantically involved, even if the possibility existed, which he was sure it didn't.

He admired her before he loved her. Only gradually did he discover that what he mistook as indifference was the cover she used to mask her fierce, passionate attachment to those she loved. He was almost surprised when, on a warm summer's evening, as they dined al fresco at Ben Marden's, he'd looked across the table at her and realized how grudging admiration had quietly, without him noticing, become something more, much more, something he resisted putting a name on because he had no intention of falling in love. Neither did she, she told him after they were married. "But isn't that always the way with love?" she said. "It just happens."

But Roberta wasn't like those penny-a-piece cherry melts candy stores used to sell, hard outside, gooey center, the soft-hearted hooker of the pulps. She was practical, not sentimental. Instead of worrying whether the glass was half-full or half-empty, she found a way to fill it. When she cared for someone, it was with clear-eyed appreciation of their faults as well as their graces, and when she loved it was with a purpose and strength that never seemed to waver or ebb. Child of a Catholic mother and Jewish father, she had no interest in any faith. But though not the slightest bit religious, she approached life devoid of doubts. Her poise applied inside as well as out. Nothing seemed to throw her.

The physical enjoyment he had with her was still real. Dunne couldn't speak for every doughboy or G.I. who went overseas, but he'd bet most came back with a different appreciation for sex than they'd gone over with, and in his experience that was especially true in the first war, the bordellos of France serving as an erotic Harvard and Yale for boys who would have otherwise never made it past grammar school. Their expectations weren't the only thing that was raised. They discovered that there was technique involved in the give and get of lovemaking, a body of bodily knowledge that if learned and applied could make the experience infinitely more pleasurable.

From the start, part of the attraction that Dunne and Roberta felt was their shared attitude toward sex. It was as though they'd been practicing all their lives for when they found one another. He left for the Second World War intending to be faithful. While it was less of an education than the first war, his final report card wasn't without its blemishes. He wasn't proud of the times he strayed but felt the circumstances made those lapses inevitable, and, besides, he'd done his bit in confession. They weren't memories that preyed on him.

Their lovemaking wasn't as intense or as frequent as when he first returned. Though she seemed almost always amenable to his advances, the initiative came more and more from her, a studied seduction, flash of flesh, high heels, black nylons with the seams up the back.

Several nights before, after they'd made love, he fell into a vivid dream in which he drove Wine's sporty Speedster fast as he could down a road he didn't recognize. He kept glancing in the rearview mirror at the black car trailing behind, ahead only an enveloping, obliterating whiteness. He turned the wheel, but the car stayed on the same course. The engine emitted a high-pitched whine, a sound he'd heard before. Where? He tried to press the brake, but it wasn't there. At that point, Roberta poked him. "Fin," she said, "wake up. You're shouting."

This morning, he searched for an excuse other than the truth: lack of interest, at least for the moment. "You're all dressed."

She took the muffins and put them on top of the stove. "That's easy to undo."

"Tonight," he said. "Be our dessert."

She walked away, grabbed her purse from the kitchen table, and lifted the car keys from the hook by the door. "Maybe you should get involved in something besides business trips. Why not volunteer at the veteran's hospital?"

He wasn't opposed to the notion. But not now. Better save it for the day when the company of addled and ailing men would be inevitable, even comforting. That evening's dance lesson put him in a better mood. They both enjoyed what followed. But the extra-long nap he'd taken in the afternoon left him unable to sleep. He sat by the still-drained pool and smoked. As day neared, one bird, up before the others, sang a frantically pitched solo. It was hard to tell if it was the proverbial early bird, or lonely, lost, bored, or just crazy. Maybe a little of everything. Stars and moon folded themselves into morning light.

He dozed on the flight to Havana. He was groggy when he got off, but his spirits quickly revived. Havana always had that effect, memories of his honeymoon with Roberta, that first day on the balcony of their hotel, admiring the cobalt sky, a color so singular it deserved a name of its own: Havana blue. It was just before the war torpedoed the tourist trade and gambling came under a temporary ban, around the time, he remembered, when the Tropicana opened. They watched the movie actor Errol Flynn, obviously plastered, as he danced with a lovely Cuban woman half his age.

Drunk or not, Flynn was steady on his feet as he and the woman laughed and glided across the dance floor. In those last evenings before phony war gave way to real, everybody seemed handsome, beautiful, happy, all painted with the lush, forgiving, silver glow of the moon. Only a little more than fifteen years before, but felt as though it were fifty.

The sky over Havana was the same, but change was in the

air. Construction cranes dotted the horizon. Influences from the north grew ever more pronounced. Thanks to the new passenger ferries, the once rare sight of shiny, big, fin-tailed American cars was now common on the city's streets. Installed by coup, with a wink and a nod from Washington, the hopelessly corrupt regime of Fulgencio Batista worked in league with American gangsters. They had the run of the city's nightlife, like New York during Prohibition when Oweny Madden and his fellow bootleggers operated nightclubs, speakeasies and gambling joints, their enterprises blessed by Mayor Jimmy Walker.

The situation in Cuba drove patriots like Wilfredo Grillo mad. Yet Dunne had yet to meet a visitor from the north who wasn't charmed by the sea-scented island city with its blazing sunlight and torrid nightlife, stately streets and wide avenues, friendly, courteous, disproportionately handsome people as multi-hued as Howard Johnson's 28 kinds of ice cream—deep chocolate, coconut, vanilla fudge, pecan, cocoa marshmallow, and everything in between. Sedate, orderly, sexy, exciting, seething, beautiful, dirt poor, magical, and everything in between. *Habana*. Name your poison, pal.

The bitter temperatures in the northeast U.S. made it impossible to get a reservation, now at the height of the tourist season, in one of the grand old hotels, the Seville-Baltimore, or Plaza, or the sumptuous Nacional. Dunne booked a room in a smaller, remodeled one—sleek, modern—that catered to the growing airline trade. At check-in, he bantered in Spanish with the desk clerk.

A retired teacher, widowed, the clerk had landed part-time work at the hotel when the tourist trade was at its peak. The management insisted he become proficient in English, a process he'd only recently begun. Dressed in an old-style wing-collar shirt, an even older-styled pince-nez attached by a black ribbon to his lapel, he gestured at the brash, shiny lobby, Formica counters, faux-crystal chandelier. "We must stay with the breasts of the times," he said. "*¿Ese es el dicho que usan en los Estados Unidos, no?*"

"*Sí.*" Dunne understood Spanish and could speak a fair amount, an ability he'd picked up from Roberta.

He ate breakfast on the balcony outside his room. He enjoyed the morning breeze, though it pushed against the pages of his *Havana Post* and made it hard to read about the new prosperity washing over the city, plans for new hotels, casinos that would finance public improvements. The ad for the Tropicana boasted that thanks to headliner Nat King Cole, it was totally booked. But he hadn't come to join the hordes of *Yanquí touristas* at the sex shows, or in the noisy, crowded nightclubs, with their gaudy-bawdy floor shows, or to gawk at the high rollers in the more well-known casinos. He wanted the distraction of Havana's relaxed rhythms, the easy gait of that pre-war city, busy but never in a hurry.

He decided to go early to the Club House at the newly refurbished Oriental Park Racetrack, before it got crowded, to watch the workouts and the first races; afternoon, single glass of rum and a cigar in a small café off the Malecón where all the U.S. newspapers were available; afterwards, join all the true *Habaneros* in a nap. That night he'd visit the Starlight Room at the Old Madrid to play roulette, the place where Roberta had spotted the usually casino-shy Ernest Hemingway. Still had a pre-war feel. Dunne called Eddie Moran, the head bouncer, to let him know he was coming. An old pal from the 69th Regiment, Moran was one of countless Prohibition-era tourists who, after several Cuba Libres at Sloppy Joe's on Zulueta Street, talked about returning for good. Eddie actually did.

Dunne decided to swim a few laps in the hotel pool but went on for longer than he planned. Afterwards, he had a session with Nestor, the poolside masseur, a tall, muscled Argentinean who raged with barely contained ferocity against Juan Perón and his dead wife, Eva, and the way they ruined his country. "Sooner or later, the bandits come to power." He pressed his fists down so hard into Dunne's shoulders that he barely choked back a yelp. "You'll see," Nestor said, "one day it'll be your country's turn."

Relaxed and aglow, Dunne closed the shutters in his room and lay down for a few moments under the hypnotic whir of the ceiling fan. He was startled from sleep by the telephone on the nightstand. The time on his wristwatch was 5:15. He'd slept the afternoon away. He picked up the phone. The hotel operator asked him to hold while she connected him to an international line. An instant later, after a burst of static, a nasally, high-pitched voice announced a long-distance, person-to-person call from New York. *Mister Bud Mulholland for Mister Fintan Dunne. Is Mr. Dunne available?*

Dunne sat up, doubly taken back. He'd presumed Roberta was calling to scold him for not calling to tell her he'd landed safely. "Let me see if I can locate him." He put his hand over the receiver.

He knew only one Bud Mulholland. Not exactly Mr. Sympathy or somebody to turn to for cheering up, Mulholland was someone you wanted around when the big guns went off. When Colonel Donovan had brought Dunne into the OSS as one of his New York micks—veterans of the first war who added a dollop of operational experience and street sense to the service's high-toned mix of Wall Streeters and Ivy Leaguers—he'd told him to be on the lookout for other prospects. Dunne recommended Mulholland, who proved a most worthwhile recruit. Tell him who had to be eliminated, time, place, mode of transportation: he'd do it or train someone who could.

It was nine years since Dunne had last seen him. Post-war partying of spring and summer subsided into grim London winter. Mulholland said little, which wasn't unusual among those long in combat. But he seemed to be suffering not so much war's impact as absence. Known for the precision with which he dispatched those marked for elimination, he'd been in continual action since 1943, behind enemy lines in Holland, with the Italian partisans, in the advance into Germany. In his cups, one of the Ivy League OSS recruits who'd been with Mulholland on several missions observed: "Bud's got two passions. Slaying the Axis's men and laying the Allies' ladies. Now, he's reduced to the latter which, unfortunately, isn't the one he finds most pleasurable."

Dunne took his hand from the receiver. "This is Fintan Dunne."

"Go ahead, please, Mr. Mulholland," the operator said. "Your party's on the line."

The voice at the other end came through clearly, except for an echo when it paused. "Dunne, you bum, taking it easy down there, while we're freezing our keisters off up here . . . *here.*"

"Bud?"

"How many other Mulhollands in New York do you know? . . . *know?*

"How'd you know I was here?"

"Your wife didn't want to tell, I think maybe I frightened her, said it was a matter of life and death . . . *death.*"

"Who's?"

"Nobody's, really, I was exaggerating, but it's important, and I'm calling on behalf of someone with a lot of clout wants you and nobody else . . . *else.*"

"I'm retired."

"So I hear . . . *hear.*" Mulholland didn't say anything more.

If Dunne wanted to end the conversation, now was the moment. "What's involved?"

"Even if I knew, I wouldn't yap about it on the phone, party in question will only discuss it with you and only in person . . . *person.*"

"When?"

"Yesterday preferably, tomorrow if possible . . . *possible.*"

"I just got here."

"Fly all the way and don't worry what it costs . . . *costs.*"

"Prefer the train."

"Suit yourself, but he wants that you should start right away . . . *away.*"

"He?"

"Come north, 'cause that's the only way you're going to find out . . . *out.*"

Holding back an answer, he mentioned business to wrap up, other options to consider. Left unmentioned: pride, genuine uncertainty, abrupt unexpectedness of the offer. He'd call in the morning with his decision.

"Suit yourself, Fin, but an opportunity like this won't come again . . . *again.*"

He ordered dinner in his room. The long nap didn't interfere with a solid night's sleep. In the morning, with his mind made up to pursue Mulholland's proposal, he went in person to let the desk clerk know he'd be checking out.

The desk clerk was busy with a guest. "*Estare con usted en un momento, Señor Dunne,*" he said. He turned the ledger to face the guest on the other side of the counter. "*Mire, aquí esta la lista de reservaciones. Su nombre no aparece en ella.*"

The young, blondish man opposite the clerk had shoulders broad and bulky enough to double as automobile fenders. Before he'd opened his mouth, the pink-and-black checkered sports jacket announced he was from up north. "Try it in English, pal."

"He says your name isn't on the reservation list," Dunne said.

"Already figured that out."

"Just trying to help."

"Much appreciated." The on-and-off flash of his smile,

which had all the spontaneity of a traffic light, said it wasn't. He aimed a finger at the courtly, gray-haired clerk. A red-and-blue serpent was tattooed on the back of his hand. "I booked this trip a month ago through Gateway Travel, so get on the horn here"—he laid his hand on the desk telephone—"and straighten this out pronto, *capice?*"

He sounded as though he was from Chicago. Maybe Cleveland. Got accustomed to flying in the service. Instead of schlepping by boat, take the $39 Pan Am round-trip puddle jumper from Miami or book one of the new direct flights from the Midwest to Havana, airfare, hotel and meals, all included for one affordable price, payable in five easy installments.

Outside, a tour bus began unloading a troop of tourists from the airport. The bellhops struggled to keep order and sort the luggage. The clerk picked up the phone. Fingers drumming lightly on the ledger, he waited for an answer from whoever was on the other end. He turned to Dunne. "*Siento hacerle esperar, Señor.*"

"*No se preocupe. No estoy apurado.*"

The clerk nodded appreciatively, equally grateful for the courtesy of an answer in Spanish and the good manners of a *turista* still loyal to the notion that visitors from the frenetic, inclement north should adjust to the easy-tempered, tropical pace of Habana not the other way around. A moment later, he rested the receiver back in its cradle and said with solemn finality, "*Lo siento, pero . . .*"

Dunne interrupted. "Look, I think I can solve this. I've been called back to the States. My room is available." He repeated himself in Spanish.

"That's nice of you, pal." The guest opposite the clerk stood back, making no attempt to hide that he was sizing up Dunne. His green-blue pupils were the color of angry Atlantic waves. "I got to tell you, you look familiar. Don't have any long-lost relatives in Cicero, Illinois, do you?"

"Not any who would admit it," Dunne replied.

The man opposite Dunne introduced himself as Jack Morello. Dunne asked where he was from. "From the place I just left." He invited Dunne to the hotel bar for a daiquiri (which he pronounced as day-kerry). "Best in Havana, even better than at the Floridita. I'm told I have to try one." He flashed another mechanical smile. Eyes told a different story: pent-up fury of a man cheated at the track, or cuckolded by his wife and knew it. "And I always do as I'm told." He made it sound like a threat.

Dunne explained he had to catch a plane. Morello gave a silent indifferent shrug and walked away.

When Dunne came back through the lobby after retrieving his bag, Morello was gone. No sign of him in the bar either. The memory of that smile, welcoming as a headstone, lingered behind like a half-made threat. Far more Cleveland than Havana. Dunne hurried through the blazing sunshine into a waiting taxi. First thing to do when he got home was make a discreet inquiry about the identity of Mulholland's employer.

He recognized Bud Mulholland right away, appointed time and place, under the clock in Penn Station: gray fedora, gray herringbone coat, black galoshes over black shoes, *New York Standard* under his arm. Plainclothesman's plainclothesman. Ordinary and unprepossessing. Just don't get too near, or mistake that subtle, cynical curve of his mouth for a friendly invitation to get close or make small talk.

"Welcome to the North Pole." Feet slightly apart, right hand clenched and hanging at his side, Mulholland seemed poised to throw a punch. Unlike so many of the vets Dunne encountered since war's end, he hadn't put on weight. If anything, he looked as if he'd lost it. The ramrod straightness that had made him seem taller than he really was had given way to a slight crouch. But maybe the hunch in his shoulders was nothing more than a reflexive defense against the arctic weather.

"Guess I'm too late for Santa." Dunne extended his hand.

Mulholland undid his fist and shook hands. He sniffed. "You been in storage?"

"Coat has." Roberta had retrieved his Rogers Peet double-breasted camel's hair overcoat and packed it in his valise. He'd taken it out to air as the train glided across the Meadowlands, but the smell of mothballs was still overpowering.

"Check your bag, and let's blow before the fumes knock somebody out."

"Where to?"

"The Iron Horse. A bar with no TV. One of the few. We can talk."

"Prefer to listen while you fill me in."

"Can't. He says it's between him and you."

"Who's 'him'?"

"He'll see you at six. For now that's all I can say."

Despite the bustle and hum of the crowds moving through the close-to-shabby station, a khaki-gray sadness haunted the vast interior, as though the memory of all those wartime partings of lovers and spouses—last-minute hugs, clutchings, sobs, tears, forebodings—had seeped into the walls. It was the same tired, worn-down feeling that by war's end was taken for granted everywhere in Europe but seemed out of place in America. It put Dunne in mind of those former residents of Berlin or Vienna who spent their last days in New York sitting stoically in the corners of Bickford's or the Automat, their dignity not erased entirely but visibly depleted, once-stylish clothes frayed and out-of-date: political exiles and genteel, formerly prosperous Jewish refugees, visitors from another time and place, stranded between here and the hereafter.

Mulholland led the way onto wind-slashed Eighth Avenue. Low in the west, the sun was ready to sink behind the General Post Office. Slush puddles were fast solidifying back to ice. Dunne raised his collar, glanced up at the vaguely familiar words carved into the façade: SNOW . . . RAIN . . . GLOOM OF NIGHT . . . APPOINTED ROUNDS.

Up close, Mulholland's quiet, retiring presence had a hard-edged authority, almost menacing, a tightly collared ferocity as charged as an electric wire. He moved a few paces ahead. "Come on," he said over his shoulder. "Move it." Short as he was, people instinctively stepped out of his way.

"How far?"

"Next corner." Mulholland paused and let Dunne catch up. "You must wish you were still in Cuba."

"Right now, I'm thinking my wife was right. Said I'd be nuts to come to New York this time of year."

"Every wife thinks her husband is nuts. Eventually, they're right."

Final blush of plum-tinged twilight filled the window beside the bar. Bartender's banging on the cash-register keys had a musical ring. Impromptu, unintended "Taps."

Day is done, gone the sun.

"At a certain age, things that once seemed important, don't." Fintan Dunne listened for slurring in his voice. *Pace yourself.* So far, so good.

"Stop making yourself sound like Methuselah," Mulholland said. "You look good, Fin. Even got a tan."

Dunne rattled the cubes in his Scotch glass. *Crackle, crackle.* Ice tumbled and fissured. *Crack.* A small sound, but sharp as a pistol shot, accompanied the slowly melting dilution of water trickling into amber-colored alcohol. Always plenty of rocks.

Part of the secret of pacing yourself. "This point I think I know more dead people than living."

"Two world wars. And the conflict or scrape or whatever-the-hell-they-call-it in Korea. Finally a fight they didn't want us in."

Cash-register music again.

Fare thee well; Day has gone.

"Only a few went that way." More than a few, but by unconscious, almost universal agreement among those who'd experienced the worst of war, a topic left undiscussed. Lately, it was getting hard to keep straight who died in which war. Nardelli, Scanlon, Haines, Billy Sullivan in the first. Long list in the second included that milk-faced first lieutenant from Iowa cut in half by a German machine gun at Anzio—whatever his name. "Cancer, strokes and heart attacks are the culprits now."

"Sooner or later something gets you." Mulholland squeezed thumb and forefinger, tweezers-like, into the pack, extracted a last bent cigarette, crumpled the empty pack into a ball, and dropped it in the ashtray. Elbows on the bar, he ripped a match from its book and lit his cigarette. "Me, I'll take the John Garfield way."

"Who hasn't heard that story?" Dunne poked the ice with a plastic stirrer, horse-shaped head, name printed lengthwise: IRON HORSE LOUNGE. He remembered Garfield in *Body and Soul.* Slugged it out with the moxie of a real boxer. *I'm the champ. It's gonna be easy.* Then it got hard. Dead five years later, not even forty. "He had a wife and kids. True or not, they can't like hearing it."

"Ever hear of a man died screwing his wife?" Mulholland scooped loose change from the bar. "Garfield croaked saddling a showgirl. Other things contributed, sure, booze, bum ticker, blacklisted from the movies on account of that stuff about being a Commie. They tried to get him 'to name names.' It ate at him.

A buddy of mine did the investigation, let me eyeball the file. Garfield was an alley cat. Poke any knothole available. Least he died smiling."

He went over and deposited coins in the cigarette machine and returned with two packs; he laid one on the bar and slid it to Dunne. Out in L.A., Jeff Wine's sordid intelligence on the movie industry came with the details of the night when Garfield's little girl died in his wife's arms, and he sprayed the backyard with an automatic weapon before staggering mad with grief into the Hollywood hills as he howled like a werewolf in a B-grade horror film. A heart that broke before it stopped.

"Whoopi-ty-aye-oh," Mulholland crooned in a low, surprisingly mellifluous voice, "let me go the John Garfield way, back in the saddle again." He opened the pack, lit a cigarette, extinguished the flame with a single hard snap of his wrist. "You've been away a while." He handed the matchbook to Dunne.

Dunne lit a cigarette of his own. "Business pretty much runs itself. It didn't need me. I didn't need it. Why should I hang around?"

"Traded the sunny southland for this ice box. You must need something."

Dunne nodded at Mulholland's reflection in the mirror behind the bar. He had a point. They exhaled simultaneously. The smoke seeped into watery yellow light above, flattening into a wavering line of gray vapor, ghostly, and conjuring in Dunne's mind the image of a ridiculously young and hideously wounded Kraut lieutenant captured (stumbled over was closer to the truth) in late 1944. Intestines oozing across the charred, shredded remnants of what had been genitals and legs, he raises two fingers to his mouth, sign language for a cigarette. Somebody sticks a lit one in the boy soldier's mouth. He utters something in German.

"What'd he say?" a G.I. asks.

A gaunt Jewish private from Yonkers (who'd be obliterated by an anti-tank gun the following week) translates: "Wants us to shoot him."

In the background, a G.I. jams an ammo clip into place. Let the Kraut enjoy a drag before releasing him from his suffering; the most basic of battlefield mercies, though it never shows up in official reports or newspaper accounts or newsreels.

Kraut takes a deep draw, exhales a long wheezing breath, speaks a few ragged, agonized words that sound devoid of any parting salute to Hitler or National Socialism.

The G.I. aims. "Is he praying?"

The soon-to-die private shakes his head. "It's a line from a poem, I think: 'The souls of dead comrades vanish like smoke.'" Kraut's last words.

The dimness of Mulholland's reflections softened but didn't erase his crooked smile. He sat with his arms folded on the bar. "Soon as I heard the need was for the 'best detective in the business,' I says, 'Fintan Dunne, he's your man.'"

"I'm out of the business." A slight exaggeration, since he hadn't sold the agency outright to ISC. But he was out of the day-to-day operations and, soon enough, ISC would amalgamate it into a highly predictable, hugely lucrative national network of franchises offering professional security services to corporations and manufacturers, about as exciting and interesting as applying for a driver's license.

"If you were, you wouldn't be here." Mulholland dragged on his cigarette, sipped his drink, and coughed a harsh, gagging rasp. He stood, hands on the bar, shoulders heaving from the effort to catch his breath.

Dunne slapped his back hard. The coughing subsided. "Went down the wrong pipe, that's all." He wiped his eyes with a cocktail napkin. "I'm fine."

Bartender handed Mulholland a glass of water. Dunne gave

another pat, lighter than the last. Resting his hand on Mulholland's jacket, he felt the sharp, prominent vertebrae beneath, angular components of a hard, spare body, repository of several slugs and jagged shards, souvenirs of wars local as well as global, several decades of blood-drenched history. He ran his hand in a casual frisk across his shoulders. No holster strap.

Mulholland retook his stool. "I said, 'Dunne don't need dough. Even if he did, that's not why he'd enlist.' I know you long enough to know that. What's it been, Fin? How many years?"

"Enough, I guess." They'd met on the NYPD after both were wounded and decorated in the first war. Mulholland's baptismal name was Ambrose, which he despised and never used. Always introduced himself as Bud. Promoted to detective, he made a name for himself as a stylish denizen of the Broadway nightlife. He got in the headlines as a result of a gun battle with two of Dutch Schultz's shooters in a dive on West 54th Street. Killed them both and took four slugs in the process. Out on his own, Mulholland was working private security for a Wall Street firm when intermission ended and war two began.

"'Only one thing'll bring you Dunne,' I said. Know what it is?"

Bartender: "'Nother?"

Dunne passed him his glass. "Ice is all."

Flanked by two crevices, Mulholland's delicate, slightly rounded nose was like a small hill between two rifts. Puffy, half-moon blotches hung beneath each eye. Brooding and care-worn, his face retained a shadow of the darkly handsome, so-called black-Irish good looks the tabloids had plastered all over their front pages.

At the height of his career in the NYPD, not long after the shoot-out with Schultz's associates, Mulholland landed back on the front pages. One morning while he was still asleep, his showgirl lover tiptoed into the bathroom with his service revolver, turned muzzle to chest, thumbs on trigger, squeezed—he'd taught her the squeezing part, at dusk, on the beach at Rockaway, the gun's report echoing loudly, like a cannon shot—and blew a hole in her heart.

The tabloids described him as "the hero cop with the map of Ireland on his face." True enough. Irish by way of Hell's Kitchen, Mulholland had the old country imprinted on his mug, all right. But over time that map had lost any resemblance to the phony-baloney, tin-pan-alley, little-bit-of-heaven version of Ireland. Mulholland's was the real thing: A map with too much history, most of it bad: conquest, famine, rebellion, civil war. Stony, sullen, the joy knocked out of it.

"The suspense is killing me," Dunne said. "What's the one thing?"

"Vanity. Fintan Dunne won't accept there's a case he can't solve."

"Spell vanity b-o-r-e-d-o-m, you got a point."

"Get the kind of ink you got for rescuing that guinea kid from the chair, you're hooked. When it comes to getting high, heroin's got nothing on fame."

"Wilfredo Grillo was Cuban, not Italian, and he wasn't a kid. He was almost forty. Besides, that was seventeen years ago."

"Bible got it right. Look it up. Book of Ecclesiastes. 'Vanity, vanity, all is vanity.'"

"When did you become a Bible reader, Bud?"

"Haven't gone Protestant, if that's what you're implying. But spend enough time in hotel rooms, you end up taking a look. Belongs as much to us as the left-footers, and once you get beyond the 'begats' and 'beholds,' there's some gems. That vanity stuff made me think of you. 'Christ,' I says to myself, 'one of these days they'll probably make Dunne's life into a movie, one I'll be sure to miss.'"

In the casual mental accounting he sometimes did of friends, acquaintances, business contacts, Dunne always put Mulholland in column one, a consequence more of length of time than any emotional tie.

"You had your share of headlines, Bud." Dunne didn't go near the showgirl suicide, an old headline but still freshly printed on Mulholland's face.

"Know why I recommended you?" Mulholland obviously intended to answer the question himself. "You're lucky, that's why. Any idiot can learn this racket. What he can't learn is luck, and that's what it comes down to: You're either born lucky or not."

Dunne used the horse-headed stirrer to swirl the shrunken ice in his drink, now more water than Scotch. He entertained pointing out that his luck was bad as well as good: orphaned, wounded, thwarted in his career as a cop, beaten, almost drowned, old wound behind his knee that made it hard to climb stairs, insomnia. But he knew Mulholland took for granted ordinary tragedies and hurts to focus on the totality of a life that included a happy marriage, business success and, if not fame, fleeting notice. Not a charmed life, but luckier than most.

"Neither of us would be here without our share of luck," Dunne said.

Mulholland's only acknowledgment of his own luck in arriving here, midway in a war-ridden century, all parts functioning—mostly—was a shrug. "You got the breaks, played them right. Not saying you don't deserve what you got, but you've been luckier than the rest." He checked his wristwatch against the clock above the bar, confirming that, like most time pieces in New York watering holes, it was fifteen minutes fast." This is how he wants it, Fin. You'll find out who he is when we get there. Said he didn't want any leaks. Promised I'd have you there six sharp." He lifted his overcoat from the back of the stool, slipped one arm in a sleeve, pointed with the other to the door. "Better go."

"Need to use the little boy's room," Dunne said.

"I'll be outside."

Dunne exited the Iron Horse as the light at the corner flashed red. Mulholland was nowhere in sight. The thought entered his mind that he'd been duped, the long-distance call and rendezvous a practical joke, a begrudger's revenge. A ragging cough came from behind. He turned. Mulholland was in the half-lit doorway of a lingerie store that had just closed. Framed by the silhouettes of twin half-mannequins dressed in front-laced black corsets with racy red garters, he raised the match in his cupped hands to the cigarette between his lips. "Get it from the horse's mouth. That's what he wants. We'll grab a cab in front of the station."

The surge of pedestrians thickened along Eighth Avenue as they neared Penn Station. The massive colonnade of the General Post Office reinforced the station's imperturbable magnitude, stone façades oblivious to the flood tide of rush-hour commuters en route from the city and work to a night's rest in the vast, fast-expanding suburban tracts of New Jersey and Long Island.

As soon as they entered the cab, Mulholland barked an address in the east 70s. Staring out the window with the intensity of a onetime occupant of a squad car, he absentmindedly handed Dunne his folded copy of the *Standard*. Dunne glanced at the screaming headline: REDS SET TO STORM FORMOSA. As a boy, he'd sold the *Standard* on the southeast corner of Bowery and Delancey, under the El, fighting off the interlopers who tried to take his spot. The *Standard*'s headlines were always the same, always like this one, large print that SCREAMED! at passers-by. Didn't matter whether a socialite/chorine shot her husband/lover or war declared/ended or a milk strike called/settled or firemen pulled a cat out of a tree, whatever the *Standard* decided was the top story of the day was made an event of epic significance.

Inside, blood-and-thunder editorials railed against radicals, bureaucrats, cowardly diplomats, blood-sucking bankers, foreign conspirator, *et al.*, an array of villains that had been hard to categorize until the Roosevelt administration, which the paper at first supported and then made an object of concentrated scorn "for its deranged desire to collectivize our economy and Sovietize our government."

Dunne couldn't remember the last time he'd bought a copy of the *Standard*. Sometimes Roberta read him an item from the gossip columns or from the daily horoscope—it had the most extensive of any in the country—or he'd pick up a copy in a dentist's or doctor's office, or find one on a train seat, in which case he'd jump to sports or the funnies, or maybe browse the society pages, a habit left over from when his bread and butter was matrimonial and divorce cases.

Beneath today's headline, in a center-page box that continued inside, was an editorial entitled "Reds Ready for War! Are We?" The gist was that the Chinese, with the assistance of the Russians, had built a vast series of tunnels in case of atomic war. The U.S., on the other hand, had almost none. "For what are the hapless bureaucrats in Washington waiting?" the editorial thundered. "Shouldn't we have leaders with the strategic sense to employ our superior arsenal of new and improved atomic bombs against the Reds before they drop theirs on us? Or does this inattention suggest more than ineptitude? Could the decision to leave the American people to be vaporized beneath a merciless deluge of Russian hydrogen bombs be rooted in treason?"

Dunne handed the paper back to Mulholland. "Wilkes never gets tired of beating the same drum, does he?"

The traffic barely moved. Mulholland stared out the window. His right hand held a loose grip on the strap beside the door. At the mention of Wilkes, the long-time owner and publisher of the *Standard*, he turned slowly toward Dunne. "I guess."

"What's he like?"

The traffic eased as they entered Central Park. Light from the full moon raised a white glow from snow that everywhere else had been trampled, obliterated, or turned the color of soot. The cab sped up.

Mulholland tightened his grip on the strap. "*Who?*"

"Walter Wilkes. That's who we're headed to see, right?"

Leaning back, the rear of his hat almost touching the window, Mulholland shifted in his seat to face Dunne. "Figured you knew." His face, impassive, gave no sign he was bothered by the news. "Didn't imagine a single call from me would do the trick. Won't waste my breath asking how."

"A bird told me."

"What kind?"

"The early bird."

"Two birds I never liked. That's one. Stool pigeon is the other." The curve of Mulholland's mouth could have been a real grin. Maybe not.

This early bird's name was Louis Pohl. (He pronounced his last name Pull. Friends, acquaintances and associates called him Pully.) Dunne had called him first thing after he got back from Cuba. They'd met a dozen years before, at the OSS office in Washington, when Pully headed one of the thirty-odd sections related to intelligence operations. His small unit of two or three recruits was focused on making statistical estimates of Germany's remaining economic and military reserves. His figures were usually at odds with what other military intelligence agencies came up with and, as events turned out, always on target.

He'd had a brief stint with the NYPD, in 1929, while

Dunne was still there, but they'd never met. Commissioner Grover Whelan hired him to head up a newly formed Office for Statistical Research and Information, a high-sounding title for an office with one chief—Pully—and no Indians. A glad-handing Wanamaker's executive who had elevated the ticker-tape parade to an art form as the city's official greeter, Whelan was Mayor Jimmy Walker's choice for commissioner in the wake of Arnold Rothstein's rub-out, when all the papers were calling for a shake-up. Whelan, an experienced department store VIP, provided a first-class job of window dressing. He refurbished the police headquarters, hired Pully away from the U.S. Department of Commerce to plan "a new scientific approach to crime fighting," staged some showy raids, then ran things pretty much as before. The corruption that flowed from Prohibition kept on flowing.

Pully lasted barely a year. He quit and took a job in Binghamton with International Business Machines. After Pearl Harbor, he offered his services to Army Intelligence and was borrowed by Colonel Donovan for the OSS. Dunne was only with him a few weeks in Washington, in 1943, before he left for London, but they came to like each other a great deal. He didn't see Pully again until the day he showed up and introduced himself as a vice-president with International Service Corporation—ISC. He had a proposition, as he put it, "you'd be most foolish not to seriously consider."

After an on-and-off courtship, Dunne agreed to the business arrangement Pully offered on behalf of ISC. Despite a slightly stiff way of talking, Pully had an easy, relaxed way. Dunne had never asked where he went to school. He suspected it was one of the Ivy League snob factories but, unlike most of their graduates, Pully never brought it up. Short, with a thick neck welded into his torso and a protruding stomach, he was shaped like a thumb. His blue double-breasted suits, which were a kind of uniform with him, hung on him like a set of cheap drapes.

"I've undertaken the assignment of turning private investigation from the rag-tag, disreputable stepchild of police work into a cadre of professional intelligence workers," Pully said the day they shook on the deal.

He didn't lie when he phoned Pully and asked if he'd nose out Mulholland's employer. Told him he was being offered a possible assignment, maybe a big one. Knew it conflicted with his non-compete agreement with ISC. He'd be glad to sign over whatever fee was involved. "Thing is, Pully, once a rag-tag stepkid, always a rag-tag stepkid."

After a half minute of silence that felt to Dunne like five, Pully said, "I'll see what I can do. No promises." He called back the day before Dunne left for New York. "I got what you asked for. Mulholland is employed by Walter Wilkes, proprietor of the *New York Standard*. He works out of Wilkes's penthouse on Fifth Avenue. Theirs is a relationship wrapped in secrecy worthy of the Manhattan Project. A piece of friendly advice: if you go ahead with this, don't sign a contract. It'll only complicate your deal with us."

Mulholland waited in front of the building off Fifth Avenue until the cab that dropped them off pulled away. They went south half a block. The harsh wind coming up the avenue stung Dunne's cheeks and pressed against his eyes, squeezing out a single tear. "How far?"

"Right here." Mulholland veered under a green canopy, into a brightly lit marble lobby where the doorman let them pass with a nod. At the end of the entrance hall was a set of brass elevator doors with the signs of the zodiac embossed in three rows. Hands moving impatiently in and out of his overcoat pockets, Mulholland glanced up at the floor indicator. "The cloak-and-dagger crap isn't my idea, but I do what I get paid to do." He pressed the button to summon the elevator several times.

"From the looks of it, you're well paid." On the door, second from the top, in the middle: a brass image of a woman with a spike of grain in her left hand. Virgo. A remembered line, like a song lyric—*Virgos should stay close to home*—came and went.

"Relatively speaking."

Relative to what, Dunne didn't ask. He followed Mulholland into an elegantly paneled elevator. A boy-sized, gray-haired operator, stiff as the starched shirt beneath his uniform, closed the door with one spotless white-gloved hand and pushed the operator's lever with the other. He didn't ask for a floor. Mulholland didn't give one. The lights on the control panel flashed as the elevator climbed from L to 28 and stopped at PH.

"Had a hunch we were headed to the penthouse," Dunne said.

"Early bird tell you that too?"

They exited into an anteroom awash in the scent of an extravagant bouquet that overflowed a copper vase, the aroma of bon voyage parties, funeral homes, first-class hotels. A maid held the door open to an immense coffer-ceiling living room filled with ponderous oak furniture. It had a stuffy, pre-war feel, old money so flush with new that it didn't worry about keeping up. A wide staircase curved gracefully to the floor above. She took their coats, carefully folding them over her arm.

Mulholland led the way into the library, a long windowless room lined on two sides by shelves of deluxe leather-bound books with gold-lettered spines, the kind to be displayed rather than read. Hands in his pockets, rocking gently on his heels, he stood with his back to the small, newly-stoked fire burning in an ancient-looking marble fireplace. The maid reappeared, and Mulholland addressed her for the first time. "Usual for me, Lena. Scotch on the rocks for Mr. Dunne here."

"Lots of ice," Dunne added. "Please."

Above the mantle, in an ornate, gilt frame, was an oil portrait of a man in a powdered wig leaning against an old-fashioned, hand-operated printing press. He had the same serious, haughty mien that wig-wearers in old paintings usually wore, with one difference: the painter made no effort to soften the raw unattractiveness of his subject's features—crossed eyes, sloping nose and undershot jaw.

Dunne stood next to Mulholland with his back to the fire. The heat radiated pleasantly against his pant legs. The maid served their drinks and left. Mulholland posed his glass in a toast to the two full-length portraits on the wall opposite the mantle and tipped it toward the younger of the figures: a lean officer in campaign hat and jodhpurs, with a swagger stick beneath his arm. In the background, artillery fired toward a line of trenches. "Our hero, Mr. Walter Wilkes."

Dunne looked up at the portrait. "Didn't know he was in the AEF."

"Let's just say he didn't give Alvin York any competition. His pop got him assigned to the general staff. Suffered a severe groin wound. Bad case of the clap contracted while leading a frontal assault on a Parisian brothel. Frogs gave him the Order of the Purple Cock, third class. General Foch himself pinned it to his crotch."

"This the pop?"

"How'd you guess?" Mulholland stepped in front of the second portrait: a stout gentleman, in top hat and frock coat, with right hand tucked, Napoleon-style, into the front of his coat. Instead of a swagger stick, he had a newspaper beneath his arm.

"Wilkes the Elder. Son of a blacksmith in some shit-ass backwater, he ran away, landed a job as a messenger for a printer, eventually graduated to typesetter and set up his own company on Maiden Lane. Within a decade, he handled most of the printing for the city's brokerages. Became an investor himself. His knack at buying at the bottom, selling at the top, which some said rested on the inside dope his printing business gave him access to, earned him the title 'the Merlin of Maiden Lane.' Started his own newspaper, the *Standard*, and before long was buying papers all over the country."

Mulholland raised his glass once more. "When the old man died, he was said to be the seventh richest man in America. Walter has moved up to sixth. Not exactly a rags-to-riches saga, although he likes to pretend otherwise." He consumed half his drink in a gulp. "Oh well, as long as the checks don't bounce, blessed be Wilkes the father, the son, and their unholy enterprise."

"And who's dog face?" Dunne turned and pointed at the portrait over the mantle.

"Him? Another thing you'll get from the horse's mouth." Mulholland pressed a button below the light switch. A shelf of tall volumes turned out to be a panel that slid back to reveal a television. He turned a dial. A pinprick of light appeared and expanded in a flash like an H-bomb explosion from the news-reels. "Millionaires are like precinct captains. Everything got to be done their way. Lucky for me, unlike the local precinct, this house has a TV."

President Eisenhower's press conference from earlier in the day was on the screen. He was being questioned about the con-frontation with Red China over the Straits of Formosa.

"Now here's the prescription for making sure John Q. Public gets a good night's rest: a daily dose of Ike." Mulholland left on the news conference but turned off the sound. He dropped into a worn leather easy chair, picked up the newspa-per from the table next to it and turned to the TV listings. "Let's see. What's your preference? 'The Pinky Lee Show' or 'Teen Bandstand'?"

"That's the choice?"

"Fifteen minutes, it'll be 'Liberace.' Wilkes keeps us waiting long enough, Bishop Sheen will be on. There's a guy knows how to keep an audience awake. If he could play the piano like Liberace, he'd probably put the whole country in the pope's pocket."

The maid came back in. "Follow me, please, Mr. Dunne. Mr. Wilkes is waiting."

Mulholland flipped the page of the newspaper. He didn't look up. "I'll be here when you get back."

Dunne put his barely touched drink on the mantle and trailed the maid up the stairs and down a thickly carpeted hallway to a set of double doors. She knocked gently and stood back. A voice, high and feminine, called out, "Come in."

The walls of the semi-circular foyer were painted with a continuous woodland scene, green hills, cypress trees, grape vines. A satyr playing a flute romped across a field. Nearby, a raven-haired girl clad in a long, wispy, see-through veil, outline of breast and thigh clearly visible, was about to enter a forest. The way her body was drawn, its curve and flow, were hauntingly familiar. He'd seen her before. But where? She looked backwards, over her shoulder, with playful, inviting eyes: *follow me.*

Beyond, in the middle of a large room, was a bed that reached beyond king-sized to emperor- or sultan-sized. Recessed lighting left the corners of the room in shadow and bathed the bed with soft illumination. A silver-maned figure in a blue silk robe sat up against a curved oak headboard, foulard handkerchief flowing out of monogrammed breast pocket. A telephone and buzzer rested beside him on a rubber mat, their black cords snaking over the left side of the bed. The tray across his lap, supported by a short metal frame, served as a desk. He scribbled with such furious concentration on the papers in front of him that the brass-colored point of his purple fountain pen sounded a nervous, hurried scratch.

A young woman snugly fitted in a gray skirt and white blouse stepped from the shadows carrying a crystal goblet. Reaching over, she placed it on the tray. "Your water." She perched on the right side of the bed and crossed her luxuriously lengthy silk-hosed legs. Left swayed atop right, Broadway-style kick, in a minor key, toe of black high heel pointing alternately to floor and ceiling. Her blonde hair was shaped to follow the line of her finely sculpted jaw. Full, glossy, ruby-colored lips that parted in a smile.

Wilkes stopped writing, sipped from the goblet and peered over the top of his glasses, eyes filled with enough mild surprise to sustain the pretense that he was unaware anyone had entered. "Ah, you must be Fintan Dunne. I'm sorry to have kept you waiting."

Too far away to shake hands, Dunne made a small, awkward bow, blushing at its unintended resemblance to the formal kowtow of those forlorn Japanese diplomats and generals who surrendered on the deck of the U.S.S. Missouri. Neither Wilkes nor the blonde seemed to notice.

Head down, as he tended once more to his papers, Wilkes said, "By now, I suppose, you know who I am. This is Miss Adrienne Renard. Her services are various and invaluable." Her gaze focused on Wilkes, Miss Renard seemed about to say something, but didn't.

"Indulge me a moment more, Mr. Dunne." Wilkes hurriedly signed the bottom of a half-dozen pages and shuffled them off to Miss Renard. "That's it, closed for the day." He twisted the cap back on his pen, dropped it on the tray. Miss Renard put the papers in a manila envelope, which she slipped under her arm.

"Please, be seated." The words were more command than invitation. He pointed to a yellow-canvas director's chair at the foot of the bed. Standing, Miss Renard put her knee on the edge of the bed, leaned across and lifted the tray. Her breasts, firm, plump hemispheres cradled in a lacy white brassiere, were visible through the unbuttoned top portion of her blouse. She stopped beside Dunne's chair on her way out of the room.

He looked up into her blue eyes, deep set above chiseled cheek bones. Eyes like those of the girl on the foyer wall. But more intense than inviting: *Look but don't touch.*

"I trust we'll get the chance to talk."

Late twenties, early thirties, he guessed. Too much makeup. "Hope so."

"I'll do my best to see it happens, Adrienne. First, I must convince Mr. Dunne to sign on." Wilkes's words sent Miss Renard on her way. The door closed with a soft thud. "Very talented girl," he said, "and in a very great hurry. One must be careful never to let one's haste get ahead of one's talents." He straightened his shoulders and shook his head sideways, as if to clear it. "I've been looking forward to meeting you, Mr. Dunne."

"Mulholland made it seem urgent."

"Ah, Mulholland. Tough, impolitic and, thanks to those attributes, useful in certain situations. He has a low opinion of most everyone, myself included. But he's an admirer of yours. According to him, when it comes to private investigators, you walk on water."

"I prefer swimming."

Wilkes either wasn't amused or wasn't listening, and he began explaining that his reason for being in bed was an old back injury inflicted in France when he was thrown by a horse escorting artillery to the front. Dunne resisted asking about the wound Mulholland alleged. Annoying but not life-threatening, the pain came and went.

Though laid up in bed, he was obviously a large man, with more resemblance to his substantial father in the portrait in the library than to the svelte young officer he'd once been. He had that jowly, self-satisfied aspect common to industrialists, bankers and cabinet secretaries; the red, blustery face of someone who'd either spent a good deal of time outdoors or was an indoorsman with high blood pressure.

Wilkes went from the specifics of his back problem ("the copulative act is an effective way to relieve such distress"), to generalizations about disease ("easier to prevent than treat") and staying healthy ("keep to a diet of fish, grains, fresh vegetables, blackstrap molasses, moderate amounts of wine, vigorous exercise"), to a discussion of vitamins and hydrotherapy. Chin up, he swept the room with his eyes, as if addressing an audience. Before long, through a union of natural healing and well-funded research, he saw no reason why science couldn't extend the human lifespan indefinitely.

As he listened patiently, Dunne realized that Mulholland hadn't been exaggerating: with Wilkes, it was all straight from the horse's mouth, everything delivered with identical authority and certainty. "America's Authentic Voice" was the motto on his newspapers. Plenty of critics and rivals disputed that, foremost among them intellectuals, professors and "respected" journalists at "reputable" newspapers who disdained Wilkes's publishing recipe of natural cures and fads (healthy bodies, especially female, were heavily featured), crime, scandal, sex and a high-powered paranoid patriotism. But none of them put a dent in his huge circulation and advertising revenues.

Over the years, Dunne had heard Wilkes described both as a genius and as a puffed-up nonentity whose supposed abilities were the product of the high-priced public relations firms he hired to build and maintain his myth. What mattered in the end was that he remained very, very rich, and as long as the money lasted, it would be taken by most as presumptive evidence of his genius.

Off in the corner, a radiator made a low hiss. Fishing in his pocket for his cigarettes, Dunne realized he'd left the pack on the bar. Instead, he came up with the horse-headed stirrer.

Wilkes segued from health and exercise to the importance of timing in human events ("history punishes equally those too early as well as those too late"), a parade of goosed-up generalities routinely transcribed by well-paid, kiss-ass editors and served daily to the reading public.

"That's why I've asked you here, Mr. Dunne. You're a doer, not a bystander, a kindred soul. So let's get to business. I had a careful check done before I asked you here. A most interesting career. Someday you'll have to tell me all about it."

"Not much to tell."

"Self-effacement, I find, is a trait shared by many men of action."

Could be, though Dunne found it was a talent for relentless self-promotion that most often got people ahead, whether men of action or not. He nodded, as if in agreement.

Wilkes went off on a new digression: the incompetents in Washington—"men of no action"—and the present occupant of the White House, another in a succession of "chickens-in-chief," same cowardly refusal to use nuclear weapons to save the French from defeat by the Communists in Vietnam previously on display in Korea.

His emphatic monotone had the grave agreeability of a statesman addressing the nation or a radio huckster selling laxatives. "Know when the moment is right, then act decisively. I live by that axiom, Mr. Dunne. It's served me well. And now the time . . ." He plucked the handkerchief from his breast pocket and wiped the trail of spittle collected on his lower lip, like a trumpet player about to give it his all ". . . has come to find out what happened to Joseph Force Crater."

For the second time in the space of a few hours, Dunne considered that he might be the victim of an elaborate practical joke. "*Joseph Crater?* You mean, *Judge* Crater?"

"None other."

"The one who went missing?"

"'Into thin air,' as they say, inaccurately in Crater's case. The day he vanished was thick with heat and humidity. A great unsolved mystery. The greatest, until now." The broad smile on his face indicated Wilkes had hit the high note he was after. He tucked the handkerchief back in his pocket with a flourish.

Crater was more of an over-used punchline than an unsolved mystery. Elevator stops at a floor. Nobody is there. One occupant to another: *Must have been Judge Crater.* Ha, ha. Bell boy parades through hotel lobby barking an urgent message: *Judge Crater call your office.* It drew fewer and fewer laughs each passing year. On the odd chance he'd heard wrong, Dunne asked again, "Judge Crater? Who disappeared twenty-five years ago?"

"Twenty-four and a half, almost to the day. The public announcement was made nearly a month after he disappeared. As a Tammany sachem, former assistant to a U.S. senator, and recent appointee to the State Supreme Court by Governor Roosevelt, who was already conspiring to seize the presidency, Crater was a veritable Noah's Ark of political secrets. His disappearance was highly convenient for some."

"Bet it sold a load of newspapers."

"We offered a $20,000 reward for information on his whereabouts, a king's ransom in those first days of the Depression. Responses poured in from all over the country. Most were fanciful. A few seemed helpful. In the end, none panned out." Wilkes lowered his head. The memory of failure, no matter how long ago, seemed to weigh on him. "It was widely regarded as 'the crime of the century.'"

"Till the Lindbergh baby was snatched."

"I suppose."

The search for Crater proved mere prelude to the three-ring circus that enveloped the Lindbergh kidnapping. Led by the *Standard*, with Wilkes as ringmaster, a troupe of rabid reporters, show-biz radio announcers, and eager-to-be-famous lawmen wrung the last lurid drop from the baby's disappearance and the trial and execution of the man convicted of the crime. *Read all about it.* The whole world did. Shepherds in the Pyrenees and fishermen in the South Seas checked each night to make sure their children were safe in bed and not the prey of the fiend who snatched the golden child from his crib in Hopewell, New Jersey.

"Even if people remember Crater, what makes you think they'll care?"

"Because they'll be reminded they should. A vital principle in my business and, perhaps, the most basic. Remember Floyd Collins back in 1925? A no-count hillbilly explorer gets trapped in a Kentucky cave for four days and the whole nation is riveted. Why? How many thousands have been lost in caves before and since without the world giving a hoot? But once the Collins story was made into headlines and radio echoed his plight across the airwaves, the particular was transformed into the universal, a single drop made to represent the sea of misfortune in which, to one degree or another, we all swim. Even the sainted Mr. Lindbergh, who came to depict himself as the innocent victim of a prurient and invasive press, wasn't above being hired to fly photos of the attempted rescue to New York.

"Once a story becomes news, everybody wants to be part of it. But news isn't every saporous event that occurs. No paper or periodical, no matter how voluminous, has room to cover that. To paraphrase the motto of one of our more pretentious metropolitan journals, we can only print the news that fits. News, then, isn't merely what happens, it's also what's published, head-lined and, if need be, published over and over again. That's been true for a century now, and been made more true by radio. We have yet to measure the real impact of television, but it will be nothing less than vast."

Dunne sucked on the stirrer as if it were a cigarette, then dropped it back into his pocket. "In my business, the trick is to know the difference between tough and impossible. If there's ever a parade of impossible cases, Crater would be grand marshal."

"Just as there are no uninteresting stories, only dull, unimaginative reporters and editors, there are no insolvable cases, only lazy, incompetent investigators."

An acid taste rose at the back of Dunne's throat, the sour dislike of desk-ensconced civilians oblivious to the muddle of deceit, uncertainty and delusion present in even so-called cut-and-dried cases. The radiator's hiss sounded like air leaving a tire. Inflated expectations that brought him north, the notion of being back again—amid a top-priority investigation, cops half-resenting, half-welcoming his presence—sagged and lost shape.

The red button on the phone next to Wilkes pulsed with mute urgency. "Excuse me. I must take this." Wilkes listened for a moment before starting to dictate an editorial attacking "the cowardly retreat in the face of Red Chinese aggression."

Dunne closed his eyes and rubbed the lids with thumb and forefinger. He saw stars, zigzags of light, flares bursting in black sky. He thought, Roberta must be at the dance lesson by now, knees bent, back, forward. Felipe, the Cuban dance teacher, takes her hand, announces to the class, *Watch Mrs. Dunne, class, her timing is perfect.* She glistens with perspiration. He offers to escort her to her car.

Wilkes put down the receiver with a hard bang. "Sorry for the interruption. Another feckless, overeducated, overpaid idiot who can't think for himself. By now, you must be wondering whether you've been lured on nothing more than a fool's errand."

Not wondering anymore. Dance instructor or not, he might stick around the city for a few days before heading back to Florida. "You wouldn't have a cigarette? Seems I left mine somewhere."

"Smoking is a noxious and destructive habit that does substantial damage to the health of this nation. But Prohibition taught us the unintended and often catastrophic consequences of turning bad habits into crimes. There's a supply of Fatimas in the box over there on the table. Though he knows I don't smoke, Mr. Billingsly keeps sending cartons of them over to my table at the Stork."

The director's chair creaked loudly as Dunne pushed himself up. He caught himself before his knee buckled and took small steps to disguise the hobble. The box turned out to be a richly inlaid miniature version of those fancy, body-shaped caskets in which the Egyptian pharaohs were buried. Probably a gift from King Farouk or one of the other mummified ex-royals or idle rich entombed in the banquettes of the Stork Club's Cub Room, in between having their pictures snapped for the society pages.

Beneath the box, pinned to a Bristol board and covered with a plastic transparency, was a glossy page that looked like a mock-up of a magazine cover. *Snap* was emblazoned in large red letters on a white background. The rest of the space was filled with a block-lettered two-line legend: MISSING NO MORE / MYSTERY NO LONGER. He took a cigarette from the casket, blew out the match with the exhale from the first drag, and dropped it in the ashtray that he carried back to his chair.

"Hear me out," Wilkes said.

It would probably be best to book a compartment on the *Silver Meteor*, Dunne decided. Arrive fresh and rested. But it was the height of the tourist season. Would any still be available? "Go ahead."

"More than a single disappearance, however celebrated in its day, this is a story about America, who we are as a people, where we've been, where we're headed. Think about it, Dunne. Judge Crater got in a cab on August 6, 1930, never to be seen again. Do you remember where you were when the story broke?"

"Vaguely." A sweltering day in the Hackett Building. Doors and windows ajar in the vain hope of snaring a wisp of air. Tuna on white. It sat on wax paper in the middle of the desk. Always tuna in those days. Voice on the radio from next door. *This just in.*

"Most people alive then and in full possession of their faculties have some memory of it. Why do you think? Because they care what happened to Crater? Hardly. Because they recall the enormous potential the case had for unfolding into a scandal that reached into the office of the governor himself, Franklin D.—for "Deceiver"—Roosevelt? A tale as stale as month-old bread. No, the reason they remember is because Crater vanished at the very moment their hopes and expectations were being vaporized.

"The reality was sinking in that the stock market crash of the previous fall wasn't a mere dip in the road but a passageway into a nightmare world of unemployment, foreclosure and bankruptcy. There were thirteen million unemployed by 1933, one-fourth of the American labor force. A thousand foreclosures a day. Two million vagabonds riding the rails or standing in breadlines.

"Crater disappeared as night descended. A man or woman who's forty-five today was twenty at the time. Today they are who they are, in most cases less than they dreamed. When they remember Crater, they recall a final spot of sunlight before depression, world war, cold war, the last moment their dreams were intact. The man who was 40 is 65 now. He is fast approaching the final twilight. He can seek no succor in the future. His sole consolation is the past. He wonders if, perhaps, Crater ran away and found the happiness that escaped the ordinary Joe."

Wilkes's eyes roved the room. "Ten-year-old boys in 1930 grew up to be soldiers in the second war. The majority returned unharmed, but not all. In addition to those listed as officially dead, there are still over 70,000 recorded as missing in action. Add to them the thousands missing in the first war, and now in Korea. Most are dead, for sure, but think of the families, friends, sweethearts, co-workers, neighbors who wonder about the fate of that pal, brother, son, husband, fiancé who they never heard from again. By some miracle could he still be alive? And among those millions, who doesn't have a memory, however vague, of Crater's disappearance, a first intimation of what an uncertain place our world can be, where even powerful public officials enjoy no immunity from evildoers, or perhaps are evildoers themselves?"

Dunne conjured up a row of editors sitting behind him, notebooks in hand, struggling to look engaged and enthused as they labored to take down every word.

"In another twenty-firver years, Crater will be little noted and not long remembered by the legion born amid our current idyll of purposeless prosperity and moral vacuity. In fifty years, he'll be at best a footnote to a footnote in the history of our time. But now, as we approach the silver anniversary of his disappearance, he lives in public memory, a touchstone and reference point. If the mystery of his disappearance is solved, the masses will be immensely entertained by the sheer showmanship of it. Most important, how many will gain a sense of the past being put to rest and turn their gaze to possibilities still ahead?"

As if on cue, a gush of howling wind clapped against the windows, a storm of applause from an imaginary row of editors.

"A lot to hang on one story," Dunne said. "Besides, nobody's been able to locate the judge over a quarter of a century. How can you expect a different result?"

"Mulholland swears there's nobody like you."

"You sure he meant that as a compliment?"

"He says you have a knack."

"It's rusted."

"Rust can be removed. Fear of failure is less amenable to cure."

"Maybe I've better things to do than help hawk a few more newspapers."

Wilkes's cheeks reddened, as if slapped. "Hawk newspapers? I employ an army of hacks, flacks and editors who see to that quite nicely, thank you. Circulation of my papers has topped ten million, up 250,000 from last year." He picked up the buzzer and played with the black cord, but didn't press it. Dunne crossed and uncrossed his legs but didn't stand. Outside, the wind reduced from howl to moan.

"I'm used to skeptics." Wilkes's sharp tone turned flat, neutral. The color left his cheeks. "Their observations are often helpful. It's the clever-minded cynics I resent, the intellectual snobs, self-appointed guardians of public morals and manners, aspiring aristocrats, our faux elite. Should they learn of this venture, they'll revel in any embarrassment it might cause. But if the risk of failure is great, the possible rewards are ever greater. Think of what a coup it will be to find an answer to a mystery that's eluded so many for so long. You're like me, Dunne. You understand that the difficulty of a thing is what makes it worth doing. And rest assured, you'll have everything you ask for. Cut the coat according to the cloth like any master tailor. The only interest this organization will take will be to ensure you have the resources you require to produce the perfectly tailored result. If you sign on, Miss Renard will spell out the particulars. She's in charge."

Instantly slipping back into his editorial-writing role, he explained that whatever was spent was an investment, then came a brief lecture from the horse's mouth about the stud farm known as the New York Stock Exchange and the similarities between handicapping thoroughbreds and shorting blue chips. What he didn't say, Dunne noticed, was what the whole country had learned the hard way: the odds of coming home with any scratch were better at the track than on Wall Street.

Dunne extended his right leg, pushed hard against the arms of the chair, which made a prolonged squeak, and stood to carry the ashtray back to the table. Placing it next to the casket of cigarettes, he mulled over the tailor kneeling to measure pants cuffs. No need to take it personally. To Wilkes, no doubt, the whole world was divided into tailors and the tailored to. "I'll think it over."

"Money is no impediment. Time is the real challenge. Break the story on August 6th, the twenty-fifth anniversary of the day Crater went missing, a moment that will resound in the hearts and minds of the American people. You see, it's also the tenth anniversary of the dropping of the atomic bomb on Hiroshima. The press will be filled with stories about that ominous anniversary and how an event that a mere decade ago was hailed as putting an end to war and ensuring American suzerainty has proved prelude to a greater struggle against the rapidly waxing powers of global Communism. Amid that dark and depressing commentary, with the accompanying photos and illustrations of the bomb's destructive capabilities—which are dwarfed by the apocalyptic potential of the H-bomb—the Crater revelation will shine in the crepuscular gloom like a shaft of redemptive light."

"One problem. August 6th is only six months from now."

"That's not a problem."

"Not a problem? After 25 years, the case is going be solved in six months?"

"The time constraints are an advantage, not a problem. The same principle will be at work as in Boyle's Law. It's as true in business as physics: the volume of a gas is inversely proportional to the pressure it's under. Like gas, the time required to do a job expands or contracts with the pressure one is under to get it done. Find Crater, and you'll be famous."

"Who says I want to be famous?"

"Every man seeks fame, even those who deny it, perhaps they most of all. Their denial is nothing more than an attempt to disguise their resentment that fame is beyond their grasp. Fame is the only form of immortality available to us. Solve this case and I warrant your name will enter the history books."

"Don't you have to be dead to get into history books?"

"If history doesn't interest you, what about television? How about hosting a weekly show, 'Solving Unsolved Mysteries,' something like that? Fame is best enjoyed by the living, and believe me, not least among its many benisons is its aphrodisiacal effect."

"And if we can't pull it off? What then?"

"Few will even know we tried. You'll get on with your life, I with mine. Tell me, Dunne, did you notice that portrait above the mantle in the library?"

"Hard face to ignore, even if you try."

"You're not the first to react that way. But I dare say the man portrayed would be neither aggrieved nor surprised. Rumored to be the ugliest man in England, John Wilkes was certainly among the most famous and charming. 'Takes me but half an hour,' he said, 'to talk away my face.' Wilkes was also among the bravest. His newspaper, *The North Briton*, was fearless in its attacks on King George III.

"Expelled from parliament, tried and convicted of libel and sedition, and sent to prison, he wasn't cowed. He was returned to parliament and elected Lord Mayor of London. His indictment of royal abuses influenced Jefferson in his writing of the Declaration of Independence. His refusal to be silenced was among the precedents the framers of the Constitution had in mind with the Bill of Rights and its guarantee of a free press. Thankfully, we haven't the same visage, but I'm proud the same English blood courses through my veins."

Wilkes's chin sunk toward his chest. The bald spot atop his head, lightly covered by artful comb-over, glowed halo-like beneath the light. Toying with the electrical cord attached to the buzzer, he looked up. "You've every right to be a skeptic. But, please, sleep on it. Give me your answer in the morning. There's a room reserved for you at the Savoy Plaza. Mulholland will see to your luggage." He pressed the buzzer.

"Mulholland know what this is about?"

"Presume no one other than Miss Renard and yourself know."

The maid reappeared. Wilkes didn't extend his hand. Dunne made sure not to bow. As he followed her out, he glanced at the fleeing girl in the mural. Body as well as eyes could be Miss Renard's. Dunne half-expected to find her in the library, but Mulholland was alone, slumped in the armchair, newspaper open on his lap. He bolted upright when Dunne tapped his shoulder. The maid switched off the silent TV.

"Damn thing puts you out faster than bourbon and a sleeping pill."

"Try it with sound."

"Put you out quicker."

The maid returned with their overcoats and hats. Mulholland put on his coat and jammed his hat on the back of his head. "Hired?"

"Tired. Been a long day. Wilkes said there's a room for me at the Savoy Plaza."

"Suite. Enough space for the Mormon Tabernacle Choir. Want to eat?"

"Sleep."

"Your driver's downstairs. So, let me guess. Wilkes told you what's up, but told you to keep it to yourself."

"Nobody but Miss Renard."

"He reads too many detective novels. Bet he also gave you the spiel about his nibs here, right?" Mulholland faced the portrait of John Wilkes over the mantle.

"Father of the free press."

"Yeah, and pornographer and all-around sex maniac."

"No reason to speak ill of the dead. Goes double when it's your great granddad, I guess."

"Great granddad, my ass. Wilkes's forebears were Pennsylvania Dutch. Name was Wiltz. The old man changed it. And one other thing. Bet he didn't tell you that John Wilkes is who John Wilkes Booth was named after, did he?"

If not spacious enough to accommodate the Mormon Tabernacle Choir, the suite at the Savoy Plaza could comfortably fit a family of six. A bell boy delivered his bag. Dunne had a desultory call with Roberta. Told her he was meeting with the bosses at ISC. They wanted him to get involved in a case.

What about that man who called looking for him when he was in Cuba—the one who'd insisted it was a matter of life and death? Was he part of the meeting? she wanted to know. On top of being persistent, he'd been unpleasant and rude.

"Nothing that dramatic. I'll fill you in when I get home."

"Are you dressed warm enough? The announcer on the TV news reported New York is in a deep freeze. He said the Hudson had frozen over near Tarrytown for the first time in fifty years. The temperature here reached eighty-one. Tonight there was a lovely breeze. After the class, Felipe saw me to my car. We stood at the water's edge. There was a party at the club across the way. The fireworks lit up the night sky. I enjoyed it."

He resisted the urge to yawn. Out the sliding glass doors, directly north, up the avenue, was Wilkes's apartment tower. "Felipe?"

"Yes, our dance instructor. Are you listening to *anything* I say?"

"I'm tired, honey. I'll call you in the morning."

"Fin, be home soon. Promise?"

"Promise."

He slid the door open and stepped out on the terrace. The wind had shriveled to a whisper; from below come the muffled but steady hiss of late-night traffic. He took a deep breath. Frigid air surged into his nostrils and lungs, stinging. He peered at the penthouse in the distance. Every light seemed to be on.

Back inside, he opened the bottle of Scotch from the welcome basket on the table by the door and poured himself a half-shot. Teeth brushed, pajamas on, he slipped into the space where the maid had turned down the sheet. He pushed his feet toward the bottom of the bed. The dull, cramping ache in his calves was the kind that usually followed a day of tracking down leads. Hadn't felt it in a while. Reaching to turn off the light, he paused. *Ecclesiastes.* Mulholland had quoted from it.

He opened the night table drawer and took out the Gideon's Bible. The Christian Brothers at the Catholic Protectory, where he began and ended his education, warned their charges against interpreting the Bible for themselves, particularly the Protestant version found in hotel rooms. Though he'd succumbed to other temptations found in hotel rooms, he'd never fallen into Bible reading. First time for everything. He searched a minute for Ecclesiastes. He found what he was looking for in the opening lines:

"The words of the Preacher, the son of David, king in Jerusalem.

Vanity of vanities, saith the Preacher, vanity of vanities, all
   is vanity.
What profit hath a man of all his labor which he taketh
   under the sun?"

If there were some dark Protestant heresy in any of this,
Dunne hadn't a clue what it was. Ecclesiastes was a short book.
Some nice lines about "a time for everything . . . to get, to lose, to
keep, to cast away." He skipped to the end:

"For God will bring every work into judgment,
   including every secret thing, whether good or evil."

It sounded as though God should be in the detective business. All-knowing. All-powerful. Nothing by chance. He book-
marked the passage with a match, tucked the Bible back in the
drawer and put out the light.

   He came to with a start, no idea where he was, how long
he'd been asleep, only what made him wake . . .
   Sensation of cold metal being pushed into his ear . . .
   A room was dark as newsprint. Dunne needed a minute to
sort out where he was. Sat up. Turned on the light. Gradually, a
piece at a time, he retrieved the dream he'd just left.
   *Caribbean beach, except more desert than beach, no ocean
in sight. Sits with back to the sun. Shadow falls. Turns. Looks.
Mulholland there. Top of his head sheared off. Miss Renard, lus-
cious figure in black corset with red garters, hangs on his left
arm.*
   *Mulholland's right hand has a snake tattooed on the back.
Lifts a Lugar from his belt, moves it close, whispers, "Good or
evil . . . evil . . ."*

The cold, uncomfortable feel of a gun barrel sliding farther into his ear . . .

Miss Renard slips out of the corset, says, "These things are secret . . . secret."

Whispered voice again: "Always do as I'm told, Fin . . . Fin."

On the way to Florida, Roberta had spent most of her time reading a book by Freud about dreams. She couldn't stop talking about it. He never really started listening, but promised he'd get around to reading it. "I enjoy hearing about your dreams," she'd said.

He told her about the ones he thought she'd enjoy. This one he wouldn't.

The clock next to the lamp indicated 3:15. He shut off the light, drifted back to sleep, sure of the answer he'd give Wilkes in the morning.

Part II

The Crater Chase: An Excerpt from Louis Pohl, "Judge Crater, Please Call Your Office," in *Where in the World? A Collection of Unsolved Disappearances* (San Francisco: The Conundrum Press, 1974).

The appropriate point from which to begin any chronicle of the disappearance of Judge Joseph Force Crater is the Great Wall Street Crash of October 1929. Historians and economists continue to argue about the exact relationship between the stock market's swoon and the prolonged worldwide economic paralysis that followed. But people alive at the time would always connect the onset of the Great Depression and the bursting of the effervescent illusion of a "New Era" of perpetual prosperity with the debacle that unfolded on the floor of the New York Stock Exchange.

The party was over, and as hosts and guests made a frantic scramble for the exits, the trickle-down theory—that the good fortune of the rich will seep southward through all levels of society until it slakes even the parched and thirsty throats of the poor—was turned on its head. Misery proved more fluid than prosperity. The effects of unemployment, bankruptcy and foreclosures poured rather than dripped down the economic ladder in a soaking, unstoppable deluge that swept all before it.

Among the first casualties of the pour-down reality of mass poverty was another booming Jazz Age activity, political corruption. (The relationship between a pumped-up bull market and unbridled greed among public officials has been a recurring theme from the Gilded Age to the present.) Slowly at first and then with swift and spreading anger, the public no longer deemed the venality and self-enriching peculations of local pols as a predictable and forgivable case of skimming off the cream, but as a felonious attempt to deprive their constituents of much-needed milk.

The change in the moral weather was signaled early on by the reaction to an incident in the Bronx that, had it occurred two months before the Crash rather than after, might have barely registered with the public. Instead, it set in motion a series of events that would lead to the resignation of New York's mayor and inflict wounds on the city's Democratic machine from which it would never fully recover. It began with a dinner held in a local restaurant in honor of a Bronx magistrate who'd also been leader of the local political clubhouse. The festivities were in full swing when a gang of hold-up men forced their way in and relieved the company—including judges, cops and reputed members of the mob—of wallets, watches and assorted valuables.

The outraged guest of honor made several urgent calls— *none* to the police—to report the robbery and seek recovery of the stolen items. *Mirable dictu*, all the loot was returned to its rightful owners within twenty-four hours. When news of the loot's speedy return leaked out, an official inquiry into the magistrate's conduct revealed he'd managed to accumulate a small fortune on a judicial salary of little more than $10,000 a year. Though the magistrate was removed from the bench, his demise only began a swelling chorus of complaints and allegations. Governor Roosevelt, his presidential ambitions hanging in the balance, could no longer resist the rising public outcry and authorized a sweeping investigation run by a stern and incorruptible blue-blood.

Just as the inquiry was about to begin—in August 1930— State Supreme Court Justice Joseph Force Crater bid two dinner companions good night, entered a tan-colored cab on a midtown street and was never seen again. (Despite an exhaustive search, neither the cab nor its driver could be found.) No sooner was his disappearance announced than Crater was assumed to be a key player in the unfolding political scandal. It was rumored the bosses had him killed to ensure his silence, or that he ran away in fear of being exposed for buying his judicial post and using to it solicit bribes. His defenders were few. A former law secretary to a state Supreme Court judge who went on to a distinguished career in the U.S. Senate, a graduate of an Ivy League law school with a successful private practice, Crater was routinely referred to as a buffoon and a hack.

The theory that Crater was a victim of political intrigue has enjoyed wide currency but remains only one theory among many. In those early days of what would become the Great Depression, what is certain is that Crater became a kind of Rorschach test for the American public. The ever-dwindling number who clung to President Hoover's assurances that prosperity awaited around a soon-to-be-turned corner tended to believe Crater wasn't dead at all. He was off on a month-long "whoopee party" in Chicago; or on a fishing trip deep in the Adirondacks; or in Montreal having a good laugh at all the wild speculation about his "disappearance"; or closeted with two hookers in an East Side penthouse until the investigations were over and everybody went back to the everyday business of getting rich.

For those concerned with the wave of gangsterism and lawlessness that had followed in the wake of Prohibition, Crater became yet another victim of the rampant, uncontrolled crime. Somebody thought he'd stumbled across his bullet-riddled body in the Ramapo Mountains, but it turned out to be only a bootlegger from Brooklyn. In Perth Amboy, New Jersey, the police disinterred a corpse from the Jewish cemetery on a tip that mobster Waxey Gordon buried the murdered Crater there as a favor to New York Mayor Jimmy Walker. The corpse proved to be the man that the cemetery authorities had insisted he was: a ninety-year-old, much-loved Hungarian rabbi who'd died peacefully in his bed.

As the slump deepened and factories closed and foreclosures spread, reports of Crater sightings poured in from across the country. Crater was on the road, hitchhiking, riding the rails, roasting a potato with the legion of footloose unemployed in makeshift Hoovervilles from Albany to Seattle. He was the well-mannered, well-spoken gent in a dusty, tattered suit who knocked on the back door of farmhouses from Ohio to Nebraska and offered to sweep the yard in return for a cup of coffee and a piece of pie.

He stood on breadlines in Chicago, San Francisco and Detroit, one nobody among millions. Shoulders hunched, hat pulled down, identical tesserae in a mosaic of misery, he smiled sheepishly and, before vanishing back into the crowd, thanked his benefactors with the cryptic remark, "You know, I was some-body once, back in New York."

Crater was all the things people were feeling—hopeful, fear-ful, doomed—as they wrestled to make sense of events they couldn't control. And while his unsolved disappearance might have been a source of pride to those who did him in (if he was done in), it caused endless embarrassment for the New York Police Department and its 18,000 members. It was one thing when the neighborhood milkman went missing. But, to para-phrase Lady Bracknell, while losing track of an ordinary citizen might be tragic, losing all trace of a justice of the New York State Supreme Court smacked of pure carelessness, or worse, gross incompetence.

Along with frustration at the false leads, blind alleys, mis-chievous miscues and deliberate didoes, the harried contingent of detectives assigned to the case soon felt the sting of public ridicule. Quipped comedian George Burns from the stage of New York's Palace Theatre, "These cops call themselves detectives? They couldn't find a rabbi in the Bronx." A headline in the *New York Standard* announced to the world: "THE FINEST ARE FLUSTERED."

The police could only feel relief when the attention of pop-ulace and press was drawn away from Crater by new crimes and new sensations. They weren't alone. Among his friends, acquaintances and patrons in political circles, Crater was somebody best consigned to public oblivion. The governor who'd appointed him to the bench was soon off to bigger things and didn't want the tin can of judicial corruption tied to his presidential bandwagon. Crater's fellow justices on the Supreme Court didn't need his ghost trailing behind them, with all his suspect baggage. Those said to have been his partners in various shady business deals, his putative lovers, and the rumored recipients of his judicial favors waited anxiously for the investigation to cease. In the end, however pleased or pained some must have felt about Crater being gone, they were all eager he be forgotten.

New York City

"I rose, and cast my rested eyes around me,
Gazing intent to satisfy my wonder
Concerning the strange place wherein I found me."

—DANTE, *Inferno*, Canto IV

FRESH FROM THE SHOWER, DUNNE WRAPPED HIMSELF IN ONE OF the hotel's plush terrycloth robes, rubbed his wet head with a towel, and massaged his gums with a pasteless toothbrush. He answered the knock expecting the coffee and toast he'd ordered. Instead, a woman in a fur coat and wide-brimmed fur hat that hid her eyes held up a copy of the *Herald Tribune*.

"Compliments of the management." She handed him the paper.

He scanned the front page, hoping he wasn't about to be asked to buy a subscription.

"Mr. Wilkes gives this hotel an inordinate amount of business, but they consider the *Standard* too spicy for the clientele and provide this bromide instead."

He slid the toothbrush from his mouth. "Miss Renard?"

"Why not invite me in?" A briefcase hung from both hands in front of her coat. "Or do you prefer to conduct business in the hallway?"

He stepped aside. "I didn't expect . . ."

"A detective's job is to expect the unexpected, no?" She brushed past, removed her hat and flung it on the sofa. "Where can I hang this?"

"I was expecting room service." He helped her take off her coat and hung it in the closet next to the door.

"Sorry, but that's not my line of work." Briefcase in hand, she crossed the room and sat in a winged chair. Her hair was drawn into a precisely braided coil at the back of her head. Winter sun, full of morning intensity, poured through the window and illuminated her face. Less makeup than the previous evening hadn't diminished her looks. A sly slant to her wide eyes, which he hadn't noticed the night before, made him think of Lauren Bacall.

Dunne tugged negligently at the sash around his robe, tightening it, aware without looking of bald ankles, hair beginning to disappear from legs, and bare, archless, corpse-white feet. He moved behind the sofa. "Give me a minute to get dressed."

"Take all the time you need." She lifted the briefcase onto her lap. "I've plenty to keep me busy."

He did a proper job of brushing his teeth, completed a quick reshave of neck and chin, slapped on bay rum, squeezed a small measure of hair cream in his palm and rubbed it into his black-and-gray-streaked mop. Leaning toward the mirror, he examined his hairline. Not even a slight retreat. He put on a starched white shirt and his best pair of charcoal slacks, and stood sideways to the dressing mirror: waistline firm as hairline.

Room service had delivered his breakfast while he was getting dressed. Miss Renard poured him a cup from the silver pot. She sat next to him on the couch, lowering herself with a graceful half-curtsy.

"How about you?" he asked. "I'll send for an extra cup. Want some breakfast?"

"I don't drink coffee. I ate breakfast two hours ago."

He smeared marmalade on a piece of toast. "Wilkes wants an answer, I suppose."

"He's sure he's got it." She smoothed her skirt with a caress of her pale, slender hand. "Once nine-thirty passed, Mr. Wilkes said, 'If Dunne were going to decline, he'd have done so by now.' He sent me to work out the details."

"A mind reader that good should've solved the Crater case by himself."

"He's an uncanny judge of character. I've never known him to be wrong."

"First time for everything."

"Not this time. Shall we?"

"Shall we what?"

"Shall we get to business and work out the details?"

"How about we start with you telling me what Wilkes is really up to?"

"Good question, Mr. Dunne. More than he let on." She retrieved her briefcase and opened it on the writing desk. "He wanted to make sure you'd take the job before he let you in on all that's involved. Have a look. It'll give you a better idea of our plans." She removed a Bristol board covered with a plastic transparency, the same one he'd seen on the table in Wilkes's room. "Did he show you this?"

"Not exactly. Came across it by chance."

"With Mr. Wilkes, nothing is by chance."

"Sounds like God."

"Mr. Wilkes has more money."

"God doesn't have a bad back."

She managed a grin, tight and small. "You're irreverent."

"Been known to get me in trouble."

"Not with me." She lifted the transparency, leaned the board against the wall, and took a step back. "Do you know what it is?"

"Looks like a cover for a magazine, but I never heard of *Snap*."

"With good reason, as it doesn't exist yet. This is a placeholder. Mr. Wilkes has hired some of the industry's top art directors to come up with as striking a design as possible. When he believes in a project, there's no limit to what he'll invest. He has big plans."

"He ever have small ones?"

"There's nothing small about Mr. Wilkes."

"I'll take your word for it."

She shot a peevish sideways glance. "He intends to launch the first issue in conjunction with a television production. It's never been tried before." She went back to looking at the board.

"And your part in all of this is what exactly?"

"You heard Mr. Wilkes. My role is 'various and invaluable.'"

"Everything from astrologer to zookeeper?"

"And more."

"But not room service?"

Hands on hips, her elbows jutted out like half-folded wings. "I resent that."

"You like my irreverence, remember?"

"But not cheap, vulgar insinuations."

"Insinuations are my business, cheap and otherwise. I need to be sure what I'm getting into. That includes knowing what your involvement is."

"I'm the project manager."

He reached in his pant's pocket and took out a pack of cigarettes. "Smoke?"

"Mr. Wilkes doesn't approve."

"I won't tell if you won't."

He lit a match from the long, elegant book embossed with the hotel's initials, SP, on the cover. She leaned her cigarette into the flame. The ends of their cigarettes almost touched. "What's a project manager do?"

She stood back. Right elbow resting in left palm, she levered the cigarette to her lips, sucked lightly, lifted her chin, and spouted smoke above his head. "Everything."

"For instance?"

"Look, if you want to understand the job he's trusted me with, you need to understand Mr. Wilkes. Like the late Mr. Hearst, he was born to great wealth and, again like Hearst, refused to settle for a life of idle enjoyment. In expanding the empire his father left him, Mr. Wilkes has avoided the humiliating setbacks Hearst suffered during the Depression. He accumulated capital the way a general builds reserves of men and weapons, waiting for exactly the right moment to throw his forces into the fight and win not merely a battle but the war."

She foraged in her briefcase, removed a business-sized envelope with scribbling on its front and laid it in front of her on the desk. Her voice tightened, taking on the slightly artificial tone of someone still uncomfortable speaking to an audience of strangers. Her manner aped Wilkes's: the same faraway, impersonal gaze.

Wilkes had already outdone Hearst, she said, and had little regard for other competitors, except for Henry Luce and his burgeoning Time-Life empire. "Consider the numbers." She looked down at the envelope. "In the last three years, magazine ad revenues have gone from $600,000,000 to $790,000,000, a rise of close to $200,000,000. In that same period, *Time* magazine's ad revenues went from $32,000,000 to $43,000,000, and *Life's* from $97,000,000 to $138,000,000. In other words, with those two magazines alone, Luce is collecting almost a quarter of the industry's ad revenues. The man prints money as well as magazines."

"I do my magazine reading in barber shops and doctors'

offices. Mostly old issues of *National Geographic*. They don't go stale like the weeklies."

Cigarette held in the slender vise of her fingers, she waved her hand dismissively, leaving a crooked trail of smoke. "The point is, Luce's competitors are intimidated and unimaginative." The discomfort was gone from her voice. She was relaxed and emphatic. "But *not* Mr. Wilkes. He knows that despite pretensions to statesmanship, Luce is really a showman. That's how he got *Life* off the ground, with articles like 'How to Undress for Your Husband.' He was brought up on indecency charges for a piece he ran depicting the birth of a child. That's why Fleur Cowles failed with *Flair*. Maybe the most beautiful magazine ever, but all high style and none of the sizzle that moves the masses."

Hearst, she continued, had no self-control. Ruled by his passions for architecture, art, and Miss Davies (his sole interest in extending his newspaper empire into Hollywood had been to advance her career), he earned the mockery heaped on him in *Citizen Kane*. Luce, on the other hand, had too much self-control. His magazines came on an average of one a decade. He had even less of an understanding of Hollywood than Hearst, and though not beyond purchasing television stations, he did so defensively, unable to get past his contempt for what he believed is TV's "innately trivial and superficial nature."

Dunne interrupted again. "Still haven't told me what a project manager does."

"First you must understand the project itself. Since you're working with us now, I'll let you in on some privileged information. Mr. Wilkes is negotiating to take control of the DuMont Television Network before it goes under. Don't ask for the details. It involves technical stuff about VHF and UHF, sub rosa talks with the studio heads, political intrigue at the FCC. His lobbyists are working to make the feds see the necessity for a third network—one he's tentatively named 'The Red, White and

Blue Network.' It's the kind of complex dealing that gets his juices flowing like nothing else."

"Nothing?"

She gave another dismissive wave. "With the launch of *Snap*, he's directly challenging *Life* with a magazine plugged into the power of television. He's also in discussions, highly confidential at this stage, to bring one of the studios under his control. Where others see the parts, he perceives the whole. He intends his publications to pulse with the immediacy and intensity of television, and his network to convey images and information with the authority of print. 'Pan-pollenization' is the term he's coined."

"Birds and bees have the copyright, no?"

She exhaled, this time making no attempt to direct the smoke above his head. "Mr. Wilkes is a genius."

"He shares that opinion."

"He's not a humble man. There's no need. He alone is ready to seize this moment. Do you realize that last year 4,000,000 babies were born in the U.S.?"

"I have an iron-clad alibi in every case."

"I'm serious." A frown creased her forehead. "That's the largest population increase in American history. The census experts project over the next twenty years our population will swell from 165,000,000 to 220,000,000. Mr. Wilkes's competitors barely seem to notice. If they do, they're at a loss what to do about it. They tinker at the fringes of their businesses and will either miss or be capsized by this wave. We alone are building an organization that will be carried on the crest. History is like that. It rewards perfect timing above all else, punishing equally those who are too early as well as too late." She rested her cigarette in the ashtray.

"Where'd I hear that before?"

"'There is a tide in the affairs of men, which taken at the flood leads on to fortune; omitted, all the voyage of their life is

85

bound in shallows and in miseries.' It's from Shakespeare's *Julius Caesar*."

"I'm more partial to *Little* Caesar, with Edward G. Robinson."

"Then try the movie version of *Julius Caesar*. It's playing at the Trans-Lux. Marlon Brando as Marc Antony is, well . . ." Her voice trailed off. "What a presence." She reached down and took hold of the cigarette, tapped it with her index finger, rapidly, as if it were a telegraph key. Western Union wire for Mr. Brando. *Bravo.*

"We were talking about the quote."

"Yes, the quote. Mr. Wilkes has an updated version. It's in his book of quotes. Privately printed, but I can get you one. Every executive has a copy. It might help you understand better how the Crater case fits into all of this, as a trigger, a device to affect a single synchronized effort—a fusion, if you will—whose long-term implication for global communications will be as momentous as the H-bomb is for geopolitics."

"And your job is to run Wilkes's version of the Manhattan Project?"

"If you care to use that metaphor."

"It belongs to Wilkes. August 6th, the tenth anniversary of Hiroshima."

"Yes, that was his idea. Brilliant and typical. My job is to see that it all comes together. Editor and publisher of the magazine, newspaper staffs, director and producer of the television show, studio representatives—all report to Mr. Wilkes through me. I control and coordinate every aspect, creative, financial, promotional, editorial."

As to Dunne's employment, she explained, Mr. Wilkes wanted an arrangement that didn't involve ISC. She produced a contract from her briefcase. Payment over and above reimbursements for expenses would be in installments: first upon signing the contract; second in three months, at which time he was to submit a full report of his findings and advise whether he was confident of producing results in time for *Snap*'s launch; final payment to follow the outcome of the investigation.

"Mr. Wilkes hates to haggle." She detached a check clipped to the contract and placed it on the desk. "Here's installment number one. I trust it's adequate."

Made out *Pay to the Order of Fintan Dunne* and signed by Wilkes, the amount was blank. "That depends."

"On what?"

"What you mean by 'adequate.'"

"I don't understand." She crushed the smoldering remnant of her cigarette with several hesitant pokes. "Decide for yourself. That's why the check is blank."

"The amount isn't inadequate, only the notion we do business his way. I avoid contracts. Nothing but legal flypaper that gets gummed up with lawyers and lawsuits. I'll bill you when I'm done." He pushed the check toward her. Pully's friendly advice had been to avoid complications. Advice worth taking. "Shake on it."

"I need to let Mr. Wilkes know before . . ."

"If I recall correctly, you're the project manager. You 'control and coordinate every aspect.' That includes hiring and firing the help no?" He took hold of her limp hand and pressed it.

She tightened her grip. "All right, as long as you understand what the deadline is, it's a deal. There's a lot at stake for me as well as the company. If Crater proves a bust, I need to be able to move ahead with the other options."

"Understood."

"Mr. Wilkes said to assure you the organization's resources are at your disposal."

"If they were worth anything, Wilkes would have unearthed Crater twenty-five years ago. Less noise and fewer people, the better."

Glancing at her wristwatch, she let out a yelp. "I'd no idea of the time. I'll be late for my weekly staff meeting. Better run along."

"Try a cab."

Another frown rippled across her forehead. She shoved the materials on the desk back into her bag. "Don't be so literal."

"I take people at their word till they give me a reason not to."

"You always find a reason, I suppose."

He helped her into her coat. "No, not always, but close."

She handed him her card. "If there's anything you need, call my office."

He rang for Mulholland. No answer. He lay on the bed and switched on the radio. No more big bands. All the worthwhile entertainment had either gone off the air or, like Jack Benny, was moving to television. He found a music station. "The Ballad of Davy Crockett" was followed by "The Yellow Rose of Texas." Thanks, but no thanks. He put on his coat, exited the back of the hotel, crossed Madison and ate lunch by himself at Schrafft's. Instead of returning to his room for a nap, he went for a walk. Chance for some exercise as well as to help rid his overcoat of its lingering mothball scent.

Along 59th Street, the faces of bundled-up pedestrians were half-veiled by hats and scarves. A city full of people in disguises. If Crater was still alive, a remote possibility but real, he might be half a world away. Or maybe he never left the city. Maybe he was the sixty-ish-looking gent walking this way, gloved hand covering the lower half of his face. One of several hundred thousand suspects. Like looking for a particular blade of hay in a stack of it.

South on Seventh Avenue, he passed the Park Central Hotel where gambler and gangster Arnold Rothstein was shot, another famously unsolved crime, though not one to resonate in people's hearts and minds and help them regain a "measure of confidence in the future." The Roxy Theatre on 50th Street, one of the grandest of the movie palaces when it opened the year before Rothstein got shot, was shut. An ice show was being dismantled and the lights were out. Had a faded, worn look, as though it wouldn't be long before the Roxy followed Rothstein into the Great Beyond.

The walk warmed up most of him, but his feet were cold as he stepped into the lobby of the Taft Hotel. Back in the Rothstein days, it was the Manger Hotel. Vice squad dubbed it "House of a Thousand Hookers." The perfectly ordinary tourists and businessmen moving through the lobby indicated that those days were long past. He checked the listings in the *Standard*. The Rivoli was featuring a revival of *The Big Sleep*. Hollywood gumshoe bunk redeemed by that impossible-to-fake magic between Bogart and Bacall. He'd seen it twice already. Spencer Tracy and Robert Ryan were in *Bad Day at Black Rock* at the RKO, Ida Lupino and Howard Duff in *Women's Prison* at the Palace.

Always had a liking for Ida Lupino, especially after he saw her in *High Sierra*. Lovely face and understated manner, as good an actress, he thought, as Bette Davis. But never got the breaks she should have. Mulholland's motto: It all comes down to luck.

The prospect of revisiting the Palace put him off. Last time he was there was sometime between Rothstein's murder and Crater's disappearance, probably around when Miss Renard came into the world. He was still a cop and the Palace, now a second-tier movie house, was the pinnacle of the country's vaudeville circuit, home to the hottest acts, Durante, Burns & Allen, Milton Berle, stuff you could now catch on television. He decided to go to Radio City and catch William Holden in *The*

Bridges at Toko-Ri. Roberta insisted Holden reminded her of him. He didn't see it. Holden was younger, sleeker, better groomed.

He bought his ticket and went in. The cavernous theater seemed even larger half-deserted. Didn't care for the movie—a thinly disguised Navy recruiting film dressed up with a cameo by Grace Kelly as a faithful, self-sacrificing officer's wife and a pudgy, aging Mickey Rooney as brave-hearted buffoon. On the way out of the men's room, he glimpsed the janitors taking a break in a storage area. They sat watching television among a squad of giant toy soldiers, props left over from the Christmas show.

Outside, a slap of cold wind was momentarily refreshing. He stood and lit a cigarette beneath the marquee on Sixth—or as the city wanted it referred to, the Avenue of the Americas, an alias designed to escape the tainted memory of the El and the Tenderloin, with its working-class saloons, dance halls and cat houses. An old trick of the municipal magicians. Call Fourth Avenue Park, make Ninth into Columbus above 59th, change the name, turn the old new, make the past disappear.

In the middle of the avenue, a thick column of steam billowed from the abbreviated smokestack poking through the canvas tarp covering a temporary worksite. War or no war, the souls of dead comrades vanish like smoke. Stay around long enough and the city becomes a ghost town. Not uninhabited, like those busted and deserted places out west, but filled with new faces. Those who came before, forgotten; buildings and people alike replaced, replaceable. More departed souls and structures each day, until the ghosts outnumber the living.

The cigarette half-finished, he tossed it overhand into the gutter. Squat brick structures on the other side of the avenue were of a piece with the Els and the low-slung areas along the East River, places like Drydock Street where he'd been born, now wiped away by housing projects and highways. Soon the wrecker's ball and bulldozers would take care of the row of buildings across the way, decayed and shabby as an old man's teeth, an affront to the soaring prominence of Rockefeller Center, the smiling future proclaimed by the shimmer and gleam of the glass towers to the east.

Close eyes: wet, dreary morning in 1930 or '31, around when Crater went missing. A train pulls into elevated stop at Sixth Avenue and 34th. Pretty, olive-skinned girl sits catty corner across the car, glances up from beneath a red rain hat. Open them: winter's dusk a quarter century later. Sixth Avenue El went in '38, the Ninth Avenue line in '40, Second Avenue in '42. And the girl, what happened to her? Husband/boyfriend/lover goes away to war and never comes back? Or does, and they marry, have babies, and disappear into one of those new developments on Long Island?

Newspapers were unanimous that the Third Avenue El would go soon, though Transit Workers Union boss Mike Quill was issuing brogue-rich threats to halt what he labeled a "businessman's swindle designed to clear out the working class and small shop owner in order to make way for corporations and the rich." Hard to imagine Manhattan without an El roaring above, like a cyclone passing overhead. The splintered light beneath was as much a part of the place as snow in Central Park, belch of fog horns in the harbor.

"Our city's progress is unstoppable," the *Standard* quoted Mayor Wagner as saying. "It's the heart and soul of New York." Lungs were another story: daily dose of exhaust from autos, trucks, incinerators, fumes from heating oil and coal, two million people smoking umpteen million cigarettes a day. He lit another cigarette. Too many too early left a stale, metallic taste. Still brought an unchanging comfort, reliably filling the empty moments.

Jeff Wine was wrong when he'd called it a "yesterday city."

Not dying but changing, as it always did, becoming something different from before. Call it progress, if you want, even though the alterations weren't always improvements. It was those who never left, citizens of the perpetual cycle of demolition and construction—houses, buildings, theaters erected, altered, demolished; neighborhoods rising, falling and being redeveloped; famous and infamous celebrated, cheered and consigned to oblivion the ones stuck in the yesterday city—who had to adjust to being unmissed missing persons, has-beens living in a town populated with ghosts. Either that or pull a disappearance á la Judge Crater, in which case, if you're somebody worth missing, people might care what happened to you: *Be remembered for disappearing, while everyone who stayed around was forgotten.* There was an article or book in that for some historian or philosopher to write.

Back in his room, Dunne phoned Miss Renard's office and asked the secretary to tell the clipping morgue at the *Standard* to send him everything they had on the Crater case. Polite and cooperative, the secretary called back almost immediately. "Miss Renard would like to speak to you. Please hold." A full minute went by. A reminder of who's employee, who's employer? He gave her the benefit of the doubt. Maybe she was just busy. After several more seconds, she picked up.

"Sorry, Mr. Dunne, I was on with Mr. Wilkes. Third time today he's called to say how pleased he is you've signed on, or at least given us a handshake."

"Now that I have, call me Fin."

"Easy to remember. Rhymes with sin."

"Or gin. And you?"

"Friends call me Nan."

"Nan it is."

"I'm phoning because a colleague canceled our dinner plans. You free?"

"Tried to reach Mulholland earlier but couldn't, so yeah, Nan, I am."

"How about 8:30 at the Coral? It's close to you, on 59th between Madison and Park. I'll be in the dining room, in the rear."

"See you there."

Dunne dialed Louis Pohl as soon as he hung up. He was direct. "Back for more, Pully."

"You're pushing it, Fin. What's it this time?"

"One last favor for a semi-disreputable stepchild. Background check on Adrienne Renard, assistant to Walter Wilkes."

"On the basis of one last favor, I'll see what I can do."

The front door of the Coral opened on a dim, narrow barroom filled with noise and smoke. The main source of light was a large fish tank behind the bar, green and glowing, its inhabitants floating serenely above a seabed of pink pebbles and white coral fragments. A pair of tan-skinned, slick-haired bartenders in puff-sleeved shirts worked with acrobatic concentration to keep up with the drink orders of the crowd packed two-deep at the bar.

Dunne threaded his way to the back. The frozen face of the maitre d' standing guard behind a bamboo lectern melted into something close to a smile when Dunne mentioned Miss Renard. He led the way through a spacious room more dimly lit than the bar. Along the walls were semi-circular booths facing out on generously spaced tables, each with a small candle and a bowl shaped like an oyster shell, an orchid floating in it. Hubbub from the front was audible but unobtrusive, a busy, lively background noise.

Adrienne Renard was in a rear booth. Her black dress was cut low enough to be alluring without making an out-and-out invitation. She raised her martini glass. "I got a head start." Her hair framed her face the way it had the previous night. Dunne sidled in beside her and ordered a double Scotch on the rocks, which the maitre d' had a waiter deliver promptly.

"Hemingway says a good café has the same aura as a church." She turned to him, scanning the room as she did. Except for a few threesomes, the tables were occupied by couples, heads leaned in, hands extended, sometimes touching. Fingers folded around the stem of her glass in a prayer-like gesture, she glided it sideways and made a gentle collision with Dunne's. A mixture of candlelight and shadow wavered across her profile. "A toast to the Church of Saints Sin and Gin."

Dunne needed no explanation of the congregation: executives from the nearby advertising agencies who'd called their wives to let them know that once again an important piece of last-minute business had come up, and they'd be late. A decade after war's end, their rise into well-paid positions and comfortable suburban lives was not without its stresses. The officer corps of the nonstop, nationwide advertising campaigns driving postwar prosperity, they had to seize and hold the public's attention for a lineup of clients that included the makers of cars, cosmetics, refrigerators, TVs, cigarettes, soap, and toys and clothes for those 4,000,000 new toddlers, as well as drum up support for a growing number of vote-seeking politicians.

The question they faced was how to avoid being smothered by the vexing demands of constantly pumping up sales and the numbing predictability of marriage and work. The answer: find an activity more compelling and pleasurable than a weekend round of golf which could be indulged without upending an entire career.

"I know what you're thinking," she said.

"Isn't Wilkes in charge of mind reading?"

"You're thinking I'm not very different from the other women in this room. It's stamped on your face. The male smirk."

"You're reading what isn't there."

"I read faces like gypsies read tea leaves. Except they're guessing. I'm not."

There was a quaver in her voice, subtle. Odds were this wasn't her first martini of the evening, but her mind reading wasn't entirely off the mark. The women were decidedly younger than their escorts. And less stiff. Pretty, stylish—if a shade more flashy than classy—graduates of commercial high schools with maybe a year of polishing in a secretarial school, they were aware of how the game was played. None was under the illusion that her companion was about to ditch wife and job for an ethnic outer-borough office girl. But each enjoyed the free meals, attention, lunch-hour trysts in hotels or cheap studio apartments, hurried but intense sex.

Evenings at the Coral were a romantic perk, light and enjoyable, one drink too many, but nothing beyond a touch, a kiss, money for a cab ride home to Pelham Parkway or Jackson Heights, time spent pondering wedding plans now that the boy friend had a full-time job or the prospect of a civil service appointment.

"Can't get it out of your head I'm Wilkes's plaything, can you?"

"Can you get it out of yours that I don't care?"

"But you think it. Admit it. When it comes to women, all men think alike."

"I'm being paid to find Judge Crater. What I think or don't think about your relationship with Wilkes doesn't make any difference." He turned, expecting to confront an angry pout, eyes charged with resentment and scrutiny.

Her face, poised and beautiful, had no readable expression. "It does to me."

"Knowing the players is part of the game. Throwing stones isn't."

She guessed correctly that he'd already ordered a background check. If he hadn't, she said, she'd save him the time and expense. Her last name wasn't Renard, and she wasn't baptized Adrienne. Wasn't baptized at all. "I'm Jewish," she said. Her mother was from Austria, now Poland, and had arrived in America as a little girl. Her father left when she was three, at the bottom of the Depression. Alone and broke, her mother turned for help to her sister. She and her husband ran a hole-in-the-wall grocery on Tremont Avenue, in the Bronx. They raised her. "Anna Resnick is my real name." She paused, raised her glass, and sipped.

She graduated from Walton High School. Her uncle wanted her to become a public school teacher. She had bigger ambitions and went to City College as a classics major. She planned to win an assistantship at some prestigious Ivy League graduate school that, gag as it might at accepting a Jew and a woman, couldn't overlook her grades and abilities. But her uncle died during her senior year, and her aunt was left with next to nothing, so she went out to get a job. She adopted the *shikseh* moniker Adrienne Renard and took the first position that came along. It was with Wilkes Communications.

After a year working in the personnel department, she was assigned to fill in for one of the secretaries in Mr. Wilkes's office. At most companies that'd be the end. Jewish girl from the Bronx gets secretarial job in corporate sanctum sanctorum, and stays till she marries or makes a lateral move for five dollars more a week. "But Mr. Wilkes," she said, "isn't bound by the old-boy snobbery that reigns at places like Time Inc."

"No need to spill all this." Dunne wondered how much of it Pully would turn up.

"Maybe you don't need to know it, but I need to tell it. I

know why Mr. Wilkes noticed me. Even to be assigned to his office you have to look a certain way. And it was no secret what he expected. When I made it clear I wouldn't act in that little play, I expected to be transferred. Instead he dropped a business proposal on my desk and said, 'You went to college, Miss Renard. Tell me what you think.'

"I did. More proposals arrived for comment. I jumped from secretary to assistant to the chairman to vice-president for special projects. The jaw-dropping among the male executives became a familiar thud in the Wilkes Building. One day he came to me with the idea for a project to flesh out a theory he'd been brooding over for some time."

"I remember. 'Birds do it, bees do it . . . pan-pollination.'"

"Yes, *pan-pollenization.* That's Mr. Wilkes's term for it. We talked it over for months before he offered me the chance to run it. I was scared. I knew if I turned it down, he'd find someone else; just as I know if I fail, I'll be out of a job. There are no second chances at the Wilkes Organization. And I won't be looking for any because I won't fail."

"What's Mulholland's role?"

"With me, none."

"With Wilkes?"

"Security stuff, bailing out reporters who get in trouble with the police, that sort of thing. Mr. Wilkes trusts him. That's no small thing."

"Any reason he shouldn't?"

"Not that I'm aware of."

"But he doesn't trust Mulholland enough to get him involved in this. Why?"

"Ask Mr. Wilkes. He's better acquainted with Mulholland's strengths and weaknesses. But I gather you know him better than any of us."

"Longer."

"My dealings with him have been peripheral, at best. He's the Billy Goats Gruff type, but that goes with the job, I suppose."

They ordered dinner. The waiter delivered Miss Renard a fresh drink. Dunne wasn't in the mood to work at making conversation. He welcomed her monologue on the multiple attributes of the many-splendored Mr. Wilkes—vision, resolve, honesty, bravery, willingness to take risks—big business meets the Boy Scouts. Half-listening, he watched as the couples at the other tables began to leave. Ignoring their colleagues and co-workers at the other tables, they left without so much as glances in their direction.

Nan Renard only played with her food, but finished her drink quickly. "I'm already over my limit," she said. "But we're celebrating, Fin, aren't we? Celebrating our new adventure." Tempted to declare his low expectations for the Crater investigation, he didn't. She went on about the future of Wilkes Communications, speaking so emphatically at one point that the couple at the next table looked over. "Oops, better tone it down." She pressed a forefinger to her lips and giggled.

"And you believe Wilkes is sincere in thinking I'll find out what happened to Crater when nobody else could?"

"Depends on what you mean by 'sincere.'"

"How many meanings does it have?'

"The literal meaning is 'without wax,' a reference to the practice of ancient art dealers who disguised nicks and cracks in the marble statuary they were trying to sell by filling them with wax. In that sense, Wilkes is sincere. Except for his ears, he's wax-free. And, yes, when it comes to making money and building his empire, he's sincere in every sense of the word."

After they ate, her body slumped softly against his and her head casually leaned on his shoulder. He moved his arm along the booth's u-shaped ledge, resting it behind, what from a distance might be mistaken for an embrace. Picking up the candle

from the middle of the table, he lit a cigarette for her, then one
for himself.

She whispered, "If we do it right, it will be glorious."

It came to him suddenly, where he'd seen the female form
depicted on the wall outside Wilkes's bedroom: Catechism class
at the Catholic Protectory.

Forty boys in rows of desks bolted to the floor listened as
Brother Flavian droned on in his heavy French accent about the
"Body of Glory" that the souls of the saved will assume at the
General Resurrection. In these "glorified bodies" of purified soul
and spiritualized flesh, rid of imperfections, the faithfully depart-
ed would live forever.

The student in the desk next to Dunne's waited until
Brother Flavian turned to write on the blackboard and passed a
folded sheet of paper. Dunne opened it on his lap. It was a hasti-
ly but artfully done drawing of a supremely voluptuous female,
nude, ascending into heaven and playing a small harp. Scrolled
across the top were the words "Glorious Gloria in Her Glorified
Body." Once, years later, in "The Cuddles & Cuties Revue" at
the Winter Garden Theatre, he'd seen a real-life body to match.
"The Venus of Broadway." Mulholland's girlfriend, Mary Claire
Richfield, the suicide.

"Penny for your thoughts." Her smile was soft and natural,
without wax.

"You'd be overpaying."

The waiter cleared the dishes and brought them coffee.
From across the room, head forward, arms swinging at his sides,
a broad-chested man in a well-tailored, chalk-striped suit
approached. Big head, big ears, thick, slicked-down black hair,
he walked with the lumbering, determined stride of one of those
upper-class ape men who'd anchored his college football team's
defensive line. Miss Renard identified him as Herb Johnson, "a
key player at Compton Advertising."

He stopped in front of their booth and exchanged a few pleasantries. She introduced Dunne as a "special assistant to Mr. Wilkes." Johnson's eyes tick-tocked back and forth, as if weighing which of them to focus on. He stuck with a known quantity. "Adrienne, my shop is abuzz with rumors of a 'secret operation' you've got under way."

"It wouldn't be a secret if I told you, would it, Herb?"

"Some secrets are better shared than kept. You care about having advertisers like Lorillard and Proctor & Gamble aboard, better not stay tight-lipped too long." He turned and went to the door where his buxom tablemate was waiting.

Miss Renard blew a trail of smoke after him. "Television has them confused. It brings in oodles of money but unlike radio and print, TV has generated a high degree of uncertainty. Don't have their bearings like they did with radio and print. They're scared of what might be next, and when men are scared they revert to their most primitive emotional state. Ever read Freud?

"No, but you're not the first one to tell me I should."

"No matter. Now you know all there is to know about Madison Avenue. It's the Kinsey Report as written by Franz Kafka."

"Haven't read them either." When it came to thinking about sex, he preferred looking to reading. *Wink. Titter. Eyeful.* The rear-rack magazines. Last month's *Playboy*, with the Betty Page centerfold.

"Everything in this business comes down to sex and paranoia."

Roberta had recommended both of Kinsey's books. The more recent one, *Sexual Behavior in the Human Female*, was on her nightstand. He thought about mentioning it, then thought again. "What about sin and gin?"

"They're included in the other two."

Another executive approached. "Here comes Ron Fuller,"

she said. "He worked on the Eisenhower TV spots. Now all the politicians are courting him." More cordial than Johnson, Fuller made passing mention of his hope that "if something big is cooking, we won't be left in the dark," and went on his way.

Soon, the only people left were several waiters loitering near the door and a couple in a corner booth in a slow-motion version of mouth-to-mouth resuscitation. "Come on," Dunne said. "Time to let the waiters go home."

"From the looks of those two in the corner, the waiters will have to stay all night."

He moved sidelong out of the booth; stab of pain in his knee made him grimace. She took his hand. "Something wrong?"

"Bum knee, that's all."

"From the war?"

"From kneeling to say the rosary."

"So you're not as irreverent as you claim?"

"Not while I'm in the Church of Saints Sin and Gin."

Stumbling slightly as she stood, she bumped against him. "You all right?"

She slipped her arm in his. "See me up the aisle, I'll take it from there."

He retrieved their coats from the checkroom and held hers as she slipped into it. His hands lingered on her shoulders. She turned her head. He bent toward her, and their lips brushed in a tease of a kiss. Waft of perfume, alcohol, cigarette smoke, distinct and seductive, the spell a good café casts, wholly unlike church. "Sorry, but I have to visit the ladies' room."

"I'll wait in the bar."

The crowd had thinned out. There was now one bartender instead of two. Dunne ordered a Scotch straight up. The tank behind the bar put him in mind of the rendezvous of Orson Welles and Rita Hayworth in *Lady from Shanghai*: glass walls of an aquarium for a backdrop, the fish inside as large and menacing as sea monsters. Not these. Except for what looked like a miniature shark moving in fretful circles near the surface, the tank's small, placid, brightly colored tenants—striped, fan-tailed, needle-nosed, and a pair of sea horses—swam in slow contentment.

The woman on the stool in front of Dunne pointed out the miniature shark to the man sitting next to her. He called over the bartender. "Carlos," he said, aiming his finger at the tank, "see that fish? What's he called?"

Carlos shook his head. "I learned long ago, you want to do good in this business, don't never ask nobody their name."

The woman and her companion laughed. "You know what I mean, Carlos," he said. "What kind of fish?"

"Unless it's filet of sole, I don't tell one kinda fish from other."

They laughed again. Carlos sauntered down the bar to serve a customer. "Poor fish," the woman said. "Must be hungry."

"If he was hungry, he'd eat the other fish," the man beside her said.

"He's too small to do that."

"Small fries are the ones to watch out for. He'd take the rest of them if he wanted, but, nah, that's not his problem. I know the look. That shark is no different. A horny fish is what he is."

Dunne stood against the wall. Horny fish, horny men. One has feet, the other fins; but their brain is the same. A rule every bit as golden as "pace yourself": *Don't think with your testicles.* Except for the times when you can't help it.

Away from Roberta for over two years, overseas, before those OSS missions, he'd had no desire to pray, confess or kneel for last-minute repentance sincere only until the threat of death had passed. Get holy and then, if you survive, renege on the deal. How smart could God be to be fooled by such a clumsy, self-serving logic? Better a round of café nights, mutual seduction and repeated satisfaction, the kind that calmed anxieties in a way nothing else could—neither booze nor physical exertion nor fear-induced piety.

If war teaches any lesson, it's that in the face of death, it isn't damnation you fear, only death itself, instant end, obliteration of self, or even worse—like that Kraut, the boy lieutenant—a self left with only death to crave. Same fear for hero and coward, the gap between the two far thinner than those who'd never been in combat imagined, a matter of seconds, inches, jumping right instead of left.

Maybe, as the saying went, there are no atheists in foxholes. Yet, if fear is the impetus for faith in God, that faith resides in the sole hope of being spared death; death so imminent and near it has a color—white, enveloping, obliterating blur—as well as taste—dry, stale, acidic—and sound: high-pitched, droning monotone that drains other sounds of meaning. In his experience, making love and facing death were the only two instances of a full, unqualified union of mind, soul and physical self.

First time he saw death face to face was in France, during the first war. At dusk, the regiment trudged up a shell-pocked road. Suddenly, the dimness filled with the menacing whine of an approaching shell; then, electric flash and concussive shock as it hit near where Billy Sullivan had gone to piss. They ran to his side, hoping he'd only been knocked down, and froze in a half-circle. The shell had taken off his helmet together with the top of his head, splattering brains and blood across the dry brown grass. Not yet equipped with the battlefield skill of looking at the dead without noticing the nature of their wounds, they peered down at Sullivan's cleaved skull.

No way to tell if he'd died with a clear conscience or not. The expression on his face was pretty much like that on all the faces of all the dead men in both wars, those not contorted by pain and agony, but a mix of emptiness and shock. *O God, why me?*

Another shell hit. Dropping to the ground, each fervently

begged not for eternal life in paradise, angel's wings, proximity to God, but for a few more ordinary hours on earth. Indiscriminate, chance-ridden, war-driven death stirred no noble feeling—no grand revelation—save the solitary urge to live. *Spare me, God, and I'll be good. I'll never sin again. Answered prayers, at least for now.* But, hours or days or weeks or months later, away from the guns, those praying, pleading, believing faces were the same flushed, fevered, pleasure-driven ones frequenting brothels.

Years later, late 1945, just before shipping back to the States, on the way out of a London pub with Jack Lynch, a Jesuit chaplain from Jersey City who'd gone ashore on D-Day—he mentioned anxiety at returning to Roberta. Happiness/regret/nagging awareness of a vow he didn't keep. Café nights in Paris, two weeks with an English nurse, among others. A sin? Maybe there was a less harsh, less bitter word for something so human, but he couldn't think of one.

Lynch took out the thin purple stole that priests wear in confession, tucked it discreetly beneath the collar of his coat, listening as they maneuvered amid pedestrians and traffic before whispering the Latin absolution. "Fin," he said as they parted, "given what's gone on these last years, I'm not sure God had time to notice sins as ordinary as yours. But what I've found is that though love doesn't always make us faithful, it always makes us suffer for our unfaithfulness. It's your wife's forgiveness you should ask for. Make it up to her when you get home." He went on his way without imposing any penance beyond that.

The scaled-down shark continued its frantic back and forth, thinking with its testicles. It was possible Miss Renard had an agenda besides the one she was pursuing for Wilkes. Or maybe Wilkes hadn't revealed his true hand. Then again, it could be

Miss Renard was lonely, attracted by a man twice her age. Maybe part of the chemistry she had with Wilkes was a grasping for the father who walked out on her when she was three. Didn't have to be Freud to speculate something was up with her. Consider Bogie and Bacall. Twenty-five years between them. She never saw her father after she was six.

Whatever was going on had to be more than Wilkes let on. More than the million-to-one odds of finding Judge Crater. A lesson every dick learned, at least those eager not to get themselves killed: listen to your gut.

The couple at the bar rose to leave. The man slapped several bills on the counter. "Half is yours, Carlos. The other half is to buy that fish a mate. I can't stand watching him anymore. He reminds me of myself."

The woman took his hand. "Come on, let's fix that."

"In a minute. First I got a song I want to hear." He took some change from the bar and went to the jukebox. Nat King Cole began to sing "Unforgettable."

Miss Renard returned from the ladies' room. Her well-formed, high-heeled frame swayed slowly, almost as though underwater, half-floating across the ocean floor. Two men at the end of the bar turned and looked. She lifted the Scotch from Dunne's hand and nestled the glass beneath her chin. "How about a night cap at the Stork? Only a short cab ride. I have use of Mr. Wilkes's table in the Cub Room, a primo spot. We'll be treated like stars."

"This star's battery is low. How about a rain check?"

"How about a nightcap at my place? I'm down the block, across Park."

"I'll see you home, but then I have to get back to the hotel."

"What's the rush?" She put the glass down on the bar with an emphatic bang.

"Have to pack."

"Pack?"

"Going home in the morning."

"*Home?*" She nearly shouted. Carlos looked up from the service sink.

She buttoned her coat, flipping up the collar with an abrupt snap. Dunne took her by the elbow and led her into the street. She pushed away his hand. "We have to start now. The deadline is impossibly tight as it is."

"Boyle's Law."

"Life isn't that predictable."

"Tell that to Wilkes."

"Don't you think I already have?" She turned and walked away.

He caught up and fell in beside her, vapor of their frozen breath all that was left of the Coral's mellow, enveloping mood. She hugged herself, head down, isolated pose directed, he surmised, as much at him as the cold. "Do me a favor," he said when they reached her building. "I called your office earlier to have the clippings from the Crater files sent to me. Make sure they're expressed to me in Florida."

"My career is riding on this, so if I seem nonplussed by your taking a break before we even start, it's because I am."

"Business to settle, that's all." Away from New York, café moods, and the sense of being seduced. By who? Mulholland? Miss Renard? Walter Wilkes? Try to get perspective on the Crater case, on the sense he wasn't seeing what must be in plain sight.

"'Talented girl, but in a hurry,' that's what Mr. Wilkes told you, right? He says that about me to everybody. Well, tell me, who in this town isn't in a hurry? And any hurry a man is in, double it for a woman. If I want to get where I want—where I deserve—it has to be *now*. For the Anna Resnicks of this world, a chance like this never came before and may never come again. I need this to work. Don't be long."

She turned and went into the building without another word. He went back to the Savoy Plaza along the north side of 59th Street. The Coral's front lights were off. The green-electric glow from behind the bar, radiating through the window, made it seem one big fish tank. There were two messages at the front desk, both from Roberta. First was short: *How was he planning to travel home? And when?* Second was longer. *Eddie Moran had called from Havana. Said it might be important. Want me to call him back with your number in New York? Or will you call him when you get home?*

Dunne laughed to himself. Eddie was undoubtedly miffed his old pal didn't show up at the Starlight Room to say hello, share a drink and some memories. That was the inviolable protocol with old buddies like Eddie. You were anywhere within a thousand miles and didn't drop by, they got insulted. He'd make it a point to see him next time he was in Havana.

He turned on the TV and stretched out on the bed. After a spate of commercials, the late show of "Million Dollar Movie" came on: *Force of Evil*, with John Garfield. Though he hadn't brought it up with Mulholland, he'd met Garfield once, a chance encounter in Danny Schwartz's gym, where Julie—that's what everybody called him—was sparring with ex-featherweight Jimmy Ryan. Garfield was back east before filming *Body and Soul*, which would earn him his second Oscar nomination.

Out in Hollywood, Jeff Wine had laughingly recounted the names of the tough-talking, square-jawed leading men who showed up early on the set so they could insert dentures, don hairpieces, squeeze into a corset and get comfortable in elevator shoes. Garfield wasn't one of them. Everything about him was real. Though, well-built and nimble, he didn't have much of a punch. Ryan went easy with him. Julie joked about it when he came out of the ring. "Jimmy coulda killed me," he said. "Instead, he waltzed me."

He didn't have any airs either, especially for a Hollywood

star. A shooting star, as it turned out, silver trail fading fast, incandescent halo of movie fame passing to his sullen heirs, Brando and that other brooding malcontent, baby-faced James Dean.

"Garfield came and went," the joke went around when he died. Or: "Did you hear? Garfield was all set to star in a remake of 'They Died with Their Boots On.' The new title: 'He Died with a Hard-On.'" The smirks and stories were legion. *He died high in the saddle. He died smiling. He got stiff and stayed stiff.*

Except maybe he wasn't smiling. Maybe he'd lost his bearings. Maybe he was afraid. Maybe he was grabbing for what was slipping away and what was already gone. Maybe he died wishing he could have his prime back, wondering how suddenly the destination that he thought was ahead was in the rear-view mirror and there was no brake to hit and no way to turn around. *Whoopi-ty-aye-oh*. Maybe that's what it meant to go *the John Garfield way.*

Dunne drifted off to sleep. When he awoke the movie was over and the station had signed off. The screen held a stationary test pattern in the shape of a Maltese cross. He got up and turned it off. He'd call Roberta first thing with his travel arrangements.

Part III

Girls! Girls! Girls! Excerpt from *Variety*, July 30, 1930.

Army of Femme Floaters

Wanderlust—Girls Go from City to City—
Never Stick in Any Spot—Employment Agencies Surprised
at Number—Girls Almost Always Broke

A horde of floaters—girls who never stay long in one spot but work their way from week to week or month to month from city to city—is flooding the country.

Employment agencies have been astounded by the number applying for positions. The male variety is no novelty, with employment agencies already accustomed to large bunches of them.

Agencies can spot the floaters by the manner in which the application cards are filed. Frequently girls are found who list their last place of business in Kansas City, second Calgary, and their last in San Francisco. They rarely ever stay more than three months in any city. Constantly on the go, in the majority of instances they say that they wanted to work their way to the big city, where they would stand a chance to get ahead.

Employment agencies express surprise at the type of femme floaters who apply for work, and the type of work and salary they will accept. Some are highly intelligent, speaking and looking like professionals, yet will work for $12 a week. This is because they are usually broke when they hit New York.

When asked how they manage to travel around as they do when they're supposedly broke, the girls reply that they go any way they can, mostly by hitch-hiking. Hardly any of them report being passengers on a train.

Femme floaters in show biz are the natural and expected thing, but their numbers have risen steeply, and the numbers of non-pro femme floaters are now just as high if not more so. The agencies expect that as times get better, the tide of femme floaters will ebb. If times get worse, the opposite is anticipated.

Playa de Oro, Florida

"Turn back and seek the safety of the shore
Tempt not the deep, lest, losing unawares
Me and yourselves, you come to port no more."

—DANTE, *Paradiso*, Canto II

THE CRIMSON SUN'S PERFECT CIRCLE BARELY TOPPED THE DISTANT
line of trees beyond the mist-covered marsh. A tumble-down
barn came into view with its three-word question painted in tall
white letters on the side: ARE YOU SAVED? Seen from the window of his sleeping compartment, the landscape and the question
told Dunne the train's nighttime progress had brought them to
South Carolina or Georgia. A moment later, another barn-side
message added a note of urgency undoubtedly intended for fast-
moving trainloads of unredeemed and/or unredeemable travelers: HELL IS REAL!

It was afternoon when the train pulled into its destination.
A long line of autos was lined up by the tracks. Roberta was in
the shade on the platform. White straw hat. Green silk blouse.
White silk skirt. She took a small oval mirror from her purse,
pouted her lips, applied fresh lipstick, put it away and chatted
with two women standing nearby. Framed in the window, the
trio of stylish middle-aged women could have been posed for a

picture spread in *Life* or *Look* (soon, maybe, *Snap*) on, say, "America's Weekday Widows" or "The New Immigrants: Northern City Folk Head to Southern Suburbs." Whatever title they put on it, Roberta was by far the most youthful and attractive of the three.

Dunne removed from his wallet the handwritten note that had been waiting for him at the front desk when he checked out of the Savoy Plaza. He read it again:

> Dear Fin,
> Sorry if I seemed rude. I had a wonderful time, but it came at the end of a long, trying day. (They're all that way in the House of Wilkes!) I'm afraid I behaved badly. Forgive me. I'm already looking forward to your return. I *know* we'll make a great team!
>
> > Fondly,
> > Nan
>
> P.S. The files you requested are on their way.

He folded the note in half, quarters, tore it into pieces and dropped it in the ashtray.

On the way out, waiting for the conductor to open the car door, Dunne faced a portly, sixty-ish man with a carefully tended head of silver hair he recognized immediately from the Savoy Plaza. Parading through the lobby, Mr. Silverhair's attention had been absorbed by the tall twenty-something redhead in an elegant mink coat hanging on his arm. She kissed him behind the ear and whispered something that made him smile.

Now, companionless, he glowered impatiently at the train car door and gave Dunne the slender, minimally cordial smile exchanged between travelers who'd never seen each other before (he thought) and expected never to see each other again. First to exit, he threw his coat over his shoulder, dashed past the porter

114

and made a showy embrace of one of the women chatting with Roberta.

Roberta drove off with the top down. They rode beneath a canopy of stately trees. Hat off, eyes closed, he lifted up his face to bathe in palm-flickered light. If Crater had engineered his own disappearance, if he'd made it out with spoils enough to start a new life somewhere, he probably wouldn't hole up in the hills or in the rear of a basement apartment with the shades drawn. More likely, he'd hide in public, using as disguise the general indistinguishability of stout silver-haired gents populating every part of the country, moving amid a ceaseless flow of strangers with the well-tested assurance that if people see what they expect to see in the context they expect to see it—milkman at their door in the morning, boy entering the bus with his school bag, silver-haired sugar daddy with young honey in the lobby of the Savoy Plaza—they really don't see anything at all.

Steering with her left hand, Roberta reached with her right and gently squeezed his fingers. "Why so quiet? Aren't you glad to be home?"

"Who's that woman you were talking to?"

"Which one? I was talking with two."

"The one whose husband gave her the bear hug."

"Louise Wilson."

"What's her husband do?"

"He's an executive at Florida Gas & Electric. Obvious he'd missed her, wasn't it?"

"Sorry. Silly question." He knew she was miffed at his abrupt tone. He put his hand over hers.

"Your hand's cold." She pulled hers away.

"Still in my New York mode. Cold place, getting colder." The reflexive coil that had settled in his bones, sunk into shoulders, and pulled shoulders toward chest, seemed to loosen. He flexed his knee.

"Maybe it's not New York. Maybe the blood doesn't flow to the extremities the way it once did."

"Depends on which extremity you mean." He moved his hand to her leg, fingering the fine silk, bump of garter snap beneath. Would the time come when such things had no effect? Could be. But not yet. "How about we get the blood flowing again?"

"Dancing?"

"That's one way."

They tried another when they reached home. He enjoyed the leisurely familiarity and practiced intimacies of their love-making, except for the consummate moment, when he closed his eyes and saw Adrienne Renard's face, a vivid illusion, more startling than arousing, almost interrupting his momentum, though Roberta didn't seem to notice.

Afterwards, he swam in their re-filled, renovated pool. Roberta had surrounded the entire area with a high fence so they could swim nude, which on occasion they both enjoyed. She made dinner. They ate on the patio. "Eddie Moran called again. Guess you never called him back."

"I will. But it was a rush in New York, and I didn't have a chance." He gave an abbreviated version of what transpired in New York, adding that the higher-ups at ISC were pleased he'd taken the case, which they would most definitely not be if Pully got around to mentioning it to them. Miss Renard, a young go-getter, was in charge. She seemed to know what she was doing.

"It's nice to hear a girl can make a career for herself in a business like that." She paused and took a sip of water. "But are you sure that business is the only motive?"

Her question came across to Dunne as an accusation. "What's that supposed to mean?" He didn't try to hide his resentment.

"Maybe she has other motives, as well."

"For instance?"

"You won't know until you look into the case, will you?" Her tone of resentment matched his.

"No, I won't."

"And you'll be headed back to New York, no doubt, as soon as possible."

"The newspaper files are being shipped here. As soon as they arrive, I'll get started reading. Once I'm done, I'll head back."

"The files arrived this morning. They're in the living room."

"You're just telling me now?"

"Sorry. I thought we could enjoy some time together before you got back to work." She threw her napkin on the table and went inside. The bedroom door closed with a loud slam.

He cleaned the table and washed the dishes. After he was done, he opened the boxes piled on the coffee table in the living room. Inside were stacks of cardboard clipping books from all the major New York papers—*Standard, News, Mirror, Times, Journal, World*, et al.—filled with chronologically arranged, day-by-day accounts of the Crater disappearance and investigation. As he lifted one of the books, a square piece of paper slipped from it and fluttered to the carpet. Joe Crater's face stared up at him.

Dunne recognized the paper as one of the police flyers that had flooded the city. They'd been everywhere, strewn across sidewalks, parks, subway cars, barrooms, lunch counters, until interest waned and they were shredded for ticker-tape parades, or used for scrap paper, or turned into toy boats, paper hats and sun visors. Several years later, on an outing to Coney Island, Dunne ordered a beer and French fries. Half-finished with the fries, he noticed that instead of newspaper, the paper cone in which they came was a rolled-up police flyer. A dollop of ketchup obliterated half of Crater's head.

Dated September 8, 1930, the bare-bone facts of the case were headlined above and below Crater's picture:

MISSING SINCE AUGUST 6, 1930
Honorable Joseph Force Crater
Justice of the New York State Supreme Court

A brief description followed of what Crater looked like and what he was wearing:

> Born in the United States – Age, 41 years; height, 6ft.; weight, 185 lbs.; mixed gray hair, originally dark brown, thin at top, parted in the middle and slicked down; complexion, medium dark, considerably tanned; brown eyes; false teeth, upper and lower jaw; tip of right index finger somewhat mutilated, due to having been recently crushed.

> Wore brown sack coat and trousers, narrow green stripe, no vest; either a Panama or soft brown hat worn at rakish angle, size 6 5/8, unusual size for his height and weight. Clothes made by Vroom. Affected colored shirts, size 14 collar, probably bow ties. Wore tortoise-shell glasses for reading. Yellow gold Masonic ring, somewhat worn; may be wearing a yellow gold, square wristwatch with leather straps.

The black-and-white photo of Crater looked as if it had been taken as an official campaign portrait. Along with parting his hair in the middle, he sported the high, stiff, celluloid collars that were mostly out of fashion by 1930. The hair style and col-

lar gave him a passing resemblance to the president at the time,
Herbert Hoover, who had the same passé fashion sense and was
also destined for obscurity, though without the mystery that surrounded Crater.

In the photo, Crater stared resolutely at the camera. He had
a fleshy face, not fat, but headed that way, and a sharp, triangu-
lar nose. The stern, properly judicial pose was belied by the smile
creeping out from the corners of his mouth as though he'd shared
a small joke with the photographer the instant before the flash
went off, and by the bulging, almost frog-like prominence of his
eyes. His brown pupils were two black dots. The hint of a smile
didn't come close to revealing his false teeth.

The overall effect was of a man ten to fifteen years older
than his stated age of forty-one, an impression probably the result
of a deliberate effort on Crater's part to project the gravity and
experience of a justice of the State Supreme Court appointed to
fill an interim term and set to run for a full fourteen-year term the
following November. Dunne guessed that this was the source of
the phantom smile, a quick aside shared with the photographer, *I
want to look grave, but not like I just came out of one!*

He was careful not to push beyond his surface impressions
of the mug on the circular: a face can be a mask as well as a
map. Hard to tell which until you know what's behind it. When
Dunne joined the police soon after returning from France in
1919, the emphasis was on learning to read mug shots for those
elements—sloping forehead, weak chin, flat nose, etc.—indicat-
ing a "criminal nature." A chart on the wall at headquarters
identified certain physical aspects with specific crimes. The only
one he remembered was crossed eyes for shoplifting. It was a
cause for laughter in the first precinct he was assigned, on Jerome
Avenue in the Bronx, where the convergent squint of the captain
in charge, a ruthlessly honest cop exiled to the Bronx for his
inability to abide even the most petty and innocuous venalities of

subordinates and superiors, earned him the name Cross-eyes Sweeney.

That same lesson—the lack of any real connection between the eugenic notion of a "physiognomy of criminality" and real criminals—was driven home in Germany, in 1945. As an OSS representative, he sat in on the interrogation of two S.S. men the Brits had snagged at the Bergen-Belsen Concentration Camp. One was a stumpy, thick-lipped corporal who wept when he described being dragooned into the S.S. only weeks before and his horror at what he saw when he'd entered the camp. His companion, a young sleek, tow-headed major—his clear-complexioned, boyishly beautiful face punctuated by luminously blue eyes that look as if they were lifted from a cherub on a holy card—refused to answer any questions. The Brits identified him as a long-time member of the staff and chief among its sadists, notorious for randomly sticking the barrel of his Lugar in an inmate's ear, hesitating a moment to enjoy his terror before pulling the trigger.

Scrawled next to Crater's picture in faded black ink was a one-line distillation of the facts: *Last seen entering a tan cab on the evening of August 6, 1930, on W. 45th Street, between 8th and 9th Avenues.* Event of yawn-provoking ordinariness no passer-by noticed or had reason to. Noted almost in passing, the cab was obviously a big part of the puzzle. The highly publicized search the police carried out failed to produce a single lead on the cab, its driver, what company it belonged to, where it came from or where it went.

Another piece of the puzzle was the date given for Crater's disappearance, August 6th, and the date the circular was issued, September 8th. At the time, there was a major fuss about how long it took before anyone notified the authorities that Crater had vanished, but Dunne couldn't recall the particulars.

The book the circular had slipped from was pasted thick

with clippings from the trademark pink pages of the *New York Graphic*, which had taken to the Crater case like frenetic hyenas in the Frank Buck jungle movies that tore apart hapless, lumbering water buffaloes. As the search went on, the *Graphic* increasingly resorted to its famous (or infamous) practice of featuring faked photos—"composographs" the paper called them—in which the heads of real people were stuck on bodies posed in provocative re-creations of supposedly real incidents.

In one, Crater's face had been cropped from the missing person's circular and imposed on a black-robed figure, arms draped around two chorines in judicial-style robes opened to reveal black garters and stockings. The caption proclaimed: DISORDER IN THE COURT. JUDGE CRATER FLEES BENCH FOR LOVE NEST. The judge's shadow of a smile now seemed a leer.

After flipping through more pages of the *Graphic*, Dunne put the volume aside. He decided to start with the *Standard* and follow the coverage it gave the case from start to finish. Seven thick volumes of clippings made it clear that, though not as imaginatively lewd as the *Graphic*, the *Standard* had outdone all its competitors in the extent of space it had devoted to the case.

Over the next several days, he read methodically through each volume and took extensive notes, looking for discrepancies among the various newspapers accounts, or the odd fact, unnoticed or unappreciated at the time, that might offer a possible opening for a new line of investigation. He noted, for example, the mention in the police circular that Crater's finger had been somewhat mutilated, due to having been recently crushed. Did this indicate, Dunne wondered, that Crater had been in an altercation soon before he'd disappeared? The explanation in the newspapers turned out to be more prosaic. His driver had accidentally slammed the car door on it.

Dunne ended by reading an expansive series of articles in the *Standard* published in 1940, on the tenth anniversary of the disappearance, written by Stella Crater, the judge's wife (and now, presumably, widow) "in order to set the record straight about my husband and me." Though the flowery, melodramatic prose had undoubtedly been goosed by a hired pen ordered to portray her as an innocent Red Riding Hood lost in a forest of wily wolves, Stella Crater's account made it immediately apparent that she didn't merely view her husband through rose-tinted glasses, which might after all slip or be removed. Hers was a case of congenital blindness.

Her Joe—the name she used throughout—was White Knight and Captain Courageous, moral paragon and noble jurist, attempting to steer a course of righteous public service through the treacherous shoals and evil currents of Gotham's toxic politics. There was an engaging lack of guile in the way she told her story. Where the newspapers quickly turned repetitious, each presenting and repeating essentially the same set of facts, her account had a refreshing novelty. Somewhere in it, he thought, might be buried some useful tidbit, an overlooked fact, a thread that no one had ever pulled.

Mrs. Crater refrained from accusing any specific person or persons of being behind Joe's disappearance. In her morality play, it was the beast called New York that killed her all-American beau—an uncouth and corrupt alliance of "swarthy skinned gangsters," pols with "beady eyes and leprous hearts," and "women of the lowest possible character," a triumvirate "antithetical to everything we call decent and Christian."

The *Standard,* however, made sure that its readers knew lurking behind it all was the governor, Franklin D.—for "Deceiver"—Roosevelt, who if he didn't carry out the crime, approved and blessed it, willing to do whatever necessary to hush up the tainted process of how judges were chosen in New

York and preserve his chances of being elected president. It was for this reason, Dunne knew, and not just to mark the tenth anniversary of the case, that the *Standard* serialized her articles on the front page through the spring of 1940, the editors doing their part to fulfill Walter Ferris Wilkes's determination to torpedo F.D.R.'s ambitions for a third term.

"Joseph Force Crater," the editors ventriloquized in Mrs. Crater's introduction, "was incapable of deceit and immune to dishonesty. In any investigation of the courts of this state, there was no doubt that he would be a fearless champion of truth. This is why I remain rock certain that persons at the highest level of our government felt it necessary he be removed from the scene and why, once he was gone, such a concerted effort was made to besmirch his reputation and drag his name through the mud."

The self-portrait that emerged from the version of events Stella Crater painted was of an ingénue from upstate, a Gretel who'd found her Hansel in Joe Crater. A former law professor and legal secretary to a State Supreme Court judge, Joe was an all-American boy from Pennsylvania who'd risen by his own merits. They met when he was fresh out of Columbia Law School and she was working as a bookkeeper in a "well-regarded millinery establishment" in which she had "little or no association with the foreign pieceworkers." She soon quit her job, since Joe's success in private practice allowed him to provide very nicely for his "dear Stell." "Such terms of endearment," in her telling, "Joe always employed in addressing me."

Eventually, after his stint as a judge's law secretary, he returned to private practice and they went from comfortable to rich, moved to a cooperative apartment on lower Fifth Avenue, employed a cook, maid and chauffeur, and purchased a "summer cabin in Maine amid the whispering pines that lined the peaceful shores around Lake Belvedere."

Approached by the Governor about accepting an interim

appointment to the bench, Joe wavered. The salary of $22,500 was less than he was currently making. (An editor's note pointed out that as recorded by the U.S. Department of Commerce the average annual wage in 1930 was $1,100.) But the attraction of public service proved irresistible. After assuring dear Stell that their drop in income wouldn't materially affect their standard of living, Joe accepted. The Governor quickly sent a "basket of roses" and a note "which much to my regret I didn't keep, expressing the expectation that this was but a steppingstone to Joe's elevation to the highest court in the land."

Two months after Joe ascended the bench, when Memorial Day weekend arrived, Stell departed for their annual stay at Lake Belvedere. This time, however, she went alone, but not before Joe answered her complaint about his staying behind with a short sermon about his new responsibilities and "the exceedingly crowded calendar before him in the court." For anyone even slightly familiar with the operations of the State Supreme Court, that line was good for a laugh. The pace of proceedings, somewhere between stately and glacial, came to a complete halt once summer settled in. But off Stell went, "hurried along by a playful spank from Joe and the firm directive to get a good rest." With a maid, a cook and a chauffeur, it was unclear to Dunne what she was supposed to get a rest from. Fred Kipps, their driver and a retired cop, drove her up. "He was a most responsible man," she wrote, "despite the one time he inadvertently crushed Joe's finger in the car door, an unfortunate accident which Joe was quick to forgive." Kipps left the car with her and "went off on a vacation of his own."

Two weeks later, "tired and care-worn, though filled with pent-up affection," Joe arrived by train. The following days were "an idyll of blue skies and summer breezes, as carefree as anything Joe and I had known since the bucolic days of youth." A small ripple stirred the placid waters of the lake on a Sunday morning in early July, while Joe lazed in his hammock and Stell paged through the week's supply of newspapers from the city. She read to him an item announcing that the Manhattan D.A. was opening a full-scale investigation into what some alleged was a widespread practice on the part of unnamed politicians to sell appointments to the bench.

Joe's only reaction was to move his hand "in the manner of a man nonchalantly shooing away a mosquito. Without opening his eyes, he said in a drowsy voice, 'If the allegations be true, it's a good thing such underhanded machinations are brought to light. But they're of no concern to us, dear Stell.'"

Another ripple stirred two days later when a telegram arrived for Joe. Telegrams were a minor event at Lake Belvedere, but this one was of no consequence, or so Joe "casually responded" when Stell "idly inquired." He picked up the poker next to the fireplace and stabbed the telegram, put a match to it, and used the poker to scatter the blackened remains. He told her it was "a message from a judicial colleague advising him to get a good rest before the new term started on August 25th." If she questioned why one judge needed the urgency of a telegram to tell another judge to relax—a telegram he then burned and obliterated—she made no mention.

It was obviously not Stell's style to question anything Joe did, and she remained in character two days later when he announced that he thought it would be a good idea if they left Lake Belvedere for a car trip to Quebec. She quickly packed and off they went on a "romantic interlude" tucked inside their "relaxing vacation," stopping at small inns where they enjoyed, being legally able, a cocktail with dinner. Joe showed no sign of stress or worry, although several times, "we stopped at out-of-the-way service stations, because he felt it necessary to make use of the phone to call his broker to ask about fluctuations in the stock market, which were often of a distressingly dramatic nature in what was for our nation a dark and uncertain period."

The markets were distressed, but not Joe "who whistled as he drove, more than once putting an arm around me to draw me close, as if we were a pair of spooning lovebirds." Returned to their nest on Lake Belvedere, Joe found another telegram waiting. This one wasn't an encouragement to relax "but a plea from several colleagues to join them in Atlantic City for a private discussion of confidential matters related to the functioning of the court in the upcoming term." Reluctant to stray once more from the side of dear Stell, "Joe was constitutionally incapable of putting personal pleasures ahead of his responsibilities to the public, his colleagues and the court." As before, he burned the telegram in the fireplace.

Joe drove to Atlantic City, but didn't come right back to Maine. Instead, he continued to New York City where he "saw to last-minute business in the court, checked on our finances and bid bon voyage to his old boss, a former judge, now United States senator, who was leaving for his annual summer visit to his native Germany."

Professional and personal obligations fulfilled, he departed New York on the early evening of August 1st, sure he wouldn't return until the opening of the new term at month's end. Driving all night, "he outraced the Bar Harbor Express and, though tired when he arrived, took me in his arms, as effusive as ever in his affections. He expressed his delight at the prospect of the several weeks of uninterrupted peace and quiet." The weeks turned out to be a day. The next morning, Sunday, August 3rd, he woke early and proposed they walk into town and have their breakfast at the village diner.

As they finished their breakfast, the Methodist Church across the way let out, the worshippers mingling with members of the Congregationalist Church from around the corner who'd also just ended their service. Each Sunday when services were done, the village general store, a combination grocery, dry goods and post office, opened for an hour, not for the convenience of the God-fearing natives, who stayed away in observance of the Sabbath, but for the heathen summer folk, who always seemed in need of something. Joe said he felt like a thick steak and some potatoes for dinner that night. They went into the store where she did the grocery shopping and he browsed about.

On their walk home, Stell noticed Joe's mood had changed. He was "unusually quiet and seemed burdened." When she asked if anything was wrong, "he stopped on the roadside, put down his bag of groceries and took me tenderly in his arms." Joe had a confession to make. While she'd been shopping in the front of the store, he'd slipped to the back and made a call on the village's sole public telephone to ensure that all was in order in the court and that he could truly relax. Alas, duty called again. Joe didn't mention the identity of the person on the other end of the phone or the nature of the business so urgent that it required him to head back to New York, which he'd just left.

Stell accepted the news of this departure as she had the ones before. "I knew the kind of man Joe was, the day I married him. As devoted as he was to me, I never doubted I would have to share him with his work." They had an early dinner. He'd decided to take the train and leave the car with her. She drove him to the station. "He was resigned but certainly not depressed. As the train pulled out, I looked up. His face was framed in the window above. The steam swirling from the engine made it seem for an instant as though he were looking down on me from a cloud. He beamed that wide, beneficent smile of his, and its radiance shone on me like a blessing. No matter the calumnies spoken and written about him, or the pain of losing him, that blessing has never gone away."

The smile might have remained (and though she didn't say so, its broad, bright beam might have owed something to his artificial choppers), but that was the last Stell ever saw of him.

Joe said he would be back by Wednesday, but the day passed with no sign of him. Ditto Thursday and Friday. Stell was annoyed. Joe's dedication to his work was crossing into wanton disregard for her feelings. Saturday was her birthday, and she was so sure he'd be on the morning train, she drove to meet it. Joe wasn't among the load of passengers who detrained.

That night some acquaintances, a Boston lawyer and his wife, stopped by to wish her happy birthday. Surprised that Joe hadn't returned from New York, "the lawyer tried to be reassuring. 'If more of our public servants had your husband's spirit of selfless dedication,' he said, 'this great country wouldn't be in the fix it is today.' His wife told him to mind his own business, and I silently concurred."

Sunday, August 10th, marked a week since Joe's departure. Instead of driving into town alone to use the public telephone, she trekked two miles to the lawyer's cabin in a "gray mizzling rain that dampened my sagging spirit even more." He'd already left for Boston, but his wife was comforting and accommodating. She retired to the kitchen to brew a pot of tea while Stell made her call.

Stell tried their New York apartment. As the phone rang and rang, she realized that "this was why I had taken so long to take so obvious a step: I dreaded there would be no answer." Pondering whether or not to call the police, she hesitated for fear of somehow hurting Joe's reputation (one way or another she had to know by now that he wasn't detained by work). She decided to phone Sylvester Berind, a political insider and secretary to Joe's old boss, the ex-judge, now senator.

Berind saw no cause for alarm or involving the police: "'You know how conscientious your husband is, and don't forget, he's facing an election this fall.'" To put her mind to rest, he promised to see what was up with Joe and prompt him to get in touch with her.

Declining the offer of a lift, Stell walked home. "The rain stopped and the sun appeared. The branches atop the pines glistened. I felt reassured." Her fears reignited when two full days went by and there was no telegram from Berind or Joe. The next morning, August 13th, Fred Kipps, their chauffeur, arrived back to Lake Belvedere.

Suddenly, without warning, her pent-up fears poured out. She wept as she explained that Joe had been called to the city and that she hadn't heard from him in nine days. He patted her on the shoulder, a small gesture but one she appreciated: "Outwardly gruff in the manner of many hardened veterans of the New York police, Fred had a kind heart. He poured a shot of whisky from his silver flask and made me consume it in a single gulp. He insisted it would help, and for a short while it did." She said that she wanted him to drive her to New York, but he convinced her that it would be easier for him to scout around for Joe if he were alone. He left in their car on August 15th.

For the next five days she heard nothing. Finally, she began throwing her clothes into a suitcase. "Wracked by bewilderment and fear, my hands shaking as though with palsy, I fixed upon a course of action: I would walk to town and catch the next train to New York." Just then, there was a knock at the door. The mailman had a special delivery letter for her. It was from Fred Kipps. "Seeing the stricken, fearful look upon my face, the mailman inquired if I was all right. I assured him I was, but my answer was belied by the trembling fingers with which I took hold of the letter and made a mangle of the envelope.

"'Everything looks okay,' Kipps wrote, 'though I haven't caught up with the Judge himself. The apartment is in order. I talked with the color [sic] girl who does the cleaning and she tells me she done the dusting that you asked. Last time was two weeks ago. She seen nothing unusal [sic]. Me neither. Nobody seems worried about your husband of them I talked to. I haven't seen him myself, but they says hes [sic] been seen around.'"

Them I talked to . . . they says . . . Kipps gave no names. But it wasn't hard to imagine the mounting panic among the city's political chieftains now that Joseph Force Crater, a sachem privy to the inner workings of their powwows and war councils, had left the wigwam. (Another editor's note recorded that on August 21st, the day Kipps's letter arrived at Lake Belvedere, Governor Roosevelt bowed to mounting political pressure and authorized a full-scale investigation of the magistrate's court.) The alternatives weren't pretty. Had Crater defected to the investigators moving in on the magistrate's court, offering them an inside look at the Supreme Court as well? Or fearing exposure, made a run for it? Best case, he'd rented a professional party girl and was off playing pattycake (a possibility that grew more far-fetched with each passing day). What mattered to the politicos was heading off disaster before the papers sunk their scandal-mongering jaws into the story and used it to reinforce a frontal attack against the Tammany machine on their front pages.

Kipps came back to Lake Belvedere the day after his letter arrived. "Friends of the judge," he reported, "advised against asking questions that might arouse the newspapers' attention and hurt his chances in the upcoming election." Leaving this bit of information unexplored (which friends?), she spent the next three days "in a state of deluded inertia, expecting my beloved would step through the door the next minute."

The next person through the door was the postman, on August 25th, who informed her a caller identifying himself as a "colleague of Judge Crater" had telephoned the owner of the general store to request "a message be delivered to the judge directing him to contact Judge Carmen Traglia by noon at the latest." Without waiting to summon Kipps and the car, Stell "practically ran all the way to the store." Breathlessly, she called the number the owner gave her.

Judge Traglia, presiding justice of the First Department, answered. "In a cold, formal tone, he said he wished to speak with Joe. Before I had the chance to say more than that I was his wife and sick with worry about his whereabouts, he interrupted me. 'Your husband, madam, assigned to preside in the calendar part, failed to appear this morning at the opening of the new term.' As my anxieties of the last weeks began to pour out of me, he interrupted me again."

Poor Stell. Nothing seemed to penetrate her twin defenses of willful ignorance and invincible innocence. She listened as Traglia ran through an obviously rehearsed script designed to establish: A) this was the first time he'd spoken to her; B) until this moment, he was unaware there was any possibility that Judge Crater would not appear for the opening of the term and C) "until informed otherwise," he would assume Crater was attending to "private business perhaps related to the upcoming election."

Dunne pictured Traglia in his chambers with a stenographer listening in to transcribe the call and Sylvester Berind coaching him with hand signals, a finger drawn across his throat to let him know it was time to thank Mrs. Crater for her call, instruct her to let him know as soon as she heard from her husband, and hang up before she could say another word. Job done: ass covered.

As much numbed as despairing after her short conversation with Traglia, Stell confessed "through the blur of the next several days the only comfort I found was in Fred Kipps's flask." On the morning of August 29th, twenty-three days after Joe failed to make good on his promised return, Stell roused herself "to do what, with the wisdom of hindsight, I should have done three weeks before." She and Kipps left for New York in the late afternoon on "a journey through night and torrential rain that took me away from excruciating uncertainty toward a discovery I had dreaded and couldn't face until now: my beloved might be the victim of foul play."

Kipps drove nonstop, "face pressed close to the window as the wipers worked furiously to part the curtain of water, and I wept most of the way, crying out at one point, 'Oh, Fred, if only those wipers could clear away my tears!' Glancing at me with those hang-dog eyes of his, he said, 'It's a hard thing, Mrs. Crater, to know how much hurt a heart can feel, but for what's it's worth, just remember, you ain't alone.'"

Once they arrived, Stell wrote, "I paused as I put the key in the lock of the apartment door, hoping I'd wake from a nightmare and find myself lying beside Joe in the bedroom of our Lake Belvedere cabin." Instead, she found the apartment as she'd left it; nothing out of place. Fred went around opening the windows to let in fresh air. She got on the phone and began furiously placing calls. To the governor in Albany (the call failed to go through), to the mayor (unavailable), to Judge Traglia (unavailable), to Joe's law secretary (no answer), to Joe's campaign manager (he was unaware anything might be amiss and presumed Joe was vacationing in Maine), to several acquaintances (no answers), to everybody, it seemed, but the one party that made the most sense: the police.

The next morning, August 31st, a plainclothes cop appeared at her door. "He introduced himself as Detective Luke Ruppert, and I instantly recognized him as an acquaintance of my husband's and long-time bodyguard for Joe's old boss and patron, the Senator." Sitting across from her, as she struggled to hold back her tears, "Ruppert worried the rim of his hat with his hands and reported that he'd learned Joe was missing 'through friends concerned about his whereabouts.'" (Were these friends the same "friends of the judge" mentioned by Kipps? Didn't they have names? And what kind of friends didn't come forward to offer his wife a single word of comfort or support?)

Detective Ruppert informed her that he was working on his own, without involving the department. (Why not involve the department? was the question Stell should have asked, but didn't. Wasn't the time long overdue for the full resources of the police to be called in?) He'd already checked with the hospitals and the morgue. The good news was that her husband wasn't in either. (Which raised the question—unasked by Stell—just how long had Ruppert been looking into the case?) He was sure the judge had his reasons for being out of touch and, once he showed up to offer them, the explanation would make perfect sense. "'State Supreme Court justices,' he told her with an assurance that would soon ring with enduring hollowness, 'don't just disappear into thin air.'"

Buoyed at knowing that at last a professional investigator was on the case and that he expected a quick and satisfactory resolution, Stell was taken aback by what came next. The wisest and safest course, he advised, was for her to go back to Lake Belvedere and wait until he summoned her. "'Don't want to rouse suspicions before your husband has a chance to get back from whatever business he's attending to, do you? He's got an election ahead, so it makes sense to be extra careful.'"

When Fred came to her apartment that afternoon, she told him what the detective recommended and confessed her befuddlement about what to do, whom to trust, where to turn. Once more, she dissolved, and this time "the tears were born not of anger or even of frustration but of a hopelessness bordering on physical paralysis." Fred waited until the tears ceased before seconding Ruppert's recommendation. "'What's to be gained by staying?' he asked. 'You can't do anything to help that detective, and the more you go asking about the judge, the more likely some lowlife reporter will poke his nose where it don't belong.'"

She remembered nothing of the return trip to Maine. The day after they arrived, Sylvester Berind, convinced the rumors could no longer be contained, and acting, he claimed, on his own initiative—and without consulting or attempting to notify her—went to the police and filed a formal missing person report for Joseph Force Crater. It was thirty-one days since he'd beamed down his "broad, bright smile" on dear Stell, twenty-eight since he'd entered a cab on West 45th Street. Whoever was behind the disappearance had time enough to take a slow boat to China—and back.

Nobody bothered to get in touch with Stell to notify her that the report had been filed and was splashed across the headlines of every newspaper in the city, almost instantly becoming a story of national and international interest. The police were thrown into a frenzy, the commissioner and mayor both demanding that the NYPD find out what happened to Crater before the press did. Missing Persons raced to follow the tips and supposed sightings of the judge that quickly flooded in, its woefully undermanned ranks augmented by every available detective the department could spare.

Adding to the intensity of the hunt as well as muddying the waters was the bevy of amateur dicks, bounty seekers, thrill seekers, cranks and well-meaning (for the most part) citizens drawn by the excitement around the case and/or by the enticement of the rewards posted by the city and the *Standard*. It was even speculated that the mob, concerned somebody (or bodies) from its ranks might be involved, was doing detective work of its own.

Unaware of any of this, poor Stell sat in an Adirondack chair staring out the screen door of her cabin, wreathed in her new-found habit of chain smoking. At dusk, she recalled, the hulking figure of Sheriff Abner Scott loomed up behind the screen. He knocked but entered before she could invite him in. Over six feet tall and 250 pounds, he removed his hat and rested his right hand on the handle of his pistol. "His mouth was frozen in a grim horizontal line, no hint of the smile he'd invariable flashed all those times when Joe and I had encountered him in the village. 'Guess you heard the bad news, Mrs. Crater,' he said."

"I nodded. It wasn't difficult to guess what he was getting at."

"'Your husband's been missing a while, it seems.' His head moved from side to side in the kind of slow, disapproving shake with which a parent reprimands a child.

"'Who told you?' I imagined it must have been the Boston lawyer and his wife trying to be helpful, though I felt a flash of anger at their interference since all I wanted for the moment was to be left in peace.

"'Told me? It's on the wireless. Whole damn world knows by now.'

"The continued movement of his head and his cold, reproving tone suddenly left me with a sense of menace. 'The *world*?' I let out an audible gasp. All at once the past month instantly fell into perspective. I'd been played for a fool while the legion of Joe's acquaintances and allies—it was clear now that, except for each other, we had no friends—covered their tracks and perfected their alibis.

"'Yep, Mrs. Crater. The world.' His hand tightened on the stock of his pistol, as though about to lift it from its holster.

"'But you don't—you can't—believe I deliberately withheld that from you, *do you*?' I heard the pleading desperation in my own voice, but could do nothing to prevent it. The walls of my nightmare pressed closer from every side.

"His head stopped moving. He raised his hand. The palm was so close I thought he might be showing the hard calluses he earned in the ceaseless work of repairing and maintaining the cabins and cottages of summer folk like Joe and me.

"'Stop right there, Mrs. Crater,' he said. 'It don't matter

what I believe. What I *know* is your husband went missing well nigh a month ago and you never breathed a word 'bout it to me or any lawman elsewhere.'

"'That's because I was sure it was all a mistake. I thought—I hoped—I *expected* that at any moment Joe would come through the very door that you just did.'

"'Reporting your husband missing to the chief lawman here in Lake Belvedere, well, that's something you didn't do but should've. Could be as you say, you was expecting him home, or it could be you're an accessory to a crime, or worse.'

"'No, you can't possibly believe . . .'

"The hand went up again. 'The court will decide what to believe or not. I got no intent to put you under arrest, if that's what you're afraid of. But I'm acting under a request from the D.A. down in New York City to make sure you don't scoot nowhere till they send somebody up."

At this point, Dunne made a note to himself to check out whether Fred Kipps, the ex-cop chauffeur, and Detective Luke Ruppert were still alive. Beyond that, there'd been nothing that jumped out at him. He kept reading. It was difficult not to sympathize with Stell. It was as if she were walking through her safe, cozy cabin one sunny summer's day and suddenly went through a hole in the floor, tumbling from her "idyllic interlude of blue skies and summer breezes" into a cross between a hall of mirrors and a torture chamber. She wasn't the first nor would she be the last to learn that hell is not only real but that you don't have to die to get there.

She recalled her trip to New York to testify before the grand jury as a blur (one in a seemingly endless series). She was whisked south in a car that was sent to fetch her. Once they reached Foley Square, she was hurried past the battery of Movietone cameras and a swarm of photographers and reporters, their damning shouts echoing in her ears as she took the stand. *Did you do it, Mrs. Crater? Did you?*

The D.A., an acquaintance of Joe's, started out his questioning in a kind, patient tone that gradually accelerated into rapid-fire questions and pointed accusations. His hunger to reduce Joe's disappearance to the machinations of a jealous wife left him agitated and perspiring heavily, "with froth on his lips." He reminded Stell of a rabid dog. *Did you suspect your husband of infidelities? Did you ever see him with another woman? Was he seeking a divorce?*

The innuendo was clear, and though there wasn't a shred of evidence to back it up, the leak in the D.A.'s office supplied enough information that the next morning, as she was escorted out of her apartment for the return trip to Maine, the innuendoes from court were in big black letters on the front pages of the papers at the corner newsstand: *A Black Widow Killer? What Has She Got to Hide? Crater's Mrs. Stays Mum. Did She Take Him for a Ride?*

It was testimony to Mrs. Crater's underlying strength of mind that after this barrage of uncertainty, anxiety and betrayal, after being abandoned and used by those she trusted, after losing the man she depended on for everything, whose faults and failings she refused to recognize, and being falsely accused of a role in his disappearance, she didn't shatter and collapse into a pile of jagged shards held together by alcohol and tranquilizers. While the evidence that emerged about Joe's philandering, as well as his shady financial dealings, left no doubt about her infinite capacity for self-delusion, there was more to her than that. She had the mortar of survival—of denial and determination—that allows some to hold themselves together whatever misfortunes or trials come their way.

The next trial (the last before the spotlight moved on and the D.A. and the press lost interest in the Black Widow Theory) arrived in the hulking, panting form of Sheriff Scott as he half-waddled, half-ran from his car across the yard and up the three steps to her front porch. He knocked and this time waited for her to invite him in.

Stell remembered him "pausing to catch his breath as he struggled to get the words out: 'Reporters . . . on their way . . . be here real soon.'"

"Finished washing the few dishes from the dinner I'd prepared for myself, the first time I'd enjoyed eating food in weeks, I was sitting enjoying a cup of coffee and a cigarette. I was glad to see the sheriff. Since my return, he'd gone out of his way to be helpful. 'What reporters?' I asked.

"'Train of 'em.' He put his palm over his heart as if about to make the pledge of allegiance.

"'By train? From where?'

"He took a deep breath. 'From Boston, New York, all points in between. They hired the whole damn rig, engine to caboose, every last seat, and they're scouring the village to hire cars to bring 'em out here. Some are already on the way. Do what you want, Mrs. Crater, stay and talk if you care to, but I figured you deserve the courtesy of being forewarned so's you can decide for yourself. Give you a ride, if you'd like.'

"I was touched by the Sheriff's concern, a lonesome but welcome reminder the world still held its modicum of decent souls, yet declined his offer and watched as he returned to his car. I walked into the woods and progressed at a steady but unhurried pace till I reached the cabin of the Boston lawyer and his wife. It was dark. A light was on. The lawyer wasn't there but his wife was in the process of packing their things and getting the place ready to close for the season.

"Though surprised to see me, she greeted me warmly. When I explained why I'd come, she put aside her chore and hugged me. She brewed a pot of tea. We sat and talked for the next several hours, and after patiently listening to my sad saga, she shared with me sorrows of her own, a gesture of solidarity that comes naturally, I believe, among women who've known both the heartbreak as well as joy matrimony can bring. I stayed the night in her guest room, and the next morning, after undertaking a scouting mission to the village, she reported that Sheriff Scott had convinced the army of reporters that I'd fled Lake Belvedere and they were crowding on the train to get home.

"Despite her kind insistence on driving me to my cabin, I preferred to walk. I told her I wanted the exercise. Although I didn't say it, the truth was I needed to be alone. I was convinced that the inquisition was only going to grow more intense, and that all those powermongers who'd betrayed me and besmirched Joe would turn their skills at skullduggery and deceit into making me their scapegoat. I knew the forest would help me find a few moments of peace, and I wasn't disappointed. The birds' tuneful whistles, playful chirps and caws blended with the wind's high and lonely swish as it moved amid the treetops to create the calming chorus nature alone can orchestrate.

"There was no sign of anyone when I reached my cabin, though the trampled grass and frenzied weave of tire marks on the dirt driveway indicated a crowd had been there recently. I stayed shrouded in the forest's shadows for several minutes. Sure that no one was about, I emerged and mounted the steps to the porch, pulled open the screen door and received a terrible shock.

Sitting in the very same chair from which I'd watched Sheriff Scott first arrive with the news that the case had gone public was a man in a blue suit and red tie. His hat was in his lap, hands rested on the armrest. He had a handsome face. His blue eyes fixed on me. He didn't speak but seemed relaxed and at ease.

"If I could have, I would have turned and run back into the forest, but I felt a weakness in my knees. I thought I might faint.

"He got up. 'Please, Mrs. Crater, have a seat.' He gestured

to the spot he'd just vacated. I fell into the chair. I tried to say something but my mind was a scramble and no words would come. 'Can I get you a glass of water?' he asked. I nodded. He went over to the sink and returned with a jelly glass half-filled with water. I was chagrined that my hand shook as I held the glass to my lips and emptied its contents.

"He brought over a wicker-backed chair, placed it directly in front of me, and sat. He leaned forward, hat hanging from his hands between his legs, and smiled. As he spoke, I noticed how straight and white his teeth were. 'The door was open, so I let myself in. Sorry if I gave you a shock, but don't be afraid, Mrs. Crater. I'm not one of those press hounds.' Dropping his voice almost to a whisper, as though there were a danger someone might overhear, he said, 'I'm a friend.'

"Still trying to gather my wits, I wondered for a fleeting instant if I was having a hallucination brought on by stress. But I could see my visitor was real enough. Whereas a month or two before, I might have presumed such a declaration of friendship sincere, recent events had cured me of such naiveté. 'I've no idea who you are,' I said. 'All I know is that you've entered my house without being asked.'

"True, yet though you don't know me, I know you. At least, I've a good idea of the person you are and the fix you're in. That's why I've come. In my line of business, I've seen too many innocent people get hurt. I don't want that to happen to you.'

"'And what line of business might that be, Mister . . . ? I don't believe you've told me your name.' At this point, despite his denial, I was sure he was a newspaperman who hadn't left with the others but decided to stay and await my return.

"He shifted in his seat, reached into his back pocket and, taking out a small leather case, said, 'For the moment, let's leave it at this, Mrs. Crater.' He flashed a detective's badge from the New York City Police Department. 'I've seen a hundred cases like yours. Oh sure, maybe they didn't have the same notoriety, but it was the same routine and same result. D.A.'s out to get a conviction so he can run for a higher office. Newspapers act as judge and jury. Cops like me pressured to do just about anything to put a case to rest. The accused bewildered and alone, sold down the river by some self-serving, low-life mouthpiece whose major concern is making sure the papers spell his name right. For the defendant it's one long nightmare that ends when they strap him into the electric chair. Hate to tell you how many innocent people have been executed for crimes they didn't commit.'

"He'd touched a chord, expressing my fear of being made a scapegoat, of being convicted of harming the one man in the world I loved passionately, in the spirit and the flesh. A surge of emotion welled up in my throat. O Joe! Dear Joe! The horror of his fate as well as mine rose before my eyes. One day strolling together through fields of bright summer flowers; the next, plunged into awful darkness. My words came out in a choking sob: 'O my God . . . my husband . . . I'm so afraid . . . afraid he's been . . .'

"'Murdered?'

"I sobbed as I hadn't since I was a little girl. He took a silk, monogrammed handkerchief from his pocket, unfolded it and gave it to me. I pushed it away. 'It's all right to cry, Mrs. Crater,' he said in a voice fallen once again to a whisper. 'Murder is a terrible word. Maybe the most terrible in the English language, and I got to think in a case like your husband's, where he's been gone for a month, without a trace, that's what we're dealing with: murder.'

"'No, no, no.' I must have repeated that word a dozen times. Though I knew its probability—that it could be the only explanation for Joe's deserting me—the horrifying finality of the word rent my heart anew.

"He pulled his chair close, sitting almost sideways to me,

and patted my knee, gently, as a parent would a distraught child. 'I want to help you get out of this, Mrs. Crater. I'm not here as a cop, but as a person who believes you've suffered enough and deserve to be delivered from this nightmare. So please listen, and try to absorb what I'm saying before you react. I'm going to point you to the surest and, I believe the *only*, way out.'

"He proffered his handkerchief again, and this time I took it. I stopped my sobbing, wiped my eyes and nose. 'Yes,' I said. 'I'll listen.'

"'I don't know whether you're involved in your husband's disappearance or not.'

"'I'm most certainly *not*,' I said with all the emphasis I could muster.

"'What I mean to say is, sure, I believe you're innocent, but so what? Remember what I said about innocent people being executed for crimes they didn't commit? Think about all those who got a vested interest in seeing you erased. Pols who want this case to go away. D.A. who wants to be governor. A governor who wants to be president. And the press, just try to imagine how they'll wring this until it's dry. Jealous wife. Oversexed husband. Make it as low and dirty as they can. You'll get sympathy from nobody, not even from the jury who'll be swayed to believe this was a premeditated murder you did your best to cover up.'

"'Joe Crater is the noblest man I've ever encountered,' I said. The urge to cry had passed, my sadness transformed into anger by not only his crude reference to Joe but the earlier insinuation that there was even a remote possibility I might have a role in his disappearance. 'I shouldn't think it necessary to have to remind a police detective that they have to find Joe, or his body, before anyone can be charged with anything, and should that dreadful day ever come, I can stand before any court, on earth or in heaven, and avow my innocence. I loved—I *love*—my husband. That's the truth, so help me God.'

"He listened with head down, right hand raised to forehead, a posture, I imagined, assumed by Roman Catholic priests hearing confession. When I'd finished, he looked up and stared at me with more intensity than sympathy. 'You know, Mrs. Crater,' he said, 'if this were a fairy tale, everything you just said, all those wonderful sentiments, they'd mean something. But what counts now isn't "the truth," as pure and perfect as it may be. No, what matters is the reality of the situation you're in.'

"Rising from his chair, he began to pace. 'You think that swarm of reporters you just fled was interested in "truth"? That's why they came? Sorry, but if sending you to the chair sells more papers, not a one will lose any sleep. Same goes for the D.A. when it comes to advancing his career. And the judge? How many do you think have the nobility of your husband? Or is it more likely they all want to end this affair fast as they can?'

"'If it comes to that, I will rely on a jury of my peers to ascertain the truth.'

"'A jury of your peers? In a fairy tale world maybe. In the world we live in, it's going to be twelve highly impressionable pinheads who get their opinions from the *Graphic* and the *Standard*.'

"He stood in front of the fireplace, hands in his pockets, rocking on his heels. "The prosecutor and his minions will concoct a convincing scenario that puts you in your apartment the day your husband disappeared. They'll threaten and browbeat that poor cleaning girl until she swears she saw you that day. They'll dangle promotions in front of ambitious cops, drag witnesses out of the city's dungeons and dives, and cut enough deals to get their testimony so that you'll begin to think maybe you were where they say you were. They'll weave a straightjacket of false testimony and circumstantial evidence Houdini couldn't wiggle out of, and they'll do it with all the skill and desperation of men who know their futures are riding on making you the scapegoat.'

"I got up and went over to where he was standing. When I spoke, it was close to a shout. 'Stop! What are you saying? That the situation is hopeless? That I'll be convicted of a crime I didn't commit?'

"'Hear me out, Mrs. Crater. If you doubt me, I'll give you chapter and verse on people as perfectly innocent as you who got railroaded into the electric chair.'"

Struggling to exert some self-control, I said with vehement firmness, 'Please leave this moment. I've had enough.'

"He smiled. 'Yes, it's exactly that tone you'll need when you preempt their well-plotted lies by relating a passion play of your own. Act one: Joe comes back to Lake Belvedere in the middle of the night and wakes you from your sleep. He's distraught. There's liquor on his breath. He won't tell you how he came, only that "a friend who wanted you to stay out of this" drove him back. You know it's a woman. You know, though you've closed your eyes to his affairs. Standing in this very spot, you listen to your husband pour out the story of his infidelities. You cover your ears and tell him to stop. He grabs you, pulls your arms to your sides and makes you listen.'

"'O God, this is obscene!' We stood face to face in front of the hearth. This time I made no effort at self-control. 'Get out, right now! Get out or I'll fetch Sheriff Scott!'

"'The very words and passionate tone that you used with Joe. You can see for the first time in memory he's drunk. He seems possessed by some fit of madness. He lets go of your arms. They ache from his grip. Suddenly, without planning it, you slap him. He seizes you by your shoulders and throws you against the fireplace. Without thinking, you pick up the poker from its stand.' He paused, reached down and took the poker in his hand.

"It crossed my mind that I was dealing with a lunatic—a

homicidal lunatic—but instead of striking me with the imple-
ment, he pressed it into my hand and closed my fingers around
the brass handle. 'You don't remember swinging it. It's as if you
blacked out. All you remember is looking down at his crumpled
body, the bloody wound on his skull. You kneel and cradle his
lifeless body in your arms.'

"The poker made a loud clang as I dropped it onto the
hearthstone. I walked to the door and opened it. 'I've heard
enough,' I said in a steady, calm voice. 'I'm going to get the sheriff. Whether you wish to go or stay is up to you.'

"My visitor stayed where he was. I suppose I should have
been frightened that he might repossess the poker and attack me
with it. But I no longer cared. As far as I was concerned this was
the last of the endlessly ugly surprises I'd endured since Joe's disappearance. If it all ended here, in a pool of my own blood or on
some distant day in the electric chair, either way, so be it, I would
be reunited with my beloved Joe.

"'I'm almost finished,' he said. 'Act two: You roll the body
in a sheet. Pull it into the woods. Heavy, yes, but somehow you
find the strength. A week goes by. There are times you think—
really believe—it's all happened in a dream. You meet the train
the following Saturday. You tell your neighbors you're worried.
That evening, unsure any longer what's real and what's imagined, you go back to the body. You're certain that if you can see
it one more time, see the decay, smell the stench, confront the
reality, you'll be driven to call the sheriff and turn yourself in.
But, incredibly, it's gone. All that's left is a few torn remnants of
the sheet. There are bear prints everywhere. You gather the fragments of the sheet and burn them when you get home. In the
morning, sunk in a mind-numbing stupor of guilt, horror and the
inability to accept the unintended consequences of an act of self-
defense, you start to sound the alarm that Joe's missing.'

"'You're insane,' I said.

"He left the poker where it was and walked toward me. He stopped to pick up his hat. 'Unfortunately, I might be the only sane person you've met in these proceedings. Everything I just said is a lie, of course, but it's your only chance to avoid the electric chair.'

"'I'll take my chances with the truth. I've put my faith in Jesus Christ.'

"'And we know where the truth got him.'

"'To heaven, if I remember correctly.'

"'The truth often will. In your case, it'll be an express, powered by 2,000 volts. Ever see somebody die in the chair? Not neat and painless like they make it out.'

"I made no answer. He walked past me, onto the porch. He put his hat on at an insouciant angle, covering his eyes. 'The final act: Black Widow becomes wounded wife. The press goes from attack to defense. Embarrassment of the police at not being able to find a Supreme Court judge turns to elation. Lynch mob becomes adoring fans. What woman, betrayed and threatened by a drunken husband, wouldn't have done what you did? The D.A. and the pols he's indebted to, right up to the governor, can hardly contain their joy at the way your story ends the affair, removes the case from their jurisdiction as well as the need for further investigation. The judiciary, burned by the present scandals, can't believe their luck in seeing the case shipped off to Maine.'

"He went down the steps into the yard. I looked around. There was no car. 'It's a bit of a walk back to town,' I said.

"He looked up at me, pushing up the brim of his hat. They say if you look hard enough into a person's eyes, you can see his soul. Peering intently into his eyes, I saw nothing. 'I'm a cop. I'm used to walking,' he said.

"'Goodbye then.' I suspected he had a car parked down the road, out of sight.

"'I'm trying to help. I hope you believe that.'

"I smiled wanly. *Trying to help.* How many times had I heard that refrain? Eventually, even the innocent grow wise.

"'Here's the happy ending: Your case is heard up here, where everybody's on your side. Most you get is six months. When you're out, the village wraps its arms around you. The play ends. Your life begins anew.'

"I went inside. The screen door slammed reassuringly behind me. I turned and locked it, putting hook into eye, a small measure that, silly as it might sound, made me feel safe. From outside, I heard his voice: 'Think about what I've said, Mrs. Crater. I'll stop by tomorrow and see if you want to talk more about it.'

"I never wanted to talk—or think—about what he'd said ever again. I lay atop the lovely, hand-sewn, red-and-white quilt that Joe and I had purchased at the Methodist Ladies' Annual Picnic the summer before, on a July day as they exist only in Maine, broad sky lit with crisp, clear sunshine. Joe's scent, masculine and wonderful, still lingered on it. Exhausted, I fell into a profound sleep and didn't awake until morning. A moment later, as the parting words of my visitor from the previous night came back to me—*I'll stop by tomorrow*—I heard a car pull up outside. I jumped to my feet, looking for a place to hide and, glancing furtively out the window, I saw it was the sheriff's car.

"Abner Scott had come to see how I was faring now that the invasion of newspapermen had withdrawn from Lake Belvedere. Reassured by his presence, I asked him to stay for coffee, and he accepted. As we sat waiting for the pot to percolate, I told him of my visitor. It sounded so strange in the retelling, almost unbelievable even to me, that I wondered if he would credit it. I ended with the stranger's promise to return today.

"'What he say his name was?' the sheriff asked.

"I went to reply but was utterly chagrined to realize that in

147

my shock and confusion, I'd never pressed him to find out. My face reddened with embarrassment, I replied, 'I don't know. He never told me.'

"'Don't matter, woulda used a phony one, for sure.'

"'He showed me a detective's badge.'

"'Five & Dime's got a full stock of 'em.'

"'It looked real. A New York badge. I could see that plainly.'

"'Extra dollar or two, you can get a badge to say what you want.'

"'It feels as though it could have been a dream.'

"'It weren't no dream, but one of those perverts follows the press wherever it goes. You always find one where you find the other, like worms in a graveyard. Probably mental. Most of 'em is. This kinda thing is irresistible for 'em. They can scare you, but they're usually harmless. Just out for thrills. I'll stick around, have a talk with him when he returns. Maybe they can get away with that guff down in New York, but not in Lake Belvedere. Be the last time he bothers you, I guarantee.'

"Sheriff Scott stayed all day, sitting in the rocker on the porch, smoking his pipe and whittling. I served him lunch, and in the afternoon, we enjoyed coffee and pie together. He left around dinnertime but promised to swing by that evening to make sure my visitor hadn't returned.

"The detective—whoever he really was—never reappeared. I suppose he might have tried but, seeing the sheriff's car parked outside my cabin, changed his mind and went in search of some other scandalous events where, if the sheriff's analysis was correct, he could scavenge amid the wreckage of people's lives in search of vicarious thrills. Sheriff Scott later reported to me that he had checked with the New York police and that they assured him no member of the department had been anywhere near Lake Belvedere on the day in question.

"When it came to the sheriff's conclusion about my visitor, I retained my doubts. It seemed to me that the carefully wrought scenario he laid out was beyond the abilities or interests of some ghoulish thrill-seeker. I detected a more skilled and accomplished practitioner of deceptions, one who might have been delegated by a powerful political player to induce me to bring a stop to the whole investigation and the machinations it might uncover. The sheriff's prediction did turn out to be true, however: Joe's case proved an irresistible attraction to a seemingly endless number of cranks, thrill seekers and mental cases, who have never ceased arriving to this present day."

Drawn in by Mrs. Crater's transparent honesty, by the way she clung to the myth of her husband's blameless life while sparing no detail of the manipulation and humiliation heaped on her, Dunne read through to the end of the narrative, which was mostly a record of her attempts to bring some finality to the case by having Joe declared officially dead and getting the insurance money that would allow her to start rebuilding her life. He was surprised to discover it was two o'clock in the morning by the time he finished. He wasn't the slightest bit sleepy.

Instead of going to bed, he stripped naked and went to the pool. As part of the renovation, Roberta had installed overhead as well as side and bottom lights. She switched them off when she went to bed. He put them back on and lowered himself into the illuminated water. First several laps, he resisted the usual urge to push hard, overreaching, arms punching the surface. *Pace yourself, match strokes to breath, synchronize turn of head.* He lost count of how many laps he'd completed, but felt strong and continued to swim.

Mrs. Crater's reconstruction of events was pieced together ten years after they'd occurred. The word-by-word recounting of conversations and exchanges was, at best, an approximation she and her ghost writer had put together. Yet her story stuck with him. And he wasn't as ready as Sheriff Scott to dismiss Mrs. Crater's visitor as "mental" or, as the story suggested, a seducer sent at the behest of Governor Roosevelt to provide a convenient solution that served the ends of New York's crooked pols. Presuming she was still available, he'd see if there was anything more he could drag out of her.

In some instances, the press clips refreshed his memory; in others, such as the various musings and allegations about the judge's financial dealings and sexual escapades, it all seemed new—although like a lot of details from twenty-five years ago, it might have faded from memory. On the morning of August 6th, Crater sent his court officer to cash two checks in the amount of five grand and change. The money never turned up. Neither did the two briefcases filled with files that Crater took with him when he left his chamber. But if Dunne imagined there was a chance that the outsized luck Mulholland attributed to him might result in a happy stumble across an overlooked clue sticking out of the mound of newspaper copy, the key everybody else missed or ignored, that possibility remained unrealized.

Given the delay in reporting the case, the pursuers began a hundred yards behind the starting line, and now—a quarter of a century later with the odds of ever catching up having gone from highly improbable to probably impossible—the final uncertainty expressed by the Grand Jury seemed beyond amendment or reversal: "The evidence is insufficient to warrant any expression of opinion as to whether Joe Crater is alive or dead, or as to whether he has absented himself voluntarily, or is a sufferer from a disease in the nature of amnesia, or the victim of a crime."

Though he didn't feel spent, he stopped, pulled himself up and perched on the pool rim, calves and feet dangling in the water. The slim hope of figuring out Crater's fate hinged on talking with whichever of the principals and original investigators were still alive. Even then, it wasn't going to be much more than a crap shoot, where he'd bust without a hard six. Unless they were loaded and the outcome already set. But by who? To what end? He peered below, swirling his sunken feet in two parallel circles. An aquarium for people instead of fish. Same back and forth. He wondered: *If it were just Wilkes who wanted him on the Crater case, would he have taken it?*

Enthroned in his oversized bed, Wilkes couldn't hide his confidence that everything, everybody is for sale or lease, the solution to every problem ultimately a matter of price, even eventually death itself, once enough doctors and scientists were rented for the job of "extending the human lifespan indefinitely." Why should the Crater case be any different? Don't haggle over what it costs, just be sure to hire the one who can get it done, another in his private army of editors, maids, accountants and tailors.

But Nan Renard was wrong that morning at the Savoy Plaza when she confidently repeated Wilkes's assertion that all she had to do was go "work out the details" because "if Dunne was going to decline, he'd have done so by now." Awaking with a start in the middle of the night, he had decided he'd call after breakfast to let Bud Mulholland know his boss should find somebody else for the job. She changed his mind. Not that palaver about "pollenization," but his sense of the spooked, uncertain kid behind those fine cheekbones and the Fifth Avenue façade. He wanted to help. That's all.

"Are you sure?" A voice from behind. Startled, he turned. Barefoot, in the scarlet silk robe from Bergdorf's he'd given her on their last Valentine's Day in New York, Roberta approached. She looked fresh and awake, as though she'd just taken a shower. She'd been standoffish, going about her own business as he spent almost all his time poring through the newspaper files. Now she leaned down and rubbed his shoulders. "Are you sure you want to stop? Maybe you better come to bed and try a less taxing exercise."

The next morning he rewrote his notes, culling the essentials he'd follow up on when he got back to New York. In the afternoon, he packed and got ready to leave. Roberta questioned why he didn't go by plane. "Why schlep on the train when a plane will have you there in a few hours?" She showed him a full-page ad in the newspaper. Lovely blonde stewardess waving from the door of a gleaming Super-C Constellation. *Just 3 hours and 45 minutes to LaGuardia Airport. Forget the train. For comfort, speed and convenience, take the plane!*

He didn't change his mind. Planes always brought back the war, the rush, anxiety, need to get everywhere in a hurry. The thrill of looking down on the world from several thousand feet wore off quickly. Preferred earth-bound view, subtle changes of landscape, as the train moves up the coast. Arrive rested and ready for whatever is ahead. "Do what you want," Roberta said. "But really, Fin, sometimes you're so old fashioned." He was going to ask what was so wrong with that, but she'd already left the room.

As they were leaving to go out for dinner, Louie Pohl called. The background check on Adrienne Renard, he said, had turned up "a bit of news." Seems she wasn't who she said she was, except, as it turned out, she was, because what Pully uncovered was what Nan had already revealed. Real name was Anna Resnick. Raised by her aunt. Promoted over the heads of most other executives at Wilkes Communications. Rumor was her relationship with Wilkes went beyond business. No way to prove it. Though he acted as if the name change came as news, Dunne was glad to hear she'd been straight with him.

"I hope you know what you're getting into," Pully said. "I

don't know about Miss Renard. But Mulholland and Wilkes play for keeps."

"That's what I play for, too."

"Just make sure you're playing the same game."

He was ready for bed when the phone rang. Roberta answered, scribbled on the pad next to the phone and held it up for him to see. *Eddie Moran calling from Havana!* Good-hearted Eddie. But with a well-deserved reputation as an endless gabber. Probably still miffed about being stood up. He grabbed the pad and scribbled *I'm asleep.*

"Just a minute, Eddie," Roberta said. "I'll see if he's out of the shower." She put her hand over the mouthpiece and said in an emphatic whisper, "This is the *third time* he's called." She thrust the receiver at him and went into the bathroom.

Before Eddie could get a word out, Dunne apologized for saying he was going to come by the Starlight Room and then not showing up and leaving Havana without even a goodbye. Eddie brushed it off. "Woulda been great to see you. Always is. But stuff comes up. I understand that. Honest, I didn't even give it a thought until a few days later when your name got mentioned."

"A good context, I hope."

"That's the thing. Got a minute? This takes some explaining."

"I'm catching an early train to New York, Eddie. But go ahead." Eddie had the same youthful tone as thirty years before and sounded every bit as talkative.

"Well, musta been the day after you called. Maybe it was two. What day you call? Was it a Sunday?"

"Does it matter?" Once this was over, he was going to have to resist the urge to bark at Roberta for insisting he take Eddie's call.

"Not really. Just that I was trying to recall the exact night when Jimmy Malacoda showed up at the Starlight Room.

'Snake' is what a lot of people down here call him. It's a double whammy, 'cause he's got a tattoo of a snake and the qualities to match. Nobody ever calls him that to his face of course. Name he goes by is 'Jimmy Bad Tail,' which I'm told is what Malacoda means in Italian. Don't look like a wop though. You seen him, you'd swear he was a Polack, which maybe his mother was, but either way he's a full-fledged, full-time gorilla with the Salavante mob outta Cleveland."

The time on the alarm clock was 11:15. Train left at 8:30 A.M. Plenty of details he still wanted to see to in the morning before he left. Now, thanks to Roberta's overdeveloped sense of etiquette, he was stuck on this call.

"Still there, Fin?"

"Yeah, Eddie, but this is an international call. Don't want you to rack up a big bill on my account."

"No matter. I'm on an office phone. Where was I?"

"Jimmy Bad Tail from Cleveland just showed up."

"Don't get me wrong, most of the Cleveland boys are quiet and respectful. Wouldn't take 'em for anything but normal tourists, except that most of them are built like beer trucks. But Jimmy Bad Tail, him you know is trouble right away. Got a smell like spoiled meat. Anyways, this one night when he arrives with a girl on his arm, he's obviously drunk and she's obviously a hooker. Why he had to pick the Starlight Room of the Old Madrid, you gotta ask him. God knows, there's no shortage of places in Havana where hoods and hookers are welcomed with hugs and kisses. Thought about keeping him out, but he's been here before and behaved—and why risk trouble with the Cleveland boys?—so I wave him through, but, to be sure, I tell one of my assistants to tag behind and make sure he stays in line."

Eddie Moran's story was on the usual track traveled by ex-cops and bouncers in recounting confrontations with tough guys that end in a moment of triumph or an anecdote that makes the whole tale funny or memorable. The older the storytellers, it seemed to Dunne, the longer and less funny the stories. Out of friendship, he didn't rush him off the line. Another five minutes, that might change.

Eddie wandered through the details of Jimmy Bad Tail's increasingly obnoxious behavior, how he abandoned the hooker he'd brought with him and almost started a fight with the croupier at the roulette table. The end came when he tried to pick up the wife of a big-time surgeon from Miami. She brushed him off. He grabbed her ass. She hurled a drink in his face, and the casino's flying squad swarmed over him, as Eddie put it, "like flies on dog shit."

"Some people never learn." Dunne was relieved Eddie's story seemed approaching a conclusion. Not exactly either funny or significant, his story was a reminder of the general decline in the way people—hoods included—behaved in public, which was the point he'd wanted to raise earlier with Roberta, about how "old fashioned" wasn't always the wrong way to go. He covered the receiver and yawned.

"Bum like Jimmy Bad Tail never knew in the first place. He's the type put the scum in scumbag. Like you'd expect, he goes for his gun, but we get that away from him pronto and haul him to the basement where I have Tito, my head guy who tips the Toledo at about 280, sit on him till he's calm and promises to be nice."

"Bet that caught his attention." In another minute, he'd make an excuse to end the call.

"You'd think. But here's where the trolley jumps the tracks. When Jimmy Bad Tail gets up, he ain't calm but raging, and I'm thinking how lucky we are he don't have that gun. Tito gets him in an Antonino Rocca-style arm lock from behind, but that don't shut him up. 'You piece of shit, Moran,' he says to me, 'you and all your flat-foot friends ain't worth a rat's ass and I could take you all out if I had a mind to, same as that broken-down dick friend of yours was here last week holed up in some second-rate dump.'

"I didn't know what he's talking about. 'What friend?' I says.

"'Wise-ass, no-class type like the rest of you, Fintan Dunne. The deal was signed and sealed. Woulda been a pleasure if it wasn't nixed at the last minute.'

"I can't believe what I'm hearing. *'Fintan Dunne?'* I says.

"'Yeah,' Jimmy Bad Tail crows. 'Too bad I didn't get the chance 'cause as far as I'm concerned every cocksucker the likes of you deserves to get it in the head.' Then, since Tito's got him squeezed so he can't punch, he lets go and spits in my face, which is when I pull him loose from Tito and belt him so hard he lifts off his feet and cracks his skull on the concrete like an egg on the side of a frying pan."

"You kill him?"

"No such luck. Took him to the Nuns' Hospital. It was a bad concussion."

"Sure he was talking about me?"

"How many Fintan Dunnes do you think there are in Havana? But just to be sure, I go back the next morning to find out. Head nun says two friends came in a big sedan and, despite her objections that he shouldn't be moved, took him away. Figure he'd be back for his gun, but nope. I let the Salavante people know what happened, but don't mention 'bout him and you. They tell me they're sorry about Bad Tail's misbehavior and say he'd been ordered back to Cleveland. Been no sign of him since."

The story's sudden twist left Dunne puzzled. He peppered Eddie with questions. *Was Jimmy Bad Tail doing rub-outs for the mob on a regular basis? Did he indicate who wanted him for this job or why it was cancelled?* Eddie had no answers. "All I know is what I told you," he said. "Didn't make no sense to me, which is why I wanted you to know about it, 'cause I figured you'd have some idea why Jimmy Bad Tail was gunning for you, or who'd go and hire him."

"No idea who or why." Dunne's mind went back to that brief time in Havana. Barely left the hotel or talked to anyone, except the morning he checked out. Momentary encounter at the front desk. That Cleveland smile. Gave you a chill just looking at it. Name began with J. It came to him. He blurted it out: "Johnny Morello."

"Who?"

"J.M., same initials as Jimmy Malacoda."

"You're losing me, Fin."

"That snake tattoo, Eddie, is it on his hand?"

"Back of the right. You met Jimmy Bad Tail when you were down here?"

"Bumped into. In a hotel lobby. You're sure he used my name?"

"'Fintan Dunne' is what he said. Don't know whether he was talking for real or mouthing off—that's the way with hoods, you never know."

Eddie promised to keep poking around and to call if anything turned up. Finished getting ready for bed, Roberta came out of the bathroom. "You two had quite a chat," she said. "What about?"

"Old times. Eddie loves to chew over the past."

"Aren't you glad you took the call? Now you'll have one less thing on your mind." She got into bed.

Dunne turned off the light. "Exactly."

Part IV

Crow the Cop: Excerpt from interview C-1487, NYPD Oral History Project: Captain John F. Cronin (ret.), NYPD 1929–1963, Missing Persons Bureau, Bureau Chief 1940–1963; conducted by Prof. Verlee Prybyloski, J.D., Fordham University School of Criminal Justice at Lincoln Center, September 5, 1966.

Q. Please identify yourself by name and present occupation.

A. John F. Cronin. If retired is an occupation, I'm a retired cop.

Q. Why did you choose a career in the NYPD?

A. I'm the oldest of eight. When my father died, I was at Regis and thinking about joining the Society—the Jesuits—but had to drop out to help my mother. Got a job as a runner on Wall Street. One day my pal and co-worker, Joey Natone, says he's signed up for the police test, and why don't I do the same? I went along on a lark.

Q. What was your first assignment?

A. The Panhandle. That's what we called the northeast Bronx. There was a small farm on my beat. Started me thinking I should've joined the Texas Rangers.

Q. What brought you to Missing Persons?

A. A fluke.

Q. Your transfer to Missing Persons was by accident?

A. You see, back in '13, Big Tim Sullivan, the Bowery leader, developed mental problems. Rumor said it was from the syph. His brother took him up to his house in the Bronx to rest, and Tim pulls a brodie and disappears. City gets itself in an uproar, wondering how somebody so well known could vanish. Word was he's been murdered by his gambling buddies or by Tammany to shut him up. About then, the patrolman on duty at the morgue takes the required last look at the bodies about to ship to potter's field, and right away recognizes Big Tim. Been hit by a train, cut in half, and mistaken for a hobo. Some say it's suicide, but there's no proof.

Q. This occurred over a decade and a half before you joined the NYPD, did it not?

A. Well, you see, because of Big Tim the city set up a Missing Persons Squad, and here's where the fluke comes in. I'm not claiming to be a saint, but I made a habit of attending Mass every morning. Still do. Also make it a habit to read from Dante's *Divine Comedy* every day, but that's a tale told another time. Anyways, when I'm walking a beat up in the Bronx, I start each morning by attending Mass, thanks to which I made the acquaintance of Mortimer J. Sullivan, Big Tim's nephew and a captain in the Chippewa Democratic Club, himself a daily communicant who never touched alcohol.

Q. Was Mr. Sullivan responsible for your transfer to the Missing Persons Bureau?

A. Yes. God rest his soul, Mortimer saw to it, but circumstances tied to those times during Prohibition, which you should understand, is what led me to accept his help.

Q. What circumstances were those?

A. I'm not talking out of school when I say there was no more anything-goes period in the department's history than Prohibition. Even abstainers like me saw no sense wringing the country dry because some Fundamentalist tub-thumpers thought it was a one-way ticket to hell. Be hard to go into any speakeasy in those days and not find one or two cops having a gargle or moonlighting as bartenders or bouncers. Corruption gushed out of the booze business like an Oklahoma oil well.

Q. This was true even in the northeast Bronx?

A. Truer there than anywhere. Beer was being manufactured and shipped all over the place. Whisky was landing on City Island and Throgs Neck by the vatful. Dutch Schultz and the other booze barons threw money at cops to look the other way or, in some cases, ride shotgun on the shipments. Believe me, no matter what bill of goods some others try to sell you, the Panhandle was awash in booze and bribes.

Q. Did this include members of the department with whom you were acquainted?

A. I'm not accusing anybody by name, but I wasn't comfortable with it, which wasn't a problem until one day when I'm directing traffic on Tremont Avenue and stop a truck with two men in the cab. The driver, though I didn't know it, is Mo Geissman, Schultz's assistant. I don't like the way he's acting and tell him to open the back of the truck. Right off, he offers me a grand "to get lost." I tell him he's under arrest. He laughs in my face, which is when I cuff him. Put it mildly, when I book him for attempted bribery, carrying a concealed weapon and operating a vehicle filled with cases of illegal gin, I don't exactly endear myself back at precinct house. Presto, I'm walking a night beat in a part of Pelham Bay nobody's lived in since the Indians left the Bronx.

Q. Is this what led you to seek a transfer to Missing Persons?

A. Missing Persons was Mortimer Sullivan's idea. I bump into him one day leaving the precinct house and he remarked on not seeing me at Mass. I tell him what's up, and he volunteers to help. This is September of '30, when the Judge Crater case first breaks, and Mortimer says to me that Missing Persons is desperate for help, and he'll speak to somebody he knows there. He was as good as his word, just like his uncle Tim.

Q. The first case you worked on at Missing Persons was the disappearance of Judge Crater?

A. Case was two or three weeks old when I got there. Didn't have time to catch my breath. Nobody did. Up till Judge Crater, Missing Persons was something of a backwater.

Q. Didn't the Crater case change Missing Persons from a backwater into a centerpiece?

A. It was a curse.

Q. A curse? Why was that?

A. Like those explorers who opened the tomb of King Tut and all suffered terrible deaths as a result, the Crater case spelled disaster for the detectives who led the investigation, good men whose careers ended because of it. They were mocked in the newspapers or used as fall guys for the politicians who didn't want Crater found but acted like they did and blamed the detectives for "incompetence." One got involved on a personal level, which is the absolute worst thing any detective can do.

Q. Do you have a theory?

A. Theories are for geniuses like Einstein. A cop sticks to the details.

Q. What were the most pertinent details of the Crater case?

A. First, given a whole month went by before his disappearance was reported, the chances of turning up Judge Crater were never better than one in 10,000. Two, dead men tell no tales, and the tales Crater could've told meant the number of those with a motive to do him in was legion. These included the governor, mayor and most of the city's politicians. The judge also turned out to be horny as a toad, and let's just say none of the girls he used shed tears he was gone. Three, there was something not quite kosher about the case.

Q. Not kosher?

A. Like being given a puzzle whose key part is withheld. I had this cop's hunch that we'd been put on the wrong path from the beginning and would never find our way back.

New York City

"So to go on, and see this venture through . . .
I entered on that savage path and forward."

Dante, *Inferno*, Canto II

A WELL-DRESSED YOUNG MAN, LEAN, WITH A PAINED FACE AND A constipated smile, approached Dunne as he came up from the tracks. Said he'd been sent by Mr. Mulholland to see to the luggage. Car and driver were waiting outside. Same suite as before was ready at the Savoy Plaza. When Dunne tried to slip a dollar into his hand, he recoiled. "That's nice of you, Mr. Dunne, but I'm an assistant editor, not a porter, though there are people at Wilkes Communications who have trouble making that distinction."

Out front, idling behind a line of taxis, was a black Buick, license plate imprinted with a lone W. The editor/porter sat up front with the driver. Save for an extended sigh, he stayed mute on the ride to the hotel. Finished taking care of the check-in at the front desk, he offered a soft handshake. "Miss Renard," he paused an instant before squeezing the next words through his lips, "*my boss* will be in touch later."

The grand and immaculate suite echoed with the same vacant, lonely silence as newly entered hotel rooms everywhere, no matter size or daily rate. On the table by the door were two swanky cellophane-wrapped welcome baskets: one cradled a half-dozen bottles of top-shelf booze; the other, expensive toiletries. Beside them, instead of the *Herald Tribune*, lay a copy of the *Standard*.

Without removing his hat or overcoat, he crossed the room, slid back the glass door and stepped onto the terrace. Gray clouds had congealed into a bland, formless emptiness. In the near distance, the windows of Wilkes's penthouse revealed no life, but neither did any of the other windows in view. It had been sunny for most of the trip, until the train neared the city, where the bleak, desolate marshlands seemed to absorb the sky. Low-key excitement and optimistic anticipation curdled into anxious suspicion. Odds were the search for Crater would be frustrating and fruitless. More likely was the possibility some of Wilkes's competitors might catch on and turn it into a public joke. Then there was Eddie Moran's story about Jimmy Bad Tail. Try as he might, he could make no sense of it.

Back inside, he changed into casual clothes, poured himself a Scotch and sat with the *Standard*. The headline banged the usual drum—REDS READY TO RAPE LAOS. The accompanying editorial demanded that the US act on Secretary of State Dulles's threat to use "all means possible against Red aggression," including its arsenal of "new and improved atomic weapons." *New and improved*. Just like shampoo and dish liquid.

The phone rang. It was Nan Renard. He'd spoken to her office several times but this was the first time he'd heard her voice since the night he walked her home from the Coral. She was business-like, apologizing for not being able to stop by in person as she'd planned, but it was another impossibly hectic day at Wilkes Communications. Besides, Mr. Wilkes had directed her to "leave our detective alone so he can do what he does, but make sure he's got everything he needs."

"So far so good," Dunne said. "Wired your office a list of names and asked for addresses and phone numbers of those still in New York. They got back to me right away."

"That's the Wilkes Organization for you, we always do as we're told."

Words he'd heard before, but not from Wilkes. Bad Tail's farewell: *Always do as I'm told.* Echoed in a dream once. Eddie Moran had brought it back in full. Innocent coincidence? Probably. What if it wasn't?

"Fin," she said, "you still there?"

On the convoy across the Atlantic, in 1943, the escort destroyers honed in on the slightest hint of something beneath the surface and fired off a barrage of depth charges as the officers on deck counted backwards from ten seconds until the charge went off. He eyed his watch. *Ten seconds.* "You sound like Jimmy Bad Tail."

"Jimmy who?"

"Malacoda." *Nine, eight, seven seconds . . .*

"What's that?"

"You mean *who.* Jimmy Malacoda. Bad Tail is a nickname. Somebody else who always 'does as he's told.'" *Six, five, four, three seconds . . .*

She laughed. "Good for him. Might like working at Wilkes Communications, but he certainly doesn't sound like your type."

Hesitation but no hint of distress in her voice. "He isn't."

"Look, Fin, I'd love to chat, but I'm busier than ever. If I don't hear from you in a few days, I'll call. At the very least, let me buy you dinner at the Coral. This time there'll be a better ending, I promise. Too many martinis last time. Lesson learned."

She sounded sincere. Why shouldn't she? Or she was doing a convincing job of faking it. Why would she? After he hung up, he ordered dinner from room service and ate in his room. Maybe he shouldn't have brought up Jimmy Malacoda. But she didn't seem to sense a challenge. Glad for that. Had to trust somebody and she was the best candidate.

He sat and reviewed the names he'd compiled for possible interviews. The researchers at Wilkes Communications indicated several were permanently unavailable: Luke Ruppert died of a stoke in 1949; Judge Traglia went from lung cancer a year later; Sylvester Berind, who eventually became a Supreme Court justice himself, keeled over on the eighteenth hole of the St. Andrew's Golf Club in Hastings-on-Hudson, New York.

Cold trail grew ever colder.

Among the living was Stella Crater, who resided in Greenwich Village. Fred Kipps, ex-cop and Crater chauffeur, was in a Lutheran old folk's home on upper Broadway. The last two people to see Crater alive were Sam Hechtman, former chief lawyer for the Schumann Theatre Organization, and Patti Leroche, a showgirl, who (depending on the newspaper you read) was either Hechtman's date or Crater's. Hechtman had a law office in upper Manhattan. No occupation was listed for Miss Leroche, who lived on Union Street, in Brooklyn. Alexander Von Vogt, the Missing Persons detective who'd led the search, was retired and resided in Far Rockaway.

The place to start was the Missing Persons Bureau, headed by Jack Cronin—universally referred to in the police department as "Crow"—an acquaintance from the pre-war days when Dunne Detective Agency's bread-and-butter business involved tracking down absconding spouses and fleeing lovers. Not having talked to him in years, Dunne didn't know what to expect when he called from Florida. He was pleasantly surprised when Crow not only took his call but agreed to see him the morning after he was scheduled to arrive back in New York.

He turned on the TV. "The Red Skelton Show" raised his spirits. As he got ready for bed, he had a premonition he was going to dream about Nan Renard. He hoped it would be in an enjoyable way, which is how it turned out.

Rain, sleet or snow seemed imminent. Dunne took the subway. Crow was at his desk in his second-floor office at police headquarters on Centre Street, a cramped, disheveled room, with files, books and newspapers piled everywhere. Yellowed and brittle as parchment, the shades were half-drawn. Walls were almost the same tint, somewhere between snot and nicotine, the color of most city offices, dispirited and dull five minutes after being slapped on.

Crow put down his book and rose from his chair in a semi-crouch. He raised a handkerchief stained with yellow blotches to a nose that ended with the prominent hook popular myth described as Jewish but that observation made clear was distributed across a wide human spectrum, from Indian chiefs to Arab sheiks, North African tribesman and Lizzie Scaccio, Grand Street madam. Crow sported the Connemara version, hooked beak that along with his slicked-back, coal-black hair earned him his nickname. He honked into the handkerchief several times, wiped vigorously, and put it away. "I won't shake your hand," he said. "I feel a doozer of a cold coming on. It's all over the city."

Slushy mix of rain and ice made a noisy rant against the window. Crow went over and lifted from the only available chair an oak, arch-shaped radio of the type popular before the war. He held the unplugged wire in snake-handler fashion, thumb pressed down behind the head. "I keep meaning to throw the damn thing out. Pulled the plug three years ago, the day they took Fred Allen off the air. Now, with television, the slide toward coast-to-coast idiocy gathers new velocity each day." He placed it on the floor and pointed at the empty chair. "Have a seat, please."

He drew the shades down all the way. Returning to his

desk, he picked up the book and turned the spine so Dunne could see the title: *The Inferno*. "A masterwork of human psychology," he said. "Even Freud admired it, though he had no use for the theology. Father Alfred DiLascia started me reading Dante back at Regis. I've been rereading all three books of *The Divine Comedy* ever since. Know parts of it by heart. I was in the third circle of hell when you arrived. A favorite spot."

He pulled on a leather bookmark and flipped opened to a page that he scanned with his finger. "Here it is: 'Water sluices through darkened air/ And soaked soil gives off a putrid stench.' That always makes me laugh. The stink of wet earth is what the Irish call the 'the sweet aroma of turf,' fragrance of the Ould Sod. To the Italian nose, it smells like shit." He swiveled in his chair and pointed to a small plaster bust of a sharp-faced figure, a nose very much like his own, on the bookshelf behind. "For Dante, hell is a cold, rainy place. The center is frozen solid, a little like New York in mid-winter."

A clerk entered without knocking, laid a folder on one of the several piles arranged on the desk, and left. Crow took no notice, continuing with his report on the weather in hell. Dunne did his best to look interested. Everybody acquainted with Crow knew about his eccentricities. They also knew he ran a corruption-free bureau whose success in tracking down missing persons guaranteed he'd be in his job as long as he cared to be. Want his cooperation, play by his rules.

He lifted a pack of cigarettes from his shirt pocket and offered one to Dunne.

"Thanks, got my own."

"You didn't come to listen to me spout about Dante, did you, Fin? Last I heard you'd made a bundle peddling your outfit to some conglomerate and fled to Florida. Sounded like a good idea to me. Why you back?" He rapped the tip of a cigarette hard against the face of his wristwatch, then lit it.

As soon as Dunne uttered Crater's name, he got the response he expected: quizzical look to the effect of *you've got to be kidding.* Once he convinced Crow he wasn't, an equally expected question followed: *How could an experienced, seemingly sane person get mixed up in such an idiotic, useless, hopeless undertaking?*

"Personal favor?"

"No."

"What then?"

"A client is paying me to."

"Who?"

"You know I can't tell you that."

Crow got up and paced the small uncluttered space in front of the windows. Crater was a curse, he said. First case he worked on at Missing Persons. In fact, the reason he was brought in, though as it turned out, he ended up working the other disappearances that continued to happen, ones the press and politicians weren't interested in, runaway kids, wives fleeing husbands, husbands escaping wives, minor mobsters like Gene Moran who bungled a hit on Legs Diamond's brother and was never seen again. You could fill a medium-sized telephone directory with the small-time hoods disposed of in ways that ensured they'd never be found. Then there were the crowds of ordinary folks trying to get away from who they were before, to use the immensity and anonymity of New York to escape their past, or the poor souls—hoboes, drifters, alkies, lonely hearts, bums—who are reported missing but nobody cares if they're found.

"If I didn't know better," Crow said, "I'd say Dante spent the years before his exile on the missing-persons beat in Florence. Here's where you see it all, murder, mayhem, malfeasance, the felonies and misdemeanors people flee, bad marriages, embezzlements, embarrassments, broken bonds of family and friendship, illusions and false hopes that lure them on, concentric circles of deceit, of betrayals major and minor, of 'wounds and woe,' as

Dante puts it, so vast his eyes 'longed to linger weeping at the sight.'"

But it was Crater who got the attention, and the brunt of the search was borne by a trinity of senior detectives who'd joined missing persons to get away from the political meddling and triple-spouted font of corruption flowing through the department from booze, prostitution and gambling. Fed up with the hounding he took from the press and higher-ups, Eddie Fitzgerald resigned and moved to Montauk, where he drowned in a boating accident. Billy Moon fell into a funk and found temporary (and toxic) solace in booze and bar girls, dying from cirrhosis. And Alexander Von Vogt, poor Allie, among the most upright cops that ever passed through the department, he did what no cop should ever do—what Virgil warned Dante against as they passed from the Eighth Circle to the Ninth—got personally involved, and it brought him down.

Crow rubbed out his cigarette on the windowsill and raised the shades. Clatter of icy rain against the glass grew louder. "*Citta dolente*, city of desolation. Dante described it having four rivers: Acheron, Styx, Phlegeton and Cocytus. So does our city: Hudson, East, Bronx, and Harlem. Coincidence, I suppose." He stared out the widow. "The damned are best forgotten. Can't do anybody any good by digging up the Crater case. Leave it be."

"Appreciate the advice. But I'm going to stick with it till I hit a wall."

"Or it hits you."

"Whichever. Meantime, I'm asking for your help in two ways. First, I'd like to read the file on the Crater case."

"*Files*. They fill half a cabinet. But technically, the case is still open, and you're a civilian, so you should apply through the commissioner's office. But you were a cop—an honest one—and I respect that. What else?"

"Tell me whatever you know or remember and point me to

anyone you think I should talk to. Already have some names and addresses, including Von Vogt's."

"Cross him off right now. He'll never talk to you."

"No harm in trying."

In that case, Crow suggested, the best way to start was to drop Von Vogt a note. Be direct. Von Vogt "respected forthrightness." More important, go to the record room, start reading the files. Too voluminous to knock off in a day. "That way," Crow said, "you'll have a better idea of what questions to ask. You won't waste my time, and I won't waste yours."

Dunne spent the day at a beaten oak table that looked as though it had been in service since the first Dutch settlers brought it from Holland. He used the calendar book, which registered the date of each written report and the identity of the officer who filed it, as a guide. In the early days of the case, as Crow had explained, the cops brought in to assist Missing Persons were assigned to different teams, each with a veteran detective at the head. Every day, they'd be given addresses or potential witnesses to visit and report back on. The lead detective gathered their information into a single report, had them initial their section and then signed the full document.

Barely into the first overstuffed accordion file, he noticed a discrepancy. The calendar registered an entry by Det. Von Vogt on September 7, 1930, but there was no corresponding report. He presumed it had probably been placed out of order, but didn't find it among the other reports, which were all correctly filed.

When Crow came down at four p.m., he seemed unfazed by news of a missing report. Up until the war, the Crater files got quite a workout. Then people lost interest. It was probably fifteen years since anyone took a peek. Wasn't the first or last time a report was put back in the wrong place. Was undoubtedly in there somewhere. He suggested Dunne quit for the day. He'd thought of somebody else who'd been involved with the hunt for

Crater. Dr. Eugene Rossiter, nephew of the late Doc Cropsey, had followed his uncle into the coroner's office. He'd called Rossiter, who said he had some time this afternoon. Crow was going up that way and offered to accompany Dunne.

They traveled in an unmarked car across town to First Avenue. Though the sleet had ceased, heavy traffic slowed them to a crawl. As he drove, Crow kept the sidewalks under constant surveillance, moving his head in a deliberate swivel and leaning over the wheel for a better view of a pedestrian's face, the feral reflexes of a veteran cop sniffing for trouble.

Dunne told Crow that the reports he'd read so far didn't differ in any significant way from the newspaper accounts. Crater's bank statements showed that he'd withdrawn the equivalent of a State Supreme Court justice's annual salary at the time of his appointment to the bench, a seeming indication he'd paid for his office. (In Mrs. Crater's telling, the money was used to help members of his family "financially distressed by the Stock Market crash of the previous autumn.")

Of the five grand that Crater had received from having his court clerk cash two checks the morning of his disappearance and the two briefcases filled with papers he'd taken from his chambers — not a trace was found. The money, Crow speculated, could have been intended to pay off a blackmailer. The files might have contained information Crater wanted to keep out of the hands of investigators authorized to look into the buying or selling of judgeships. But if they were so private and potentially dangerous why was he so obvious in removing them?

In the month-long lapse between when he disappeared and when it was reported, there was no telling who'd entered Carter's apartment, what they'd been after or what they'd removed. If Carter had left the cash behind, who knows who might have taken it. "The year was 1930, don't forget," Crow said. "People were scared and desperate. Five grand was a fortune. Even a saint would have been tempted to take it. And if Tammany got wind that Crater removed a bunch of papers from his chambers—and you bet they did—they would have slipped someone into his apartment to see what they contained and, if necessary, seen to their disposal."

Though in sync with published accounts of the case, the police reports added another level of detail. Detectives Fitzgerald and Von Vogt made it clear that the carefully coordinated responses of Crater's judicial colleagues were intended to keep the investigation from going where they didn't want it to go. No judge would speak with them unless another judge was present. A stenographer recorded their answers. Whether Crater had been done in for reasons unrelated to his position or was hiding in fear of an investigation, his colleagues' first concern was to avoid any involvement. If a single one had the slightest concern over Crater's fate, he made no mention.

Interviewed in his chambers, in the presence of Justices McCarthy and Mandel, Judge Carmen Traglia volunteered that when Judge Crater hadn't appeared for the opening of the term, he'd attempted to reach him at his summer residence in Maine. Since he was calling in his capacity as presiding judge and not merely as a friend, he had a stenographer record the call (and, yes, he assured them, he'd done so with the consent of Mrs. Crater). He had some difficulty reaching her, but she confirmed that her husband had returned to the city to attend to "private business related to the upcoming election." Convinced that "despite this lapse, Joe Crater was a superb jurist," and not wanting to jeopardize his chances in the fall, Judge Traglia simply assigned another judge.

At this point, the detectives noted in their report, Judge Traglia excused himself to see to some pressing business in his courtroom and left them to examine a wall covered with framed and autographed pictures of himself with celebrities like "Lou Gehrig, Babe Ruth, John McGraw, Mae West, Jack Dempsey, Eddie Cantor, Jimmy Durante, Norma Talmadge, as well as the present governor, the present mayor (and two of his predecessors), several congressman and both senators." It was an unnecessary reminder, Dunne knew, for the detectives to avoid any overt aggression or skepticism in their questioning or risk reassignment to the far reaches of the Bronx or Staten Island.

"You ask me," Crow said, "Crater wasn't murdered by politicians seeking to ensure his silence. In the state investigation of the magistrate's court, there were plenty of canaries, but none was ever burked or flushed without a trace. Besides, when made to explain his visit to see Mrs. Crater, Detective Luke Ruppert testified he did so at the behest 'of friends from the regular Democratic organization.'"

Alas, though memory failed Ruppert when it came to their names, Crow was confident he told the truth and that the party chiefs were genuinely worried about Crater's whereabouts, which they wouldn't have been if they'd already had him eliminated. (Ruppert denied entering the apartment before Mrs. Crater returned from Maine but Crow thought he probably had. "Ruppert had spent a decade on the burglary squad, which is probably why his Tammany friends chose him in the first place." Ruppert did admit that the day before he went to see Mrs. Crater at her apartment, he'd inquired whether a passport had been issued in Judge Crater's name. But he couldn't remember if he'd done so on his own initiative or at somebody's request.)

It seemed more likely—Crow thought—that whatever happened to Crater involved his insatiable appetite for sex. Blackmail was probably part of it, which would explain additional monies he'd withdrawn from his bank that were never accounted for. ("Joe was generous with his friends, generous to a fault," was his wife's explanation.) Maybe he refused to pay any more. Maybe he threatened to go to the police.

The newspapers had lavished attention on revelations of Crater's liaisons with showgirls and single women ("practiced traffickers in prostitution and prevarication," wrote Mrs. Crater). Missing Persons not only turned up several female acquaintances of Crater's that the press had missed, but also obtained information for some of those who'd already been interviewed. Alice Wayne (real name: Mary Jane McGinty), age nineteen, a chorine with The Artists & Models Show who told the press she'd regarded the judge as a "sweet, kindly uncle who took an interest in my career," confided to Detective Moon she'd consented to have sex in return for Crater's help in getting a better job, but cut off relations when he demanded she do things she described as "degrading and unsanitary."

A visit by Fitzgerald and Von Vogt to Atlantic City established that the judge's visit there in late July, which he told his wife was "for a very private discussion of confidential matters related to the smooth functioning of the court in the upcoming term," was for the purpose of bedding several showgirls who were working in the Schumann Theatre Organization's summer circuit.

According to the papers, Elaine Dove (real name Edith Woll), a twenty-two-year-old "cabaret performer" who'd been seen on several occasions in Crater's company, was recovering at the Polyclinic Hospital from "an injury to her knee." Detective Von Vogt reported the injury was in fact "gonorrheal rheumatism." Though she denied having had sex with Crater, she stated that "on several occasions she met him at an after-hours joint on West 54th Street, and that the last time she saw him was in the early hours of August 4th and that he'd been by himself. She'd been introduced to him by Sam Hechtman, chief lawyer for the Schumann Theatre Organization, and Patti Leroche, her ex-roommate in the Hotel Plymouth, and swears she knows nothing about Crater's whereabouts."

As the last two people to see Crater alive, Sam Hechtman and Patti Leroche (real name: Bernadette Larocca) had been objects of special interest to the police. Crow described Hechtman as a street-savvy lawyer who'd worked behind the scenes to craft a good part of New York's entertainment law and then cultivated the judiciary to see to it the law was interpreted and applied in the best interests of the Organization. Thanks in good part to Hechtman's legal skills, the Schumann brothers managed to keep their empire afloat during the Depression. When things improved, they showed their appreciation by firing him.

A twenty-five-year-old chorine, Leroche was fifteen years younger than Hechtman. Though neither admitted it, the police speculated she was helping him provide those whose support and cooperation the Organization wished to have—cops, judges, politicians, reporters, suppliers, ticket agents, etc.—with the kind of female company that would keep them satisfied and well disposed. "Technically, since it was favors being traded and not money," Crow said, "it wasn't prostitution. But the girls had little choice. If they didn't work, they didn't eat. Beauty was a buyer's market. Despite those who like to paint that time in romantic hues, the truth is Broadway was one big brothel."

The cops grilled Leroche and Hechtman several times, but neither wavered from their original statements: On the sultry evening of August 6, 1930, at around 6:30 P.M., Leroche stopped by the offices of the Schumann Theatrical Organization to inquire about a job she hoped to land with a road company of the "Artists & Models" review scheduled to leave on the western circuit. She bumped into Hechtman, a casual acquaintance, who said he was headed to Bobby Duncan's Café, on West 45th Street. He invited her to join him and she accepted.

They were at Bobby Duncan's Café only a short while when Crater arrived. Hechtman knew Crater from the Democratic political circles in which they both traveled. On several occasions he'd helped Crater, a well-known theatre buff, obtain hard-to-get tickets for hit shows. Crater was about to sit at a table by himself when Hechtman asked him to join them. (The waiter staff confirmed this version of events.) Leroche had met the judge "once or twice before" at a local club but had never had a conversation with him. She said that she'd always presumed he was a bachelor and was surprised when he announced he was leaving first thing in the morning to join his wife at their summer cottage in Maine.

The wilting, oppressive heat, Hechtman remembered in his statement to the police, affected them all. Hechtman noticed at one point that sweat was dripping from Crater's neck onto the high, stiff shirt collar he favored. He wiped it away with his napkin, but didn't loosen his tie. Their desultory conversation mostly concerned the glum prospects for the upcoming theatrical season, which would begin after Labor Day. Hechtman and Leroche both thought Crater seemed distracted but not upset.

At about 9:30 p.m., Hechtman paid the check, refusing to let Crater contribute. They exited the restaurant. Crater looked up and down the street. A tan cab turned onto West 45th from Eighth Avenue, headed west, and Crater hailed it. He shook their hands and, stepping into the gutter to enter the cab, turned and said, "I'll be glad to get away." Leroche recalled catching a fleeting glance of the back of the taxi driver's head; Hechtman didn't bother looking. As they went on their way, she looked back and saw the cab turn onto Ninth Avenue, quickly slipping out of sight, out of time, out of history, to carry Crater to wherever it was he was going.

Crow pulled up outside the morgue and stuck his NYPD

identification on the dashboard. "That cab was what drove Von Vogt and the others nuts. The way it vanished without a trace."

"Were they sure Hechtman and Leroche were telling the truth?"

"If they were involved in Crater's disappearance, it doesn't seem likely they'd meet him in a public place, walk outside and watch him get in a cab, letting the whole world know they were the last to see him alive. They'd have to be stupid or crazy, and Leroche and Hechtman were neither."

Instead of the twenty minutes Crow said it would take to get to the morgue, it took forty-five. Rossiter, the doctor whom Crow said had been involved with the hunt for Crater, was in his surgical whites and waiting at the front desk. Over six feet tall, burly and overweight, he had thick red hair streaked with white sidewalls vaguely shaped like horns. He threw his cigarette on the marble floor, squashed it like a cockroach beneath his right heel and exhaled smoke through his nose like a steam-snorting El Toro from a Bugs Bunny cartoon. "You should've told me you were coming by way of China."

Crow mumbled about the traffic and how intolerable it would stay till the city put in a cross-town expressway. "I'm not going to shake hands" he said. "I have got a cold and a slight fever." When he introduced Dunne, it sounded like an afterthought.

"That makes two of us." Rossiter turned toward a pair of swinging doors at the end of the corridor. "I don't usually talk to private dicks," he said over his shoulder. "Almost as big troublemakers as reporters. But Crow here called in a favor." He barreled through the doors, head down, like a bull entering the ring. They followed him into a narrow room with metal shelves and glass jars on one side, folded gowns and sheets on the other. The pungent, medical odor of formaldehyde, invasive and bitter, caused a slight irritation in Dunne's eyes and throat.

"Nurse!" Rossiter boomed. "Where the hell is the nurse?"

The door at the other end opened. A diminutive nurse entered. "I've been waiting for you inside. Everything is ready." Her white gown was tied in the back. Her hair was tucked beneath a white cap that covered her forehead. Only above the mask was her face visible: youthful olive skin, deep, brown eyes, extravagant lashes. She looked directly at Dunne. "I'm an M.D., a pathologist, *not* a nurse."

"A rose by another name." Rossiter handed her the file. "Nice thing about autopsies, the patients are never late." He donned a white cap and draped a rubber apron over his neck. She tied it in the back while he pulled on a pair of rubber gloves. "I intend to catch the 5:27 to New Rochelle—where I will enjoy the warm embrace of my wife and the cold kiss of a martini— and since the commissioner frowns on taking cadavers home, especially homicides, it's off to work I go."

"Forgot this." She held out a mask.

"Idiocy."

"Rules."

"Same thing." He snatched the mask and tied it on hurriedly. "If you want to talk, follow me." His voice was only slightly muffled. He stalked into the other room.

The assistant pathologist whom Rossiter insisted on calling a nurse handed them each a set of whites. She waited until they dressed and led them into a white-tiled room with a floor of black and white hexagons, an oversized drain in the middle. Formaldehyde was more oppressive here. There was a row of altar-like marble slabs. On top of the nearest one lay a sheet-covered body. Rossiter and a young male assistant were examining the same file. The "nurse" wheeled a tray of instruments into place that looked more like gardening tools and kitchenware than surgical implements. The overhead fixture, buzzing intermittently like a lazy insect, shed a harsh light.

Rossiter lifted the sheet. The dead man appeared to be in his forties. Face as white as the tiled walls; in contrast, hair so black it seemed dyed. Lips slightly puckered, a trace perhaps of a final sour taste or thought: lemon, betrayer's kiss, last regret. He rolled the sheet down to the man's waist; poked with a scalpel at the puncture wound beneath the right breast, dry crust of black blood surrounding it. "The perfect place to stab a man. Keep the shiv out of sight, bring it up from below, stick it in, jerk it up, bingo. Probably done by a pro. Or one lucky amateur."

Crow squared his shoulders, sucked in air with a noticeable inhalation that pasted the mask to his face. He plucked it with his fingers. Sounding slightly out of breath, he crossed himself in a quick, furtive way. "What is it St. Paul wrote? 'For this perishable nature must put on the imperishable, and this mortal nature must put on immortality.'"

"Put a sock in it, Crow. You sound like some fearful Jesuit." Rossiter continued to poke around the wound and didn't look up.

"'Fearful Jesuit'? Spare me the epithets of that apostate, James Joyce."

"I speak from experience. Those pious sophists spent four years at Fordham trying to stuff my head with their Thomistic gibberish."

"'Gibberish'? No philosopher has ever surpassed the intellectual achievement of St. Thomas Aquinas. Dante based his opus on Aquinas."

"Medieval claptrap. Superstition over science. Do you think our friend here . . ." He reached for the tag attached to the corpse's big toe and read from it: "Do you think Mr. Gene Halloway is dead because his 'quiddity' has gone elsewhere?"

"His soul has left his body, yes."

Rolling down the sheet, Rossiter exposed the corpse's genitals. He lifted the limp penis with the scalpel. "Well, here's his 'dity.' I'll bet a bunch of ripe bananas that while Mr. Halloway was enjoying the floor show at the Black Hat Café, said dity was stiff and standing, and he was aiming to stick it in somebody else's girlfriend or wife, which is what led him to his untimely demise at the hands of 'assailant or assailants unknown.' Where his 'quid' went after that is anybody's guess."

He leaned over the body, pressing down the fiercely sharpened blade like a floor layer with a linoleum knife, and made a long central cut from the top of the rib cage to just beneath the belly button. Crow turned away. As he folded back the flaps of flesh to expose the chest cavity, Rossiter raised his head. The deep, intense blueness of his eyes was accented by the isolating whiteness of cap and mask. "Doesn't bother you, Dunne?"

"Seen worse."

"War?"

Dunne nodded.

"Which?"

"Both." First time: in the Argonne, jagged metal panel from an exploded caisson tore open the sergeant atop the trench, toppled him back. His insides spilled across the wooden walkway, a vivid outpouring instantly trampled and kicked aside by desperate, frightened soldiers, slipping and sliding in the gore as they hurtled for cover.

"Three years as a Navy doctor in the Pacific. Once you work wholesale, you barely notice the retail." Rossiter went back to work, barking out anatomical data that the male assistant copied on a chart. The nurse/pathologist brought over a bowl that fit into a holder on the side of the table. He lifted out the heart and lungs and placed them in it. He stood back. "Nurse, where's the saw?" His irritation was unmistakable.

"I didn't think a cranial was called for . . ."

"Didn't think! The two most fatal words in the medical profession!"

His bull-like bellowing sent her scurrying to the other side of the room. Rossiter pulled down his mask. "Feel free to take yours off, too. Its only purpose is to provide our hack commissioner and his imbecilic, rule-crazed toadies the opportunity to hand down yet another utterly inane regulation, as if I might give our friend here my cold. But that's what administrators do, isn't it? Add unnecessary rules? How else to justify their entirely unnecessary existence?"

He took the saw she brought him. She slipped a tray under the corpse's head and raised a brace that pressed against the cheek bones. "You won't report me, will you, nurse?"

"Rules are rules." Her lush black lashes rolled slowly up and down. She didn't remove her mask. "And I'm not your nurse."

"Don't tell me you were educated by the Jesuits?"

"Ursuline nuns."

"Worse." He turned to his male assistant. "Please note for any Jesuits or Ursuline nuns who might inquire that, in Mr. Halloway's case, as in all that have preceded it, I once more failed to find any evidence of a soul." He laid the fine blade of the saw across the top of the cadaver's forehead. "And get a trocar in the abdomen and start draining. For Pete's sake, that should have been done already." The male assistant, who Dunne guessed was a medical student or intern, put down his notes and quickly returned with a slim-headed tube attached to a large opaque glass container.

Crow stood staring down into the cadaver's empty chest.

Drawing the saw back and forth with long, steady strokes, Rossiter worked nonstop for several minutes. Despite the room's dank chill, a bead of sweat skied down the side of his nose. "I pity the patients of tomorrow. The medical schools are turning out a uniformly timid crew. So afraid of making mistakes, they won't do anything on their own and live in fear of taking risks. How the hell can anyone practice medicine if he's afraid of making mistakes?" He put down the saw. "So, Dunne, what's the urgent business brought you to this shambles?"

"He's on a case." Crow was still staring.

"I figured that out by myself." Rossiter stopped sawing and wiped his face with his sleeve. The blade of the saw was at the rear of the skull. The nurse/assistant pathologist stepped forward and carefully removed the severed top. He rested the saw on the tray, dug into the pocket of his gown and took out a lighter and a pack of cigarettes. "Nurse, here's another mortal sin to report to the Ursulines." She was conferring with the male assistant about an annotation he'd made in the file and paid no attention.

He offered the pack to Dunne, who declined. "Homicide, I presume."

Dunne removed his mask. "Probably. But still listed as a Missing Persons."

"How recent?"

"Wait'll you hear." Crow transferred his gaze from chest to skull.

"Joseph Force Crater," Dunne said.

The sudden, unexpected clap of Rossiter's thunderous laughter made his female assistant's eyes dilate with surprise.

"Little early for April Fool's, don't you think, Dunne?"

"Exactly what I told him," Crow said. "A fool's errand."

"A job. Nothing more." Or maybe something more. Memory of Nan Renard returning from the ladies' room with a rhythmic sway of hips.

The nurse/assistant pathologist handed Rossiter a shallow metal bowl to use as an ashtray. "Yours is not to reason why. Yours is but to do and get paid. An admirable sentiment. But whoever hired you needs a psychiatrist, not a dick. Crater long ago became the cynosure of cranks and crazies, the kind who report being abducted by Martians. In fact, that's what you say: Crater's holed up on Mars. Then cash the check and blow."

"Crow tells me you were part of the investigation."

"A cameo. I was fresh out of medical school."

Crow hooked his mask with a forefinger and pulled it down. "Doc Rossiter is a nephew of Doc Cropsey."

"Was. Doc Cropsey passed into the void thirteen years ago. Good man and a great coroner. Cut up more corpses than you could put a number on."

"He was a friend. I was at his funeral." St. Agnes's church on 43rd Street, a solemn high requiem mass, three priests in black chasubles, choir chanting the *Dies Irae*. The crowd that packed the church included the health and police commissioners. No recollection of meeting Cropsey's nephew.

"I was already on my way to vanquish Tojo and the Japs." Rossiter took a voracious drag on his cigarette, tapped the ash into the bowl. "Doc Cropsey was too clever to get embroiled in the Crater case. From the start, it stunk of politics and behind-the-scenes shenanigans. Don't solve it, you're an idiot or part of a cover-up; do, it's a frame-up. Political cases were like polio, he said. Safest course is to keep your distance."

"But he stuck you in the middle." Crow had lost interest in the cadaver. "You couldn't have been happy about that."

"What you have to remember is when the case broke, the reporters outnumbered the cops ten to one. There was one cop assigned to check out the reports of Crater's body being found, and let me tell you, it was like tulip time in Holland, bodies blooming everywhere, especially in New Jersey where we had three reports a day of Crater's body being dug out of a dump, fished out of a river, or found in somebody's basement. The police commissioner had been warned by the mayor that if the press scooped the cops on this story, his head would be the first to roll. Right away, the commissioner asked that a coroner be assigned to travel with the cops—or, as it turned out, the cop—and give an immediate opinion about the probability of the corpse being Crater's.

"Sure that his political connections would brand him a tool of Tammany, Doc Cropsey knew exactly what he was doing when he picked me for the job. I was a medical tyro. Yes, I was his nephew, but the press didn't have to know that, and given their innate laziness and the urgency of the case, they'd probably never find out. Even if they did, he was sure they'd have so much invested in me as the fair-haired boy, a young Doctor Kildare, they wouldn't let that relationship get in the way of a good story.

"Doc believed it likely Crater was done in by professionals and would never be found. Yet if by some remote chance one of these claims proved true and Crater's body was found, the reporters would do everything in their power to shaft the cops and anoint me as the idealist doctor and boy sleuth who put the flatfoots in their place. As it turned out, after several weeks of false alarms, the merry band of scribblers lost interest, and Detective Billy Moon and I spent several months traipsing from Jerksberg to Moronsville. Moon got cockeyed drunk every night and hired the occasional harlot. I stayed in my room and read Darwin."

"Never turned up anyone who remotely resembled Crater?" Crow asked.

"I thought Dunne is the one interested in this case?"

"Crow's asking the same questions I would."

"Turned up plenty. A banner year for dead men in their early forties. Good many suicides. Several corpses were half-rotted or chewed up by animals or badly burned. Often the whole town had a stake in it being Crater. The reward offered by the *Standard*, added to what the city put up, made the body like a lottery ticket. Individually and collectively, with the

Depression settling over the land, the desire to claim that money was desperate."

"Nobody did, did they?"

Rossiter extinguished the cigarette against the side of the bowl and immediately lit another. "Tried as hard they could, but I had a simple test. Crater had all his teeth removed and been fitted with false ones. It was right there in the police circular, but that didn't stop people from believing otherwise. The desire to believe is the strongest desire of all, especially when money's involved. Ask the Jesuits. There are none better at exploiting that desire. First thing I did was pry open the mouth. Not a single one of the cadavers fitting Crater's general description passed that test."

"Got a best guess about the case?" Crow continued to ask the questions.

"It's been a long time since I gave it any thought. The Roosevelt haters always whispered he was behind it because he was afraid his presidential run would be scuttled if Crater confessed to paying for his judgeship. But the Republicans were implicated as often as the Democrats. You don't think those upstate judges weren't paying Republican bosses for their jobs? If F.D.R. was interested in a cover-up, he'd have to make nine-tenths of the judges in the state disappear. No, I say it was sex. Crater was a notorious bladesman, and to paraphrase the Galilean, he who lives by his blade stands a good chance of perishing because of it."

Rossiter picked up the scalpel and touched the corpse's penis. "Like our friend here, Mr. Halloway, Crater's blade was probably too sharp for his own good."

Dunne took out his pocket-sized, wrote down his room number and the general exchange of the Savoy Plaza. He ripped out the page. "Anything else comes to mind, here's where you can reach me. I'll leave it out at the desk."

"Funny thing, Dunne, but by one of those small coincidences that lead the gullible to discern the hand of fate, I was at Missing Persons the day the case broke. We did a good deal of business and that day I was delivering papers for somebody or other's signature. The first reaction in the office was that a woman was involved. Most times when a middle-aged man went missing, that was the case. Only one cop disagreed, said it was the wife up in Maine did it. He was adamant."

"Remember his name?"

"At this point, I'm lucky I remember my own. Anyway, he was assigned somewhere else. He was there, like me, on some other business."

"Been generous with your time, doc," Crow said. "Now it's me owes you."

"My pleasure, Crow. But before you go, one favor." He stood behind the corpse and crouched, palms on thighs, face almost level with the topless skull. "Come here."

Hesitantly, Crow went over to Rossiter.

"Take a peek in there."

"Where?"

"In Mr. Halloway's skull."

Crow crouched next to Rossiter. "What am I looking for?"

"I was hoping you'd spot his soul. Never been able to find one." As Rossiter straightened up and let out a single loud laugh, the assistant pathologist threw down her file on the instrument tray. This time, it was his turn to be startled.

"I've had just about enough of you having fun at the expense of the dead. You're worse than unprofessional. You're a disgrace." She took off her mask. Except for the cap covering her hair, her full lips and white teeth completed her lovely Mediterranean face. "Your behavior is indecent. I won't report you only because it would be useless. Nothing would happen. But maybe, this once, you might find it in that shriveled soul of

yours to put aside your arrogance and examine your conscience."

"Nun talk."

"No, shocking as it may be to hear, this is the way human
beings talk. Do yourself a favor and try it some time, if only for
the sheer novelty." She walked out of the room.

Rossiter pulled off his cap. "That girl, Linda DeMarco, is
one hell of a pathologist. Best I've ever worked with. She's the
one figured out how that doctor in Inwood killed his wife by poisoning her with curare. Fooled everybody but her. Poisons are
her specialty. Probably learned that from the Ursulines, too. Or
maybe from the Dominicans. Official poisoners to the Vatican.
But she's too sensitive to survive in a profession like this, where
all the egos are bloated and stilettos double as elbows. I'll fix
that. When I'm finished, she'll be tough enough to overcome
whatever she comes up against. Mark my words, both of you."

Crow gave Dunne a lift back to his hotel, resuming his careful cop watch on the streets as Dunne continued to prod him on
the Crater case. When he brought up Mrs. Crater's account and
the tale of the detective who visited her in Maine, Crow cut him
short. "Typical newspaper crap." He went off about the garbage
they printed and the trouble they caused, a complaint that wend-
ed its way, predictably, to Dante, for though there weren't newspapers in his day, he knew the type, those who prostitute words
and language, feasting on scandal, corrupting the public mind
with myths and lies, and smoothing the way to the final abyss,
where truth and trust can't exist. "He sticks them in the Eighth
Circle, in a pit where they're covered in shit. Just imagine what
he'd make of television."

"Somehow I was left feeling Mrs. Crater didn't make it up.
Seemed so real."

"The whole story is far-fetched. A person shows up in her house claiming to be a detective from New York and she doesn't even ask his name. Give me a break. Besides, there's no record of a cop from New York within 300 miles of Lake Belvedere at the time she claims. We showed her pictures of any detective who had even a remote possibility of having made the trip. She couldn't identify anybody. The woman's totally delusional. She marries a sex fiend she imagines is a cross between St. Francis and Sir Lancelot. Soon as she tells her fantasy to Wilkes's scriveners, they write it up like a scene in a Faith Baldwin novel."

Wilkes name was dropped casually enough that Dunne was sure Crow attached no special significance to it. He asked Crow about the telegrams Crater received in Lake Belvedere. Weren't there copies on file in the local office or some record of who sent them? Crow shook his head. The record-keeping up there was a mess. The Methuselah in charge had been at it since the last century. Got fired as a result and lost his pension. Another victim of the Crater curse. Sadder still, his successor located the log book. The telegrams were sent by "John Jones, New York City."

Crow parked in front of the side entrance to the Savoy Plaza, on 58th Street, flashing his badge at an officious doorman who blew his whistle and signaled him to move. The sleet had resumed. He got out with Dunne but declined to come in for a drink. They stood beneath the steady *wap, wap* of icy rain on the canopy. "You got a reputation for having been a good cop, and that counts for a lot with me. It's also been widely advertised you can be a pain in the ass."

"Two go together, don't you think?"

"I'll give you what help I can, Fin, but you heard Rossiter. He agrees. You're wasting your time."

"I guess I've got it to waste."

"Then be careful what you waste it on." He took off on another commentary on *The Divine Comedy*, how Dante put

Ulysses in the Eighth Circle of Hell, a decision that horrified admirers of the great hero of *The Odyssey*. But in Dante's eyes, when Ulysses tired of retirement in Ithaca and left to seek what lay beyond the Gates of Hercules, where he and his crew meet their end, he committed a great sin. "The Greeks had a name for it," Crow concluded. "*Pleonexia.*"

Dunne nodded. Crow and his eccentricities. Play by his rules or don't play. "Sounds like a skin disease."

"A disease, all right, but of the soul, not the skin."

The doorman repeated his attempt to get Crow to move, this time as plea rather than command. "I beg you, please stand aside. You're making it difficult for guests to enter or leave."

"Yeah, yeah," Crow said but didn't move. "Ulysses' sin is the vanity that drives him to overreach, wandering the world 'all human worth and wickedness to prove,' rather than staying at home to fulfill his debt of love to Penelope."

"I'm looking for a missing person. Isn't that what you get paid to do?"

"Far as Crater's concerned, that check was cashed a long time ago."

"Crater can't be found, no harm done. But if by some wild chance he can, Missing Persons has one less person to look for."

"The chances of solving it are zero or below."

"My client thinks otherwise."

"Otherwise, Fin, all you have is the probability of waking ghosts best left in peace."

"I don't believe in ghosts, but I appreciate the advice."

"But you're not going to take it. I knew you wouldn't, but I felt it must be said."

As Crow turned to walk back to his car, a small boy in a shiny yellow rain slicker and coonskin cap was being dragged along by a stout woman wrapped in a thick blue coat who had the plodding gait of a prison matron or nanny. "Stop dawdling."

Her exasperated tone edged toward furious.

The boy pulled his hand away and crashed into Crow. He said in a loud but good-natured way, "Hey, Daniel Boone, easy does it."

"Daniel Boone? Don't you watch TV? I'm Davy Crockett, you jerk."

"Watch who you call a jerk, you little putz." Crow seized his arm, squeezed hard and let go. The boy ran to the woman, wailing, and hugged her legs. She wagged a finger in Crow's face. "How dare you! I got a good mind to call a cop!"

"Call the marines, for all I care. They're all brats. An entire generation of spoiled brats. They're going to turn out rotten, all of them, just wait and see."

Over the next several days, as he read through the files, Dunne couldn't help but feel the mounting frustration and eroding morale of the detectives as they tracked down the calls and letters, everyone certain about Crater's whereabouts, the newspapers all the while yammering away about "police incompetence" and the politicians hammering on the commissioner to wrap up the investigation before it blew up into another scandal.

Judge Crater is relaxing on a yacht parked off Southampton, Long Island. He's held against his will at a sanitarium in Ridgefield, Connecticut. The mob has him prisoner in the backroom of a candy store on Manhattan Avenue in Brooklyn. He's spied sipping cocktails at the Clifford Inn on the Jersey Shore on the same day that a town clerk in upstate New York sees him hop a Montreal-bound freight train.

Soon he moves west, driving with the top down in a DeSoto Six Convertible Coupé through Whiting, Indiana, and strutting out of a theater in Des Moines, Iowa, after watching the film *Cimarron* with a woman bearing an uncanny resemblance to its star, Irene Dunne. He shacks up in San Francisco with a curvaceous brunette at the Hotel Robins on Park Street, under the name Joseph Owens, Jr. Simultaneously, he travels south, dining in Augusta, Georgia, plays golf outside Jacksonville, Florida, and rents a villa in Havana, Cuba; and north, to Niagara Falls, where he rides between two "swarthy, foreign-looking types" in the front seat of a Buick sedan with Pennsylvania license plates, and to Minot, North Dakota, where he hides out at his brother's place; and east, sailing first class on the Ile de France and setting up residence at 9 Padre Avenue in Seville, Spain.

Or maybe he never leaves the city. Maybe he's in Room 1630 at the Dixie Hotel, or in a suite at the Concourse Plaza Hotel in the Bronx, or sleeping off a bender in the Holy Name Mission on Bleecker Street. The files bulged with carbon copies of letters to police departments around the country asking them to follow up leads or to supply more information, and with reports on the endless footwork of following up on Judge Crater sightings in and around the city.

Finally, about a month after the hunt started, an official directive was issued (probably in response to the detectives' pleas) authorizing them "to file without further action communications concerning the Crater investigation that you deem to be from persons of low mental condition, or pranksters, or utterly lacking in material relevance to the resolution of the investigation."

The relief this provided, welcomed as it undoubtedly was, didn't save them from the manipulations of the many cranks, pranksters or people of ill will who were clever enough to couch their anonymous tips in credible terms. Off the detectives went to Brooklyn, Hoboken, New Rochelle, by subway, car and foot (and occasionally bumming rides with reporters who never seemed to lack for automobiles), through hotels, asylums and reeking basements. More than once the tip was from wives or girlfriends out to embarrass husbands or lovers by sending the police to knock on doors and interrupt wayward mates in the middle of trysts with other women.

In the first week of November Detectives Moon and Von Vogt followed up a letter from "Tommy the Cabbie" who claimed he not only knew the taxi driver of the cab that picked Crater up the night he vanished but had been told by that same driver that Crater was in a private room in St. Elizabeth's Hospital in Washington Heights where "the one in charge is being paid a bundle" to let him stay. "I don't want no trouble," he wrote, "because I got a family but I was raised to do right and help out our polise [sic]."

The one in charge was a tall Irish nun. A tight virginal smile turned into an indignant grimace at the suggestion she or any of her sisters might be complicit in hiding someone from the law, never mind Judge Crater. She expressed her intent, the detectives noted in their report, to call the commissioner, whose niece happened to be a sister on the hospital staff, to express her shock and displeasure. Taking note of the fat, cigar-chomping janitor who stood in the background smirking, Moon and Von Vogt grilled him. He vigorously denied knowing anything about Tommy the Cabbie and his letter.

The more time Dunne spent with the reports, the more the personalities of the three detectives came through. Detective Edward Fitzgerald's signature had a florid, artistic quality that didn't seem to match his subdued, straightforward prose. Once, when the commissioner's office dispatched him to Albany to interview "noted criminologist Dr. Algernon Vandeleer"—who turned out to be the resident of an old folks home eager to sell the department his newly invented device "to disclose the perpetrators of all crimes"—Fitzgerald's frustration rose to the surface. "Assignments of this sort," he noted at the bottom of the report sent to his higher-ups, "will continue to guarantee an unsuccessful conclusion to this investigation."

Plodding, competent and quickly dispirited by the internal confusion and external pressure that were part of the case, Detective William Moon typically got right to the point. "Acting on anonymous letter received 10/16/30 checked out 15 Highland Place, Yonkers. Boarding house run by Angela Baldasari. Widow. Gives age as 71. English poor. Five boarders, all elderly Italian men. She's got no idea why anyone would report Crater as being on the premises except as a stupid joke." The reports got even briefer and more pointed when Moon accompanied Dr. Rossiter on the search for Crater's remains.

The stalwart of the squad was Detective Alexander Von Vogt. Tucked in the files was a letter from the chief inspector to the commissioner complaining that the newspapers were libeling his men and himself when they pictured the Crater investigation as being conducted by a band of hapless amateurs and/or lackeys of corrupt politicians. Defending the integrity of the investigation, the chief inspector wrote that the lead detective, Alexander Von Vogt, "is as respected an investigator as the police department possesses. He consistently displays a degree of originality in matters which he handles that takes him from the beaten path usually followed by detectives and as a result, not infrequently, secures results where others fail."

Filled with sharp observations about the physical and emotional characteristics of those he interviewed, Von Vogt's carefully typed reports were usually two or three times as long as the other detectives'. They revealed an educated man able to dismiss one would-be tipster as "purveying the usual persiflage of an inveterate imbiber" and describe another as "filled with the illusory excitement of a recent benedict." (When Dunne inquired, Crow was glad to provide the definitions of persiflage: frivolous, insignificant talk; and benedict: a newlywed.)

Von Vogt came across as honest, smart, seasoned and blunt.

In a letter he wrote to Stella Crater, he reported that a headless torso with only the right leg appended had washed ashore on Jones Beach. The coroner judged it to have been in the water for well over a month. On the leg were the remnants of a blue silk sock attached to a Brooks Brothers blue garter "badly faded through the effect of the water." Another important feature, he added, was the "male appendage had been circumcised." Could she please confirm "whether or not your husband owned such garters and whether he was circumcised or not."

His obvious unfamiliarity with Stella Crater's delicate sensibilities and the steadfast, impenetrable defensiveness she maintained in all matters pertaining to her husband indicated Von Vogt had never met her. This was confirmed in the follow-up letter he sent when, unsurprisingly, she didn't respond to the first. In it, he apologized for not being with his partner, Det. Fitzgerald, when he'd interviewed her during her return to the city. "I'd just lost my wife," he wrote, "and needed time with my young sons."

If moved by Von Vogt's explanation, Mrs. Crater kept it to herself. For Von Vogt's part, the files indicated the time he took to be with his boys was exceedingly brief. Instead, he threw himself into his work, inching away from grief not through isolation but through grinding away at the Crater investigation. Yet the fact of Von Vogt's being a widower at age forty-six helped explain how he came to be pilloried in the press and ended up in a desk job at the Police Academy on Hubert Street.

The parts of the story that weren't in the files or newspapers were supplied by Crow. "Allie was one of the best detectives the department ever produced," he said. "He did the work of four while he was on the Squad. Sure, he could be thick the way Krauts tend to be, but he was as upright as sunlight and never demanded anything of anybody he didn't demand of himself."

Allie Von Vogt was raised by German immigrant parents on

Park Avenue in the Bronx (a poor cousin to the prestigious, wealthy avenue in Manhattan). Despite the aristocratic preface of "Von," his old man was a carpenter. An only child, Allie did very well in school but to his parent's great disappointment dropped out of the engineering program at City College to marry his girlfriend, who gave birth to the first of their three sons six-and-a-half months after the wedding. He entered the police department that same year, in December 1914.

With the war raging in Europe, Crow reported, the Prussian ring to Allie's last name led to him taking much good-natured ribbing, which became decidedly less good natured after the U.S. entered on the side of the Allies. Anything and everything smacking of the Kaiser and his Huns became suspect, causing thousands of German Americans to anglicize their names and sauerkraut to be dubbed "liberty cabbage." Von Vogt, however, stayed Von Vogt. He was a loyal American, he maintained, and his name had been passed on by his father, an honest, hard-working naturalized citizen who lived by the laws of his adopted country.

By dint of diligence and intelligence, Von Vogt rose quickly, becoming one of the NYPD's youngest detectives. When Prohibition arrived, he requested a transfer to Missing Persons with the intent of staying away from the grafting uncorked by the illegal booze industry and its attendant rackets. His wish granted, he made a name for himself through the intensity and quality of his work. He was the clear choice to head the Crater investigation, and the volume and thoroughness of the reports he filed were proof that no one else, whether assigned on a short- or long-term basis, might have matched his efforts.

The trouble started about three months into the case when, with public interest cooling, the newspapers paid belated attention to the squawking of an inmate in the Federal Penitentiary in Atlanta who claimed his ex-wife, a former department store model by the name Connie Newberry, had been Crater's long-term mistress until he dumped her. According to her ex, a convicted counterfeiter, embezzler and bigamist, Connie had bragged to him about using her mob connections to have Crater quietly strangled in the back of a taxi and his body hidden in a shallow grave in the Adirondacks.

Accustomed to jail-house braggadocios eager to retail pumped-up allegations and outright fabrications to bargain for reductions in their sentences, the police were slow following up. The *Standard*, on the other hand, hoping to stoke renewed interest in the case, dispatched a reporter to Atlanta. Next day, it touted a decisive break: *Mistress and Murderer: Crater Culprit Identified.* Tipped off about what was coming (the police speculated it was by her ex who knew that if she went on the lam it would only help prove her guilt), Connie Newberry disappeared from the room she shared with a cosmetics model in the Mayflower Hotel on Central Park West.

In a flash, the *Standard* and its competitors ploughed up all the dirt they could on Connie Newberry, and luckily for them, her life yielded a bountiful crop of lurid stories and speculation. Born Estelle Ludgemann, she was the daughter of Herman Ludgemann, a German-Swiss immigrant who settled in Hartford, Connecticut, and worked as a watch salesman. He perished in a hotel fire in Providence, Rhode Island, in 1904, when Estelle was six. At the time, he was hailed in the local papers as a hero for having vainly attempted to save his bedmate, who was registered as Mrs. Ludgemann. Except she wasn't. Burned beyond recognition, her body was never identified.

Connie Newberry worked in the small bakery her mother operated until she headed for New York at sixteen, where she landed a job in the Ziegfield Follies as a chorus girl. After two years, at age eighteen, she struck gold and married a successful furrier twice her age. That marriage ended in an acrimonious divorce. In 1919, at age twenty-one, she married Maxfield Newberry, the twice-divorced, forty-year-old scion of an old New York family. Charming and well-dressed, a former captain of Princeton's equestrian team, and a lawyer who served as a major with the Seventh Regiment and had been decorated twice, Max Newberry was a playboy alcoholic who, upon learning he'd been cut out of his mother's will, blew his brains out.

Connie's next marriage, in 1926, was a six-month affair with an up-and-coming stockbroker who as well as turning out to be a counterfeiter and embezzler also proved to be a bigamist. Off he went to the Atlanta Penitentiary, leaving Connie single, broke and faced with doing what she had to do to stay afloat. This included a stint in a traveling burlesque show in which she starred as "The Jazzy Jezebel." (Although she vigorously denied it, the *Standard* suggested she had a featured role in a cheaply made indecent film—a "naughty flicker"—that, though never publicly distributed, was widely circulated at stag clubs and bachelor parties.)

It was after returning to New York and getting work as a department store model that she was introduced to Joseph Force Crater, who set her up in an apartment on Jane Street in the remote reaches of the West Village. A year or so later, either unduly nervous about a potential disclosure scotching his chances for appointment to the bench or, more likely, tired of the arrangement, Crater cut off their relationship.

Feasting on the cornucopia of salacious details in Connie Newberry's background, the *Standard* dubbed her "The Jilted Jezebel." The *Graphic* ran grainy, blurred stills from the blue film, inviting readers "to contact the police if you've seen this woman." Meanwhile, the editorial writers accused the cops of being deliberately derelict in trying to track her down because the politicians, afraid of all the secrets she might reveal, had ordered them to go easy. Von Vogt took up their challenge and within a few days located Connie Newberry at her sister's apartment in Sunnyside, Queens.

Maybe if Von Vogt hadn't been so recently widowed he wouldn't have fallen as completely and quickly for Connie Newberry as he did; and maybe if she weren't feeling so abandoned and vulnerable, she wouldn't have reciprocated so strongly. "It was obvious to us all," Crow said, "that Allie had ceased seeing things objectively. If he'd left well enough alone, it would have all come out in the wash. But he couldn't help himself and wouldn't let us help him either. Off he went in a barrel over Niagara Falls."

He insisted on being present when the police commissioner conducted his own interview of Connie Newberry and was seen holding her hand as they left. In an act of uncharacteristic indiscretion, he snapped back at the press, striding into the Shack— the reporters' den behind police headquarters—and announcing that the speculation about the "Jilted Jezebel" was "unmitigated dog crap." Instead of backing off, the newspapers counterattacked, scoffing at what one editorialist called "love-struck, bleeding-heart investigators," and demanding the D.A. begin an immediate inquiry into why it had taken the cops so long to locate and interrogate Connie Newberry.

As accusations flew back and forth, Miss Newberry slipped out of her apartment and vanished. The sniping from the press blended into a symphonic howl. Speculating that she'd fallen in the clutches of the people behind Crater's disappearance, the *Standard* blamed the "incurable corruption and invincible incompetence of the NYPD." The *News* and *Mirror* repeated the rumor that she'd gone off to join Crater wherever he was hiding. The *Times* lamented "the growing sense of insecurity felt by law-abiding citizens in this city and across the country." Stunned and chagrined, Von Vogt was taken off the case and stuck behind a desk at headquarters.

At week's end, she telegrammed the NYPD that she was in Havana and on her way home. Panicked at seeing every detail of her life—from her father's death to the painful particulars of her marriages—paraded before the public, afraid of being indicted by the D.A. for a crime she had nothing to do with, and upset and guilty over the criticism directed at Von Vogt, she used a friend's passport to flee on a cruise ship to Cuba. Now, however, realizing her flight had only made matters worse, she voluntarily returned.

It didn't take long before it was established to everyone's satisfaction that her ex-husband was a self-serving windbag. The newspapers moved on. Vindicated in his assertion of Connie Newberry's innocence, Von Vogt was put back on the case. Yet his brief stint as the "love-struck detective" left a permanent taint. He saw Connie Newberry a few times after she returned, and though he made it clear he didn't hold her rash decision against her, she was done with New York and left to start over again on the West Coast. "To paraphrase Dante's lament for the lovers Paolo and Francesca," said Crow, "'Love to a single end brought him and her.'"

Von Vogt's last entries were two letters and responses filed on January 30, 1933. The first, from Rev. F. Roland Grovesnor Phelps, at 9 Route Kaufman, Shanghai, raised the possibility that maybe Crater really had taken a slow boat to China. Von Vogt let the Reverend down gently, thanking him for his inquiry and informing him that Judge Crater didn't fit the description of a "rotund, notably garrulous fellow fluent in several of the Oriental languages"; the second, from C.S. Weatherholt, director of the Malay Archipelago Expedition, called attention to a local river pilot who claimed "he'd been a judge in New York." Von Vogt wrote back requesting more information.

After leaving Missing Persons, Von Vogt bounced around the department for several years before being shuffled off to a job at the Police Academy. His oldest boy, Alexander Jr., was killed at

Anzio in 1943; the next oldest, Carl, died at Iwo Jima in 1945. In October 1946, Von Vogt, a widower with his remaining boy gone off to college at M.I.T., retired from the Department after a thirty-two-year career with only a single blemish. According to Crow, "He never again uttered another word about the Crater case or Connie Newberry, and we all knew never to bring them up."

Finished reading the files for the day, Dunne made his first foray to interview the players in the case who were still alive and available. He began at the beginning, with Patti Leroche (neé Bernadette Larocca), one of the last two people to see Crater alive. The *Standard*'s info was bare bones: she'd been married to a grocery store magnate but was now separated, went under the name Pat Roche, worked as a salesgirl at A&S in downtown Brooklyn. Lived on Union Street. No listing in the phone book.

He rode the subway to Fourth Avenue and walked up Union toward Prospect Park. A brisk wind blew what he took at first for a small snow flurry but soon realized was incinerator ash from the apartment buildings atop the hill. Miss Leroche's address turned out to be a rooming house, one in a row of dowdy brownstones with room-to-let signs in the front window. Another neighborhood awaiting the wrecking ball.

He went up the stoop and rang the bell. The curtain on the front window parted enough to signal somebody was home. He waited for whoever it was to open the door. Nobody did. Rang again. Nothing. He held down the button on the doorbell with his thumb until the door opened with an angry jerk. A squat, muscular, middle-aged woman in a bulky, gray, loose-sleeved sweater and black tights stood before him with folded arms. "Rooms are all rented. If you're selling something, we don't want it." Her voice was deep and gravelly; her black hair was closely cropped, like a boy's.

"I'm looking for Pat Roche."

"She moved."

"Where?"

"She didn't leave a forwarding address."

He gestured over her right shoulder to a row of brass rectangular mailboxes. "Name's still there." A bluff. He couldn't read the names.

"I forgot to take it off. Thanks for reminding me."

"I need to talk to her. That's all."

"Wish I could help, but can't. So long."

He planted his foot on the door sill. "Make it worth your while."

Her right hand rushed up the left sleeve of her sweater and withdrew a letter-opener-sized knife, with a shiny blade that looked as if it could double as an ice pick. "Move that foot or else you'll be sorry you ever rang my bell."

Stepping back, he put up his hands. "Hey, no need to…"

"It's all right, Maria." Behind him, a woman carrying a bag of groceries came up the stoop. Topped by a brown beret, her long, olive-skinned face was vaguely suggestive of an acorn. She stepped past Dunne and handed the bag to Maria. "I'll take it from here. Why don't you get dinner started?"

"Want this, Pat?" Maria held out the knife. "He tried to stick his foot in the door."

"I don't need it, do I, Mister . . . ?"

"Dunne. Fintan Dunne. You Pat Roche?"

"Let's talk about it inside," she said. "It's cold out here."

He followed her into the closet-sized vestibule. Maria went through the inner door without another word, the knife handle accessibly sticking out of the top of the bag.

She took a pack of cigarettes from the pocket of her blue pea coat and looked him up and down. "You're not a cop, obviously. Maria would be in handcuffs if you were. No book bag or sample case, so you're not a salesman." He accepted the cigarette she offered, shared the flame of her gold lighter. "The gas man doesn't wear a suit, and if you were wearing a better suit, I'd say you were a lawyer. If you had a partner, you might even be one of those holy rollers in search of converts, but you're solo. Only one other possibility. Private investigator."

"You should be in the business."

"Except girls aren't allowed, are they?"

"No such rule."

"Not in writing, just in practice. I know why you're here."

"Why?"

"Marty sent you." The cigarette tip flared like a tail light in the dimness. She exhaled and drew the smoke up her nose. "Marty the Grocery King wants to verify I'm living in Park Slope with another woman. 'Boston marriage' is the polite term. 'Dyke duet' is less polite but more popular."

"Don't know Marty."

"Look, let's drop the disguises. Tell his highness he can have his annulment, divorce, whatever. He should feel free to go ahead and marry the virgin martyr he's chosen to serve as consort for the chief of the Delfino Foods Corporation. Tell him he doesn't have to waste his money on a detective. He doesn't have to pay me a dime so long as I never have to see or hear from him again."

Down the stoop, by the curb, in a lone square of earth, was a frail, wasted sapling. The bark at its base was stripped away. A car attempted to parallel park and backed into it. She opened the door and stuck her head out. "Hey, asshole, watch the tree!" She turned and looked at him. Her pupils were the color of dark chocolate. "Do me a favor, will you? Tell Marty, that miserable cocksucker, I'd rather take my chances on the meanest street in this borough than spend another minute in the same room as him."

"I don't work for him, Miss Roche. Here on another matter entirely."

"And that'd be what?"

"Crater case."

Her long, thin face was severe and glum. No makeup. But clear, smooth skin. The remnant of an angular beauty. "You're not kidding, are you?"

"Just a few questions. No notes. No quotes. I won't bother you again."

She dropped her cigarette on the black-and-white tiled floor, covered it with the toe of her shoe and pirouetted. "Who gives a fuck about Joe Crater anymore?"

"My client."

"Who else besides your client?"

"That's his business. Mine is to look for leads that might've been overlooked in the original investigation."

"Nothing was overlooked. Crater was a greedy, crooked politician and all-around prick. Problem was there were so many leads and so many suspects with so many good motives, cops could never narrow down the field to a manageable number."

"You and Sam Hechtman were the last to see him alive."

"We were never suspects."

"What were you?"

"Ask the cops. I said all I have to say on the subject twenty-five years ago. You like ancient history? Go buy a shovel and dig for dinosaurs in Prospect Park. Meanwhile, I have to help Maria get dinner ready."

"Was Hechtman your boyfriend or your pimp?"

She turned around and unlocked the inner door. "Fuck you, Dunne."

"Look, I appreciate you were in a tough spot back then."

"No, you don't. You can't know what it was like. More and more girls, fewer and fewer shows. That summer, something like 2,000 showed up to try out for Earl Carroll's 'Vanities.' He made them audition nude. Earl's motto was 'Women don't want to be loved. They want to be taken, ruled and raped.' He was true to his word."

"You worked for the Schumann Organization, no?"

"The Schumann brothers weren't any different. Tryouts for their 'Artists & Models' review wasn't show business. It was a slave market."

"What part did Hechtman play?"

"Sam wasn't the worst. For starters, he preferred boys to girls. But as chief lawyer for the Schumanns, his job was keeping judges and pols well disposed. You know the old saying. 'Better to know the judge than the law.' Crater wasn't the only one. I got set up on a couple dates with Judge Traglia. A certified caveman."

"Was Sam setting you up with Crater that night?"

"No way. I bumped into Sam earlier. He asked me if I wanted to grab a bite. He was as surprised as me when Crater walked in, especially since we'd just been talking about him. Sam had told me Elaine Dove, my ex-roommate, was in the hospital with the clap. He guessed Crater gave it to her. The guy was a dirt bag. Handed out infections like Santa's candy canes. Some girls couldn't take it. One committed suicide." She slipped the key out of the lock and stepped from the vestibule into the hallway. "All on the record, Dunne, and has been for twenty-five years. If I was you, I'd get another client."

"What about the cab Crater got into?"

"What about it?"

"Anything."

"Tan, like lots of other cabs."

"Could it've been waiting down the block for Crater to leave the restaurant?"

"How would I know? Ask the cabbie."

"What do you remember about him?"

"Who?"

"The cabbie. You told the police you saw the back of his head."

"He wore a cap. Didn't turn around."

"Nothing else?"

"Oh, for Christ's sake, it was dark. It wasn't like Sam or me was soaking up every detail because we had an inkling Crater was about to vanish from the face of the earth."

"Thin neck or thick? Shape of head?"

"Maybe his ears bent. Or maybe it was just his right ear. There. Are you happy?"

"Bent how?"

"Stuck out. At least that's the impression I had. I can't be sure. I could only see one side of his head. Tell you what, stop by in another twenty-five years and I'll tell you what else I can remember." She closed the door. The lock snapped into place with a metallic *click*.

Dunne called Nan Renard when he got back to his room. She'd left for the day. He had her home number but didn't try. He rang Mulholland. No answer. He ordered dinner from room service and ate by himself. Instead of watching television, he had several Scotches, smoked, stared out the glass doors at the graceful, generously spaced city above the cheek-to-cheek hodgepodge of people and buildings below: crenellated towers, spires, temples, glass conservatories, electric glow of their windows hanging like stars in the black, motionless sky. From here, New York was serene, graceful, imperial, no sign of Crow's (and Dante's) *citta dolente*, Gene Halloway's mortal stab wound, Alexander Von Vogt's broken heart, Pat Roche's well-earned bitterness.

He went out on the terrace, rested his forearms on the ledge and looked down. Banked by the park wall on one side and buildings on the other, the reassuring hum of traffic was interrupted by honks, occasional screech of brakes, distant siren whine. A fragment from the *Salve Regina* came to him, a prayer they said every morning at the Protectory, the only one he ever found comfort in: *To thee do we cry . . . mourning and weeping in this vale of tears.*

Crow's reluctance to pry open the Crater case was understandable. A city with sufficient mourning and weeping as it was. No need to add old tears to new. But the relatively short time he'd spent filling in the background was enough to convince him an answer wasn't out of reach. No crime was a riddle beyond solution, a mystery with no answer. The culprit or culprits had the answer all along. The phantom cab and the thoroughness with which Crater disappeared made it probable that more than one person was involved. His gut told him they weren't all dead or moved away. The only question was whether it was too late to gather the pieces to the puzzle, as well as how far those with the answers would go to stop the poeple trying to find them.

The room felt overheated when he came back inside. Too much Scotch didn't help. He put the bottle away, turned on the TV and fell promptly asleep in a wing chair. Awoke in the morning with a stiff neck. He finished his usual breakfast of coffee and toast, and remembered he hadn't talked to Roberta since he arrived. He had the hotel operator place a long-distance person-to-person call.

The operator connected him. "Honey," he said, "sorry I didn't call sooner."

A male voice on the other end, foreign sounding, said, "Roberta is not here, Mr. Dunne."

"Who's this?"

"This is Felipe."

"Who?"

"Felipe Calderon, your dance instructor."

"Where the hell is Roberta?" He hadn't intended to sound annoyed.

"The store. She says if you call while she is gone, I am to answer and tell you to try again tonight."

He looked at the clock: just after nine. "What store?"

"Food."

"Breakfast?"

"No, no. Food for the *excursion*."

"The what?"

"You know, the, eh, picnic. The class, we are all going to the park by the river. I am driving Roberta."

"Tell her I phoned." He moderated his tone. "I'll try again later."

Soon as he hung up, he called the front desk and had them send up the masseur, a hulking Norwegian who worked with slow intensity to erase the pain in his neck that had grown worse during the brief phone call. He took a hot shower when the massage was finished and lay down for a few minutes to enjoy its effects. Wouldn't say he was upset that Felipe answered the phone. Surprised, that's all. Probably Roberta's way of letting him know she was peeved he hadn't called earlier. Couldn't blame her.

He schlepped to the Bronx on the IRT. First appointment was with Robert Emmet Murphy, a retired cop living in Parkchester with his ninety-year-old mother. Crow set it up. Murphy had been transferred from the Traffic Division to Missing Persons in the early days and weeks of the case, he explained, "to work under Allie Von Vogt. Allie would go out with two or three of us. We'd concentrate on a certain neighborhood, follow up all the reports of Crater sightings. And believe me, there was no shortage. Seemed Crater had Santa Claus' knack for being everywhere at once. Then Allie would sit down and go over them. Anything that showed any possibility, he'd personally revisit."

Murphy didn't mask his skepticism about the odds of turning up anything new. "The man to talk to is Von Vogt. Best cop I ever worked with. He had more than his share of tragedy, poor guy. But nobody was smarter or better informed on the Crater case. Problem is, I know Allie and there's no way he's ever going to talk to you."

He took a cab to Kingsbridge to have lunch in a German restaurant on 231st Street with Bernie Sampson, who'd been Crater's law secretary. A retired Municipal Court judge and former Democratic district leader, thin and smartly dressed, Sampson went short on food and long on drinks. Sampson liked to talk and was filled with amusing stories, the predictable M.O. of a widowed jurist who lived alone and missed delivering monologues from the bench. Didn't have anything new to add about the case, except he wasn't ready to rule out the possibility Crater had engineered his own disappearance.

"He was sighted all over the country. Not that it meant anything in the Depression, since if a reward was involved, people would've reported seeing King Kong on their neighbor's roof. On the other hand, maybe they weren't all making it up. He became a kind of cult figure among the hoboes and all those who joined them on the road in the worst of those years. They actually sang a song about him, 'The Ballad of Judge Joe.' It had a verse that went, 'Was a wife, a life left you weary/ Judge Joe, Judge Joe, you're forever free."

Last time he saw Crater was when he stopped into his chambers the morning he disappeared. "He looked depressed. Strike that. He looked o-ppressed. The possibility of an investigation, money, women, work, all the usual baggage weighed on him. And, remember, those weren't happy days for anybody." Sampson ordered his fourth martini. "He was a very smart man—don't let anyone try to tell you differently—and entirely capable of masterminding his own escape." He gazed out the window of the restaurant. "Wouldn't that be delicious? Us stuck in our routines and him 'forever free.' If that's the case, then I say, 'Good for you, Joe.' At least somebody got away."

Traveling downtown on the Broadway subway, Dunne got off at 149th Street to visit Fred Kipps at Melancthon Manor, the Lutheran old people's home where he'd been living for the last few years. He found the five-story brick building a block west of Broadway, the outside grimy and worn, inside spic-and-span bright. The head nurse, a tall, starched blonde with Shirley Temple dimples, was friendly but inquisitive. *What was his connection to Mr. Kipps? Did he know any of his family? How long since he'd last seen him?*

Dunne didn't bring up the Crater case nor mention that though their careers on the NYPD had overlapped for a few years, he and Kipps never met. Said he was an ex-cop who lived in Florida now. On a visit to New York. Staying at the Savoy Plaza. Let her fill in the rest.

"You're the first of his police acquaintances to stop by," she said, "and you might be somewhat surprised by his appearance. He had a stroke two years ago, and I'm afraid his condition has deteriorated dramatically. As I'm sure you know, he was shell shocked in the First World War, which hasn't helped."

"I honestly can't remember the last time I saw him."

"Mr. Kipps doesn't have many visitors. His only daughter lives in L.A. It's been quite some time since she came to see him. She phones at Christmas and Easter, but Mr. Kipps can no longer speak. Until very recently he could scratch a few words on a pad with his left hand, but lately he's stopped doing even that."

"I won't stay long." He wished a ready excuse for backing out of the visit came to mind, but it didn't. "Just pay my respects."

"Stay as long as you like. Though he might not be able to express it, Mr. Kipps will appreciate every minute you spend with him. All our patients welcome company. The sad fact is, the lack of it shortens their lives."

The ancient elevator wheezed and creaked its way to the top floor. Directly across the hall was Kipps's room. Slumped in a wheelchair facing the window, he was bent over so far he appeared at first to be headless. The nurse put her hand on his forearm, rubbed it with a slow, gentle touch. "Mr. Kipps," she said, "you have a visitor. An old friend from the police force, Mr. Fintan Dunne." She rolled the wheelchair back a short distance from the window, reached her hands beneath his armpits and propped him up.

Lifting a chair by the wall an inch or two from the floor, careful not to scratch the linoleum, she placed it next to him and rubbed his arm once more. "And, Mr. Kipps, in case you get the inclination." She took a pad and pencil from the pocket of her uniform and laid the pad in his lap. "I brought you this." She folded his fingers around the pencil. "There. Now let me leave you two old friends together so you can have a nice visit."

Kipps stared at the pad in his lap. There wasn't much left of the round, beefy figure whose picture ran on the front page of the *Standard* twenty-five years before when he'd railed at reporters to stop hounding Mrs. Crater ("Judge's Chauffeur Calls Mrs. Crater 'An Angel'"). Sunken chest. Hollow cheeks. Gray strands plastered to a white, freckled skull.

Dunne raised the window a few inches, let a sliver of cold air slip into the room, and lit a cigarette. Kipps raised his head, sniffed. Dunne put the cigarette to Kipps's lips. The hollows in his cheeks deepened as he inhaled. Dunne repeated the process until Kipps dropped his head. Tossing the butt out the window, he sat beside Kipps, who leaned back and gazed into his face. Kipps's left eye was almost closed; the right, closest to Dunne, was wide as a fried egg, blue yoke surrounded by blood-shot white. Hard to tell what the mind behind it was thinking. Or not thinking. Maybe only the fair and obvious question: *Who the hell are you?*

"Well, Fred," Dunne said as if in answer, "like you, I'm an ex-cop, but we've never met. So here's the deal. I'll gab, you do whatever you like, and we'll call it a visit." Kipps showed no reaction. Dunne laid out the story of his involvement with the Crater investigation, from Mulholland's phone call to his interview with Wilkes, Nan Renard's role, research and reading he'd done. Felt almost like going to confession.

He lit another cigarette. No use in offering a drag to Kipps, who seemed to be asleep. In the distance, atop the Palisades, a lustrous reddish-blue winter sunset was reminiscent of that last visit with Izzy Bleier, late winter 1941, in the Veterans Hospital outside Poughkeepsie. Izzy looked up at the sky with a faint spark in his eyes, the hint of momentary ignition, but the engine wouldn't turn over.

Hometown hero of the Lower East Side and one-time middle-weight contender, Izzy had been buried alive for several minutes during the German offensive at the Aisne, in May 1918, by the same shell that wiped out the rest of his company. Another shell blew him free. Spent the next twenty-two years sitting by the window, elbows planted on armrests, palms pressed against ears. He went the week after Pearl Harbor. There were five people at his memorial service in a dinky synagogue on Madison Street. Old soldiers never die. They just rot away, alone and dazed, in hospital rooms.

Wasn't until the nurse pressed her hand down on his shoulder that he realized he'd fallen asleep. Evening had arrived. She turned on the light by the bed and whispered, "It's wonderful you've spent all this time, Mr. Dunne, simply wonderful. Now I wonder if I could impose on you to help me lift Mr. Kipps into bed?"

She turned the sheet down, fluffed the pillow, and deftly

maneuvered the wheelchair up to the bed. In one quick motion, each taking a firm grip on an arm, they lifted him up and sat him on the mattress. She guided his head onto the pillow as Dunne raised the legs, removed the slippers and covered him with the sheet and blanket. Walking over to the window, she reached down and picked up the pad, which had fallen to the floor. "Well, look at this," she said softly. "He's written something." She handed the pad to Dunne. "How encouraging."

On it, printed in a wobbly, spidery hand, was a simple, almost indecipherable word.

He gave the pad back. "I can't make it out without my glasses. What's it say?"

"Let's see." She held it at arm's length and squinted. "Looks to me like 'taxi.' Were you talking to him about taxis?"

"I might have mentioned one."

Head resting in the center of the pillow, eyes shut, mouth agape, Kipps let out a loud snore. Standing at the bottom of the bed, Dunne noticed for the first time that there was a pronounced bent to one of Kipps's ears. His right ear stuck out.

First thing in the morning was a phone conversation with Sam Hechtman. They arranged to meet later that afternoon, after five. Dunne lay back down on the bed. Hadn't gone to sleep till almost dawn. Kept going over the visit with Kipps. By itself, a bent ear wouldn't mean much; but that word Kipps had obviously gone to such effort to produce, what was it? A random thought that wandered out of his wrecked brain? A regurgitated fragment of the recounting of the Crater story that he'd just heard? Or a final enfeebled attempt at confession?

He looked at the notes he'd taken while reading Stella Crater's account. Hadn't paid close attention to Kipps's role the first time around. Now he did. After Kipps drives her to Lake

Belvedere, he leaves the car and goes off on a vacation of his own. Doesn't return until August 13th, a week after Crater vanishes. Ex-cop and chauffeur, he doesn't seem upset or even very curious when Stella tells him she hasn't heard from Joe in nine days. Pats her shoulder and pours her a shot of whisky, like a cop might do at the wake of another cop. When she asks him to drive her to New York, he talks her out of going and goes himself, but doesn't contact the police, all the while letting the trail get colder.

She hears nothing from Kipps until a special delivery letter arrives, offering her the slender assurance that *everything looks okay* at their apartment, and though he hasn't seen the judge himself, *nobody seems worried about your husband of them I talked to.* He returns afterwards, tending to Mrs. Crater's frayed nerves by offering her tugs on his flask and finally, at her insistence, driving her to New York on August 29th, only to encourage her to take the advice of Det. Luke Ruppert and return to Lake Belvedere two days later.

Dunne skipped breakfast, showered and dressed, ready to try Roberta again, when the phone rang. Nan Renard's secretary wanted to know if he could meet Miss Renard for dinner at the Coral, at eight that night. He agreed. Instead of calling Roberta, he took the subway to police headquarters and went right to Crow's office. Didn't bring up his visit with Kipps the previous day, but pressed Crow for what he remembered about him.

"Sad case," Crow said. "Left the department to join the army in 1917. Returned a decorated vet and was welcomed back to his old job. Unfortunately, having been gassed or shell shocked, Fred could get a little fuzzy at times, not cracked or scrambled, but vague, a bit slow. Occasionally overfond of the grape. Retired on disability, he was hired by Crater as his driver. Got his name in the papers a few times for championing Mrs. Crater's innocence. When the circus moved on, he dropped out of sight."

"Is there a personnel file on him?"

"As long as he's still alive and getting a pension, there is."

"Could you check?"

"That's a department matter."

"Once a cop, always a . . ."

"Smart cop wouldn't waste his time like this."

"I've got a reputation as a pain in the ass, remember? Don't want to lose it."

Crow shook his head. "Dante put it best. 'A mind sequestered in its own delusions is to reason invincible.' I'll see what I can dig up."

In the record room, Dunne combed through the files to find the references to Fred Kipps that he'd previously skimmed. The interview with Detectives Fitzgerald and Moon was dated September 7, 1930. Kipps, they noted, was entirely cooperative and vigorous in his insistence on Mrs. Crater's innocence. He accounted for his movements between the time he dropped off Mrs. Crater in Lake Belvedere and his return six weeks later, stating he stayed with his mother at her bungalow in Rockaway. (Penned in the margin of the report was the notation "Confirmed, phone conversation, Mrs. Bertha Kipps, 9/9/30.")

Kipps told Fitzgerald and Moon he never imagined anything bad had happened to Judge Crater. Certain that Crater was involved in "the usual political shenanigans," which he wanted to steer clear of, he returned to the city in August mostly just to calm Mrs. Crater's nerves. The only people he talked to were the Craters' colored maid and "some court officers." Nobody seemed very concerned. Last two days of the trip he spent in "McGurk's, a speak on Lexington and 43rd Street." (Confirmed in person by Det. Moon in an interview with Jerry McGurk, proprietor and bartender, 9/11/30.)

It didn't seem likely Kipps carried off an abduction as professional as Crater's by himself. But if he'd been an accomplice, whoever chose him chose wisely. He was perfect for the role. Total access to Crater's movements. Trusted by both Crater and his wife. Well liked by his former colleagues in the department who not only felt a little sorry for him but would, as a matter of course, give him the benefit of the doubt. It would have been easy to have slipped out of his mother's bungalow on August 6th to drive the taxi.

But where would he get it? And what would he do with it afterwards? And what possible motive could Kipps have for agreeing to be an accomplice? There was no ransom involved. He didn't seem to bear a grudge against Crater and was genuinely protective of Mrs. Crater. Crater in turn seemed to have relied on Kipps. Why else would he have kept him on as his driver after Kipps accidentally slammed the car door on his finger? So what stake did Kipps have in seeing Crater removed? Whatever the answers, whether they implicated him or not, Fred Kipps was no longer in any condition to offer anything more than a word haltingly printed on a piece of paper.

Late afternoon, he went back to see Crow. "There's next to nothing in those files about the cab Crater got into," he said.

"For good reason. All anybody was able to turn up was 'next to nothing.'"

"I talked with Patti Leroche. She got a fleeting glimpse of the back of the cabby's head. Said his right ear stuck out."

"Matter of fact, if I remember correctly, she wasn't sure if it was only his right ear, since she could only see that side, and Sam Hechtman couldn't even corroborate that impression. Just so you know, a couple of detectives spent weeks interviewing cabbies on duty that night. You'd be surprised at how many taxi drivers in New York have an ear—or two—off kilter. In the end it went nowhere, like everything connected to the case."

Sam Hechtman's law office was on Third Avenue and 101st Street, a second-floor walk-up above a bowling alley. Hechtman's cubicle, the only enclosed space in the long, capacious, desk-filled room, was situated at alley's end. Knowing that Patti Leroche had probably warned Hechtman what was up, Dunne didn't try to catch him unaware.

When he'd called that morning, Hechtman's secretary put him right through. "Mr. Dunne," he said, "I believe you've already spoken to Patti Leroche—or whatever the hell name she goes by now."

"Pat Roche."

"I'm not mistaken, she recommended you go fuck yourself."

"Words to that effect."

"Well, I second her recommendation."

Dunne expected Hechtman might hang up, but he didn't. He stayed on for several minutes to rehash the raw deal he got from the Schumann brothers, how despite the transparent irrationality of it, they blamed him for being with Crater the night he disappeared, which unleashed a torrent of noxious press stories quoting anonymous showgirls and disgruntled actors about what sex-crazed skinflints the Schumann brothers were. "They acted as if I'd deliberately decided to be with Crater that night, as if I knew what was about to happen and could have avoided it. Of course, they kept me on long as they needed my help, but the minute business got better, it was, 'so long, Sam Hechtman.'"

Mid-sixties, frail, with skin wizened from one-too-many suntans, Hechtman didn't have to be prompted or provoked to tell what he knew. Lit a cigar, put his feet up on the desk and, after Dunne turned down his offer of a shot of rye, poured one for himself; he knocked it back and poured another. "Joe Crater was no schlemiel. Don't let anyone tell you different. Then as now, there were a lot of putzheads on the bench, but he wasn't among them. He was smart, very smart. Remember, he wasn't from the city but from some one-pump, hayseed burg in Pennsylvania. He could have returned there after finishing law school, been a lawyer for the railroads, town big shot, mayor or something, elder in the church, Republican county leader, maybe run for the Congress. But he stayed in New York, joined Tammany, a Daniel in the lion's den. He volunteered in a club, worked the polls and proved himself an ace at arguing New York's election laws. That led to him being made the law secretary to a Tammany bigwig, which led to him being recommended to the governor for an appointment to the Supreme Court at the tender age of forty."

Without being asked, Hechtman started on what he remembered of the night of August 6, 1930. "Wasn't as if me and Patti Leroche started out by asking, 'What makes this night different from all other nights?' It was as dull as a Saturday in Philadelphia. Never noticed if a taxi was waiting at the end of the block."

"What about the cabbie?"

"Never saw him."

"Patti Leroche caught a glimpse. She thought his right ear was bent."

"Bent, schment. You been a professional snoop long enough to know all about 'eyewitnesses.' They're about as reliable as a paper hat in a hurricane. Usually remember seeing what's been suggested they remember or what they *thought* they saw or what'll satisfy whoever it is needs satisfying. We couldn't agree on what kind of hat Crater was wearing when he said goodbye. I could swear it was brown felt. She swore it was a Panama. We both saw what we saw. I'm not saying Patti Leroche is a liar. But the screws were turned pretty tight on us to come up with something useful. Not being a lawyer, Patti felt the pressure worse than me."

Hechtman re-lit the cigar. "What you got to admire about

whoever did the Crater job is how professional it was. These weren't amateurs. Forget about Tammany having Crater killed to keep him quiet. Tammany had a lot of tricks, but murder wasn't among them. Except for hardcore right-wingers and Coughlinites, nobody believes F.D.R. arranged it to hush up a scandal." He finished his second shot of rye and poured another.

This time Dunne joined him. "Patti Leroche says you told her Elaine Dove, her ex-roommate, was in the hospital with the clap, and you guessed Crater gave it to her."

"Crater couldn't keep his schvantz still—this is news? Had plenty of company in that department. But this was no crime of passion by a jilted lover. This was as cold and premeditated as it gets. It takes a pro to erase every shred of evidence, never mind a cab, and it takes the mob to enforce a code of total silence. There were some smart cops on this case. Any slip-ups, they'd have jumped on them. But there weren't any, which means it was the mob. At some point, Crater must have crossed them. What that was—what he did or didn't do to get them to act—is buried under *omertà*. My advice? Let it lie. Otherwise, if by some miracle you find the answer, it's going to be the last thing you do on earth."

Hechtman gulped his rye. Devoid of the reluctance that others had to revisit his involvement with Crater, he'd come to his own conclusions and wasn't interested in entertaining anybody else's. (He had to be reminded of who Fred Kipps was.) When he polished off another rye and started repeating himself, Dunne said he had a dinner appointment to keep. Hechtman escorted him past half a dozen desks stacked high with folders. "I employ five lawyers," he said. "Second-raters to a man. But this is volume work mostly, two-bit personal injury, routine landlord and tenant. The big ones, the ones that go to trial, I take myself."

He went ahead of Dunne down the stairs and yelled at a

group of leather-jacketed teenagers loitering in the doorway. They strolled away at a leisurely pace, their greased-back hair glistening under the street lamp. He went outside without a coat and picked up the candy wrappers that the teenagers had littered on the ground. Wide flashy suspenders and garters on his sleeves gave him a dated look.

"Everything went to shit after Crater disappeared." He chewed and twisted the cigar stump, rolling it from one side of his mouth to the other. "The economy. The city. The world. But Broadway took the biggest hit. The minute Wall Street went bust, financing for plays dried up. The action moved to Hollywood. Broadway survived, but wasn't the old Broadway no more. Theatres became movie palaces and grindhouses. Great White Way went gray, tawdry and cheap, no different from Coney Island. The golden age was over, and Joe Crater wasn't around to see the end. Lucky him." He crushed the litter in his fist and went back inside without another word.

The Coral was less crowded than the last time. He arrived early. Had a drink at the bar. The fish tank held two miniature sharks. They moved slowly, in concentric circles. Nan Renard tapped him lightly on the shoulder. "Mr. Malaconda, I presume." Her face was as lovely as he remembered, but tired.

"Mala*coda*."

A slender, fleeting smile crossed her lips. "Was that a test?"

"You passed."

"Some day, when there's time, you'll have to fill me in. Let's sit."

She signaled to the maitre d'. He led them to the same rear booth as before. A waiter placed drinks in front of them without even being asked.

"Long day?" Dunne asked.

"Endless. I'm not even sure what day it is. Tuesday?"

"Close. Yesterday was Tuesday." He picked up the flower floating in the oyster-shaped bowl at the center of the table. "Here, this orchid is for you."

"It's not an orchid. I don't know what it is. But it's delicate and beautiful." She put it to her nose and sniffed. "The fragrance makes me think of funerals."

"Let's think of other things." He raised his glass.

"I can't have more than one. I'll fall asleep and have to be carried home." She tapped her glass to his. "You look tan and rested."

"Few more days, I'll be as pale and spent as everybody else."

"I wasn't sure you'd come back." She placed the flower back in the bowl.

"Did my homework."

"What'd you find?"

"Not much."

She sighed and closed her eyes, lush, mascara-brushed lashes fluttering, as though fighting back tears. "I'm under more pressure than you can imagine. You saw Mr. Wilkes's persuasive, gentlemanly side. When it comes to getting what he wants, he's not always so calm and reasonable. Crater is a long shot, at best. Maybe it's time to focus on some other cover piece for launching *Snap*, something less far-fetched."

"Maybe." Using the candle, he lit two cigarettes and handed her one. "But maybe not. It isn't as if some supernatural force whisked Crater away. There was a well-thought-out plan. Cops were beset by all sorts of distractions, false leads and bad luck. The case became a tangle of loose ends. But time cuts both ways. As well as dimming memories and obscuring clues, it can simplify and clarify. Grab hold of the right loose end, it becomes the missing thread."

"Which loose end?" She brushed her hair back. The fatigue left her face.

"Can't say yet."

"You mean *won't*."

"I mean it's too soon."

"So Mulholland's right; you are the luckiest investigator alive."

"I'm working on it."

"On being lucky?"

"On staying alive."

She finished her drink. "We've reason to celebrate."

"Let's have another."

"Another reason to celebrate?"

"Another drink."

"You'll carry me home?" The gentle shine of candlelight gave her skin a golden hue.

"I've had worse assignments." Turning to signal the waiter, he scanned her face. Her eyes had the same intensity he remembered from that night in Wilkes's apartment.

One drink turned into two. When they left the Coral, it was misty, warm, spring-like. She slipped her arm into his. They reached the entrance of her building. "Promised to carry me all the way home, remember?"

"We're there."

"The National Safety Council claims that nine out of ten serious accidents take place in the home. What if I fall on the way to bed?"

"Be sure you fall *onto* the bed."

Her laugh had the raucous pitch of someone not quite drunk but not quite sober. She put her arms around his neck, kissed him on the lips. He kissed her back, long and hard enough so the doorman turned away and pretended not to watch. "I knew you'd come back," she whispered. "I knew you'd see this to the end. That's the kind of man you are."

She went into the building. Almost called out to invite himself up for a nightcap. But didn't. Roamed aimlessly, not tired, enjoying the unseasonable warmth, the moist kiss of dense night air. New York felt like his city again. Not a ghost town, but alive with excitement and possibility that belonged to him as much as anyone.

Part V

Just the Facts: An excerpt from Erwin Schrödinger, *What Is Life? The Physical Aspect of the Living Cell, with Mind and Matter and Autobiographical Sketches* (New York: Cambridge University Press, 1992).

Every scientist knows how difficult it is to remember a moderately large group of facts, before at least some primitive theoretical picture about them has been shaped. It is therefore small wonder, and by no means to be blamed on the authors of original papers or textbooks, that after a reasonably coherent theory has been formed, they do not describe bare facts they have found or wish to convey to the reader, but clothe them in the terminology of that theory or theories. This procedure, while very useful for remembering the facts in a well-ordered pattern, tends to obliterate the distinction between the actual observation and the theory arisen from them. And since the former always are of some sensual quality, theories are easily thought to account for sensual qualities, which, of course, they never do.

New York City

"... This deceitful world whose vanities
Win many souls and ruin all they win."

—DANTE, *Paradiso,* Canto XV

THE WAITER WHO DELIVERED BREAKFAST HANDED OVER THREE letters received at the front desk. Recognizing Roberta's distinctive script, Dunne opened hers first. Brief note. Curt and cold. *Fin, going to Tampa to visit Elba and her kids. Felipe Calderon has offered to drive. We need to talk when you get back. Roberta.*

He sat on the bed and reread the note several times. Ready to pick up the phone, he resisted. A call would solve nothing. He took the Bible from the night table drawer, opened it and stuck in the note. A match he'd used as a bookmark fell out at the verse Mulholland recommended. He wasn't sure if his eyes flashed on it or he simply recalled it: *vanity of vanities, all is vanity . . .*

He avoided looking at his reflection in the mirror above the bureau; couldn't avoid the question: *what kind of man?* Felt like a foolish adolescent even asking but knew the answer: the kind Nan Renard thought he was, the kind who'd see this to the end. Afterward, he'd answer the other questions.

The second, postmarked Far Rockaway, was a reply from Allie Von Vogt to the letter Crow suggested sending. Von Vogt, it seemed, not only "respected forthrightness" but practiced it. His note was even briefer than Roberta's. And colder. *I will not speak to you under any circumstances, so don't even try.*

In the last envelope, folded inside a piece of official ISC stationery, was a ticket to the Golden Gloves quarter-finals that evening at Madison Square Garden. Louie Pohl had scribbled a brief message: *See you there! It's important!*

He put the ticket in his wallet. He guessed that Pully wanted an update on the deal with Wilkes and some reassurance that ISC's interests weren't being unduly compromised. He'd put him off, if he could, except with the debt he already owed Pully for his assistance and advice, a ticket to the Garden was as good as a summons. Besides, it beat sitting around watching TV and sipping Scotch. Maybe there'd be a real boxer in the mix, somebody worth watching.

Late morning, he left the hotel on the way to pay Stella Crater a visit. Hoping if possible to get a spontaneous, unrehearsed version of events, he didn't call ahead. He stopped at police headquarters on the way downtown to check with Crow on the Kipps file. Crow was in his office. "I know what you're here for, and I don't have it. But I got something else that should make you happy."

He flipped a piece of paper across the desk. Dunne picked it up: the report from September 7, 1930, that he couldn't find in the files. Three separate street addresses were listed, each followed by a paragraph about why it had been visited, who'd been interviewed and what, if anything, of interest was found. (In all cases, the leads had proved false.) Each paragraph bore a separate set of initials: R.E.M., A.I.M., F.X.T. At the bottom, it was signed in full by Det. Alexander Von Vogt.

Crow grinned. "I told you it was in there somewhere. Had a clerk look. Found it in with the newspaper clippings."

"Whose initials are these?" Dunne asked.

"Let me see."

Dunne handed him back the paper.

"God knows. There was any number of cops who volunteered or were dragooned into helping the Missing Persons Squad during those days. F.X.M.? Francis Xavier Somebody. R.E.M.? My guess is that's Robert Emmet Murphy. I know he worked the case. A.I.M.? Got me. Von Vogt would probably know, but after all these years, he might have trouble himself."

Stella Crater, five years younger than her beloved Joe, was sixty and worked part-time as a secretary at the Health Department office on Seventh Avenue and Clarkson Street. After Joe was officially declared dead, she'd been able to collect on his insurance. Along with her job, it was enough to allow a modest existence in a small apartment on Downing Street. (The cabin at Lake Belvedere was sold years before, at the depths of the Depression, for half what Joe paid for it.)

At first, she'd been accessible to anyone who wanted to talk about (or, more often than not, listen to) her take on her husband's disappearance. But as the years went by, and the stories became fewer but more sensational, with detective and true crime magazines competing to outdo each other in their lurid accounts of Joe's supposed connections to mobsters, madams, swindlers, etc., Stella Crater stopped talking to the press. The last clip on her in the *Standard*'s file was a brief piece dated August 6, 1945, the fifteenth anniversary of the case—and the day the atomic bomb was dropped on Hiroshima: "Judge Crater's Missus Still Keeps Vigil/ Says 'Joe Was a Hero.'"

Dunne had a cup of coffee and a sfogliatelle at an Italian bakery across from the office where she worked. At noon, when the office closed for lunch, she wasn't hard to pick out from the people leaving the building: face predictably older than in the newspaper photographs but easily recognizable; coat, shoes and hat neat but entirely out of fashion, very possibly part of her wardrobe since the days when Joe was on the scene.

He left the bakery and followed her. Passers-by took no notice of the woman once featured in headlines and newsreels, and besieged by a trainload of reporters. Trim, meticulous, slow-moving, in out-of-date clothing that gave her the air of a widow or spinster in no hurry to get to the rooms (or room) where she lived alone, she appeared a full-fledged citizen of the yesterday city, unnoticed and unmissed.

She stopped to look in the window of a florist. He stood next to her. Speaking in a soft, friendly voice, so as not to startle her, he said, "Excuse me, but are you Stella Crater?"

She gazed at his mirrored reflection in the window. "And you are?"

"Fintan Dunne." He tipped his hat. "I'm a private investigator. I've been hired to look into your husband's case."

"Is that so?" Instead of startled, she seemed serene. "By whom?"

"Someone sincerely interested in what happened to your husband."

"'Sincerely interested'? I've heard that before. She turned and looked at him. "What is it you want?"

"To discuss some aspects of the case."

"It's all on the record." She went back to looking at his faint image in the glass.

"I've read the record, police files, newspapers and your articles in the *Standard*."

"And what did you learn?"

"Enough to know that the investigation was botched from start to finish."

"The world's known that for twenty-five years." She resumed her stroll.

He fell in beside her. "But the case isn't without an answer."

"I agree with you there."

"Whoever was behind it was careful to erase the trail."

"And successful."

"Until now."

She stopped in the middle of the sidewalk, took a step back. In bright sunlight, the dusting of powder, rouged cheeks and cherry-colored lips gave her face a doll-like quality. "And *you* have the answer?" Her sharp, contentious tone didn't match the face.

"Only the person or persons behind the disappearance have the answer. But others, some without knowing, have the pieces that, when fit together, form an answer."

"And you think I'm one?"

"I think you recorded the facts exactly as you experienced them."

"I'm immune to flattery, Mr. Dunne."

"Is it flattery to point out your story has been dismissed as the deluded fantasies of a hysterical wife?"

"You share that view?"

"No, but the police do."

"You've talked with the police?"

"I've met with Captain Cronin, at Missing Persons."

The one they call 'Crow'?"

"None other."

"Typical of his ilk."

"I don't agree with him on this case. But he's an honest cop."

"It's his timidity that disturbs me. Always quoting Dante. I think of him as less a crow than as the raven of Edgar Allen Poe's poem. 'Quoth the raven, *Nevermore.*' If you ask me, he's afraid of repeating the mistakes of his predecessors. He'd rather do nothing than risk being unsuccessful. That was his attitude as well as the entire police department's to any attempt to get them to persist with the investigation. 'Quoth Crow and his cronies, *Nevermore*.' They don't care who suffers as a consequence."

"I know what you've been through, and it's not my intention to add to your burden. I think your story has never been given the serious scrutiny it deserves."

"Nobody knows what I've been through." She bit her lip and resumed walking, but at a pace slow enough it was obvious she wasn't trying to escape.

He walked beside her. "Maybe not. But I'm not here to add to it. If it's still possible to find the answer, I'll do my best to find it. If not, I'll go away."

"I've learned from experience to be frugal with my trust."

"You know what Ecclesiastes says?" He paraphrased, "There's a time for everything, a time to save, another to spend."

"You read the Bible?"

"On occasion." He felt no need to say what that occasion was. "I'll be upfront with you, Mrs. Crater. I started this job thinking it was a lost cause. But it's not a job anymore. I'm after the truth. I can't guarantee the truth will please you. But isn't that what you've been after all these years: to be done with the uncertainty, to overcome the lies, to know once and for all the truth about what happened to Joe?"

She glanced at her wristwatch. "Perhaps you could come back at a more convenient time?"

"This is as convenient as it gets. I don't have a lot of time."

"I'm on my lunch hour."

"I'll buy you lunch."

"I prefer to eat at home."

"Do as you please. There are a whole lot of other people eager to talk about your husband's case."

After several seconds of hesitant silence, she added, "If you don't mind a peanut-butter-and-jelly sandwich and a cup of tea, you can join me."

Her apartment was up a steep, creaking staircase, on the third floor. Into the small living room was crammed a green-velvet-covered couch in an elaborately carved wooden frame, an easy chair with a similar covering, and a well-worn oriental rug—all that was left, Dunne supposed, of the furnishings from the spacious digs she shared with her husband on Fifth Avenue.

Joe's portrait hung above the bricked-up fireplace. A painted reproduction of the black-and-white photo taken as his official head shot for his campaign posters—same pose, clothes, prominent eyes, sharp nose—it was obviously the work of a less-than-first-rank portraitist. The only liberty he'd taken in reproducing the photo was that, instead of a phantom grin, he'd spread Joe's mouth so wide it resembled the lunatic crescent worn by Steeplechase Jack, the long-time symbol of the Coney Island amusement park.

Dunne supposed it was a clumsy attempt to answer Stella Crater's instruction that Joe be portrayed with the very last expression she'd seen on his face, the "beneficent smile" that "shone like a blessing." But she seemed happy with the result. Pausing reverently in front of it, she said, "That's how I remember him."

She talked the whole time while making the sandwiches and tea, relating her story in practically the same sequence and detail as in the *Standard* articles. Knees almost touching, they ate at a table that just fit in the kitchen. From where he sat, Dunne could see her bed, which was covered with a red-and-white quilt like the one she mentioned lying on in Lake Belvedere.

He interrupted when she mentioned Kipps's name. "What'd you think of him?"

"Of Fred? If ever there was someone who fit the description of 'a diamond in the rough,' it was he." She poured their tea.

"How'd he come to be your chauffeur?"

"We'd just purchased a Chrysler automobile. Neither Joe nor I liked to drive in the city, and his practice was such we could afford a driver."

"Did Joe know Kipps previously?"

"I've no idea. He simply asked around. Someone recommended him, I suspect. He was an ex-policeman. Very reliable. Jobs were already becoming scarce. Fred was grateful for the work."

"When was he hired?"

"I couldn't tell you exactly. It was soon after the crash on Wall Street but before Joe went on the bench. Sometime around the autumn or witnter of 1929."

"Did your husband like him?"

"Joe was upset that one time when he got his finger caught in the car door. But he quickly realized it was his own fault as much as Fred's. He let it pass. Joe had loftier matters to occupy him."

"Did you?"

"Did I what?"

"Like Fred Kipps?"

"Are you suggesting Fred had a role in my husband's disappearance?"

"No. But I was struck by your account of the way he stood by you."

"Yes, he did. Through the whole ordeal." She sipped her tea.

"Did he ever speak to you about what he thought might have happened to Joe?"

"We didn't have that kind of relationship where we talked about such things. He treated me with the utmost respect. Ours was a warm but proper acquaintance." She put down her tea cup and studied the wet leaves at the bottom. "There was once . . ." She stopped herself. "Would you care for more tea?"

"No, thank you. What happened that once?"

"Nothing, really. It was months after Joe disappeared. The police no longer considered me a suspect. I'd put the cabin at Lake Belvedere up for sale and returned to the city. I'd already notified Fred by mail that I could no longer afford a car, never mind a driver. I thanked him for all he'd done and included a check for what we owed him. I was surprised, then, when he showed up one morning at the apartment I'd rented on Bank Street. He wanted to give me back the check. He said I needed it more than he."

She poured herself more tea, added a drop of cream, stirred. "And then he . . . he asked me to marry him." Bowing her head and lifting her apron to her face, she let out three anguished, muffled sobs.

It took her several minutes to compose herself. Finally, she wiped her eyes and had several sips of tea. "I'm sorry to be so emotional."

"Please, don't apologize. I can imagine how difficult this is for you."

"It was all so absurd. A simple man who'd been affected by the war, Fred was so unlike Joe. That's why I was touched. It was the kindest gesture of support I'd received. Silly, of course, but deeply caring."

"How'd he take your refusal?"

"It was a gesture, Mr. Dunne. Fred was already married. I believe he had a daughter. He never expected me to say yes. He felt sorry for me, that's all. I told him how grateful I was, but even if I never saw Joe again, he'd always be my husband. Fred understood. He said that if I ever needed anything, I should call. I've no idea what happened to him after that. I hope he had a happy life and, if he's still alive, enjoying the company of his daughter and her children. He deserved to be happy."

She began to clear the dishes. "I'm afraid that's all I have time for. I can't imagine I've been much help."

"Let me do this," Dunne said.

"Thank you. Just put them in the sink. I'm going to freshen up."

"One more thing. That detective who visited you in Lake Belvedere."

"What about him?"

"The police were skeptical."

"*Skeptical?* I wouldn't have minded them being skeptical. Demeaning, insulting, condescending is more like it. Not satisfied to attack the notion that the person who visited me was a real detective, they spread the word that I was out of my mind, a wounded wife driven over the edge by the pressures put upon her by her husband's disappearance. I must have been under the influence of alcohol and sedatives, a hysteric lost in her own 'deluded fantasies.'"

"I was impressed with how vividly you remembered his visit."

"It was burned into my mind. It still is."

"But the police could find no corroborating evidence?"

"They didn't try."

"Did they ask you to look at photographs of detectives?"

"They threw some random photos on the table, and when I couldn't identify any of them, they were done. They never had any intention of pursuing the matter seriously. It cut too close to the bone. They knew, I suspect, that the detective was acting on behalf of the political higher-ups, trying to get me to be the scapegoat and put an end to the whole affair. They probably thought it would be easy. But I wouldn't go along. Now, if you'll excuse me, I need to get ready. I don't want to be late for work."

She went into the bathroom. He cleared the dishes and rinsed them in the sink, emptied and washed the teapot. What if Fred Kipps's marriage proposal was no mere gesture? Then he had a motive for wanting her husband off the scene. But it was a big leap to believe he put together a scheme that he carried out alone, flawlessly, disposing of a body and a cab by himself. And if his desire for Stella Crater had been the motive, why would he walk away so readily, without a murmur, when the woman he committed murder in order to possess rejected him?

Exiting the bathroom, she pulled a chair to the hall closet, stood on it, and rummaged through the linens on the top shelf. She extracted a small wooden box with a hinged lid.

"Can I give you a hand?" Dunne said.

"I'm fine, thanks." She carefully stepped off and returned the chair to its place.

He removed his coat and hat from an oak stand that looked as though it might have stood in Joe's chambers. "I'll walk back with you, if that's all right."

"That's fine." She held the box in her cupped hands. "You read everything I wrote?"

"Yes."

"Well, I left one detail out."

"What's that?"

"It happened a good deal later, when I'd sold the cabin and was gathering our old clothes, Joe's and mine, to donate to the thrift store run by the Methodist church. Going through the pockets, I extracted raffle tickets, matchbooks and the like, small mementos of the life we'd shared. The last item of clothing was the dress I'd worn the day of the detective's visit. Sickened by its associations, I was surprised I hadn't already given it away or thrown it on the fire. Hurriedly, I went through the pockets, and I found this."

She laid the box on the table and removed what looked like a handkerchief wrapped in cellophane. "At first I didn't realize what it was. I almost threw it away." She peeled away the cellophane: it was a handkerchief. She placed it in her palm. "Remember?"

"Remember what?"

"I was crying. He offered me his handkerchief. I didn't take it."

"He offered it again?"

"I accepted."

"And he forgot to ask for it back?"

"Here it is. I forgot at first I even had it." She moved her hand up and down, as though it was a weighing pan. "Once I realized what it was, I felt a great relief. They'd almost convinced me I was mad, delusional. Now, I had proof I wasn't."

Joe's Steeplechase-Jack smile loomed directly behind her head. Although she clung to her view of Joe as a modern-day Sir Galahad, at some level she had to know the truth of the allegations against him. Small, spare, immaculately clean, the room testified to all she'd lost: husband, wealth, summer cottage, chauffeur, certainty of growing old with a man she loved and trusted. Everything had been stripped away. She cradled the plain, white handkerchief in her hands as if it were a sacred relic, a holy piece of cloth, like Veronica's veil, that could heal the ache of all that had been taken from her.

Instead of pointing out that such a nondescript handkerchief proved nothing, that it might have belonged to anyone, he said, "How'd the police react when you showed it to them?"

"Show it to them? So they could destroy or lose it? Or more likely, claim that I got it from someone else and it proved nothing more than my capacity to cling to fantasies?" She started sobbing again, exposing the raw pain that time hadn't healed or even lessened. "It's mine." Gulping air, she spoke through her tears. "Proof of who is sane, who delusional."

"That's all right, Mrs. Crater. Put it away. It's yours. No one can take it from you."

"Mine." The sobs grew louder. She extended her hands and transferred the handkerchief from left to right, flipping it over. "Proof."

At the upper edge of the handkerchief, stitched in blue thread, were the initials A.I.M.

By the time he left her apartment, it was nearly 3:30 p.m. He'd sat with her until she ran out of tears. Face drained and sickly pale, she accepted his advice to call work and say she was ill and needed to take the afternoon off. She went into the windowless bedroom and lay atop the quilt, carefully tucking the box with the handkerchief beneath her pillow.

"I'll show myself out." He tiptoed into the kitchen, opened the window and lit a cigarette, careful to exhale into the cold, deepening gloom outside. A network of clothes lines was strung across the barren yard of crumbling concrete below. On the other side, from within a shroud of casement light, a pair of bony arms emerged, pulled a squeaking wire and reeled in a solitary sheet, pure as snow. Cleanliness is next to loneliness.

He stood outside her bedroom and listened to the soft but certain hum and buzz of her breathing. She was asleep. He put on his coat and hat, and gently shut the door behind him.

He stopped at police headquarters, but Crow wasn't in his office. The surly, moon-faced sergeant at the front desk said he was off on a job. Couldn't (more likely, wouldn't) say where. "Be back in the morning" was all he offered. Hoping Robert Emmet Murphy might have some idea of who A.I.M. might be, Dunne went to a bar on Broome Street and called him. The woman who answered said she was his niece. Murphy had taken his mother back to Ireland for a visit. She wasn't sure when they're return.

The bar was in an afternoon lull. It would change, he knew, when the shifts changed at police headquarters. For now, he was the only customer. The bartender left him alone. He enjoyed the quiet. Dunne had another beer before he remembered the ticket for the fights. If someone besides Pully had sent it, he'd cancel.

At least there was time for a shower and nap before he had to be at Madison Square Garden. He caught a taxi back to the hotel. The driver had a bent ear. His left.

The head desk clerk accosted him in the lobby. "Mr. Dunne, please, may I have a moment with you?"

"Sure." Dunne stepped away from the elevator. "There a problem?"

"Not a problem, sir. A guest. You have a guest waiting for you." Like his clothes—striped trousers, black swallow-tailed coat and pearl gray vest—the studied formality of his face gave him the air of a diplomat or banker.

"What guest?" Dunne glanced around. There were no likely candidates in the immediate vicinity. "Where?"

"Over there." He motioned discreetly with his head toward the front lobby, which was shielded from the elevators by a row of palms in elegant Chinese pots. "Her name is"—he glanced down at a paper slip in his hand—"Miss Caroline Mueller."

"Don't recognize the name."

"I informed her you were unavailable and invited her to leave a message. But she *insisted* on waiting. She's been sitting there a good forty-five minutes. If you wish, I'll tell her you've called to say you're elsewhere and will not be reachable for some time."

"I'll take care of it. What's she look like?"

"She's a nurse, I believe, or some kind of medical assistant or hygienist."

"A nurse?"

The head clerk's thin lips and nose constricted slightly, as if a mildly unpleasant odor had just reached him. "So I gather from the white outfit she's wearing." Obviously not his type, or the hotel's, which no doubt preferred a front lobby filled with visitors who looked as though they'd been outfitted at Bergdorf's, across Grand Army Plaza. "She's camped out in the front lobby, by the window, reading the *Herald Tribune*."

As soon as he got to the other side of the palm plants, Dunne recognized her as the head nurse at the Melancthon Manor. She put down the paper and stood, draping her coat over her arm. "Mr. Dunne, I hope you don't mind me intruding like this. I don't mean to be a bother."

"Please, Miss Mueller, have a seat. It's no bother at all. Would you like a drink?" He sat catty-corner.

"No, thanks. I'm on my way home from work. I live in Ridgewood, Queens. They told me at the front desk you were out. I thought I might as well take a breather. Such nice surroundings."

"What can I do for you?"

"I'm afraid I'm the bearer of bad news. Mr. Kipps is dead."

"When?"

"An attendant discovered him yesterday morning."

"He died in his sleep?"

"Yes, sometime in the night."

"Alone?"

"They usually do." She leaned over and touched his sleeve. "I know it's always hard to lose a friend. But Mr. Kipps was so lonely these past few years. His daughter never came. His friends were either dead or moved away. No one ever visited, except you, and your visit meant a great deal to him. He seemed more alert and animated after you left."

"I'm glad to hear that."

"He was the sweetest man, so gentle and considerate. Some of our residents are quite the opposite. From the moment he moved in, Mr. Kipps was always trying to brighten the day with a kind word or generous gesture. But then, slowly at first, his condition worsened until he was reduced to the person you saw the other day."

"Is there something you'd like me to do?"

"I thought perhaps you might alert his acquaintances in the police department."

"Sure. A friend of mine is head of Missing Persons. He'll know who to contact. Are there funeral arrangements?"

"His daughter is having the body shipped to Florida. She made the arrangements by phone. It's terrible the way children nowadays treat their parents. I see it all the time, and it's only getting worse."

"Can I help in any other way?"

"No, that's sweet of you, but that's not why I'm here. I just wanted you to have this." She reached in her coat pocket, took out an envelope and handed it to him. "We're shipping everything else to his daughter, but this was so special to him. He stared at it everyday, like it was a holy card. I want you, as an old and faithful friend, to have it."

Inside, worn at the edges, was a faded black-and-white photograph: woman in slacks and a blouse on a dock; a lake stretched out behind her to a backdrop of tall pine trees. She looked to be in her thirties, slim, pretty, smile too wide to be posed. On the back, in flowing, feminine script, was written *Lake Belvedere, June 1, 1930.*

"It was obvious how much he loved his wife. And how much he missed her, too. Though she died twenty or so years ago, he found it too painful to talk about her. If there is such a thing as an afterlife, I'm sure he's with her now. Did you ever meet her in person?"

"Yes, once." Whoever poor Fred was with now, it wasn't this woman, photographed enjoying one of the last happy moments of her life. Wounded and hurt, Stella Crater was still very much alive. The mention of the crushed tip of Crater's right index finger as noted in the police circular came back to Dunne. It had been a careless mistake on Fred's part, closing the car door without checking before. And that's how Crater had apparently regarded it. But maybe it hadn't been a mistake. Maybe at some level, Fred was giving vent to his rising anger at Crater. Anger at the constant betrayal of the woman in this photograph, a woman for whom Fred felt adoration, affection and something more.

"What did Fred die of, Miss Mueller?"

"Heart failure was what the doctor wrote down."

"Is there going to be an autopsy?"

"No need. He's been dying in stages. It was only a matter of time."

"I understand." A twofold understanding, one beyond doubt, the other highly probable: Fred Kipps had been made an accomplice in the disappearance of Judge Crater by a person or persons who knew his feelings for Mrs. Crater and convinced him he was acting in her best interests by helping get rid of a man utterly unworthy of her love; and, sick and broken though he was, Fred Kipps had probably been murdered.

Miss Mueller stood and put on her coat. As he walked her to the entrance, the head desk clerk swept by with two bell boys in tow and through the revolving door.

"It's a long subway ride to Ridgewood, Miss Mueller. Let me pay for a cab."

"That's very thoughtful of you. But I'm used to it."

A knot of reporters and photographers pressed close around the Cadillac limousine that had just pulled up. The head clerk flailed his arms and ordered the doormen to push them back. When the two passengers exited, they surged forward again. Flash bulbs popped. A crowd gathered.

Shielded by a phalanx of doormen and hefty porters, the clerk escorted a tall, regal blonde in a long silver-fox coat and her aged husband/lover/patron into the hotel as the bell boys and doormen piled two carts with leather luggage.

"How exciting!" Miss Mueller said. "That's Eva Buttenheim,

the Austrian film star. I was reading about her in the paper not five minutes ago."

"Dr. Goebbels's favorite actress."

"She says she was young and naïve. Never joined the Nazi Party. They forced her to act in their films."

"With champagne and roses. A real reign of terror. It's a miracle she survived."

Intent on following the entourage as the head clerk led it across the lobby, she paid no attention to his remark. "And that's her husband, the industrialist William Cook. He unloaded his stake in the American Steel Corporation for $50 million. Now he says he's devoting himself to helping her restart her career in Hollywood. Isn't that romantic?"

"Given her history, $50 million might not be enough."

The couple had reached the front desk. The head clerk regained his air of impassivity. Dunne shook her hand. "Appreciate your stopping by like this."

"Oh, it's nothing. It was a pleasure to meet you." Turning to leave, she hesitated a moment. "You know, when I was sitting there waiting, I thought about how when Mr. Kipps got morose, he'd say he deserved to be alone and sick. It was punishment for his 'terrible sins.' But I never believed that. He was too good a man to have done anything truly terrible, and though I'm not sure what if anything comes after death, I know in this life, just as often as not, it's the bad people who prosper and the good who suffer."

"Can't argue with you there," Dunne said.

After showering, he laid down. He hadn't planned on falling asleep but he did, and awoke suddenly, after only twenty minutes. He'd been in the middle of a demented dream involving Roberta, Felipe Calderon and Fred Kipps. Couldn't remember the details, didn't care to try.

Dinner was a turkey sandwich and a glass of milk delivered by room service. Already a half-hour late, he got into a cab that inched its way through the snarl of midtown traffic. He got out a block east of the Garden, at the corner of Seventh Avenue. Faster to walk.

The crowd out front wasn't the buzzing mass that congregated before a big event, but the Eastern quarter-finals of the Golden Gloves wasn't exactly the same as a title bout between Carmine Basilio and Sugar Ray Robinson. He hadn't examined the ticket to see where he'd be sitting, but presumed that it would be ringside or close. Instead, he found himself climbing to the upper balcony.

From the top step of the balcony's steeply pitched stairs, he surveyed rows of empty seats. Far below, beneath a faint milky film of smoke, the ring floated like a stationary raft in a pool of white, unsparing light, suitable for fights and autopsies. The trio of referee and fighters moved in a lazy, ungraceful circle, oblivious to desultory shouts, boos, and catcalls.

No usher in sight, he went down the steps to row E, seat 21, as indicated on the ticket, which was in the middle of an entirely empty row and an equally vacant section. He studied the ticket to see if he could have possibly misread it. *Upper balcony. Section 3, Row E, Seat 21.* He was in the right place. More likely, Pully or one of his underlings at ISC had stuck a freebie intended for the firm's messengers or mailroom boys into the wrong envelope and had it delivered to the hotel.

Pully was probably sitting at ringside, where the seats were mostly full. Farther back, there were empty patches; lots of people in the aisles, moving around, schmoozing, showing no interest as the tuxedo-clad announcer at center ring began to intone the judges' decision on the fight that had just ended. There was another round of boos when he held up the hand of the winner.

"Next fight will be livelier."

Slightly startled by the unexpected comment, Dunne turned. Pully had arrived. He was two rows back, standing, hands in the pants pockets of his loosely fitted blue double-breasted suit as he surveyed the arena.

"Wasn't sure I was in the right place," Dunne said.

"Perfect view from up here. You can see everybody, everything."

"Any higher, we'd need airplane tickets."

"Sometimes there's more privacy in public places." The nearest occupied seats were an entire section away. Across the way, the spectators were just as lightly scattered.

Instead of sitting, Pully announced he was going to get something to eat. Carefully placing one foot at a time, he went back up the stairs, his waddling, hesitant gait the trademark of a man with bum knees and too much weight. Several minutes later, he descended even more carefully, a large paper cup of beer in one hand, three hot dogs bundled in tin foil in the other. He sat directly behind Dunne.

Resting his arm on the back of his seat, Dunne swiveled to look up at Pully. "If you try, I bet you can find a seat in this row."

"I like the view from here." Pully looked to his right and left. "No obstructions." He chomped off half a hot dog in a single bite, chewed, swallowed.

Down in the ring, the fighters were introduced, went back to their corners and took off their robes. The one in black trunks had big ears, olive skin, a compact build not unlike John Garfield's; his opponent, in green, was red-haired, slightly taller, and as white as one of Doc Rossiter's cadavers. In contrast to the lackadaisical ballet that preceded, they started swinging hard as soon as the bell went off. The crowd below roared its approval.

Pully let out a loud burp. "Pardon me." He reached down, extending his arm over Dunne's shoulder, the last hot dog in hand. "Want this? I'm full."

"Thanks, already ate."

Black trunks parried a left hook and shot a straight right cross that caught green trunks on the side of the jaw. He staggered back. Black trunks moved in, but before he threw another punch, green trunks landed one to match what he'd just received. The crowd was on its feet. Earnestly aggressive but nervous and unsure of themselves, the fighters exchanged another volley of blows, most of which missed.

The cup of beer came over Dunne's shoulder the same way the hot dog did. "Take all you want." This time he didn't turn down the offer.

"You probably think this is an odd way to meet."

Dunne took a long sip of beer. "Crossed my mind." He raised the beer cup over his head so Pully could take it back. "You think I'm here to fill you in on the matter I'm handling for Walter Wilkes, you're wrong. Grateful for your help and for keeping ISC off my back, but this is between Wilkes and me."

"The other way around, Fin. I'm here to fill *you* in."

"On what?"

"Bud Mulholland."

After backing off, the fighters were back trading punches, some of them wild, some direct hits. Black trunks went down on the canvas but was up before the referee got to a count of two; he faked with his right and delivered a left that almost sent green trunks through the ropes.

"Looks like we're in for a low-budget punch party."

Dunne finished the beer. "Not exactly Dempsey versus Firpo."

"More like Dumbo versus Harpo."

The bell rang. The crowd gave a round of applause.

"Still young. They've got potential. You were about to fill me in on Bud Mulholland."

"You've known him a long time?"

"Met Bud when we were both with the police department. I brought him into the OSS. Went overseas together in '43. When the war ended and Truman put the OSS out of business, we hung around London for a while. But I thought it's you going to tell me about Bud, not the other way around."

"I don't know him as long as you."

"Crossed paths in the OSS, didn't you?"

"We didn't meet until after the OSS closed down. I stayed in Washington to run research and analysis for the Strategic Services Unit. The whole intelligence operation was pretty much a mess until '49, when CIA was set up to put everything right. That's when I met Bud."

"Bud was in CIA?"

"You might say he was in the delivery room when it was born. He was exactly what the cowboys in the Office of Policy Coordination were looking for. We shared an office back then. He never talked politics. Mostly he talked about the best ways to kill people. His expertise was impressive."

The bell for the second round sounded. The fighters raced to the middle of the ring and resumed pummeling each other. The crowd cheered.

"It looks like this is going to be a short fight," Pully said.

"Short but hard-fought. How long did Bud stay in CIA?"

"Well, he didn't stay long in Washington. The other higher-ups sent him right into the field to help train recruits from behind the Iron Curtain to return to their homelands and lead guerilla movements. 'What we want is bullets, not bullshit' is what I was told when I objected to wasting resources on their overwrought, ill-considered schemes. Looks like they're slowing down."

The fighters clinched. Green trunks almost seemed to be resting his head on black trunks' shoulder. The referee pulled them apart. They exchanged several punches, then clinched again.

"Blitzkrieg turns into trench warfare," Pully said. "Where was I?"

"'Ill-considered schemes.'"

"I argued that we needed to develop a capacity for long-term intelligence gathering, not short-term sabotage and half-cocked attempts at subversion; nurture agents with language skills and a deep knowledge of the cultures, peoples and parties within the Soviet empire; put aside preconceptions and stereotypes to deal with the real complexities of the situation; and establish a first-rate, reliable research-and-analysis operation that doesn't mask its incompetence with high-priced gadgetry and political gimmickry."

"Tall order."

"Far too tall for the midgets in charge, I'm afraid."

When the fighters clinched a third time, the crowd began to boo.

Pully tapped Dunne on the shoulder with a cigar. "Want one?"

"Sure."

"You see it a lot in fights like this. Kids who let the excitement of fighting in the Garden for the first time drive them to shoot their bolt in the opening round. Now they'll either drag themselves through the rest of the fight or one of them will end it with a lucky punch." Pully lit the cigar already in his mouth. He reached down and handed the book of matches to Dunne.

Separated once again by the referee, green trunks backpedaled, black trunks in pursuit. Backed into a corner, green trunks did a successful job of defending himself against a flurry of hard blows. The bell ended round two.

Pully puffed on the cigar, producing a small cloud over Dunne's head. "I made my case right up to Allen Dulles but was told, 'We're not interested in NATO agents—no action, talk only. We want men that can get things done, and fast.' They got their wish. Every last agent sent East was caught and killed as fast as they were sent in."

"That's when you quit?"

"I still believed there were enough smart, clear-thinking people to push our intelligence operations in the right direction. But it got worse once the fighting broke out in Korea. Swash-buckling tactics that bordered on the insane. They were running Chinese and Koreans through the training camps and dropping them behind enemy lines with little or no sense of what their mission was. It was an utter waste of resources and lives. The net result was that our capacity for gathering intelligence in the Far East was just about zero. That's when I quit and came back to New York. I took a position with ISC, but I'm still in contact with colleagues who shared my disgust at where things were going. Year or so later, in '53, I bumped into Bud. Or rather, he bumped into me."

"He'd quit too?"

"He never said so directly. He just wanted me to know 'my friends in Washington' didn't appreciate me nosing around in their business. 'Once you're out, Pully, you're out. Leave it at that. Guys like us should get on with our lives and not interest ourselves in matters that no longer concern us.' Made it sound as if I were some sort of subversive for following the activities of an agency of the United States government. He did it with that little threatening fuck-you smile of his."

At the sound of the bell, the fighters approached each other more slowly and warily than at the beginning of the last round. They traded a few light, innocuous punches. Successfully avoiding a sudden right hook, black trunks snapped a hard left that sent green trunks reeling backwards; moving in close, he delivered several hard body punches that put green trunks on the ropes.

"This could be it." Puffing away on his cigar, Pully exhaled what looked like a series of smoke signals.

"As much luck as skill in a fight like this. It's not over yet."
Green trunks ducked an intended knockout blow and
escaped to the center of the ring.

"How'd you respond to Mulholland?"

"I didn't. I got on with my new responsibilities at ISC.
There was no time for anything else. Then you called and asked
me to find out about Mulholland's employer. At first, I suspected
a set-up. But I figured I know you better than that, Fin. You're
not the type that betrays his friends. So I went ahead and did
what you asked."

"And connected him to Walter Wilkes."

"I knew right away what that was about. Allen Dulles has
operatives in every major news organization, CBS, *New York
Times*, *Chicago Tribune*. Hearst and Luce were eager to help.
They all jumped into bed, running fake news items, muzzling
reporters, killing stories, giving a cover to agents so they could
travel as journalists. No one jumped more enthusiastically than
Wilkes. He couldn't do enough, especially if there was a chance
to fan the hysteria the *Standard* thrives on."

Black trunks caught up with green trunks, who stood his
ground. The crowd was on its feet once more. Black trunks gave
green trunks a relentless pummeling.

Dunne lit his cigar and reached up to return the book of
matches. "So Mulholland is the agency's point man in the Wilkes
outfit?"

"He's doing exactly what he did before, running covert
operations, but now he travels under the well-tailored guise of
guardian angel, disciplinarian and head fixer for Wilkes's far-
flung operations, bailing out reporters, greasing palms that need
to be greased, smoothing things over with the police. He's got a
license to go wherever he likes. That's how he was able to stay in
Havana through last spring and summer."

"Havana?"

Green trunks grabbed black trunks, holding on like only a desperate fighter or departing lover will, clinging hard in the knowledge that to let go was to risk losing what couldn't be regained. Black trunks held him, if not tenderly, then with the peculiar intimacy fighters display amid their brutal give-and-take. The referee pried them apart. Green trunks shook his head and managed to summon enough strength to back away before black trunks could land a punch.

"The end is nigh," Pully said.

"What about Mulholland in Havana?"

"The Batista government pretty much allowed the CIA to use Havana as a base to do whatever it wanted for planning the coup in Guatemala. Mulholland went down ostensibly to take care of some problems in Wilkes's South American news bureaus. In reality, he recruited a crew of burglars, hit men and assorted felons to break into embassies, steal code books, kidnap and interrogate potential intelligence sources, the secret dirty work the gentlemen types didn't want to soil themselves with. Before Havana, it was Istanbul. Same deal. That was his base for helping pull off the coup against the Mossadeq government in Iran."

Body lowered in a half crouch, black trunks moved in for the kill. Green trunks stepped back, feinted with his right and hit black trunks with a left upper cut that almost lifted him off his feet.

"Lucky punch," Pully said.

"Appreciate what you're telling me. But it's got nothing to do with why I've been hired. They're entirely different matters. Mulholland has absolutely no involvement."

Now it was green trunks who seemed to be closing in.

Pully stood. He looked right and left. "Maybe not. All I'm telling you is to be extra careful. You're treading near a behemoth of 15,000 people, with an untold amount of secret funding to spend as it pleases, running its own prisons, brothels and airlines, employing mercenaries, assassination squads and thugs of its own choosing, equipped with an array of weaponry that ranges from artillery to lethal gases and poison."

Black trunks seemed dazed. Green trunks drew nearer. The crowd was cheering wildly. Suddenly, as if a cloud had passed in and out of his head, black trunks stood erect and delivered a devastating right to the side of green trunk's head.

"Think of it this way, Fin. Sooner or later, the day of reckoning will come. I intend to help see it does. Meanwhile, you're dealing with a drunken, rampaging elephant with a twenty-inch erection. My advice is to get out of its way."

Green trunks fell to his knees and toppled face down onto the canvas.

"Luck can take you only so far."

The referee counted to ten. Green trunks lay absolutely still. His handlers rushed out from the corner and rolled him over.

"Don't doubt what you've told me. Just can't see what it's got to do with the case I'm working."

Pully made no response. Moving with none of his previous awkwardness, he headed up the steps to the exit.

A message from Nan Renard waited at the front desk. *Please call.* Back in his room, he had the operator place a long-distance, person-to-person call to Eddie Moran at the Old Madrid, in Havana. She called back immediately: bingo, she got Moran on the first try.

"Hey, kiddo, glad to hear from you!" Moran reported he had nothing new on Jimmy Malacoda. He hadn't been seen or heard from since he returned to Cleveland. Wasn't exactly a fan club trying to bring him back. The Salavante crew never brought him up.

Dunne mentioned he'd run into Bud Mulholland. "Knew him back in your cop days, Eddie, didn't you?"

"Yeah. Cast-iron balls, that's Bud."

"Bump into him when he was in Havana?"

"You know about that?"

"He mentioned he was down there for the Wilkes outfit. Helped out with hush-hush work on the side."

"Hush hush, my ass. Those CIA boys are the biggest spenders and blowhards in town, traipsing around with lowlifes of every kind—kidnappers, smugglers, gangsters, second-storey men, tin-pot mercenaries."

"Bud ever mention Malacoda?"

"Bud mentioned nobody. Kept to himself, the way he always done. That's why he stayed the same place you did when you was here. No flashy hotels or nightclubs for Bud. Unlike them others, Bud never drew attention to himself."

"Stayed in that hotel the whole time?"

"Sure. Wasn't he the one recommended it to you?"

"Now that you mention it, yeah, I guess he did."

"All them spyglasses was like Bud, there'd be no problem, but most is a lot of showboat college types." Eddie launched into a story about some ninny from CIA who landed reeling drunk in the Starlight Room bragging about the razz they'd played on the Reds in Guatemala and how if the stuffed shirts in Washington would only get out of the way, they'd deep-six the whole commie enterprise. "Ask me," Eddie concluded, "they were lucky. These clowns couldn't get laid in the Women's House of Detention with a handful of pardons."

He went to bed without calling Nan. Drew the curtains. Turned out the light. Sat wide awake in bed. Maybe Bud Mulholland's involvement in CIA had nothing to do with the Crater case. How could it? Strange he'd never mentioned, even in passing, having been in Havana. Maybe Malacoda was blow-ing hot air when he went off about having a "signed and sealed" deal to bump off some stiff he happened to meet in a hotel lobby.

Tired but unable to sleep, he realized Stella Crater had probably undertaken this kind of exercise in frustration every night as she lay in the dark for the past twenty-five years, trying to put together a jigsaw puzzle with so many unmatchable pieces that no matter how you moved, switched or turned them, they never formed a coherent picture.

Crow was hanging up his overcoat when Dunne arrived. "Glad you got here early. No sooner did the Kipps file land on my desk, the pension office calls and wants it back. Seems the old guy expired a day or two ago." He picked up a shoe box from his desk and searched among the files beneath. "Here it is. I'm going to the john. When I return, the file is going back, so make it quick."

Dunne skipped past pages of promotion letters, medical reports and retirement papers until he located Kipps's assignment record. Routine transfers up to 1926, when he was one of several cops detailed to work with enforcement agents from the Federal Bureau of Prohibition. The record indicated he'd been part of the raid on Texas Guinan's 300 Club, on West 54th Street, which netted two U.S. senators and golfer Bobby Jones.

Next year, he was moved to the Bureau's Transportation Section on Pier 57, at West 15th Street. At the beginning of 1928, he was transferred to the Property Clerk's Office on Broome Street, across from headquarters. Retired not long after.

Crow returned from the john wiping his hands with a paper towel that he rolled into a ball. "Hand it over."

Dunne laid the file on the desk. "What was the Transportation Section?"

"The what?" He tossed the paper ball into the wastepaper basket.

"Here." Dunne placed his finger on the entry. "Says Kipps was transferred to the Bureau of Prohibition's Transportation Section, on Pier 57."

"Fancy name for a parking lot. That's where the Feds kept all the cars, trucks, and even speedboats caught and impounded for transporting booze. At one point, they had a real stagecoach used to promote a rodeo show at the Garden. Oweny Madden had it loaded with his own brew and made deliveries."

"Taxis, too?"

"Plenty. A favorite way of moving beer and booze."

"Thanks." He handed the file to Crow. "One more thing."

"Always is with you."

"Initials A-I-M. On that report that was missing, from September 7th, remember?"

"Misfiled."

"On that *misfiled* report, any idea?"

"You already asked me that. I told you I don't know. Could've been Anthony Mascone, Austin Murray, Andy Mickelman. On second thought, nix that last one. Andy's name was Nickelman, not Mickelman. Anyways, they were all detectives around that time. No idea about middle names. And it wasn't only detectives were drafted into the search for Crater. Especially in those early days, they pulled cops from everywhere, which is how the likes of me and Robert Emmet Murphy wound up here."

Returning to the file room, Dunne pulled the report filed on September 7th and reread the section initialed by A.I.M, this time carefully:

Re: Anonymous letter addressed to Missing Persons received Sept 6. Handwritten contents as follows: "Judge Crater liked to visit the girls more than once at 39 East 38th Street. Look out for the Supt. That's a clever one."

10:30 A.M. Visited premises. Interviewed Mrs. Mary King,

superintendent of building for last 5 years. Irishwoman. Widow. Gives age as 51. Makes an account of everyone living on premises. Denied any "disreputable types" reside there. Only "decent people on the up and up." Calls the allegations of Crater's visits "a bald-face lie," typical of the spite directed at her by the wives of the supers on the block who resent her for having a job as good as their husbands.

Building is 4-floor lodging house. 12 rooms. Most tenants at work. Interviewed Mrs. Alma Parker, age 78, widow, tenant in 1B. Lives with crippled daughter, Margaret, age 55. Never saw anybody resembling Crater in the building. Spoke to super in neighboring building. Never saw any sign of Crater in or around 39 East 38th. A.I.M.

A not untypical entry among the hundreds of interviews and visits by the cops in the early day of the investigation, as they struggled to deal with the flood of Crater sightings and tips; but it was the sole one initialed A.I.M. As he went through the files once more, Dunne noticed that it wasn't the only instance in which a cop had been called in to help Missing Persons follow up a single lead—another indication of how rushed and impromptu the police had to be as they played a seemingly hopeless game of catch-up.

He slipped the page beneath the table, folded it and tucked it in the breast pocket of his jacket. On the way up the stairs, he bumped into Crow on his way down. The shoe box from his desk was under his arm. "Find what you were looking for?"

"Not yet."

"Could be I got it here." Crow patted the box.

"Got what?"

"This." He removed the lid, stuck it beneath his arm and lifted out a dirt-colored skull missing its jaw bone and posterior wall. "Could be Judge Crater or maybe some Canarsie Indian, or unremembered Dutchman. Maybe one of Washington's soldiers.

Or a Hessian. Or a woman buried in one of those private plots that got paved over as the city rushed north. Arrived this morning from a construction site in East Harlem. They sent it to Missing Persons. Go figure. I'm taking it to the forensics lab, where it belongs."

He raised the skull. "I suppose I could make the same request that Dante did of the dead: "Tell me who and whence you be/ And let not your sad and shameful state prevent/ Your free unfolding of yourself to me." He rotated it slowly. The bulb in the wall fixture glowed eerily through the sockets. "The difference is, Dante got an answer, and it doesn't look like I will." He placed the skull back in the box. "Whoever he was, God's mercy on him," he said and went on his way.

Before heading out to Far Rockaway to make a try at talking with Alexander Von Vogt, Dunne paid a visit to 39 East 38th. Neither Mrs. Mary King nor Mrs. Alma Parker was in residence. The building itself, a once-stately four-story brownstone off Fourth Avenue (the local merchants, the *Standard* reported, were working hard to get the name changed to Park Avenue South), wasn't going to be around much longer, either. Along with its brownstone neighbors on either side, it was a boarded-up, roofless hulk. A sign mounted atop the plywood wall that corralled the buildings announced:

COMING SOON!
MURRAY HILL MEWS
66 Deluxe Rental Apartments
All Modern Conveniences
Occupancy June 1956

Dust-covered demolition workers banged away with sledge hammers at the interior walls and filled metal carts with the debris. Load by load, they hauled away the remnants of the multiple lives sheltered in what were originally single-family homes, substantial places of permanence and elegance, that were refigured and subdivided to house several generations of transient lodgers.

He walked down Fourth Avenue to 34th Street, turned west and continued to Penn Station. A mild morning ripened into an unseasonably warm day, the sun noticeably stronger than just a few weeks before, winter backpedaling like a fast-tiring boxer entering the late rounds, capable of damaging hooks and punishing jabs, but faced with a relentless, invincible opponent and the inevitable knock out.

He bought a copy of the *Standard* and entered the Eighth Avenue subway. He didn't have to wait long for the train to Far Rockaway, one of those far-off corners of the city, like Tottenville or Baychester, which he could locate on a map but had never visited.

Though dented and worn, the subway car didn't look all that different from when it was put into service in the years before World War I: deep-green iron walls, lacquered wicker seats, leather hand straps. Bare light bulbs overhead periodically dimmed or went out altogether, plunging the car into darkness and interrupting his reading of a feature article about the $3.1 billion for highway construction President Eisenhower was asking Congress for, the first installment in a $30 billion, ten-year road-building effort.

An accompanying map illustrated the projects for the New York region, planned as well as possible: new bridge across the Hudson, another over the Narrows, two across Long Island Sound, inter-borough and cross-town expressways (an answer to Crow's complaints), an elegant intersection of looping lines, Manhattan at its center like a fat fly caught in the middle of a spider's web. Not to be outdone, the Port Authority of New York and New Jersey had announced a $60,000,000 appropriation that would turn Idlewild Airport into "the most beautiful, efficient and functional air transportation center in the world."

The train emerged from the tunnel and ran as an El above a flat plain dotted with neighborhoods of one- and two-family homes. The car was uncomfortably warm. He took off his overcoat and wrestled the window next to his seat open a few inches. Pungent salt smell of marshland wafted in. Houses grew scarcer. Clusters of shacks and bungalows that clung to the sides of canals and creeks looked better suited to a Louisiana bayou than a borough of New York City.

He went back to the paper. A two-page spread probably commissioned a month or so earlier, in the depths of the cold snap, quoted a number of scientists on the possibility a new Ice Age was on its way. A drawing depicted wooly mammoths on a bleak, icy plain out of which stuck the tops of Manhattan's skyscrapers.

The train rattled across the trestle over Jamaica Bay and rose to a point where the city was silhouetted in the distance against the cloudless, sea-blue sky, no ice or mammoths in sight. Off to the east, a steady flow of planes descended and ascended from Idlewild, soon to be the world's most beautiful, efficient, functional airport. He wouldn't hold his breath. Dunne skipped the horoscope and turned to the sports pages, which featured a picture of Dodger manager Walter Alston at spring training camp in Vero Beach, doing his best not to stare into the yawning cleavage of Miss Florida.

Turning left, the El ran parallel to the beach and the ocean, rows of summer bungalows boarded up for the winter. The Atlantic appeared as tame as Central Park Lake. He got off at Far Rockaway, the last stop, walked aimlessly in and out of stores around the station, making sure he hadn't been tailed. He stopped at a firehouse and asked about the location of the address he had for Von Vogt.

"Looking for Von Vogt?" the fireman replied.

Taken back, Dunne didn't hide his surprise. "How'd you know?"

"Short block. Von Vogt's is the only house on it. You a bill collector?"

"No, an ex-cop, like Von Vogt."

The fireman gave him directions. "If you don't want to walk, you can wait for him in Brophy's." He pointed at the bar and grill across the street. "He stops in every afternoon at 5:15. We set our clocks by it."

Von Vogt's place was a tidy, aluminum-sided cottage converted to year-round use and surrounded by a chain-link fence. Parked under the car porch, a waxed and polished Ford V8, a '37 or '38 model, looked as though it had just rolled off the showroom floor. A flag hung limply from the pole in the front yard. Confident it would be better to approach Von Vogt in Brophy's than knock on his front door, he strolled past.

With three hours to kill, he stopped in a luncheonette for a sandwich and coffee. Afterwards, he cruised the boardwalk. Despite the spring-like weather, it was deserted except for an old man being pushed in a wheelchair. The wind picked up. He kept walking, concentrating on the sea, consciously trying to avoid turning a partial collection of facts into a theory so neat and satisfactory you become wedded to it, choosing to recognize only what bolstered it and letting it lead you further and further from the truth. Cops and prosecutors were particularly susceptible, and there were plenty of innocent people who'd spent long, hard years behind bars as a result.

Edged with a raw, wet chill, the wind grew as daylight diminished, winter rising from the canvas ready to show the wallop it still packed. He reached Brophy's at five minutes to five, glad to get inside. The lone customer was a woman in her sixties who sat at the bar reading the *Daily News*. He ordered Scotch with plenty of ice and carried it over to the booth by the window.

The burly bartender shouted over to him, "Hey, bub, beginning at five we got waitress service at the tables. You're going to have to order from her."

The customer at the bar turned out to be the waitress. She stood and tied on an apron. "Shout when you're ready." She sat down and went back to the paper. The bartender wiped and rewiped the bar with a wet rag. His unhappy, scrutinizing stare made clear he didn't suffer an excess of excitement at the prospect of a new bit of business. "What brings you here?" he said.

The waitress looked up from her paper. "Brings who?"

"I'm not talking to you, Florrie."

"Nice day," Dunne said. "Figured I'd get a taste of ocean air."

Several customers drifted in, all locals from the way the bartender greeted them. Florrie dropped a menu on the table. "Soup and sandwiches, that's it. Pie, too. All made on the premises by yours truly." She checked to see that the bartender was busy with his customers. "Don't pay no mind to Brophy," she whispered. "About as friendly as a clam. Like the rest of them, been here all their lives, treat anybody from the city like they got leprosy. They're worse now, after they've been all winter by themselves."

More customers arrived. Promptly at 5:15, a stout, dignified man in brown fedora and herringbone overcoat arrived, went to the corner farthest from the window, hung coat and hat on wall hook, and sat on a barstool. Running his hand across a closely cropped, transparent topping of white stubble, he nodded wordlessly at Brophy, who mixed and served him a Manhattan.

Though not instantly recognizable as Alexander Von Vogt, the thin, slick-haired detective with the pencil moustache identified in newspaper pictures of a quarter-century ago as lead detective in the Crater case, the facial features were substantially unchanged: thin lips, high cheek bones and forehead, prominent ears, sad, inquisitive eyes.

Brophy climbed atop a stool to turn on the television over the bar. The sound was drowned out by the trio beneath loudly arguing about whether the Giants would repeat their '54 World Series victory or whether '55 would bring the Dodgers their first victory ever.

"Don't matter which of them gets to the Series." Florrie stopped with a tray of drinks she was delivering to a booth. "The Bronx Bombers will demolish them."

Gathering coat and hat, Dunne walked to the other side of the bar. He sat on the stool next to Von Vogt.

Von Vogt sipped his Manhattan.

"I'm out for the day," Dunne said.

"Nice day for it."

"You a native?"

"Resident."

"How long?"

"Long."

Dunne pushed his empty glass forward. "Can I buy you a drink?"

"You walked past my house earlier." Von Vogt took another sip.

"Didn't know anybody was watching."

"Short street, single house, scarcity of passers-by. You weren't hard to spot."

Brophy poured Dunne a refill. "Everything okay down here?" His scowl suggested maybe they weren't.

"Fine," Von Vogt said. Brophy sauntered away. "You're the one sent the letter, aren't you?"

"I wanted to respect your privacy but hoped you'd agree to talk."

"So much for my privacy. I knew you'd be by sooner or later."

"All I need is to ask a few questions."

"You read English, I presume, then you understood my answer. It hasn't changed."

"Recognize this?" Dunne reached in his breast pocket, took the paper he'd slipped from the police files and smoothed it on the bar.

"Dunne's the name, isn't it?"

"Fintan Dunne, yes."

Von Vogt drained his drink and stood up.

"I think you were tricked," Dunne said.

"If you haven't already, talk with Captain John Cronin at Missing Persons. He knows all there is to know about the case."

"Look. September 7th. These initials: A.I.M. I think he derailed the investigation."

Glancing down at the paper, Von Vogt donned coat and hat. "That's police property, Mr. Dunne. Being a pest isn't a crime. Purloining official records is."

Brophy returned. He gripped the bar with hands the size of bear paws. "Something the matter?"

Von Vogt slipped a quarter across. "I'm going to make it an early evening."

"The cop who reported on his visit to 39 West 38th Street, who was he?"

"You seem like an intelligent man, Dunne. I suggest you find an assignment worthy of your intelligence." Von Vogt went out the door.

"What's your problem?" The boom of Brophy's voice turned the barroom silent.

"No problem." Dunne put on his overcoat. "Just a private discussion."

"Ain't private when you harass a steady customer."

"Nobody was harassed."

"Von Vogt's got an honored place here. Decorated cop. Lost

two boys in the war. You made such a nuisance of yourself, you chased him out. That's harassment."

"Whatever happened was between him and me."

"That's the problem with you pushy city types. You think you can come out here and act however you please."

The patrons were all watching. Several nodded in agreement. Dunne eyed the door. Shuffle of feet from behind was followed by an angry voice: "Tell him, Brophy, go on, tell him."

"You float in like the trash that stinks up our beaches and think we got no choice but to stomach it. Well, maybe it's time you learned a lesson."

"Past time." A hand came from behind and took hold of Dunne's shoulder. He drove his elbow into the soft belly of his attacker, who groaned loudly and doubled over.

Last thought before Brophy's bat descended: *Go for the door.* Last feeling: *black-and-white tiles of barroom floor against his cheek, cold and unyielding.*

Eyes opened, he took a few minutes to bring the object directly overhead into focus. Gradually, a featureless oval gained eyes and lips, and became a face. The waitress's. It took another minute to remember her name: Florrie. A streetlight shone above. Moths swirling around it turned out to be snowflakes.

"Thank goodness you're awake. Can you sit up?" She extended her hand.

He was on a bench. Traffic went by in a steady stream. He rolled from side to side, put his feet on the ground, took her hand and pushed with the other. He sat, ran his fingers over the throbbing egg-sized lump on the back of his head.

"They dumped you here, the bums. No need for what they done. You were about to leave on your own."

"Wasn't fast enough. Where am I?"

"Block from the train."

"Any cabs around?" Plump, wet snowflakes fell on his face.

"Car service is across the street."

He stood. A wave of dizziness surged through his head. He took her arm to steady himself. "Will they take me back to Manhattan?"

"Take you to Manchuria if you pay the fare."

He checked to make sure he still had his wallet. "I'll settle for Manhattan."

"Don't blame you. I'm thinking of moving back to the Bronx." She handed him his hat. "You wait here. I'll have the car pick you up. He'll take you home."

The hotel doctor stopped by in the morning. "A slight concussion" was his diagnosis. He recommended going to the hospital for an X-ray. Aspirin and bed rest in the interim. Dunne told the desk to hold his calls and slept most of the day. Late afternoon, he took a walk in the park. There were no messages when he got back. He told the clerk to put his calls through again.

The phone rang as he came out of the shower. He ignored it. It kept ringing. Peeved, he picked it up. "Where's the fire?"

"I'm sorry. I'm trying to reach Fintan Dunne."

"Who's this?"

"Von Vogt."

He almost hung up. But didn't. "I'm not dead, if that's what you called to find out."

"Florrie told me everything that happened."

"I remember up until the baseball bat."

Von Vogt mixed an apology with an explanation. "My neighbors are insular—in a literal rather than pejorative sense," he said. "They're not vicious, but sometimes they're overprotective of each other's privacy. What occurred last evening was entirely uncalled for. I've told them so. Any medical expenses should be sent to me."

"All I got was a bump on the head." Clad only in a towel, he felt a chill. "Tell Brophy I'll add it to my collection."

"Another thing, Dunne. Those initials."

"What about them?" He sat on the bed.

"I'd be a liar if I said I remembered for sure to whom they belonged."

"I'll settle for an educated guess."

"I don't give the past much thought."

Dunne pulled the coverlet close. He imagined Von Vogt in the living room of that small house on the empty block, black receiver pressed to his ear, looking at the mantle with the pictures of his dead wife and dead sons, all gone, but like the memory of Connie Newberry, never far away, the ghosts of what was, what could have been; a past more alive and vivid than the vacant present; a future that didn't go beyond a nightly visit to Brophy's bar. A resident of that same vanished world as Stella Crater, what did he have but the past?

"But I thought all day about those initials. There are probably more, but all I can recall are two. Anthony Mascone. Tony was with us for a good month, but never really had his heart in it. He felt we were wasting our time kicking around a political stink ball that would only hurt the reputations of those who got involved. Tony was smart. Retired a few years ago and moved to Hampton Bays. Last I heard he was pretty sick. The big C."

"The other?"

"Bud Mulholland."

"Bud Mulholland?"

"Yeah. His baptismal name was Ambrose. I remember because that's my brother's name. He never uses it either. Goes by Frank, his middle name. I've got no idea about Mascone's or Mulholland's middle names."

"Mulholland worked with you on the Crater case?" He lay back and stretched out on the bed. His headache from the morning was replaced by a slight buzz.

"He was on the homicide squad. Our paths crossed numerous times. I can't say exactly when and where he got involved, although I'm sure it was in those early, early days. He's retired, too. I don't know where he ended up. Why don't you see if you can locate him? Ask him yourself."

"I'll work on it."

"I'd ask what you expect to find, but the truth is, I don't care. Lots of people thought they'd found the missing piece to the Crater case. Nobody did. They all ended up sorry they ever got involved."

"I appreciate the call. And the advice."

"An observation, not advice. I wouldn't waste my breath giving you advice."

Dunne tucked a pillow under his head. The buzz had turned back into a headache. He stared at the ceiling for a long time after he put down the phone. *Ambrose Mulholland.* He was angry with himself for not having recalled his first name. But he'd never in any way connected Mulholland to the Crater case before and couldn't remember the last time he'd heard Mulholland called anything but Bud. Crow could supply the middle name. His body grew warm and limp under the coverlet. No use getting angry. Get some rest, then get moving.

Part VI

Glad to Get Away: An excerpt from Sanford Teller and Richard Blaine, *Nothing to Fear but Fear Itself: Myths and Legends of the Great Depression* (New York: Center for the Study of Popular Culture, 1967).

The artist Everett Ruess, who disappeared in the southwestern desert in 1934, was remembered as a regional folk hero and creative visionary who fled the encroachments of civilization and embraced the solitary freedom of the untamed West. But the myriad fates of the unprecedented numbers forced on the road by the Great Depression found special resonance in the myths that grew up around the era's two most famous missing persons, aviatrix Amelia Earhart and Judge Joseph Crater.

Earhart won international fame in 1932 when she became the first woman to duplicate Charles Lindbergh's feat and fly solo across the Atlantic. She disappeared five years later, in 1937, on the last leg of an attempt to circumnavigate the globe. The fact that Earhart and her plane were swallowed without a trace our the Pacific Ocean made it easy for the inevitable theorizers to concoct alternate explanations of the event.

According to one theory, acting on orders from President Roosevelt, Earhart faked her disappearance in order to set up a secret spying operation on the Japanese. (In view of the successful surprise Japanese attack on Pearl Harbor four years later, this putative operation must be deemed a rank failure.) A more widely believed—if equally unlikely—story is that she used the opportunity to escape a marriage she'd tired of and a celebrity she'd come to detest, and start anew.

Inevitably, within days of her disappearance, sightings poured in from around the country. Earhart was spied racing a sporty coupe across San Francisco's just-completed Golden Gate

Bridge; she stared wistfully at the plane traffic at Floyd Bennett Field, on Long Island; in black wig and sunglasses, she gave the slip to a would-be pursuer at Marshall Field's State Street store in Chicago. Sporadic sightings continued right up until the public mind was redirected by the global drama of World War II.

The gold-medal winner among Depression-era disappearances, however, is New York State Supreme Court Justice Joseph Force Crater. The circumstances surrounding the case have been repeated ad nauseum in newspapers, magazines and books. Among the least examined but most interesting facets is Crater's status as an embodiment of the archetypal wanderer who isn't forced on the road by poverty or eviction— á la the Joad family in *The Grapes of Wrath*—but who, in the tradition of Johnny Appleseed, chooses his fate. In this telling, Crater becomes the hero instead of the victim, leaving behind the stifling security of respectability in pursuit of happiness only the vagabond's life could offer.

Though students of the case almost unanimously agree that Crater was a victim of foul play, there are those who claim his true intent was revealed in the parting words he spoke to the last two people to see him alive, on August 6, 1930. The police report records the scene this way: "He shook their hands and, stepping into the gutter to enter the cab, turned and said, 'I'll be glad to get away.'"

The sheer volume of sightings from every part of the country—greater than that for Earhart—is partly accounted for by the substantial reward offered by the New York police and the *New York Standard*. But there's more to it than that. Often enough, those who claimed to have encountered the judge expressed no interest in a reward other than their vicarious satisfaction, even delight, in reporting Crater's happiness at having escaped the grim realities and insecurities of life amid the post-Crash wreckage of the 1930s.

Judge Crater was even turned into something of a legend among the hoboes and vagrants of the Great Depression, his meanderings celebrated in oft-repeated stories and songs. The most widely known of these is the anonymously composed "The Ballad of Judge Joe," which was collected in July 1937 by folklorist Albert Jenkins as part of a WPA project in an impromptu encampment near a ferry crossing along the Missouri River, two miles below Decatur, Nebraska.

The camp's two dozen inhabitants insisted to Jenkins that Judge Crater had spent several days with them the previous spring and were quite specific in their description of him: tall gent in a dust-covered brown suit with narrow green stripe. Though faded and worn, his collarless blue-and-white shirt was obviously of good material. On his right hand he wore a gold Masonic ring. His soft brown hat was tilted at a rakish angle. His only possessions were bed roll, package of clean but oft-mended socks and underwear, straight razor and eating utensils.

Though he never identified himself by his last name, he spoke of having been a "somebody" in New York, and they could tell from his "gentlemanly ways" and "excellent speech" that he had indeed been a person of high station. He encouraged them to move west, telling them that's where the future lay, and after a few days he hit the road, assuring them they'd meet again "in a better time and a better place."

An itinerant with a banjo played a song he claimed to have learned in an encampment outside South Bend, Indiana. Jenkins subsequently heard variations in camps from Fargo, North Dakota, to Stockton, California, but none differed in any significant way from the version he heard beside the Missouri. It was sung, he noted, to the tune of Stephen Foster's "Hard Times Come Again No More," which was composed amid the economic depression caused by the Panic of 1857. As set down by Jenkins, the lyrics—expressive of a willful acceptance of the peripatetic circumstances experienced by millions during the Depression—are as follows:

THE BALLAD OF JUDGE JOE

Let us pause in our journey, our voices raised as one,
And all sing of one man's destiny:
This lone and happy wanderer following the sun,
Oh, Judge Joe, you're forever free.

CHORUS:
Was a wife, a life left you weary,
Judge Joe, Judge Joe, you're forever free,
Many days you have journeyed in search of liberty,
Oh, Judge Joe, you're forever free.

He came at dusk one evening, whistling soft and sweet,
"Happy and unhurried," said he, "I always travel light";
A man of noble stature streaked by dust from head to feet,
who greets all men as brothers, no matter black or white.

"I'm on the road now, boys, traveling just like you,
Rid of life's illusions, lures and burdens;
Rid of bills and debt, and all that's overdue;
Free at last of sadness and false havens."

When cold dawn broke, he arose, bundle neatly stowed;
"I'm off today," said he, "on a journey new;
Lord willing, we'll meet again down some distant road,
Or maybe even sooner, when frost dissolves to dew."

New York City

"The luster which already swathes us round
Shall be outlustred by the flesh, which long
Day after day now moulders underground;
Nor shall that light have power to do us wrong,
Since for all joys that delight us then
The body's organs will be rendered strong."
—DANTE, *Paradiso*, Canto XIV

NO DREAMS THAT HE COULD REMEMBER—AND NONE OF THE
distressing and exhausting kind that leave you more tired than
when you went to sleep—Dunne awoke feeling far better than
the day before. He again had the hotel masseur come to his
room, and then took a long shower and had breakfast at
Schrafft's, on Madison. He walked down Fifth Avenue to the
42nd Street Library.

Bright sun said spring; temperature, in the low 20s, said otherwise. At the library, he asked for the reverse directories for the
Manhattan white pages (the listings done by address instead of
last names) from 1925 to1931. The librarian at the information
desk told him that they were kept at the Library's newspaper division at 43rd Street and Eleventh Avenue. He took a cab there.

Starting with the 1925 directory, he paged to 39 East 38th

Street. Sixteen names were listed for that address. Mrs. Mary King, the superintendent interviewed by A.I.M. five years later, on September 7t, 1930, is already in residence, her number listed as Caledonia-9-5517. Twelve of the remaining 15 were females.

The 1926 listings told a similar story, Mrs. King one of sixteen names, 12 females—but only six of the 12 were the same females as the year before. Ditto 1927: Mrs. King, twelve females, five different from the previous year. It wasn't until he'd read down the column of names a second time that he fixed on two he'd passed over. He ran his forefinger beneath each letter, making sure he wasn't misreading the entries. The twelfth name in the column was

Richfield, Mary Claire.........Lexington-9-6247;

three above that, at ninth, was

Lane, Merry.....................Caledonia-6-9360.

The first time he'd looked, he realized, he'd read Merry as Mary. It was the familiar ring of Richfield, Mary Claire, that made him pause. An instant later it registered: "The Venus of Broadway," she of the glorified body, who ended up shooting herself with Bud Mulholland's revolver. Still absorbing what was on the page, his eyes went back up the column. His finger tapped each letter of Lane, Merry. Memory of what had taken place in L.A. recent and distinct: Jeff Wine's prized photos of the poolside coupling; the unplanned visit to the Silver Moon Tea House: PALM REA ER AND ORTUNE TELLER TO TH STARS.

Neither Merry Lane nor Mary Claire Richfield could have any idea of what lay ahead. But living in New York, in 1927, amid the tide of single young women flooding into the city in search of independence, excitement, and a piece of the new life the Twenties seemed to be bringing into existence, hordes of them drawn by the lure of the booming theatrical business along "The Great White Way" ("The Great White Lie" Crow called it), they must have learned quickly what the men in charge expected of them.

Included in the exhaustive collection of newspaper clippings shipped to Florida had been a file of miscellaneous pieces from various publications that were related or potentially related to the Crater case. One recounted the "Army of Femme Floaters" pouring into the city. The limited number of clerical and sales positions open to them meant supply increasingly outran demand, and nowhere was the competition tougher than on Broadway. They did what they had to do to eat.

Places like 39 East 38th Street dotted the city. Not formal brothels but houses filled with single women where favors could be discreetly exchanged. A few, like Merry Lane and Mary Claire Richfield, would make it to the top, at least for a while. But at what price? "It was a slave market," said Patti Leroche. Crater was among the buyers.

Merry Lane and Mrs. King were there the next year, in 1928, but Richfield was gone. Right around then, she made her breakthrough in "The Cuddles & Cuties Revue" at the Winter Garden. The turnover in women continued in 1929 and 1930, but Merry Lane and Mrs. King remained. There was no listing, however, for the tenants A.I.M. had claimed to interview, *Mrs. Alma Parker, age 78, widow, and crippled daughter, Margaret, age 55.* Maybe they didn't have a phone. More likely, they were imaginary creations designed to reinforce that 39 East 38th Street needed no further investigation. If so, the ploy worked. In 1931, Merry Lane and Mrs. King were gone, as well.

He looked up the newspaper accounts of Mary Claire Richfield's suicide. Remembered it as happening in the summer of 1929. He was right. The story ran on June 21st with the headline in the *Mirror* reading: "Venus Vanquished: Gunshot Self-Inflicted." The picture that ran with it—Mary Claire in a short, flimsy, diaphanous dress—was a reminder that the Venus title was well earned.

No immediate destination in mind, he walked back to Broadway, falling into the rhythm of a comfortable pace, mind and body in sync, not unlike swimming. The more he walked, the better his knee felt, in direct contradiction to what several doctors had advised, their unanimous recommendation to avoid unnecessary foot travel and drive whenever possible. He followed Broadway downtown, turning the accumulation of facts over in his mind, fitting pieces together, forming a picture that, though not yet complete, was more than a wild guess or a highly speculative theory. For the first time, he was certain, he could hand Nan Renard her "pan-pollinating" scoop, the key ingredient in bringing together a "single synchronized effort." The explosion that resulted would be bigger than either she or Wilkes expected.

Stopping at Child's, across from City Hall, he had a cup of coffee and called Nan Renard's office. Left a message: *Be at the Coral at nine o'clock tonight.* He continued south to Trinity Church, and turned left onto Wall Street. Already wrapped in afternoon shadows, the narrow, gloomy space reverberated with sporadic honks and cast-iron rattle of loose manhole covers as the traffic rolled by. Isolated, forlorn sounds, like the last sad echoes of the wild party that ended so suddenly and so badly twenty-six years before.

He went north at Pearl Street. The recent razing of the tail end of the Third Avenue El had unmasked ancient storefronts and façades for the first time in seventy-five years. Still-standing relics of the vanished city, they looked depressed and doomed, as if they knew their demise was only a matter of time. He got on the El at Chatham Square, which was now the last stop, and stood next to the motorman's cabin, in the front car, the same spot where, as boys, he and his friends had shoved and pushed, each trying to claim it for himself. The train moved rapidly, curving from the Bowery onto Third Avenue. Rundown flophouses and fleabag hotels lining the route yielded to tenements and commercial buildings. The track ran in a straight line up the rest of the island, a river of wooden ties and steel rails, past the towers of midtown to the Bronx. He was at 42nd Street in fifteen minutes.

Old as it was, and as sure as the city fathers were they could do without it, there was no faster or more efficient above-ground transportation in the city. Downstairs, he bought the evening papers and ducked into the Automat, which was starting to fill with dinnertime customers. He had enough change to pop open the glass door for a chicken salad platter, filled his cup with coffee and sat by the window. He refilled his cup several times, smoked cigarettes and read the papers, filling the time until rush hour was over.

Woolworth's down the block was about to close but he had time to buy a screwdriver, flashlight and a whisk broom that fit into the pocket of his coat. He took his time walking to 38th Street; he strolled the block between Madison and Fourth Avenue on the south side, returned on the north. The demolition workers at No. 39 were gone for the night. The streetlamp on the east corner was out, adding to the darkness. Traffic was light, pedestrians few.

The hinge holding the lock on the wood-panel gate in front of the construction site was easily pried off with the screwdriver. The house was noticeably colder and damper inside than out. He groped his way down the hall before he switched on the flashlight—a lucky decision since the floor in the next room had been removed. Stepping carefully to the left, into what had been the parlor, he circled to the back of the house. The stairway to the basement was intact. The dank air was so thick with moisture it swirled in the flashlight's beam.

He skewered two rats with the light as they darted into a corner. He crossed the floor to the front wall, where the coal chute, now sealed shut, led up to the street.

Crouching down, he used the whisk broom to clear the space where the coal bin had been; he brushed it several times and slowly moved the light over the area he'd cleared. The patchwork repair job done to the floor was unmistakable. The rough surface indicated it had been a hasty, amateurish one. Bits of black were embedded in the concrete, as though it were still wet when the coal was piled on. He ran his finger over the slightly raised ridges, tracing a slightly irregular rectangle the size of a grave.

Nan Renard was in the usual booth. The room was nearly deserted. The waiter delivered a fresh martini and removed the old glass. Unsmiling and sad, she seemed either preoccupied or mildly stunned by the martini's effect on an empty stomach. She nodded but said nothing as he slipped in beside her on the banquette.

The maitre d' deposited a Scotch on the rocks in front of him, plenty of ice. He was annoyed to find her this way, glum, silent, on her way to getting drunk. He wanted her sober and clear-headed, attentive as possible to what he was going to say.

She lifted her glass and touched it to his, but put it down without taking a drink.

He sipped his Scotch. "What's wrong?"

"Everything."

"For instance?"

"Mr. Wilkes."

"Worse than usual?"

"He said the most terrible things. He thinks the project is going nowhere. He's threatening to close down the whole operation."

"Let him."

"Just what I need, a dose of Irish fatalism. Fortunately for you, your entire future isn't about to make a giant sucking sound as it circles down the drain." She consumed half her drink in a single gulp.

"Go easy."

She finished her drink. "I'll go any goddamn way I please."

The waiter went to pick up the empty glass. "Another," she said.

Dunne covered the glass with his hand. "Not yet."

She moved far away enough that she could face him. "My, my, you're getting good at giving orders. 'Not yet.' 'Be at the Coral at nine.' That's something all men seem good at, no matter how inept they are. Well, I can issue commands too, so go to hell."

The waiter stared with practiced attention at the far wall, as if searching for something. Dunne kept his hand over the glass. "It's important you hear me out. After, you can have all the drinks you want."

She sat in silence for a few seconds, as if deliberating; she took out a cigarette and lit it. "Say whatever you're going to say. Just don't take all night."

Dunne said nothing until the waiter walked away. "Any case I take, I try never to let myself spin theories from a limited number of facts. Before long, the theory wins out over the facts; the ones that don't support or advance the theory get tossed or ignored."

"Sounds like the opening lecture for 'Detective Work 101.'"

"The Crater case is no exception. Depending on which facts you select, you can believe that he was murdered by the mob, by his girlfriends, by his fellow politicians, by his wife, or that he engineered his own disappearance. At one time or another, a select number of facts have been used to support all these theories."

"But nothing's ever come of any of it."

"Because the investigators kept looking outside the investigation when all the time the crux of the case lay *inside*. Missing that fact, the investigation set off in the wrong direction, a mistake aggravated when the lead detective, a man who might have found his way back to the starting point, was compromised and lost interest in the case."

"Does 'crux' have a name?"

"For now, let's call him X."

"I'm not in the mood for games, Fin."

"It's not a game. I want you to provide the answer for yourself."

"Go ahead." She took an impatient puff on her cigarette. "Just don't take all night."

"Let's start with X, a young cop making a name as a hard-nosed detective. Meets a chorus girl. Before long they're in love. He proposes to her. But she prefers to postpone marriage until her career is established. In 1927, she gets a part in a Schumann brothers' revue at the Winter Garden—a walk-on—but she's gorgeous, amd people notice. By 1928, she's up for the lead in a show called 'Cuddles & Cuties.' Meanwhile, a politically connected lawyer, close to the Schumanns, is pressuring her to have sex with him. A familiar routine. Give him what he wants, he puts in a good word; don't, he blackballs you. She refuses. He goes to her bosses in the Schumann organization, who lean on her the way they've leaned on a thousand other girls. Finally she gives in, gets it over with. The part is hers. Then she learns she has syphilis, a gift from the lawyer. She doesn't tell X. But it eats at her until one morning, while X waits for her in bed, she sneaks his revolver into the bathroom and blows a hole in her heart."

"Am I supposed to guess who X is?"

"Not yet."

"Good, because I'm stumped."

"Distraught at her suicide, X can't figure out why she took her own life. Didn't she have everything to live for? The answer comes when a close friend and former housemate of his dead lover comes pleading for help. She's the next target for the lawyer's attentions, and she blurts out that she doesn't want to happen to her what happened to X's girlfriend.

"X starts to plan revenge, but not the kind that will send him to the electric chair. He watches the lawyer carefully and renews his acquaintance with the lawyer's chauffeur, an ex-cop who he worked with briefly when they were assigned to the Prohibition Bureau's Transportation Division. X notices the chauffeur's disapproval of the lawyer's sexual antics and his growing regard for the lawyer's innocent wife.

"X's desire for revenge is complicated when the governor elevates the lawyer to the bench of the State Supreme Court. His removal will result in a massive outcry and manhunt, so the plan has to be absolutely watertight. The lawyer, now a newly minted judge, has made the girl his main interest. Repulsed and scared but desperate to keep her job, she doesn't know what to do. X does. Summer recess is just beginning in the courts. He induces her to telegram the judge in Maine that she has to see him. The judge doesn't panic—this has undoubtedly happened before—but now he's facing an election in the fall and more worried than usual.

"When the chauffeur returns to the city after depositing the judge and his wife in Maine, X works on him insistently, tells him how the judge has hurt so many women and how much better off his wife would be free of such an ogre. He doesn't mention murder but suggests they scare the hell out of the judge, make him leave the bench, set his wife free.

"Another telegram arrives in Maine. Annoyed but concerned, the judge arranges to return to the city but, never one to

separate pleasure from business, meets some colleagues for sexual recreation in Atlantic City. Back in the city, he goes to see the
woman who's sent him the telegrams. She threatens blackmail.
Says she doesn't care if he goes to her bosses. She's fed up. She
wants money or she'll go to the newspapers and to the officials
who've already threatened an investigation into the magistrate's
court.

"He warns her that if she does she'll only wreck both
their careers. He needs a little while to return to Maine and
allay any suspicions his wife might have. Once he does, he'll
be back, and they can have a reasonable conversation about
the best way to proceed for both of them. Having been confronted with similar situations in the past, he's not surprised
when he succeeds in calming her down, unaware it's all part
of a trap.

"He arrives back in Maine, sure the situation is in hand.
He'll put in a call to the Schumanns— keep her happy by seeing
to it she gets a ripe part. If she wants money, he can always get
enough to keep her quiet. He slips away from his wife and
telephones the woman, just to reassure himself things are under
control. But they're not. She tells him she was about to send
another telegram. She can't wait any longer. She's got a boyfriend, and he's caught wind of what's going on. She needs to get
out of town. She needs five grand right away. She has to talk with
the judge. He should come to her place on the evening of the 6th,
at ten o'clock.

"Back in the city, but determined not to arouse any suspicions about the business he has to attend to, the judge goes about
his normal routines. X keeps careful tabs on him all day on the
6th, watching as he goes into Bobby Duncan's Café. He calls the
chauffeur and tells him where to rendezvous. At 9:15, in a cab
borrowed from the Prohibition Bureau's impoundment yard on
Pier 57, the chauffeur pulls up to the northwest corner of West

45th, facing south on Eighth Avenue. When the judge exits, the cab arrives to pick him up."

"But why take that risk? Why not let him make his own way?" There was no trace of anger or sadness in Nan Renard's face, or any trace of the several martinis.

"A couple of reasons. One, if he gets in a cab on his own, there'd be a witness to where he went and when. Second, there was always the chance he'd change his mind at the last minute, go back to Maine and pressure the Schumanns to take care of the matter for him. Third, however unlikely, he could decide to bring along hired muscle, somebody to make clear that there was only so far he could be pushed."

"Wouldn't he recognize the taxi driver as his chauffeur? Wouldn't that alert him something was up?" She rubbed out a cigarette and lit another.

"Not at first. By the time the cab turned onto Ninth, it didn't matter. Crouched in the well of the front passenger seat, X springs into action. The judge presumes he's the boyfriend the woman mentioned, but X reassures him that his only goal is to arrange a satisfactory outcome.

"The judge isn't happy with the development and, maybe now, recognizing his chauffeur, realizes he faces a significant blackmail attempt. Yet, on another level, he's probably not entirely displeased by X's presence. The man is calm and direct, maybe even affable. Instead of an outraged, irrational female, the judge imagines this is someone he can reason with; and as betrayed as he may feel at the collusion of his chauffeur, he doesn't feel in physical danger. As they pull up to their destination, he's already figuring how best to finesse the situation and what it's going to cost him.

"The chauffeur imagines X will put the fear of God into the judge, scare him into leaving the bench and ending the fraud he's perpetrated on his wife. Never supposes X plans to kill the judge.

How could anybody be crazy enough to think they're going to kill a State Supreme Court judge and get away with it? The woman thinks the same thing. When X and the judge come to her apartment, she pours them drinks. She enjoys the judge's discomfort. It's nice to see him squirm for a change. She figures that at the very least they'll get a quick five thousand out of him.

"They start to talk money. The judge paces the floor in front of the fireplace, raises his voice. He hasn't brought the cash with him. He quibbles about the sum they're asking for, reminds them that if he loses his job, they lose their hold on him. Maybe X planned to do away with the judge by drugging him first or knocking him out, but, at this display of arrogant self-confidence, X grabs the poker next to the fireplace and with one tremendous blow crushes the judge's skull."

Nan put up her hand. "Excuse me, Fin, but you sound as if you're reading from X's signed confession. Do you have any eyewitnesses?"

"Some of the details are conjecture, but not the basic facts. When it comes to the murder, X gave an account of it himself when he visited the judge's widow in Maine and had her reenact it."

"Now the sixty-four thousand dollar question: what did X do with the body?"

"I suspect the original plan was to wrap it up and bury it in some remote part of the countryside. But confronted with the reality of getting the bloody, brain-leaking corpse back into the taxi, X thought better of it. He summoned the super, a widowed, working-class woman, who not only abetted the sex trade in the building but knew the judge as a frequent visitor. He tells her there's been an altercation and she now has a justice of the State Supreme Court lying dead on the floor of the apartment. If the police are dragged in, they'll rip apart the building from ceiling to cellar. The newspapers will make a sensation of it and put her at the center of it.

"She agrees to help get rid of the body. X summons the chauffeur, who discovers he's become an accessory to the murder of a state judge. The super guides them to the basement, where they empty the coal bin and dig a grave. They do a hasty patch job on the floor, and when it's barely dry, they pile the coal back in. X reminds them the slightest slip up on their part and they'll take turns getting zinged in the electric chair in Sing Sing.

"X had factored in that the judge probably wouldn't be missed for a day or two and this gave them time to cover their tracks and settle into their ordinary routines. The next night, in one last brazen act, he slips through the service entrance of Crater's building and into his apartment. He finds the five grand and change and sees the two briefcases filled with files. He takes them as well as the money for the single reason that their disappearance will provide the police a false lead. He burns the contents without even looking at them. He gives the five grand to the landlady. Tells her not to spend any of it. For now, just sit still.

"Remarkably, a week later no public alarm had been sounded. Uncertain about the judge's whereabouts and afraid he might be spilling his guts out to state investigators about judicial corruption, the politicians were doing their best to keep his absence under wraps till they had a handle on what had happened to him. To keep things looking normal, X has the chauffeur return to Maine on the day he's expected. For her own sake, he says, the judge's wife should be encouraged to remain there as long as possible.

"When the alarm is raised, X is back working his regular beat on the homicide squad. He shows up at Missing Persons as one of the first among the many cops who offers or is summoned to help. Before the investigation can find its way to the murder site, X acts preemptively. He sends a letter calling attention to the location, then volunteers to check it out. Finding nothing of interest, he reports there's no need to return.

"He worries about how reliable the chauffeur is. But as well as having a solid alibi, Kipps is protected by his reputation as a retired cop made slightly goofy by shell shock. In the end, he stays mum. A more substantial worry is the lead detective, a highly intelligent, tenacious cop with the kind of nose that just might smell an inside job. In a moment of weakness, X visits the judge's wife in Maine and tries to convince her the only way out of her predicament is to take the fall for her husband's disappearance. One of the few mistakes he makes. He gets nowhere with the judge's wife but exposes himself to possible identification. Yet it turns out to be a coup. The story of his visit reinforces the notion that she's a self-deluded hysteric whose testimony is worthless.

"The following spring the lead detective ends up undercutting his role in the investigation. The woman in whose apartment the murder took place goes to Hollywood where she enjoys a brief stardom but is never free of her fear of being found out. The super moves to another city, happy with her obscurity and the added comfort of her $5,000 nest egg. The chauffeur spends the rest of his life regretting his part in the murder and in love with the judge's wife."

"And X, what happened to him?"

"He stays a detective. Develops a reputation for fearless confrontation, someone who not only doesn't avoid shoot-outs and showdowns with gangsters and robbers but seeks them out, and leaves them dead. When the war comes, he gets in on the action and gets better and better at his work."

"Is he still alive?"

"Very much so. He does so well in the war that the government brings him back to deal with a new set of enemies. As a cover, they help get him a job that gives him license to continue traveling and do what he does best. Kill people."

"How did you manage to uncover all this?"

"I had an assistant."

"Who?"

"Time."

"You're losing me."

"Before time eradicates, it exposes what's buried or hidden. Ancient artifacts. Nuggets of gold. A misplaced file. An old man who takes a last opportunity to make a one-word confession. A woman tired of the world's scorn who produces a hidden relic."

"Are you sure you can substantiate it all?"

"The general outline is correct. But we're going to have to bring in more people to nail down all the details. And we have to start right away, beginning with the excavation of the basement at 39 East 38th Street."

"Mr. Wilkes will be ecstatic. He'll pay whatever it costs."

"Wilkes can't know."

"He *has* to know. This was his idea."

"No, it wasn't. It was given to him."

"By whom?"

"X."

"Fin, what are you talking about?"

"After twenty-five years, interest in the case had diminished into occasional pieces in newspapers and magazines. X was certain the truth lay buried forever until one day, out of the blue, a call comes from L.A., a panicked voice at the other end, one he hasn't heard in a long time. It's the woman whose apartment the murder took place in. Someone had show up where she worked. Obviously, a cop. New York accent. She's unnerved. He tries to calm her. She tells him that the janitor got his name. Fintan Dunne.

"Now it's X who's taken aback. He knows Fintan Dunne. But he can't imagine why he'd be interested in the Crater case. Probably a coincidence. Just to be sure, he puts a tail on him, and next thing you know, Dunne is off to Havana, where X has been working for the last several months, even books himself into the same hotel. X's paranoia shifts into high gear. In a moment of panic, using his outfit's mob connections, he orders a hit on Dunne. But he quickly comes to his senses and rescinds it.

"X figures a better way to get to the bottom of the matter: It's possible but not probable that Dunne is interested in the Crater case; more likely, his trips to L.A. and Havana were entirely innocent. It's also true that if anybody was looking to hire someone for a last crack at the Crater case before everybody involved was dead and gone, they couldn't do better than to hire Dunne. So, once again, he decides to act preemptively.

"His boss is in the middle of planning the launch of a major new project and is searching for the right story to hang it on. X comes to him with the perfect candidate. A great American mystery, one emblematic of an entire era, solved at last. It's a long shot but, says X, if anyone can deliver, it's Fintan Dunne. Have the story ready for August 6th, the 25th anniversary of the case, when the competitors are all tied up commemorating the grim anniversary of Hiroshima."

"But you're wrong, Fin. The Crater case was Mr. Wilkes's idea."

"How do you know?"

"Mr. Wilkes told me so himself."

"I'm sure he did. And I'm also sure that the man who gave Wilkes the idea counted on him claiming the idea was his own. He played on Wilkes's ego. I bet he's had a lot of practice."

"You mean Bud Mulholland, don't you?"

"Ambrose Mulholland, or to employ the full name he used in the memorials that ran in the newspapers after Mary Claire Richfield's suicide, 'MCR, my love now and forever, Ambrose Ignatius Mulholland.'"

She folded her hands in front of her face, as if praying. "I need that martini."

He signaled for the waiter and ordered her drink, double Scotch for himself. "What do you know about the work he does?"

"Just what I told you. Helping reporters who get in trouble. Behind-the-scenes stuff."

"Nothing about what he does for the government?"

"Rumors, sure. But Mulholland's activities were never of interest to me."

"They are now."

The waiter delivered their drinks. When he'd gone, Dunne gave her a condensed version of what Pully told him about Mulholland. Two questions, he said, remained: how willing would Wilkes be to turn in one of his own—a liaison with a powerful government agency—in pursuit of an answer to the Crater case? And at what point would Mulholland, realizing the investigation was focusing on him, do whatever necessary to stop it?

"There's been one murder already," he said, "though Mulholland probably regards Fred Kipps's death as a mercy killing."

"He must be off balance. He can't have expected you to move so quickly."

"You can bet he'll move fast to make up for lost time."

"That means we have to move faster. I'll put off Wilkes as long as I can. You have to leave the Savoy Plaza. Lie low."

"I need to bring others in. Cronin at Missing Persons has to pay an immediate visit to the basement at 39 East 38th Street."

"What about Mulholland? What do we do about him?"

"For now, nothing."

Except for the background hum of conversation from the bar and the faint murmur of an instrumental playing on the juke-box, the room was quiet.

"This could get you fired," he said. "That's among the more pleasant outcomes."

"I know." She dipped her fingers into her glass. "Do you like olives?"

"Yes."

"Open." She removed the olive from the glass, leaned forward and placed it delicately on the slope of his tongue.

He chewed—piquant, pleasant taste, trace of gin; swallowed. "What now?"

"Let's go to the bar."

There were only a few other patrons. Carlos, the bartender, greeted Nan Renard by name, served them their drinks and stood by the window. In the aquarium behind the bar, the fish moved slowly, gliding up and down; two miniature sharks traveled side by side in mellow circuits. One by one the other patrons left.

Rain suddenly lashed the front window. Carlos peered at the watery blur; a smudge of pink neon sign blinked across the street. He turned out the front lights and locked the door, ambled back to where they sat. "Take your time, Miss Renard. Enjoy your drinks. But tonight very slow. Once you finish, I close it up." He turned back to the window. "Few weeks ago was the snow. Now rain. A good sign. It means *adios*, winter."

"Yes, Carlos," she said. "Let's toast that: *Adios*, winter."

When they left, the downpour had diminished to drizzle. "How about a nightcap?" she said.

"At the Stork?"

"My place."

He glanced both ways, west toward his hotel, east toward her building. He thought of the *reasons not to*: didn't need another drink; what could/would follow, complications, expectations, implications; Roberta. A taxi raced west on 59th Street, swish of tires over drenched, glistening asphalt, speeding recklessly before the light at the corner changed to red. "Why not?"

She put her arm in his. Neither said anything. The doorman nodded a neutral acknowledgment when they entered. They rode the elevator to her floor. She stabbed at the lock several times with her key. Giggling softly, she handed it to him. "Here, steady Eddie, you give a try."

He slipped it in on the first try, opened the door, entered, and groped for the light switch on the wall. Before he could find it, she reached past, covered it with her hand. The door shut behind her. Darkness surrounded them. Sound of her breathing—feel of it on his neck—told him where she was. Uninvited, *the reasons not to* were back. "Nan," he whispered, "maybe if we . . ."

Her upright finger formed a cross with his lips. "No maybes, no ifs, not tonight. I knew the first time I saw you, in Mr. Wilkes's bedroom. Like it or not, I thought, it's going to happen." She rushed her lips across his cheek until they reached his lips. He kissed her. Hard. Pressure of her lips on his: harder. Flicker of her tongue on his; his on hers. Mouths splayed, incapable of speech.

Eyes adjusted to the dark, they went into the living room, threw their coats on the sofa. He pulled her close, glided the zipper down the back of her dress. She pulled off his tie, undid the buttons on his shirt. She took his hand, pulled him into the bedroom. "One minute," she said. She went into the bathroom.

He undressed, got into bed. Out the window, lights on the Queensborough Bridge traced the graceful sweep of its supporting cables, the middle curve stood against the night sky like a gigantic version of the Steeplechase-Jack smile in the portrait on Stella Crater's wall. Too late for caution, too early for regret. A thought darted across his mind like a mouse into a hole: *Grow up, Fin*. It went as fast as it came.

The door to the bathroom opened. She was framed in the light: long, shapely legs enmeshed in black nylons, fastened to red garters that hung from a front-laced black corset. She walked to the bed, pulled on the laces, revealing the upward

297

tip of her breasts, erect nipples. She pulled back the covers.
Adios, winter.

He opened his eyes. No idea of how long since they finished. Bridge lights, bright in the distance, like the constellations
in the zodiac—Aries, Leo, Virgo—traced the great, wide smile.
He rolled over. She was lying on her side, awake. They kissed.
She straddled him. He ran his hands up her firm, flat belly,
rubbed her breasts, took the nipples between thumb and forefinger. They made love again.

Dawn: he woke again. She wasn't in the bed. The bathroom door was closed. She came out wearing a robe, and
beckoned as she let it drop to the floor. He followed her into
the shower. "I like my men clean all over." She opened an
unlabeled vial—shampoo especially made for Mr. Wilkes, she
explained, "frightfully expensive." He almost asked her what
Wilkes's shampoo was doing in her shower, but didn't. She
lathered his hair, ran her hand down to his crotch, stroked
him. "Stop," he said finally, "or I'll finish right here." She
smiled, kept stroking, "That's all right, Fin, *come, come, go
ahead and come.*"

Clean and dry, he got back in bed. She dressed hurriedly.
Didn't want to be late for an early appointment, she said, but no
need for him to leave. She'd call him at the hotel. She bent down,
kissed him, nuzzled his hair with her nose, smiled. "You have
Mr. Wilkes's scent."

"The scent of money?"

"Destiny. I like it."

He was glad she told him to stay. Too late to undo, doubt
or second guess what they'd done. But for now, before doubt,
regret, remorse, this was enough: void, inertia, body at rest con-
tent to stay at rest, the lack of desire that follows the culmination

of desire. He lay on his back, folded his hands on his chest, the posture of the dead. The John Garfield way. He went back to sleep.

He walked back to the hotel. Brisk, clear, sunny day. Very unlike the mood that settled over him. He stopped at Schrafft's for a pot of tea and a turkey sandwich. Sat in a corner, away from the sunshine, smoked, moped, brooded. He'd violated all his own rules. Crossed a line he shouldn't have. He knew better. But how often did knowing better translate into acting better? Not often enough. Working with Nan in the days ahead would be inevitably complicated by last night.

Roberta had tried to save him from himself with that simple advice: *Grow up, Fin.* But he didn't listen because deep down, though he hadn't admitted it to himself, until now, he blamed her for his discontent. It was his idea to retire, not hers, and he'd been surprised when she'd gone along. Unconsciously, he supposed, he'd expected her to talk him out of it. Instead, she went to Florida, scouted ahead, bought the house, and when they left New York, she was the one who traveled smoothly into their new life.

In good manly fashion, he'd behaved like a boy. He didn't voice any qualms, didn't talk to her about his doubts, but grew petulant, moody, restless, like an adolescent, until it brought him to this moment. The thought of her with Felipe came to him as a sharp pain. He'd been denying it because he couldn't admit he was the cause.

The possibility of losing her was more than he could bear. But Jack Lynch's advice from ten years ago—*It's your wife's forgiveness you should ask for. Make it up to her when you get home*—wouldn't be good enough this time. He hadn't been away at war. He'd been proving to himself that he hadn't lost anything, that he was as good as he'd ever been, that retirement was a silly mistake. In the process, he'd called into question their future.

Forgiveness would no longer be enough. Now, if she'd let him, he'd have to figure out how to rebuild what he'd destroyed.

Only one message at the desk: *Please call Mr. Louis Pohl. Urgent.* The only urgency he felt was to lie down. He sat on the bed, took a pad and pencil from the night table, tried to draft a note to Roberta. Couldn't. Put the pad back in the drawer, beside the Bible. A time for everything under heaven, for contentment, for contradictions, for contrition. On the verge of breaking open the biggest case of his life, he was sorry he'd gotten involved.

Dunne chalked up blurred vision and slight dizziness to a mild hangover. Napped for half an hour and awoke wearier than when he fell asleep, as though he were coming down with something. His stomach began to cramp. The phone rang. It was Crow. Von Vogt had called to tell him about the encounter with Brophy's bat. "You all right?"

"Fine." The wheeze in his voice was pronounced.

"You don't sound fine."

"Nothing a good night's sleep won't cure."

The cramps worsened. He was sweating. On the way to the bathroom, he had to lean against the wall for support. He called the front desk. The receiver trembled in his hand. Asked that the house doctor be sent to his room. No recollection of the answer. He must have passed out. Suddenly, someone was pressing on his chest; nearby, wearing his funeral director attire, the front desk clerk shouted in the phone. "Yes, this *is* an emergency. Send an ambulance immediately."

What followed was a blur of conscious and unconscious moments; doctors and nurses in hurried conversations; glaring lights, pitch darkness, Roberta and Felipe shaking their heads, Mulholland in gray fedora, gray herringbone coat, black galoshes over black shoes, *New York Standard* under his arm. *Welcome to the North Pole, Fin.* Did he dream the priest in his purple stole? He was sure he felt the pieces of oil-rich cotton wool touch him softly, eyes, mouth, nose, palms, bottoms of his feet; saw candles, crucifix; heard the Latin words of the Last Rites.

His first awareness of the incision in his neck and the tube inserted in his windpipe was hearing the loud purr of the air pump next to his bed. A trio of grave faces loomed above: Crow, Dr. Rossiter, the third—a woman—with short black hair, lovely face. Who? It came to him: assistant pathologist Linda DeMarco. Another illusion, he thought, as if he were lying in the morgue about to witness his own autopsy. But her hand touched his forehead, cool and real. She flashed a light in his right eye, then his left. "Severe contraction of the pupils," she said. She took a sample of blood. Crow and Rossiter stood in the corner. She barked at the nurse beside her, "Right now, begin the atropine injections, *right now*."

The sweating stopped. He sat up. But soon the dizziness returned. He lost consciousness. He didn't know for how long. She was hovering over him. "It's as if he got another dose of the toxin." She was speaking to someone behind her who he couldn't see. Her face came so close to his that he felt her exhalation on his eyelids. She sniffed around his head the way a dog would, put her nose into his hair, pulled back the bedclothes and smelled his crotch.

She stood erect. "Smell that?"

Rossiter stepped from behind her. "Smell what?"

"His hair."

He leaned down, sniffed. "Garlic?"

"Organophosphate. It's on his pubic hair as well." She turned her back to him, said to someone in the background, "He's to be shaved from head to toe. *Now*."

Dunne wasn't sure if the man who did the cutting and shaving was a male nurse or a barber, but he was thorough and quick, using scissors and straight razor on head, arms, legs, chest, crotch, not worrying about the occasional nicks he inflicted.

Afterwards, they carried Dunne to a large tub filled with hot, soapy water, rubbed, scrubbed, rinsed and dried. An injection of sedatives put him in a deep, restful sleep.

When he woke, the tube had been removed from his throat, and the breathing machine was out of the room. He was able to sit up. Had a cup of tea. Not long after, Crow's head poked around the door. "Nice to see you're back from the netherworld. For a time, it looked as though Charon was about to ferry you across the Acheron."

Alarmed by their last phone conversation, Crow explained, he'd stopped by the hotel and learned that "an ambulance had already taken you to the hospital." Doctors had diagnosed "acute respiratory distress" but seemed at a loss about the cause or how to reverse it. For a while it was touch and go. Crow called Rossiter and asked him to recommend someone. Rossiter came in person and brought Dr. DeMarco with him. "She's the one saved your life, Fin. No doubt about it, you'd have been a goner without her. Her only question is how you managed to get a fatal dose of organophosphates in your hair."

"Organo what?"

"I'll let her explain."

Dr. DeMarco stopped by later. After examining him, she mentioned that the lack of any discernible cause for his distress was what made her suspect some sort of poison was at work. But it was unclear at first that, instead of being ingested, it was being absorbed through the skin.

"The garlicky smell tipped me off. Disguised but not obliterated, it told me I was dealing with organophosphates." Developed by IG Farben, she said, the German chemical cartel, for deployment in World War II, the Nazis refrained from using them, afraid of the retaliation the Allies might inflict. They were manufactured as a nerve gas under various names, Tabun, Sarin, Soman, and increasingly used in insecticides, in DDT and the like. More and more cases of poisoning were showing up among farm workers. "So tell me, Mr. Dunne, how did you manage to work such a potent toxin into your hair?"

"Guess I used the wrong shampoo."

"I searched your bathroom and sent shampoo, soap, lotions to the lab. Nothing."

"Showered at a friend's. Maybe I mistook insecticide for shampoo."

"Not likely. What you used was a highly concentrated form of organophosphates. Laced with perfume and a gel, it was intended to ensure the compound remained on your skin as long as possible—in other words, to kill you in as subtle, sophisticated fashion as possible. Can you think of anyone who wants you dead, Mr. Dunne?"

"I'd rather not."

"You better. The shampoo is still out there. The next victim might not be as lucky."

The day he was being discharged from the hospital, he sat dressed in his room reading a copy of *Readers' Digest*. The feature piece was on the U.S twenty-five years from now, in 1980. Predictions included coast-to-coast highways, atomic cars, dishwashers, submarines, jet planes and trains, artificial hearts, lungs, limbs—better than the originals—the same dreams touted at the 1939 World's Fair, but new and improved for a world that had come close to destroying itself in the six years that followed.

Pully appeared at the door. "I hope I'm not interrupting anything."

"I was reading about the future. Looks better than I thought."

"Never turns out as good or bad as people think. Best advice? Stick with the present. At least you know what you've got." He sat next to Dunne. "I didn't think you'd look so good."

"Sorry to disappoint."

"I checked at the hotel when you didn't return my message. They told me you were here. Crow filled me in on what happened. I warned you to be careful."

"I was."

"Not enough, it seems." He handed Dunne a manila envelope. "I shared the preliminary report on Nan Renard with you on the phone. I told the investigators at ISC to keep digging. The full version was slow in coming. It arrived on my desk the day I tried to reach you. I've made you a copy. Give it a read. I think you'll find it interesting."

When he got back to the hotel, he opened the envelope and glanced over the contents. The few words underlined or marked with an exclamation point were all he needed. Daughter. Mother. Father. A trinity that he'd never guessed. He tossed the file in the wastepaper basket.

She'd played her several parts with the seasoned professionalism of an actress twice her age, ingénue, career girl, seductress. How could he have missed it, he asked himself. Other questions, as well:

Q. That face across the table in the Coral, so lovely, sincere, what was it made of?

A. Insincerity. Mask of wax. Molded to fit the moment.

Q. What was behind the mask?

A. Countenance of marble, heart of stone, like her father's.

Q. What had she really felt? Contempt? Amusement? Fear?

A. Unknown. Unknowable. What did it matter?

She must have grown more and more confident as time went on, right up to the last act, the lamb going willingly, happily to the slaughter, bleating with pleasure as the butcher's blade stroked his throat. *That's all right, Fin, come, come, go ahead and come.*

He winced at the memory.

He ate dinner in his room. It was after nine when, on the third try, he reached Bud Mulholland. "No problem," Mulholland said when Dunne proposed they meet at the Iron Horse the next day at three o'clock. It was as if he had been waiting for the call.

Mulholland didn't turn around but followed Dunne's approach in the mirror behind the bar. "Can I buy you a drink?"

Dunne mounted the stool next to him. "Club soda. Plenty of ice."

The bartender refilled Mulholland's glass, served Dunne's drink and walked away. One other patron was at the far end of the bar.

Mulholland directed his question to the mirror, reflected hand gesturing toward the bandage on Dunne's reflected throat. "What happened?"

"Cut myself shaving."

"Looks like you shaved everywhere. You should be more careful."

"Now you tell me."

"I warned you about vanity, remember?"

"But not about murder."

"I suppose you want some answers."

"Got the answers, Bud."

"All of them?"

"All I need."

"About Nan?"

"Everything."

"I didn't put her up to it, you should know that."

"Didn't exactly discourage her, either."

"She's not susceptible to discouragement."

"Not even from her father?"

"I didn't want it to happen like this."

"How did you want it to happen?"

"You really interested in hearing?"

"Try me."

Mulholland peered in the mirror: real eyes into reflected ones; he lit a cigarette, dragged, exhaled, blew a trio of O's toward the reflection. "From the beginning?"

"From the beginning."

A speakeasy on 52nd Street, just before closing time, winter thirty years ago. Recovered from the shoot-out with Rothstein's boys, back at work only a few days, having a nightcap when she walked in.

—*The most beautiful girl I've ever seen, and funny and easy to talk to. It's as if she doesn't know or care how gorgeous she is. And when I ask her out, she laughs and says, "You don't even know my name, you silly ape!"*

He knew it soon enough: Mary Claire Resnick (Richfield is the name she uses), a Bronx girl now living in a rented room in midtown, professional dancer, last girl on the left in the chorus line, little roles, big hopes. One date turned into three.

—*Never been with anyone like her. Wasn't only outside beauty she had—though she had that in spades—but inside too.*

He never thought about marriage before. Now that's all he thought about. Settle down, buy a little place on Long Island by the water, with a fireplace and a front porch. Except she wasn't ready. Bigger parts were coming her way; directors taking notice.

—*"What's the rush?" she says. "We got all our lives for that."*

And then she got pregnant. Seemed certain she'd get rid of it. Easy enough to do in those days. But she decides to go through with it. Delivers a baby girl in '26. *Anna.*

　—*But there's no way a cop and a chorine are going to raise a kid the proper way. Her brother and his wife, who ran a grocery store, agreed to keep Anna until we had the time and money to take on the responsibility. But we went up to the Bronx every Sunday to be with her. Mary Claire insisted on that. And when the day came when we could afford it, Anna was going to have everything her parents didn't—toys, nursemaids, vacations in the country, trips to Europe, tutors, the best schools.*

Back at work, she picked up where she'd left off. More notices. Bigger parts. Mary Claire Richfield was becoming an attraction. Tried out for starring role in "The Cuddles & Cuties Revue," the new Schumann brothers' production. Got the part.

　—*"Oh, by the way," she's told, "on one condition. That lawyer who's been at the tryouts, the one who sent the roses? Well, along with being politically connected, he's a real friend to the organization, a valuable ally in helping navigate the endless lawsuits and legal squabbles that are the bane of the theatre business. A devoted admirer of yours, Mary Claire, he asks one small favor."*

Not small to her. She knew how the game was played, but got where she was without playing it. Until now. To say no was to turn her back on her dream, all she'd worked for, on being able to choose the roles she wanted, offers from Hollywood, on wealth, stardom, beautiful home, wonderful life for her daughter.

　—*"Come now, Mary Claire," they said, "don't act the shy virgin. Maybe you've succeeded in hiding the birth of that child from the newspapers, but not from us. You know how things work around here. There are a dozen girls dying to step into that part. All of them eager and willing to do what's necessary to get it."*

She got the part. Audiences and critics loved her. Newspapers hailed her as "The Venus of Broadway." Advertisers started clamoring for her to endorse their products. But away from the flashbulbs and spotlights, she was sad. Depressed.

—*I didn't know what she'd had to do. She kept it a secret because she was afraid how I'd react. All I knew she was distant, didn't want any part of making love. Figured she was having trouble handling success.*

He waited for her in bed after a night on the town when she seemed her old self again. He didn't notice her slip his gun out of its holster. Had no idea what had happened when he heard the explosion in the bathroom. Had to break the door open. Saw her sprawled there, red stain spreading across her chest. His first thought was: I'm in the middle of a nightmare. Turned out it was a nightmare, but not the kind that morning and daylight could deliver him from.

—*I should have picked up the gun right there and ended it.* But didn't. Why?

—*I'd like to say it was because of our baby, because of Anna, but I'd be lying. She never entered my mind. What wanted was to know why this gorgeous woman with so much to live for, at the moment when her dreams were coming true, would do such a thing to herself—and to me.*

Didn't find out at first. The girls who knew—livelihoods precarious enough as it was—kept it to themselves. But when Merry Lane, Mary Claire's best friend, came to him he learned the truth. She'd become the next target of the lawyer's unwanted attention, and she was desperate something be done right away to scare him off.

Yet it couldn't be done right away, not if it were going to be done correctly—especially after the lowlife was elevated to the bench—in a way that extracted revenge and meted out justice but didn't lead directly to the electric chair.

—*And it was done correctly. Not perfectly—there's no such thing as a perfect crime. It's a little like war. The winners make blunders. But the losers make more. I made blunders. Going to see Mrs. Crater, for instance. But the police made more. Gradually, interest faded, and Crater went from celebrated case to curiosity.*

The hole inside him, however, was too big to be filled by a single act of revenge. He threw himself into being a cop, the toughest, most fearless detective on the force. Took every opportunity he could to put his life at risk, shoot it out with gangsters and robbers to the point where the worst and hardest of them did their best to steer clear. He wished he could say that he'd also taken charge of their daughter's life and made a home for Anna. He sent money, that was it. Didn't see her. Couldn't stand being reminded of her mother.

—After a while, if you want to know the truth, I hardly gave her any thought.

Anna Resnick was seventeen when the woman she thought was her mother died. Going through her things, Anna discovered an envelope tucked in a drawer. In it were newspaper clippings that chronicled Mary Claire Richfield's rise on Broadway and her suicide in a cop's apartment. Beneath was a birth certificate for Anna; mother listed as Mary Claire Resnick, father: unknown. There was also a death certificate for Mary Claire Richfield (AKA Resnick). Cause of death: gunshot (self-inflicted).

Stunned, she confronted who she thought was her father—Mary Claire's brother—and he told her the truth. The war was on, and her father was already serving with the OSS. She wrote him. He didn't answer. She kept writing. Finally, he wrote her back, and they struck up a correspondence.

—First time I saw her was in '46. Like seeing Mary Claire again. Anna was beautiful, smart and ambitious, just like her mother. We got close. She was trying to make sense of her mother's suicide, and eventually I told her everything. Didn't hold anything back. She said she was glad I did what I did. Took it upon herself to visit Merry Lane on the West

Coast. Merry wasn't thrilled at the idea, but they hit it off and became friends.

Pretty soon I was away again in a new job, one I'm sure Louis Pohl filled you in on that night at the Golden Gloves. I didn't go back into clandestine work because I'm some super patriot on a crusade against the Reds. God knows, the Agency's got no shortage of zealots. Me, I've never given a shit about politics. What the Agency did was offer me the only kind of work I've ever been good at. After a while, I got sent back to New York, embedded in the Wilkes's outfit.

The irony is, I knew Wilkes's old man. Had a real eye for females. At one point, the old goat offered Mary Claire a hefty sum to model for a mural he wanted painted on his bedroom wall, scene from Greek or Roman mythology. She had me come along to make sure it was on the up and up. It was. The old man couldn't perform anymore but still liked to look. Told us all about his career. He was a titan. His son is a pygmy, and a pompous ass to boot.

I didn't pull Anna into Wilkes's business. It was her idea. Asked for my help, the first and only time she ever had. How could I say no? Wilkes had no notion she was my daughter. But he liked her, and she went up the ranks fast—on her own merits, not my pull. He made her the project manager for a new venture he was planning.

Not long after came the frantic call from Merry Lane. Somebody had come to where she worked and asked for her, like he knew something. Sounded like he was from New York. She had his name written down. Fintan Dunne.

He knew a Fintan Dunne. Knew him well. Former cop. Served together in the OSS. Had his own agency. What the hell was he doing in L.A. trying to find Merry Lane? Hadn't talked to Dunne in a while, but asked around and didn't like what he heard. He'd hooked up with ISC. If he was doing a job for them, it could be something big. Anna raised the possibility that some newspaper or broadcast company might be trying to make a splash with the upcoming anniversary of the Crater case.

—I didn't think so, but to be on the safe side, I ordered a tail. And what do you know? Dunne flies off to Havana and books himself into the same hotel where I always stay.

You don't need to be in my job very long before you get a little paranoid. Helps keep you alive, long as you keep it under control. I started losing control. Couldn't get it to add up. I ask myself, Is Dunne interested in the Crater case because Anna's right and he's been hired by some press hound? Or has Louie Pohl brought him into ISC so he can enlist him in his one-man crusade against the Agency?

I'll admit it. I did something stupid. Called my contacts in Havana and ordered a hit. After a couple of hours I came to my senses. Decided to just wait and see. But Anna thought that was a terrible idea.

"Look," she said, "you can't simply sit and wait. It might be too late when you decide to do something. Sooner or later, the odds are that some editor or publisher is going to order a new look into the Crater case. If they don't hire Dunne, they'll hire somebody else; and if they do hire Dunne—and if he's as good <u>and</u> as lucky as you say—isn't there a chance he'll stumble his way to an answer?"

Nan Renard (Anna Resnick Mulholland) was clear with her father. They had to take control of the situation. Bring in Fintan Dunne, see if he got anywhere. If he didn't, then the matter was essentially closed. Nobody would. Before long, all the witnesses would be dead. The public would forget.

In the unlikely event Dunne did get somewhere, well, he'd be performing a service, exposing all the traces that should be obliterated. Let him do the work, and when he was done, do what had to be done with him.

She came up with the plan. Told her father to take a back seat, stay out of it. She'd play the wide-eyed innocent with no other interest than to advance her own career. She sold Wilkes on the Crater story right away. It wasn't hard. Despite appearances, he was drowning in debt, bad investments, uncontrolled expenses. He jumped on it.

—*She was sure you'd agree, and you did, right away. At first, as expected, things went nowhere. She seemed confident you'd give up. She'd write a check, send you away, assure Wilkes she'd find another story. But suddenly, the remotest of possibilities became looming certainty, and the unavoidable question arose: What to do with Fintan Dunne?*

It was when she told me Fred Kipps had to be eliminated that I realized Anna had become more my child than Mary Claire's. Said it so matter of factly. Wasn't hard to carry out. Slip in and out in the middle of the night. Pillow over the face. Still, I felt bad. I'd known Fred a long time. When I came back, she saw I was upset. All she said was "You should have done it years ago."

Your success, Fin, guaranteed you were next. She asked me about the possibility of using poison, something that could be subtly administered and was quick acting. I didn't try to stop her. Wish I could tell you otherwise, but I'd be lying. Got what she asked for, shampoo the Agency has used successfully on several occasions.

When I gave it to her, I explained how simple it was to use and how important to make sure it was directly and generously applied. I didn't ask for any details about how she intended to do that, and she didn't supply any.

As I watched her leave, I thought about the dreams Mary Claire and I had for our daughter and what that daughter had become. It made me feel old and tired, very tired, like I could lie down and sleep forever.

"No," Dunne said when the bartender returned, "no more club soda. Make it Scotch on the rocks."

"Same," Mulholland said. The bartender served their drinks and moved to the customer at the far end.

"Do what you got to do." Mulholland addressed the mirror. "Anna left this morning for Mexico. All I ask is that you don't drag her in."

Dunne took a sip. Bitter on tongue. Sting in throat. No taste for Scotch today. Pushed the glass away, got off the stool. He almost put his hand on Mulholland's round, drooping shoulder, almost said, *You could have tried to talk to me as a friend, not a target, somebody you've known for thirty years, who'd been in the war with you, who you could risk trusting.*

But Ambrose Mulholland could no more change who he was than he could think and act differently from his mirror image behind the bar. He'd spent the better part of a lifetime trying to undo what couldn't be undone, to heal the hole in Mary Claire's heart, put her back in his bed, make love on winter nights and summer afternoons, find peace with her in that cottage on Long Island, with the fireplace and front porch. Impotent and bereft, he'd raged against a world he couldn't change. Crater paid the price, but he was only the first. The killing went on, as if revenge, endlessly extracted, could fill the void left by her vanished love, his banished hopes, exploded expectations: the anguish a single bullet can inflict.

"So long, Bud."

"Take care, Fin."

Dunne turned when he reached the door. Mulholland was watching in the mirror, his reflected eyes same as the real ones, neither happy nor sad. Empty.

"Bring Out Your Dead: West Side Remains Identified: No, They Don't Belong to Judge Crater," by Billy Sternberg, *The Knickerbocker Journal: A Weekly Review of What's New and Old in New York City,* **September 14, 1980.**

Last week's news that a fairly intact set of remains had been unearthed at a West Side construction site near the restaurant (demolished several years ago) where Judge Joseph F. Crater was last seen almost exactly fifty years ago generated a good deal of interest. Though the memory of the judge's disappearance has faded in recent years, he continues to be an object of fascination to many New Yorkers.

As it turns out, the city's Office of Chief Medical Examiner quickly dispelled the excitement. According to Dr. Linda DeMarco, the Office's Deputy Chief, the bones proved to be those of a malnourished adult male who probably perished in the cholera epidemic that struck the city in the 1840s. At the time, the site was well outside the city and was home to immigrant squatters who erected crude shanties. It later housed an icehouse, which probably helps account for the relatively well-preserved condition of the bones beneath.

Dr. DeMarco speculated that the man was quickly interred by friends and family anxious to avoid contagion (the cause of cholera was still unknown) and, unable to afford formal interment in a graveyard, still wished to avoid consigning him to potter's field.

Dr. DeMarco refused to offer a guess about how many unmarked graves are within New York City. "It could be negligible or it could be significant. The truth is, no one knows for sure," she said. What is known is that the burial sites of the city's original Indian population were shown no respect by early setters who plowed them up or paved them over. The graves of the early settlers as well as of negro slaves, in turn, were often shown equal disrespect by the generations of ruthlessly energetic developers and builders who followed.

Murder and mayhem, never in short supply, have undoubtedly made their own contributions to the city's supply of unmarked graves. There's an enduring legend, for example, that many of the looters killed during the infamous Draft Riots were secretly buried in basements and cellars by relatives who wanted to prevent the police from identifying them and seeking restitution from their families.

The time-honored tradition among mobsters of fitting rivals and enemies with "concrete overshoes" and depositing them in the city's waterways is well known. Other victims have been tucked under construction sites, empty lots, abandoned buildings, garbage dumps, parking lots, etc.

Dr. DeMarco ventured that it is her personal opinion that the number of hidden graves in the city is probably small. But students and chroniclers of organized crime insist the number is substantial. It is also a matter of conjecture how often, in the interests of saving time and money, developers' construction crews ignore or destroy remains they stumble across.

When brought to the attention of officials, remains are hardly ever identified or claimed. With rare exception they are taken to the potter's field on Hart's Island off the Bronx and re-interred. Such is the case with the remains discovered last week on the West Side.

Whether Judge Crater is among those consigned "to sleep with the fishes" or beneath the city's streets remains unknown. Yet, unlike most of them, he hasn't been entirely forgotten. For the city's history buffs and mystery mavens, he remains an object of curiosity. If the interest of the living brings some comfort to the dead, Crater continues to have an ample portion.

EPILOGUE

Playa de Oro, Florida

"And the end of all our exploring
Will be to arrive where we started
And know the place for the first time."

—T.S. ELIOT, "Little Gidding"

Dunne exited the train amid a happy confusion of laughter, chatter, hugs, handshakes as passengers reunited with spouses, friends, children. They made their way to the parking lot and pulled away. He was the only one left on the platform. A negro taxi driver approached. "Need a ride, mister?"

"I'm waiting for someone."

He handed Dunne a card. "If someone doesn't show, call."

He put the card in his pocket. Roberta's reply to his letter had been one line: *Let me know when you're arriving.*

Didn't expect a line-by-line response to the four-page letter that he'd worked on for several days, writing and rewriting, trying not to excuse but explain—to himself as well as her—all he'd done and failed to do over the last several months. He hated writing. Always had. Thoughts that seemed clear and logical became garbled, disjointed, inane when translated onto paper. But aware that however awkward his written words might be, they'd be far less awkward than if he tried to speak them, he soldiered on.

In the end, he laid it out as best he could: ambivalence about retirement and relocation; irrational resentment at not being talked out of it; inability to make an honest reappraisal. Instead, driven by restlessness and seduced by his own overconfidence, he'd allowed himself to be sucked into the Crater case, and manipulated and directed like a marionette.

He was honest about what had transpired with Nan Renard—all of it—but played down the seriousness of the poisoning. He wanted her back, but not out of pity. He understood now that what he saw in Nan—or what he *thought* he saw, the balance of integrity and toughness, of intelligence, poise and beauty—was what he'd always loved in Roberta. Nan had the freshness of youth. But Roberta was for real, and Nan Renard wasn't. Maybe she had been once. Maybe she could be again, evolving into a person capable of trusting and being trusted. But for now she was like one of those reproductions in Madame Troussard's, a wax replica with a hollow core.

Every time he tried to compose a concluding paragraph, out came a gush of overwrought, sentimental clichés, so he ended by dashing off some lines about his stupidity, regret, embarrassment, his love for her, his desire to come home and see if he could repair what he'd broken. He ended that he'd wait to hear from her. A botch of a letter but the best he could do. He mailed it special delivery. Whatever her response—if there was one—he knew that he didn't want to stay in New York.

While he waited, he tied up loose ends. Called Jeff Wine in L.A. and asked him to check out the Silver Moon and see if Merry Lane was still fortune-telling there. When he paid a visit to the offices of Wilkes Communications, the place was in an uproar. The *News* and *Mirror* had run stories that morning reporting Walter Wilkes's bad back had turned out to be a highly aggressive form of prostate cancer. He was under treatment at an undisclosed locale in California with the experimental drug Laetrile.

Nan Renard's replacement as project manager, the assistant editor she'd sent to pick Dunne up when he returned from Florida, stood behind a table littered with a disordered shuffle of proposed covers for the August 6th inaugural cover of *Snap*. They all featured the same mushroom-shaped pillar of fire that accompanied the atomic incineration of Hiroshima; only the headlines varied: "1945: Hiroshima/ 1955: Where Next?"; "Is an Atomic Pearl Harbor Ahead?"; "Are We Ready for Atomic War?" etc. Written across each was some higher-up's short critique: "Crap." "Trite." "What idiot came up with this?"

Trying not to appear unnerved by the published reports about his boss, which no one had yet denied, he did his best to live up to his new role by being curt and dismissive. "The Crater project was an inane undertaking from the outset. Mr. Wilkes feels he was willfully deceived into pursuing it. If Nan Renard hadn't quit, she'd have been fired." He handed over a check. "Your room at the Savoy Plaza is taken care of. This should cover any other expenses. Consider yourself lucky to get anything."

Dunne handed it back without looking at the amount. "Consider yourself lucky I don't shove it up your ass."

The next day when Pully called with the news of Bud Mulholland's suicide, neither the deed nor the method—a single bullet to the heart—came as a surprise. Pully invited him to dinner and suggested the Coral. He didn't object to Dunne's preference for Cavanaugh's.

"A shame about Mulholland," Pully said. "I always appreciated his bluntness. But I don't imagine losing him will slow the Agency down one bit. Believe me, the worst is still to come."

They followed dinner with cigars, puffing away as they walked up Third Avenue. The familiar and furious rattle of the elevated train periodically passed overhead. Pully knew cigars. They savored the rich taste; the lavish smoke wafted into their nostrils; true scent of destiny, it rose into the night and vanished, like the souls of dead comrades.

He spent the next few days playing tourist, attending a play, riding the Circle Line around Manhattan on a foggy day when the city appeared and disappeared in the gray drizzle. He caught Gene Krupa at the Copa. The weather stayed wet and drab, the usual prelude to spring. In the evenings, he strolled through the park. As ever, the young were the first to twig to the change of season, kissing and embracing, minds uncluttered by the past, focused on what was to come.

Soon as Roberta's note arrived, he packed and got ready to leave. On his last morning, Jeff Wine called back. He'd gone to the Silver Moon. "You should have warned me about the wonderfully hospitable staff they have there. Only after threatening some unfriendly persuasion and waving a twenty could I get the old piss pants who runs the place to tell me anything."

"What'd he tell you?"

"Merry blew town. No forwarding address. Daughter or niece or somebody like that came by and collected her. Off they went. Sad, when you think about it, what the future once held for her and how it turned out."

Crow drove him from the hotel to the station. "I'm not going to ask about how you got poisoned or why Mulholland shot himself. My guess is they're connected some way, but I don't care. Some cop, eh? I should be jumping all over you, demanding answers. But like I told you from the start, the Crater case is a curse. It's never done anything but spread misery and death in its wake. I'm glad you're going home. I was afraid for a while you'd become one of those nut jobs who ruins his life trying to find him."

Dunne asked Crow if he wouldn't mind driving across 38th Street, between Fourth Avenue and Madison. Crow shrugged. "Sure," he said. He didn't ask why. The brownstone at No. 39

as well as its companions had been demolished. The foundation for their replacement, Murray Hill Mews and its 66 deluxe apartments, was already poured. If the excavators had come across a body they hadn't called attention to it. Time is money—nowhere more so than in New York's construction trade.

He shook hands with Crow in front of the station. "Ulysses goes back to Penelope, like he should. Let Crater rest in peace, wherever he may be," Crow said.

When Crow was gone, Dunne ducked into the nearby Franciscan church. During the war, with soldiers and sailors passing through Penn Station at all hours, the friars had begun hearing confessions around the clock, and they'd kept up the practice when peace came. The penances they imposed were so lenient that the place had come to be called "the-two-Hail-Marys-for-homicide church." Dunne made his confession but didn't feel forgiven when he came out, only reminded that though love doesn't always make us faithful, it always makes us suffer for our unfaithfulness.

Sitting alone on the platform with his luggage, he reached into his pocket for the card with the taxi's number, and took it out along with his notebook. Pages of scribbled notes. Dates. Names. Addresses. Phone numbers. Let them rest in peace, all of them. Stella Crater with her precious illusions. Allie Von Vogt, wanting only to be left alone. Patti Leroche, trying to make a new life in Brooklyn. Merry Lane, wherever she was. Anna Resnick Mulholland, a whole lifetime ahead to wrestle with what she'd become.

What use would it be to them for the past to be resurrected and for the world to learn the truth about Judge Crater's disappearance? Soon enough, after the circus played out, the world would forget Crater and turn its attention to whatever new scandal, war, homicide, championship, police action, earthquake presented itself. Those few directly connected to the case would be left to nurse old wounds, bloodier than ever.

He dropped the notebook in the trashcan and walked to the phone booth at the end of the platform, pushing away the thought of Roberta sitting beside Felipe as they drove to the beach. As he dialed the number for the taxi, her convertible entered the parking lot.

"I'm glad you came," he said.

"You look terrible. Get in."

He got in.

The radio was on. News of the latest atomic test in the Nevada Proving Ground. Army, navy and civil defense participating. He played with the dial. Knew what he wanted: Nat King Cole singing "Darling, Je Vous Aime Beaucoup"; instead, Tennessee Ernie Ford rumbling through "Sixteen Tons," followed by Leo Durocher shilling for a brand of cigarettes he probably didn't smoke.

"Mind if I turn this off?" he said.

"Go ahead."

Words that came into his head arrived like a just-remembered lyric, but they weren't from a song:

"'Vanity of vanities, saith the Preacher, vanity of vanities, all is vanity/ What profit hath a man of all his labor which he taketh under the sun?'"

They rode in silence. Give it time. She's sitting next to you. That's a start.

Pace yourself, Fin.

Author's Note

"To disappear enhances –
The Man that runs away
Is tinctured for an instant
With Immortality."

—EMILY DICKINSON

"A NOVEL," A SAGE CRITIC ONCE OBSERVED, "IS A PACK OF LIES IN pursuit of the truth." Based on the still-unsolved disappearance of New York State Supreme Court Justice Joseph Force Crater, who entered a taxi on August 6th, 1930, and was never seen again, *The Man Who Never Returned* is a novel. When facts fit the purposes of the pursuit, I use them; when they don't, I alter, invent, lie. This is what novelists do. Sue me.

The real-life Judge Crater, like the fictional character in my book, was only forty-one when Governor Roosevelt appointed him to fill an interim vacancy on the State Supreme Court. A Protestant from Pennsylvania and a graduate of Lafayette College, Crater attended New York's prestigious Columbia University Law School (F.D.R.'s alma mater). According to his wife Stella, Crater's parents had been violently opposed. "'New York is a wicked town,' his mother protested. 'It is a den of iniquity.'"

Crater graduated from Columbia in 1916 and got married the following year. To supplement his salary as a law clerk, he started to teach law part-time at City College as well as lecture at NYU and Fordham. He enjoyed teaching but one day informed Stella that "there are many things I would like you to have out of life and mere teaching will not provide them."

Though his education and background qualified him for entry into the city's white-shoe law firms, he chose a different path. Undeterred by the city-bred, street-wise heavily Irish/Jewish mix that ran the Tammany machine, he told his wife with pragmatic bluntness (and with a refreshing lack of idealistic bluster), "I have decided that the best way to get ahead is to go into politics."

Crater joined the Cayuga Democratic Club on the West Side. Along with proving a loyal and hardworking party regular, Stella reported, he "volunteered his services for any matter concerning elections which arose in the courts." This brought him to the attention of Tammany sachem and State Senate majority leader Robert F. Wagner.

In 1919, Wagner was elected to the State Supreme Court. (New York's Supreme Court is the highest court of original jurisdiction but the ultimate arbiter of the law is the Court of Appeals.) He chose Crater to be his law secretary. Crater stayed until 1926 when Wagner made a successful run for the U.S. Senate. J. Joseph Huthmacher, Wagner's biographer, described Crater as a "brilliant young lawyer" who was responsible for writing many of Wagner's significant judicial decisions.

Franklin Roosevelt, who'd been elected to a two-year term as governor in 1928, appointed Crater to fill an interim term on the State Supreme Court in March of 1930. Stella Crater—admittedly not the most reliable source when it came to a candid appraisal of her husband's abilities and actions—maintained that F.D.R. told Joe he had it in him "'to go all the way to the United States Supreme Court.'"

F.D.R.'s re-election as governor was widely recognized as a

prelude to a 1932 presidential run. But allegations of rampant corruption in the New York City's magistrate's court and demands for a state-run investigation threatened to complicate those plans. Reluctant to antagonize the big-city bosses, whose support he needed, and wary perhaps (justifiably, as it turned out) that the investigation might lead to damaging revelations about the anything-goes regime of Mayor Jimmy Walker, F.D.R. hesitated.

In August, Roosevelt finally bowed to growing public outrage and agreed to an investigation headed by Judge Samuel Seabury, who harbored his own ambitions for the presidency. News of Crater's disappearance, which broke almost simultaneously with Seabury's appointment, threatened not only to expose an even higher and more damning level of judicial corruption, but had the potential to derail F.D.R.'s presidential ambitions.

My interest in the case dates back to childhood. My father, who attended Fordham University Law School and once heard Crater give a lecture there, was admitted to the bar in 1930. He spent his career in Democratic politics, serving as a New York State assemblyman, a U.S. congressman and a justice of the State Supreme Court. Whenever the elevator in our Bronx apartment building stopped on a floor where nobody was waiting, my father would say, "Judge Crater must have pushed the button."

I don't remember precisely when my father explained to me who Judge Crater was, but it must have been in the early 1950s (I was born in 1947), because I understood the reference as long as I can remember, and it frightened me. If Crater could suddenly vanish so completely, why not my father?

The Crater case stayed with me over the years. In 1974, I visited my father in his chambers on Foley Square. At one point, a note of sadness in his voice, he remarked apropos of nothing,

"I'm told these were Judge Crater's chambers." Though he hadn't yet been diagnosed with the lung cancer that would kill him, the melancholy reference to Crater indicated to me that he suspected his own imminent demise.

While a speechwriter for Governors Carey and Cuomo, I made frequent forays to the State Library, in Albany. Mostly, I focused on researching speeches, except when I digressed and followed my promiscuous fascination with the history of New York City and wandered with aimless delight through the microfilms of old newspapers. At one point, I stumbled on the accounts of Crater's disappearance and briefly considered writing a book about it.

I also made the acquaintance of William Kennedy, whose novel *Legs* added another level of nuance to the era. (Both Legs Diamond and Crater were known to frequent the Club Abbey, on West 54th Street). I soon got sidetracked and ended up going down the path that led me to write *Banished Children of Eve*, a novel set in Civil War New York.

In January 2005, after I'd finished my second novel, *Hour of the Cat,* I had lunch with Paul Browne, a fellow Bronx native and acquaintance from Albany, where he'd been bureau chief of the *Watertown Times*. Browne, who served as NYPD Deputy Commissioner for Public Information in both the Dinkins and Bloomberg administrations, is a fellow devotee of New York City history and political folklore.

Amid a discussion of the latest recrudescence of judicial corruption, I made a passing reference to the *plus ça change* nature of New York politics and mentioned I'd once considered writing a book about Crater. Paul needed no explanations about who Crater was or what happened to him. Most people born and raised in New York City before 1960 have at least a passing familiarity with Crater. For geezers like Paul and me, he's a subject of enduring fascination.

I wondered aloud whether the police records from the case still existed. Paul said he'd look into it, which he did. He put me in touch with Lieutenant Eamon Deery, head of the NYPD Missing Persons Squad (it was a bureau in Crater's day). Bright, savvy and college-educated, Lt. Deery had none of the hard-boiled gruffness of the sterotypical Irish cop; and, true to his demographic—he was born after 1960—he'd never heard of Judge Crater. Although he doubted the records of the case still existed, he promised to have a look and get back to me.

After about a week, when I'd heard nothing, I presumed Lt. Deery had come up empty-handed and returned to the urgent business of tracking down persons who'd gone missing more recently than Crater. That's when Lt. Deery called to report he'd made a discovery. The case had been officially closed in 1979, just shy of its golden anniversary. But instead of tossing the files, the person in charge had done only half the job, removing them from the drawers but leaving them atop the cabinet. There they sat for the next 26 years, three thick accordion files, gathering dust.

Whether as historian or historical novelist, I've always found research to be the most satisfying part of the enterprise (far more than writing). To come across firsthand accounts that have been long neglected and unexamined is a special thrill. The police files were no exception. They offered an intimate and immediate view into the pressures and frustrations endured by the men of the Missing Persons Bureau as they struggled with a case that, if they solved it, could cause a political explosion; and, if they didn't, would bring accusations of incompetence and, worse, corruption.

I extracted a few leads I considered tantalizing, which suggested avenues of investigation the police, in the hurry and confusion of the moment, hadn't pursued. But with the principals of the case as well as the investigators long dead, I didn't see much hope for turning up any definitive and final answers. It came as an utter shock, then, when on the morning of August 16, 2005, I exited the rear of Grand Central Terminal and saw the front page of the *New York Post*, with a picture of the Judge and the headline "I KILLED JUDGE CRATER."

The long-missing break came, the *Post* reported, in a sealed envelope left by a recently deceased Queens woman to her daughter. Inside was a note in which the woman claimed that her husband had been a drinking buddy of a former cop who'd confessed that he and his brother, a cabbie, had picked up Crater on the evening of August 6th and murdered him. They supposedly stashed the body on Coney Island, under the board-walk near the present site of the New York Aquarium. Their motive was unclear.

The NYPD Cold Case Squad confirmed that the note had prompted a reopening of the case. Over the next several weeks, newspapers in New York and across the country ran follow-up stories. It seems that several sets of bones had been turned up during the excavation for the Aquarium in the 1950s but signif-icantly predated Crater's demise. The cop's story of Crater's end seemed more barroom braggadocio than heartfelt confession. The investigation quickly fizzled out.

The previous year, in 2004, Richard Tofel had published *Vanishing Point: The Disappearance of Judge Crater, and the New York He Left Behind*. An eminently readable, worthwhile account of the case that summarized the exist-ing evidence, the book broke no new ground and ends with the unsupported—and unsupportable—conjecture that Crater died *in flagrante* in the midtown brothel of the famous madam Polly Adler.

A critical but often overlooked aspect of the case—Crater's relationship to William Klein, head lawyer for the Shubert Brothers, and one of the last two people to see Crater alive—is brought to light in Foster Hirsch's fine history, *The Boys from Syracuse: The Shubert's Theatrical Empire.* Though Crater isn't Hirsch's main subject, the book lays bare the tangle of sex and politics in the Broadway world that was Crater's playground. It's indispensable for understanding what might have happened to him.

Barring the unlikely discovery of Crater's remains, the final truth about Crater's fate will never be known. But that won't halt the speculation. Today, a hard core of history buffs, mystery fans and cold-case aficionados continues to search for new leads and spin new theories. Maybe the Judge has appeared in his last headline, but as long as people are fascinated by sex, crime, politics and the big city, Crater will continue to be of interest.

For my part, I confess that on more than one occasion, I've retraced Crater's steps on the evening of August 6, 1930, as he went from the Arrow Ticket Agency (long gone) on the corner of 45th Street and Broadway, where he reserved a ticket to a play he never attended (although it appears someone used the ticket), to Billy Haas's Restaurant (long gone) off Eighth Avenue, for what would turn out to be his last meal (that we know of, anyway). Unconsciously, I suppose, I was hoping for some spirit to whisper in my ear. But the ghosts stayed silent.

Like the half-remembered chorus of an old, familiar song, I could never get Crater entirely out of my head. Sometimes, walking the New York streets or riding the subways, I find myself wondering if maybe Crater hadn't outfoxed everyone and hidden in plain sight, living out his days cloaked in the mass anonymity of the city.

I reread John O'Hara's novel *BUtterfield 8*, with its evocation of New York in the early 1930s as the leaden atmosphere of the Depression descended. O'Hara's book is built around party girl Starr Faithfull (Gloria Wandrous in O'Hara's telling) and her mysterious demise, which followed Crater's by a mere nine months. I wondered what magic he might have wrought if he'd made Crater the subject of his novel.

One day, sorting out old books (I have a lot of them), I came across a brown and brittle paperback copy of Stella Crater's 1960 memoir—written with Oscar Frawley—*The Empty Robe: The Story of the Disappearance of Judge Crater*. It had belonged to my father. I'd read it years before. Now I reread it. Poor Stella was hopelessly blind to her husband's womanizing, but I was moved by the strength she displayed in the face of the shameful abuse and manipulation that she was subjected to by her husband's so-called friends as they scurried for cover.

Her account of events is mostly dismissed by students of the case as the deluded notions of a betrayed spouse unable or unwilling to face the truth. I wasn't so sure. I thought there were facets of her account that might be a good starting point for a novelist, especially in conjunction with evidence in the files of the Missing Persons Bureau. I went ahead and made up a memoir that puts her back at the center of the case.

Encouraged by my nonpareil publisher, Peter Mayer, who has seen all three of my previous books into print, I decided to bring Fintan Dunne, the detective-protagonist from *Hour of the Cat*, out of retirement and put him on the case. Dunne, it seemed to me, could go where the historian couldn't, far offstage, into the shadows, away from the spotlight in which the main players strut and fret.

My Judge Crater never makes an appearance in these pages. The reader only sees him through the eyes of other characters, all of whom are fictitious. If there's a distinct New York tone to their voices, it's because it's the tone of a city I love and regard as part of my birthright as a native son of the Bronx. These whole-cloth creations are meant to speak for the unspoken for, those whose existence usually goes unnoticed and unrecorded. It's their lives—their aspirations, evasions, elations, deflations, truths, lies and regrets—that are the subject of *The Man Who Never Returned*.

PETER QUINN

Hastings-on-Hudson
June 1, 2010

ALSO BY PETER QUINN
AVAILABLE FROM THE OVERLOOK PRESS

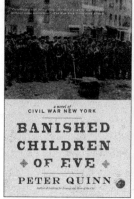

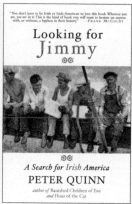

BANISHED CHILDREN OF EVE by Peter Quinn
978-1-59020-057-5 · $16.95 · PAPERBACK

"Convincing and intriguing...Hardly a page of this book is without
some revelation." —*The New York Times Book Review*

HOUR OF THE CAT by Peter Quinn
978-1-58567-799-3 · $14.95 · PAPERBACK

"Extremely readable...deserves a place next to classic
World War II mysteries." —*The Chicago Tribune*

LOOKING FOR JIMMY by Peter Quinn
978-1-59020-023-0 · $14.95 · PAPERBACK

"[An] exceptionally thoughtful and interesting inquiry
into Irish America." —*The Washington Post*

THE OVERLOOK PRESS
NEW YORK
WWW.OVERLOOKPRESS.COM

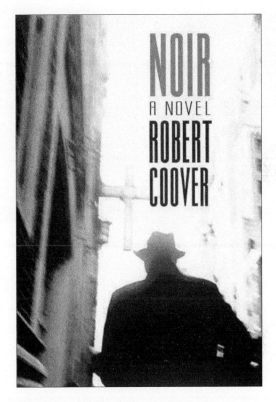

 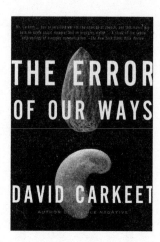